THE FORBIDDEN TOMB

Chris Kuzneski is the international bestselling author of numerous thrillers featuring the series characters Payne and Jones, including SIGN OF THE CROSS and THE SECRET CROWN. He is also the author of THE HUNTERS, the first novel in a new electrifying series that continues with THE FORBIDDEN TOMB. Chris's thrillers have been translated into more than twenty languages and are sold in more than forty countries. Chris grew up in Pennsylvania but currently lives on the Gulf Coast of Florida. To learn more, please visit his website: www.chriskuzneski.com

Praise for Chris Kuzneski:

'Riveting and relentlessly paced'   James Rollins

'Kuzneski does it again with another terrific tale, filled with action and deception, bringing the unimaginable to life. Definitely my kind of story!'   Steve Berry

'Excellent! High stakes, fast action, vibrant characters . . . Not to be missed!'   Lee Child

'If Indiana Jones joined the crew of *Mission: Impossible*, you'd get the action, history, and wicked sense of humor in *The Hunters*. With a thrill ride that pins you to your seat until the very last page, Chris Kuzneski sets a new standard for adventure'   Boyd Morrison

'*The Hunters* is taut and fierce . . . It could just be Kuzneski's breakthrough novel. It deserves to be'   *Daily Mail*

BY CHRIS KUZNESKI

Payne & Jones Series
The Plantation
Sign of the Cross
Sword of God
The Lost Throne
The Prophecy
The Secret Crown
The Death Relic
The Einstein Pursuit

The Hunters Series
The Hunters
The Forbidden Tomb

Get **more** out of libraries

Hampshire
County Council

First published in 2014 by
HEADLINE PUBLISHING GROUP

First published in paperback in 2014 by
HEADLINE PUBLISHING GROUP

1

Cataloguing in Publication Data is
available from the British Library

ISBN 978 0 7553 8657 4 (B-format)
ISBN 978 1 4722 1456 0 (A-format)
ISBN 978 1 4722 1970 1 (A-format)

Typeset in Monotype Garamond
by Palimpsest Book Production Limited, Falkirk, Stirlingshire

Printed and bound in Great Britain by Clays Ltd, St Ives plc

Headline's policy is to use papers that are natural, renewable and
recyclable products and made from wood grown in sustainable
forests. The logging and manufacturing processes are expected
to conform to the environmental regulations of the country of origin.

HEADLINE PUBLISHING GROUP
An Hachette UK Company
338 Euston Road
London NW1 3BH

www.headline.co.uk
www.hachette.co.uk

Acknowledgements

Here are some of the wonderful people I'd like to thank:

Scott Miller, Claire Roberts, Stephanie Hoover, and the whole gang at Trident Media. They sold this project/series long before it was written, and they sold my next one, too. That means I get to eat for another year. Sweet!!!

Ian Harper, my longtime friend/editor/consigliere. He reads my words before anyone else – and then reads them again and again until they're perfect. And if we ever disagree, he usually wins because he's twice my size and kind of scary.

Vicki Mellor, Emily Griffin, Darcy Nicholson, Jo Liddiard, Ben Willis, Mari Evans, and everyone at Headline/Hachette UK. They took my story and turned it into a book – one with a fancy cover, cool maps, and consecutively numbered pages. As an English major, this last one is particularly helpful because I can barely count to ten.

All the fans, librarians, booksellers, and critics who have enjoyed my thrillers and have recommended them to others. If you keep reading, I'll keep writing. And if you stop reading, buy my books anyway and give them to friends. They make awesome gifts.

Last but not least, I'd like to thank my family for their unwavering support. Then again, maybe they're just too worried to say anything bad about me. Let's be honest: I am kind of twisted, and I do *love* killing characters.

Speaking of killing, it's finally time for the good stuff. Without further ado, please sit back, relax, and let me tell you a story ....

ALEXANDER THE GREAT'S EMPIRE

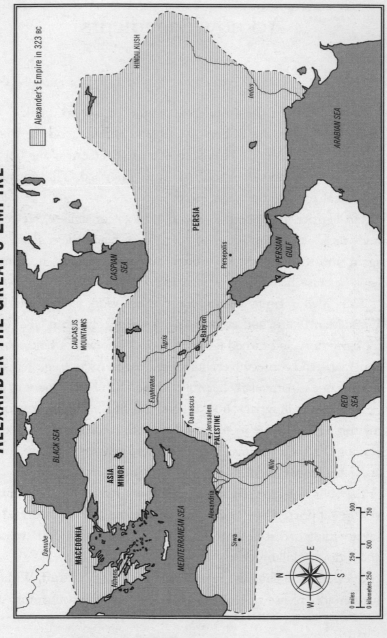

Alexander's Empire in 323 BC

HINDU KUSH

Indus

ARABIAN SEA

PERSIA

Persepolis

CASPIAN SEA

PERSIAN GULF

CAUCASUS MOUNTAINS

Tigris

Babylon

Euphrates

Damascus

BLACK SEA

Jerusalem

PALESTINE

ASIA MINOR

RED SEA

Nile

MACEDONIA

Danube

Alexandria

MEDITERRANEAN SEA

Siwa

Athens

N
W   E
S

0 miles   250   500
0 kilometers 250   500   750

EGYPT AND THE EASTERN MEDITERRANEAN

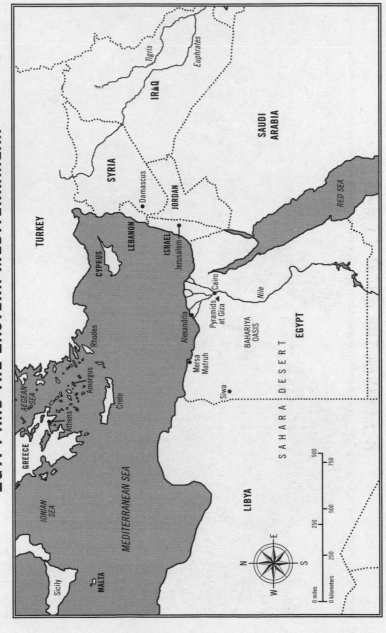

Prologue

Tuesday, April 11
Bahariya Oasis, Egypt
(180 miles southwest of Cairo)

The desert didn't scare him. He knew the dangers of hiking alone in the Sahara, but he had been doing it for so many years that he was prepared for anything.

At least, he thought he was.

A veteran explorer with more than two decades of experience, Dr Cyril Manjani had taken all the necessary precautions before leaving camp. He had notified his team of his travel plans and told them when he would return. He had packed food, water, a GPS unit *and* a compass, and even some glow sticks in case his flashlight failed. They were the same essentials that he always packed before his nightly walks.

His hike had nothing to do with adventure.

He just needed some time to think.

An expert in Egyptology, Manjani had handpicked the members of his team. Though most were graduate students, they represented the cream of the academic crop from some of the world's finest schools. Together, they covered a wide range of scholarly pursuits that might come in handy on his latest expedition.

Manjani didn't want identical opinions on this project.

He needed unique perspectives in multiple fields.

They had been toiling in the desert for three long weeks before things started to get interesting. First they had discovered a stone wall around the perimeter of an ancient site. Then came a series of small huts that had been almost perfectly preserved under the sand. Eventually they had found a much larger structure housing the desiccated remains of several soldiers and a mishmash of objects from several ancient cultures.

That had been yesterday.

Today's discovery was even more exciting – so much so that he had refused to leave it at camp.

Resting atop a towering dune, Manjani drank from his Thermos before tightening the drawstrings around his neck. The April breeze was chilly, and he was grateful for the warmth of his tea and his jacket. Staring out across the vast emptiness of the Sahara, he felt a sense of wonder wash over him. Undulating waves of sand stretched out for miles in every direction. Most saw the bleak terrain as an adversary that must be overcome, but Manjani saw it as a place of opportunity. The landscape was literally filled with the answers to mysteries that had gone unsolved for centuries.

These were the moments he cherished most.

Nothing stirred his emotions in quite the same way.

Manjani checked his watch. He had planned to be gone for ninety minutes at most, and he was quickly running out of time. Before heading back, he turned his attention to the nighttime sky. He was always amazed by how much the city lights obscured his view of the heavens. But out here, in the heart of the desert, the celestial bodies glowed against the darkest black he had ever seen. The contrast was so great that he swore he could see stars he had never seen before.

Though he would have preferred to stay on the dune a little longer, gazing at the panorama above, he felt a sudden chill run up his spine. He pulled his drawstrings tighter and cursed under his breath. He knew a sudden drop in temperature often preceded drastic changes in the weather, and out here, in the middle of nowhere, those changes could be deadly.

Wasting no time, he started his journey back.

The closer he got to camp, the more the breeze picked up strength. He covered his eyes as sand pelted his face, stinging like hordes of microscopic insects. The wind whistled past his ears, drowning out all other sounds around him. Despite the clear sky, Manjani could sense that things were about to turn nasty. As he crested the final dune, he was glad his journey was nearly over.

Unfortunately, his nightmare had just begun.

As the camp came into view, so did the carnage. At first, Manjani assumed that his colleagues' excitement – and the case of brandy that they had insisted on bringing – had gotten the better of them. They appeared to be frolicking about the camp in a state of mass delirium, yelling and tripping over each other like teenagers on spring break. But looking closer, he suddenly realized his mistake. Their movement was an act of desperation, not celebration. Their screams were born of terror, not triumph.

All caused by the demons that swarmed the camp.

Everywhere he looked, cloaked men set upon the members of his team like bloodthirsty butchers. Manjani could not hear the cries of pain above the wailing gusts, but he didn't have to. He could see the murderous rampage unfold in front of him. He watched in horror as his comrades were mercilessly dispatched, the assassins striking them down with methodical precision. Their deaths were slow and agonizing, inflicted with startling ease by the razor-sharp blades wielded by the intruders.

Familiar with the folklore of the region, Manjani had heard the stories of bogeymen that guarded the desert, but he had paid little attention to the tales. People had been disappearing in the Sahara since the beginning of time, and he had refused to believe that they had all suffered a violent death at the hands of monsters.

Now he wasn't so sure.

In his heart he yearned to charge forward, to defend the men and women whom he had convinced to join him on his quest. But in his head he understood that it was a fool's errand – one that would result in certain death. Without weapons or training, there was nothing he could do against these armed savages. Charging into camp would not save his friends; it would only ensure that he died with them. He realized the only people he could possibly save were those who might have fled before the slaughter.

Though he was ill-equipped to take on the approaching sand-storm, there was no way he could risk returning to the camp for additional supplies. He would have to face the elements with only what he carried on his back. It was a daunting proposition. Manjani knew that desert winds had killed fitter, more prepared men than he. Given the distance to the nearest settlement, he gave himself a ten percent chance of survival, at best.

But those odds were much better than the ones he faced in camp.

That was a war he couldn't win, and Manjani knew it. He would rather die searching for others who might have escaped

4

– colleagues who lacked his experience with desert survival or equipment of any kind. He owed his team that much. Their lives now rested on him, as did the legacy of those who had already perished.

Someone needed to tell the world what had happened here. Someone needed to know what he had found.

I

Few people knew of the private road through the swamps of south Florida, and fewer still had driven on it. Several harshly worded signs warned trespassers that they weren't welcomed on the property and would be severely punished when caught. Not by the police or a court of law, but by the owners of the land itself.

In the glades, it was known as *jungle justice*.

And it was just how things got done.

The longhaired biker ignored the warning signs and turned off the dirt road, eager to take advantage of the smooth stretch of asphalt in front of him. The moment his back tire reached the pavement, he twisted the throttle on his customized Harley and held on tight. His engine roared its approval and he rocketed forward at a dizzying rate of speed, laughing as the trees whizzed past him. Mosquitoes (the size of birds) and lizards (the size of poodles) darted out of his way to avoid a messy death.

Not that he would have cared.

He had killed many things over the years, most of them quickly.

It was what he had been trained to do.

At the end of the road, he slowed to a halt as he approached the massive steel gate that protected the waterfront property beyond. He was familiar with the entrance, having passed through it several times before, but he suddenly realized that he had never actually opened the gate by himself. He had always been with someone who had done it for him. Intrigued, he parked his Harley in the middle of the road, dismounted, and stepped toward the odd-looking control panel.

Strangely, there were no buttons to push, numbers to tap, or switches to activate. All he could see was a flat rectangular touch screen mounted on a futuristic metal stand. At least that's what it looked like to him. Given the sleek look of the device and what he didn't know about technology, it might have been a biometric sensor capable of reading his thoughts.

Just like the genie that lived in his iPhone.

Unsure what to do, Josh McNutt swiped his hand above the surface, hoping it was a simple motion detector like one of those fancy faucets. Next, he pressed his fingertips on the screen itself, wondering if it would scan his prints and let him in like the armory at Fort Bragg. When that didn't work, he tried both palms, one at a time.

But nothing happened.

McNutt stroked the three-day stubble on his cheeks, pondering his next move. 'Hello,' he said to the device. 'Anyone in there? Heeeelllloooooo.'

Eventually, he knocked on the unit as if it were the front door.

Still, no response.

'Stupid robot,' he mumbled under his breath.

Growing more and more frustrated, McNutt walked toward

the steel gate and reached out to shake the grate. An instant before making contact, he snapped his arms back to his sides, as if the bars had suddenly transformed into venomous snakes. In truth, his reaction was caused by something more deadly. In the past, he had been told that the gate was only the first of the security measures surrounding the estate. The grounds were also encircled with highly electrified wire mesh that could deliver a lethal current. At the last second, he wondered if the gate was armed with the same type of charge.

A high-voltage 'fuck-you' to those who didn't belong.

Ultimately, he decided not to find out.

* * *

'Crap! I thought he was going to do it,' Hector Garcia blurted from behind his computer screen. He had been watching McNutt on a variety of closed-circuit security feeds ever since he had turned off the dirt road. A seismic trigger embedded under the pavement had set off an alarm, alerting those inside that someone was approaching.

'Thought *who* was going to do *what?*' asked Jack Cobb, a former major in the US Army. As the unquestioned leader of the team, he had more pressing concerns than watching surveillance video. That was Garcia's responsibility. That, and notifying Cobb if someone was headed their way.

'McNutt,' Garcia answered. 'He's been trying to figure out how to get through the gate for the last few minutes. So far, he's losing.'

'Can you put it up on the big screen?' Cobb asked.

'Sure.'

After a flourish of clicks and keystrokes, the entire collection of security footage was displayed in a grid on the ninety-inch television that hung above the fireplace. Cobb watched as McNutt stepped back to the gate's control panel and lowered his face to the surface. Cobb pointed to feed number three – the view from the camera underneath the touch pad. A few clicks later, McNutt's bloodshot eyes filled the entire screen.

'What's the hillbilly doing now?' asked Sarah Ellis from a nearby couch. Trained by the CIA and a master of security systems, she could only shake her head in embarrassment as her colleague tried to open the gate. 'What's he looking at?'

'Nothing,' Garcia guessed. 'I think he thinks the pad is a retina scan. He's trying to press his eyeball on the glass.'

Sarah burst out laughing. 'Oh . . . my . . . God. He's dumber than I remember – and that's saying something because I've had pet rocks smarter than him.'

'Than *he*,' Jasmine Park said as she entered the room. As the lone academic in the group, she was the only one who noticed Sarah's improper grammar. 'If you're going to make fun of his intelligence, you should use proper English.'

'Says the chick from Korea.'

'Actually, I was born in America.'

'Then you should know that it's rude to correct someone's grammar – particularly someone with my skill set.'

Jasmine smiled and glanced at the video feed. McNutt had turned away from the screen and was walking back toward his bike. 'Is he leaving?'

'I hope so,' Sarah said as she crossed her fingers. 'I've been giving it some thought, and I have the perfect candidate to replace him. Not only is *she* great with guns and explosives, but she's smart enough to make ice. And that *isn't* an expression. McNutt once asked me if ice cubes came from Alaska.'

Garcia turned from his computer. 'When did he do that?'

'When we were *in* Alaska. He wanted to bring some back as souvenirs. He was going to pack them in his suitcase.'

Garcia stared at her, unsure if she was joking. 'Really?'

Sarah shrugged, her blank face revealing nothing.

Jasmine pointed at the television. 'Seriously, is Josh leaving?'

Garcia looked up at the screen and realized that McNutt still wasn't in view. He quickly tapped a button on his keyboard and switched to a wider angle, this one from a camera mounted on top of the gate. It showed McNutt returning to his bike and unbuttoning the cover of a large golf bag that was strapped to the sissy bar.

Sarah hopped to her feet. 'What's he doing now?'

'I have no idea,' Jasmine said.

'I do,' Cobb said with a growing sense of alarm. 'Zoom in.'

Garcia did what he was told, and the group watched in horrified fascination as McNutt lifted the cover from the bag.

Instead of clubs, it was filled with his private arsenal.

McNutt, an ex-Marine sniper and weapons expert, made his selection and lifted it from the bag. The Vampir – a Russian-made rocket-propelled grenade launcher – was designed to immobilize armored tanks. The gate was sturdy, but it wasn't *that* sturdy. The owner hadn't considered missile attacks when he had designed it.

Grinning with childlike delight, McNutt aimed the shoulder-mounted launch tube at the base of the gate as Cobb sprinted across the room and activated the intercom.

'Stand down, soldier!' Cobb shouted.

On the screen, a startled McNutt spun on his heels.

'Who said that?' he demanded as he aimed the tube at the touch pad.

'Lower the RPG,' Cobb directed. 'We'll open the gate.'

McNutt approached the intercom. 'Major, is that you? You in there?'

'Yes, Josh, I'm here.' Then, just to be safe, Cobb clarified his answer. 'I'm in the *house*, not the *box*.'

McNutt laughed at the comment. Unlike some members of the group, who viewed McNutt as a mentally challenged psychopath, Cobb knew most of it was just an act – a way for McNutt to amuse himself when he was away from the battlefield. Some people picked up on his sense of humor right away while others, particularly Garcia, didn't. This only made things funnier to McNutt, who always looked for ways to mess with him.

Like threatening to use a grenade launcher on their home base.

Cobb hit the button that opened the gate. 'See you soon.'

'Thanks!' McNutt shouted, his mouth no more than an inch from the touch screen. 'Give me a minute. I gotta pack my missile first.'

Garcia switched the angle back to the control panel's underside camera. Suddenly McNutt's mouth filled the television screen. 'Look at that. I can see his tonsils.'

Sarah rolled her eyes. 'Oh my God. I'm surrounded by idiots.'

2

McNutt gunned his engine through the winding driveway that led to the main entrance. Surrounded on nearly every side by a man-made inlet, the house was designed to be easily defensible. The lone bridge across the moat was a small isthmus that looked completely natural but was actually artificial and layered with explosives. With the touch of a button, the peninsula could be quickly transformed into an island.

Were it his estate, McNutt would have built a Mediterranean palace to rival the mansions on Star Island in Miami Beach instead of the 4,000-square-foot ranch that served as their headquarters. It looked more like a bunker than a beach house. But it had been built with practicality in mind, not prestige. Not only could it withstand an aerial assault, but the squat construction was perfect for the coast. The hurricanes and tropical storms that threatened Florida every year had nowhere to sink their teeth — and neither would zombies if they ever decided to attack.

Though he disapproved of the architecture, McNutt was downright envious of the house's features. After years in the military, he could recognize an Echelon-class Signals Intelligence satellite receiver when he saw one. This wasn't a standard household satellite dish. It was a top-of-the-line, military-grade device used to transmit secure SIGINT communications. Combined with its own freshwater treatment plant and electrical substation, it was clear that the house was envisioned as a base of operations.

McNutt parked in the roundabout driveway and cut the engine. As he did, the front door opened and Cobb stepped outside.

'Howdy, chief. Long time, no see.'

'You're late,' Cobb growled.

McNutt frowned and checked his watch. 'No, I'm not. You said to be here by five. By my count, I've still got thirty minutes. I'd have been here sooner if it weren't for that stupid gate.'

'I said to be here by five o'clock on *Monday*.'

'It's not Monday?' McNutt grinned sheepishly. 'Sorry, Major. Time flies when you're on leave. One day you're having a couple of beers with your buddies, the next day you're running naked through the streets of Tijuana with the mistress of a pissed-off Federale while being chased by a gang of midgets. You know how it is.'

'As a matter of fact, I don't. And I've told you before: stop calling me "Major". You never know who's listening.'

'Sorry, chief.'

'And at what point in your escapades did you decide that a rocket launcher in a golf bag sounded like a good idea?'

'The night the midgets almost caught me. They're small, but surprisingly quick. Their little legs are like propellers.' McNutt laughed at the image in his head as he unstrapped the makeshift gun case and slung it over his shoulder. 'You have to admit: it's the perfect cover down here. Even on the back of the bike, no one gives a golf bag a second look. You should see what I have in the pouches.'

'Later,' Cobb said. 'We'll talk about that later. Come inside. We've been waiting for you all day.'

McNutt nodded and entered the house.

The opulent home had a spacious floor plan, including a living room, library, kitchen, and parlor. Valuable paintings hung on the walls. The furniture that once seemed cold and sterile – as if the protective plastic from the factory had only recently been removed – now seemed familiar and comfortable. The team slept in sparsely appointed bedrooms off a hallway in the northern end of the house. McNutt wondered if the clothes he had left in the dresser drawers were still there or if they had been discarded in his absence.

If they had, he would have to go shopping.

The final area was a formal dining room that looked out on a magnificent terrace. Interlocking swimming pools, landscaped with palm trees and adorned with sculptures, gave the space the feel of a fancy resort. As they walked past the huge picture window, McNutt glanced at the private marina to the rear of the property. A single yacht was parked in the slips. He knew from his past visit that the boat's name, *Trésor de la Mer,* translated to 'Treasure of the Sea'.

McNutt smiled. It meant that his employer was here.

He hoped that he had remembered to bring his checkbook because the team still hadn't been paid for their first mission.

* * *

McNutt followed Cobb into the kitchen where three anxious faces stared at them from across the countertop. As with most homes, the space had become the de facto meeting point. Whenever they all needed to gather in one place, it was inevitably the kitchen.

'Holy shit, the gang's all here,' McNutt said.

To the untrained eye, they looked like a mismatched set. Cobb was broad-shouldered and handsome, with a narrow face and piercing gray eyes that gave him a 'leading man' quality. McNutt was strong and scruffy, with hair and clothes that almost always looked like he had just slept under a bridge. Meanwhile, Garcia represented a new wave of hacker. He wasn't pale and frail like the stereotypical nerds who never left their mothers' basements. He was tan and athletic and reasonably attractive.

'Where the hell have you been?' Sarah demanded.

'We were getting worried,' Jasmine added.

Their comments couldn't have been more fitting.

Sarah was tall, sleek, and agile, a physically gifted athlete who stood in stark contrast to the softer features of the much shorter Jasmine. Of all the team members, the two women had the least in common – not only physically, but also emotionally. Sarah was aggressive and combative, always looking for a weakness that she could exploit to her advantage, whereas Jasmine was kind and respectful, more concerned about others than herself. Part of that was their upbringing, and part was their training.

Sarah had learned her craft at Quantico.

Jasmine had learned hers in a library.

'Where he's been is not important,' Cobb said before McNutt could regale them with tales of debauchery from south of the border.

'It is to me,' Sarah countered. 'We're all in this together. I don't need him going off on a bender and announcing what we found to a crowded bar.'

Garcia shrugged. 'Even if he did, do you really think anyone would believe him? I mean, c'mon. Ancient trains? The occult? Covert operations in Transylvania?'

'Exactly!' McNutt said. 'Thanks, José, for the vote of confidence.'

'Actually, it's Hector.'

'Close enough. They both start with the same letter.'

'Actually, they don't.'

'They don't? Since when?'

'Since, um, they invented the alphabet.'

McNutt fought the urge to grin. He knew damn well what Garcia's name was; he simply chose not to use it. 'Well, that explains it. I don't *know* the alphabet.'

'That's enough,' Cobb announced. He didn't raise his voice. His tone alone let everyone know that he was done with their banter.

The group gave him his due respect and stopped at once.

'Sarah, keeping things to ourselves was never part of the arrangement. You're all free to say whatever you want to whomever you want. But you all know the risks of letting this information get out.'

Sarah started to object, but Cobb cut her off.

He glanced at McNutt. 'That being said, I'd consider it a personal favor if you would keep your mouth shut about team activities.'

McNutt nodded. 'I haven't told a soul.'

'Good,' said Cobb, who had figured as much. McNutt wasn't a trained spy like Sarah, but he was a former Marine who was programmed to be loyal to his unit. 'Hector, is there anything on the Internet about our recent activities?'

'Nothing,' the techie replied. 'It's like there's a coordinated effort to keep our news out of the news. It's actually a bit odd, if not altogether disconcerting. Nothing stays off the radar like this – *especially* not something as interesting as what we went through.'

Cobb glanced at their host – a Frenchman named Jean-Marc Papineau – who had quietly entered the kitchen through a back hallway and had listened to the tail end of their conversation. Impeccably dressed in the finest clothes from Europe, he carried himself like royalty, as if he were the king and the world was his playground.

Ever since they had met a few months earlier, Cobb had wondered how far Papineau's reach extended. He had worked wonders in Eastern Europe, obtaining everything that the team had needed for their mission, including a retrofitted train. As impressive as that was, it paled in comparison to his latest trick. In an age of camera phones and social media, how did he keep their major discovery from the rest of the world?

It took more than money to do something like that.

It took influence and power.

'Jasmine,' Cobb continued, 'have you heard anything from your sources?'

As the resident historian, she had connections at several universities around the globe. Even if their quest had not made the newspapers, the academic community had their own channels of communication. If anyone had gotten wind of their historic discovery, she would have heard about it from one of her peers.

'Yes and no,' she admitted. 'The rumors about a major find are out there, but it's just scattered rumblings. I've heard so many versions of what might have happened that I don't even know where to begin. We've been credited with finding everything from the Amber Room to the lost city of Atlantis. The stories are unbelievable.'

Cobb stared at Papineau. 'Anything to add? Can we expect an official confirmation of our discovery anytime soon?'

The team whirled around, surprised by his presence.

'Nothing official,' he said as he took his place next to Cobb at the front of the group. 'In fact, I plan on crafting a few more rumors that I would like each of you to spread through your sources. The more, the better.'

'What kind of rumors?' Sarah asked.

Papineau smiled. 'Given that it involved the Russians and a famous treasure, I thought my tale about the Amber Room was particularly poetic.'

'Your tale?' Jasmine asked, confused.

'Yes, my dear. *Mine.*'

'But why?'

Cobb answered for him. 'Because it is far easier to lie about an event than to deny it took place. The world knows something happened, so it's up to us to control the narrative. To put it in spy terms, this is disassociation through disinformation. We need to keep the world off our scent until our mission is complete. Correct?'

Papineau shot him a glance but said nothing.

'Wait a minute,' Sarah hissed. 'What are you talking about? We already completed our mission when we found the treasure. That was the deal.'

Cobb shook his head. He knew that wasn't the case. 'That's what we were led to believe, but Romania was only the first step. Isn't that right, Jean-Marc?'

'It is,' he confirmed.

Sarah slammed her fist on the counter, and then stormed toward the Frenchman. 'You lying sack of shit! You promised me five million dollars for my services. I did everything you asked and more. You owe me my goddamned money!'

Cobb stepped in front of her before she reached her target.

Papineau took a step back. 'Calm down, my dear. You're absolutely correct. You earned your money. Five million dollars to each of you, as promised.'

'That's more like it,' Sarah blurted.

'Or . . .' A grin returned to his face. 'You can double your take.'

The room grew still as the comment sank in.

McNutt was the first to speak. 'Did you say *double*?'

'I did indeed. Ten million dollars. Each.'

'What's the catch?' Jasmine asked.

'The "catch", as you say, is that none of your money – including that which you are already owed – will be available to you until *after* you have completed the next task. It will remain in trust until the mission is over.'

'And if we fail?' Sarah demanded.

'You will have the original five million waiting for you upon your return,' Papineau assured her. 'However, our relationship will cease to exist. We will sever all ties, immediately and permanently.'

'Meaning the *next* task may not be the *last* task.'

Papineau shrugged. 'I wish I could tell you what the future has in store for us. Unfortunately, I cannot. There is only so much I can guarantee this far in advance.'

'That's not good enough,' Jasmine said. A few months earlier, she had been timid and vulnerable, but after surviving multiple attacks in the field she had emerged with a new level of confidence. 'I'll do it, but I have a condition.'

'Being a nerd *isn't* a condition – it's more of a life choice,' Sarah teased.

Papineau ignored the comment and focused his attention on Jasmine. She wasn't the type to make outrageous demands. 'What is it?'

'Bring my family to America.'

'No problem. I'll have them on the next flight.'

Papineau knew that Jasmine's involvement was motivated by her desire to rescue her extended family from the clutches of poverty. All her life she had saved her money, hoping to finance their trip from the slums of Seoul to a new life in America.

He could make that happen overnight.

'I need a new laptop,' Garcia stated boldly. If Papineau was meeting terms, he didn't want to miss out. 'Custom-built to my specs.'

'Done. Anyone else?'

'A new Harley,' McNutt said.

'Same for me,' Sarah added.

McNutt raised an eyebrow.

'What?' Sarah snapped. 'You're not the only one who likes to straddle something powerful on the weekends.'

McNutt opened his mouth to speak, but thought better of it.

'Also granted.' Papineau turned toward Cobb, the only one left. 'And what about you? What is that you would like?'

'Me?' Cobb answered. 'I'd like to know what you want us to find.'

3

The kitchen conversation was over. It was time to get down to business.

The group descended the hidden flight of stairs that led to the 'war room' in the basement. The heavy door of the bunker wasn't just similar to that of the White House Situation Room, it was identical. When properly sealed, it would keep out water, gases, and toxins. Much of the room on the other side of the door was also copied from the blueprints used in Washington. The main difference was that the President's foxhole was furnished with efficiency in mind; Papineau's didn't skimp on luxury.

The space was climate-controlled to museum-level perfection and decorated with fine art and other expensive trappings. A short railing separated a long glass conference table from the leather couches and amply padded easy chairs, providing two distinct meeting areas: one formal, one far more casual.

The team took their seats around the hi-tech table as Papineau stood at the head, waiting for them to settle in. Then, without a precursory explanation, the lights began to dim. He stepped to the left as the massive video screen that covered the entire wall behind him sprang to life. The map of Eastern Europe that had been used for their first mission was gone, replaced by an image of the Balkan Peninsula.

The countries were not labeled, but Cobb knew the area

well enough to know that the borders were not accurate. Or, at the very least, not current. The southern portions of Albania, Macedonia, and Bulgaria were shown as a single area. And what should have been Greece was divided into several distinct territories.

Papineau let the silence linger, waiting for someone to hazard a guess.

Instinctively, the group turned toward Jasmine.

'That map is at least two thousand years old,' she said.

Papineau smiled and nodded. 'Two thousand three hundred and fifty years, to be exact.'

Jasmine did the math in her head. 'The League of Corinth. Philip's unified force, at war with the Persian Empire. The Kingdom of Macedon.'

'Excellent,' Papineau said.

'Can someone translate her translation?' McNutt asked.

Jasmine took it upon herself to clarify her statement. 'Philip the Second of Macedon was a brilliant military tactician. By 336 BC he had conquered most of Greece. In doing so, he brought the various factions together under his rule. He put an end to their internal conflict and unified their strength against the Persian forces across the Aegean Sea.' She pointed toward the map on the screen. 'The area may seem divided, but it was actually governed by a single man.'

'For how long?' Cobb wondered.

'Philip's reign lasted more than twenty years – a remarkable feat for the time. The map we see here was from the end of his rule, not the beginning. Upon his assassination, all of this land was left to his son.'

'And his son was . . .?' Sarah asked.

'Alexander the Third of Macedon,' Garcia answered.

As the team turned toward him, they realized for the first time that the conference table was not made of ordinary glass; instead, the surface was the same material as the touch-screen control panel at the gate. What they couldn't see was the myriad of electronic technology housed in its narrow depth. Manufactured by Payne Industries for US Central Command (CENTCOM), the advanced rendering of the futuristic computer was used to plan military strikes with depth of field.

Eager to show off his new toy, Garcia had entered keywords and dates from Jasmine's briefing into a government search engine displayed on the tabletop in front of him. Then, with a flick of his wrist, he was able to distribute copies of that information to virtual screens at each of their seats. The 'virtual reports' looked like they had been slid across the top of the desk when, in fact, it was nothing more than a fancy special effect. The graphics were so realistic that team members actually tried to catch the reports before they slid off the end of the table.

'I love this thing,' Garcia said with a laugh.

McNutt was so captivated by the technology he put his face against the glass and tried to see the gadgetry underneath. 'Can I play Pac-Man on this?'

Sarah ignored McNutt and concentrated on the name. 'Alexander the Third. Never heard of him.'

'Me, neither,' Cobb admitted.

'Yes, you have,' Jasmine assured them. 'You probably know him by his nickname: Alexander the Great.'

McNutt sat up, suddenly focused. 'Hold up! You're telling me that Alex was given all of that land when his father died? Hell,

I could be great, too, if I had that type of real estate. All my dad left me was a six-pack in the fridge and some beef jerky.'

Jasmine frowned. 'When did your dad die?'

'He didn't. He just left.'

'Anyway,' she said, suddenly uncomfortable, 'Alexander wasn't content with his inheritance. He had a much bigger kingdom in mind.'

As if on cue, Papineau changed the image on the wall display to a much larger map. The outline stretched eastward from the Adriatic Sea to the Himalayan Mountains along the border of India. It extended south to the Indian Ocean and Persian Gulf, and into the northern territories of the Arabian Peninsula and much of Egypt. The original Kingdom of Macedon was little more than a speck in the northwestern corner of this new map.

Jasmine continued, 'Alexander the Great controlled the entire area – more than two million square miles in total. It was one of the largest empires in history.'

Sarah whistled. 'That's a lot of land.'

'Indeed,' said Papineau, who knew a thing or two about real estate. 'But that's only part of his story. Alexander was trained by generals and tutored by none other than Aristotle himself. Their combined efforts resulted in the most brilliant military mind in history. Hoping to reshape the world, Alexander quickly set his sights upon the expansion of his territory. By the time of his death, he was known far and wide as a conquering hero: an unyielding, yet merciful force that swept across the land, leaving unity and prosperity in his wake. To many, he was seen as a god in human form.'

Papineau changed the image on the main screen.

To ensure their focus, all of their workstations went dark.

The group turned in unison as the giant map disappeared and was replaced by an ancient engraving. At first glance, it appeared to be a stone chamber being pulled by more than a dozen horses. The structure was nearly two stories in height, with a round, vaulted roof, and surrounded on three sides by ornate pillars.

'Upon his death, Alexander was placed inside a coffin of hammered gold. It was then placed inside a magnificent funerary hearse that was nearly twenty feet tall.'

'How magnificent?' Sarah wondered.

Papineau changed the image again, this time to an ancient painting that highlighted the ornate design of the hearse. 'A vaulted ceiling made of gold and precious stones was supported by a row of solid gold columns. Gold molding adorned the tops of the walls, and intricate gold figures decorated each corner. According to legend, the hearse was lined with a collection of golden bells to announce Alexander's arrival. They could be heard for miles around.'

McNutt grimaced with disgust. '*Bells*? The greatest general of all time and they honored him with *bells*? What kind of bullshit is that? This is a guy who rode elephants into battle. You'd think they'd come up with something more manly than that. Like drums. Big-ass kettledrums, played by naked chicks in high heels. Now *that's* a funeral.'

'No,' Sarah said, 'that's a strip club.'

'Anyway,' said Papineau, who was rarely amused by McNutt's antics, 'the golden hearse weighed a staggering amount. It required the combined strength of sixty-four of the legion's sturdiest mules to transport the structure on its journey.'

'To where?' Cobb asked.

Jasmine answered. 'His body was to be taken from Babylon

– where he died – to Macedon, the place of his birth. Unfortunately, he never made it home. The processional was intercepted by a Macedonian general named Ptolemy Soter, who directed the hearse to the Egyptian city of Memphis. By seizing the body of the dead king, Ptolemy could legally claim rule over Egypt and the bulk of Alexander's empire. Many years later, Ptolemy's son, Ptolemy the Second Philadelphus, moved the remains to the north where he was entombed in the coastal city of Alexandria, a city named for the ruler himself.'

Papineau picked up from there. 'As all of you know, the Middle East is one of the least stable geographic regions in the world and has been for several millennia. During the past two thousand years, control of Alexandria has changed hands multiple times. And not just ruler to ruler – also culture to culture. From the Greeks and the Romans to the Christians and the Arabs, the city has been built and rebuilt more times than you can possibly imagine.'

Papineau nodded to Garcia, who pushed a button on his virtual keyboard. The image on the big screen was replaced by an animated video that focused on the land around the Mediterranean Sea. A giant red dot pulsated in the sea south of Greece.

'In July of 365 AD, a massive underwater earthquake near the island of Crete triggered a tsunami that devastated the region.' As if on cue, the red dot erupted on the screen, sending virtual shock-waves in every direction. The camera zoomed to the south, following a path of destruction that led to the city of Alexandria. 'On the Egyptian coast, the surging water was so powerful it hurled ships more than two miles inland. To this day, construction crews still find chunks of boats in the desert.'

The team grew silent as they watched the video.

Jasmine was particularly moved by the devastation, which reminded her of the recent tsunamis in Asia.

Papineau continued. 'As you can imagine, the loss of life was substantial; and so was the loss of antiquities. Temples fell, buildings crumbled, and tombs were obliterated.'

He smiled as his statement lingered.

It washed over them like the tide.

Sarah caught on first. 'Are you saying what I think you're saying? You want us to find the tomb of Alexander the Great?'

Papineau nodded. 'I do indeed.'

Cobb leaned back in his chair. 'Why?'

'Why?' repeated Papineau, surprised by the question. 'Because the discovery of the tomb would be a significant historical achievement, one that would bring closure to one of the greatest mysteries of our time. And if that isn't reason enough, allow me to remind you and your team of five million other reasons.'

'I'm not talking about *our* reasons,' Cobb explained. 'I'm talking about *yours*. You're not doing this for the fame – I'm certain of that. And you have more money than you could possibly spend in ten lifetimes. So why tackle one of the greatest mysteries of the ancient world if you don't care about the glory or the reward?'

'The question is moot,' Jasmine said, her tone full of frustration. 'People have been scouring Alexandria for clues for more than a thousand years. Historians have devoted their lives to finding the lost tomb. Every myth, every angle, every hunch, has been thoroughly exhausted by the world's best scholars, and they have found nothing. I'm telling you, there is nothing left to pursue. No new evidence. No new leads. Heck, there aren't even any maps of the ancient city in existence. A mission like this is pointless. It would be easier for us to visit Mars.'

'That's not true,' Cobb assured her.

Jasmine stood her ground. 'Unfortunately it is true, Jack. People have been looking for the tomb for centuries, and as the only historian in the room, I can assure you—'

He cut her off. 'I meant the part about the maps.'

'The maps? Wait – what are you saying?'

'I'm saying at least one map of ancient Alexandria exists.' Cobb turned his chair and stared at Papineau. 'Isn't that right, Papi?'

4

Papineau was surprised by the insinuation. Confusion filled his face. He stared at Cobb, who stared right back. 'I don't know what you mean.'

Cobb set his jaw, angered that his host would rather play games than admit he knew anything about the map. 'And if I call your friend, will he give me the same story? Will he claim that we never met, that he has no idea who I am?'

Papineau blinked rapidly. 'My friend? Who are you talking about? Really, Jack, I'm not sure what you mean.'

Cobb had interrogated better men than Papineau. Men who had kept their composure through unbearable stress and physical 'coaxing', long after Cobb had lost track of the hours. Men who had taken their secrets to their graves. Papineau was an experienced liar – that much Cobb knew for certain – but he had yet to master the craft.

The flicker of emotion in his eyes gave him away.

It was genuine surprise and panic.

He honestly didn't know what Cobb was referring to.

It was a development that Cobb hadn't expected, but one that he was prepared to exploit nevertheless. For now, that meant playing things close to the vest about his recent trip to Switzerland and his dinner with a well-known historian.

Cobb chose his words carefully, giving Papineau as little as possible. 'At least one map from ancient Alexandria still exists. I know this for a fact, because I've seen it.'

Jasmine gasped – literally *gasped* – with excitement. It was the type of sound rarely heard outside of a bedroom. 'Oh my God! Do you know what this means? It means that we can— wait! Just to clarify: you're saying you've actually seen a map that was created *during* the era itself?'

Cobb continued to study his host. 'Yes.'

She gasped again. 'Where? When?'

Papineau tried to remain calm, but his anxiety was palpable. He more than wanted to know the name of Cobb's source – he *needed* to know.

But Cobb wasn't ready to let him off the hook.

He liked having something that Papineau wanted.

He liked being the one in control.

Not for himself, but for the sake of his team.

Cobb addressed Jasmine. 'Where and when is not important, but I can assure you that it meets our needs. Furthermore, I can assure you that it is authentic.'

'Can you borrow the map?' It was less of a question and more of a plea. 'Or, at the very least, can I spend some time with it so I can sketch my own?'

Cobb nodded. 'I think something like that can be arranged.'

Her eyes lit up in anticipation.

Sarah leaned forward. 'Let me see if I got this straight. We have access to the only known map of ancient Alexandria, and somewhere in the city is a golden hearse protecting the golden coffin of a famous king?'

Cobb shrugged but said nothing.

'Hector, if we assume ten tons of gold – which seems like a

conservative estimate to me – how much cash are we talking about?'

Garcia calculated the amount in his head. 'At today's market value, we're looking at a minimum of four hundred million dollars.'

Sarah whistled. 'Not a bad score.'

Papineau agreed. 'It would be, but most historians believe that the hearse was dismantled more than two thousand years ago. The gold was then melted down and pressed into ancient coins that fueled the local economy. Even Alexander's sarcophagus was eventually replaced with one made of glass. Logic dictates that the hearse would have been completely consumed before they turned their focus to the casket.'

'But there's still a chance?' Sarah asked.

'Sure,' he conceded. 'There's always a chance.'

McNutt signaled for a timeout. 'Hold up. I'm confused.'

'Tell me something I don't know,' Sarah mumbled.

He didn't miss a beat. 'The geek watches you when you sleep.'

It took a few seconds for the comment to sink in.

'Wait! *What?*' she demanded.

Garcia turned bright red. 'No I don't! I swear I don't!'

She glared at him. 'You better not, or I swear to God I'll shove your laptop up your ass. Then I'll pull it out and shove it up there again.'

Garcia didn't know whether to be scared or turned on.

Cobb cleared his throat and the group calmed down. There was a time and a place for threats, and this was neither. 'What's confusing you, Josh?'

'What?' McNutt asked.

Cobb smiled. 'You said something was confusing you . . .'

'Right!' he said with a laugh. 'If the hearse was stripped for parts and the gold is long gone, what are we looking for?'

'Good question – one that I was about to ask myself.'

'Thanks, chief.'

Cobb turned toward their host. 'Well?'

Papineau ignored Cobb and spoke directly to McNutt. 'Joshua, you were in the service for several years. How often do you visit your fallen brethren?'

'Often.'

It was an honest response from a former Marine.

In the United States, there are 131 national cemeteries that are recognized for their burials of military personnel. The largest two – Arlington National Cemetery in Virginia and Calverton National Cemetery in New York – cover more than 1,700 acres and serve as the burial grounds of more than 750,000 soldiers and their families. McNutt made it a point to visit several of these locations every year.

'And when you pay your respects, what do you leave behind?'

McNutt pondered the question. His boisterous demeanor was momentarily somber and reserved. 'Sometimes it's a personal memento. Sometimes it's shell casings. Sometimes I pour them a drink from my flask. It all depends on the guy.'

'You leave them tribute. You honor them with an offering.'

McNutt nodded but said nothing.

'Alexander was honored as well,' Papineau said as he began to pace around the table. 'For centuries after his death, great leaders from far and wide made pilgrimages to his tomb to pay their respects. Julius Caesar, Caligula, Augustus – they all came to honor him. It is a tradition that we continue today, bringing tokens of appreciation for the sacrifice of mortal men, particularly those we admire. Therefore, I ask you this: what would you bring to honor one of the greatest conquerors of all time?'

'Chocolate?' Sarah said with a laugh.

McNutt made a face. 'Don't be ridiculous. You can't bring chocolate on a trip to the desert. It would melt on your camel. I suggest virgins. Lots of virgins.'

Jasmine shook her head. 'I think you're confused. Alexander wasn't a Muslim.'

'Neither am I,' McNutt said, 'but I wouldn't turn down a bunch of virgins. They travel well, and they're good for any occasion.'

Garcia nodded in agreement, but wisely said nothing.

Sarah rolled her eyes. 'Anyway, what's the answer?'

Papineau shrugged. 'No one actually knows what was brought. If any records were kept, and there's no way of knowing if they were, they are no longer available.'

'Why not?' Garcia wondered.

'Are you familiar with the Library of Alexandria?'

'Of course I am,' said Garcia, who frantically tried to pull up information on the historic landmark. 'Just give me a second.'

Jasmine wasn't about to wait. 'The Library of Alexandria was the finest collection of information in the ancient world. It was a repository of every significant text known to man. Scholars heralded it as the center of knowledge, a place where the rulers of Egypt could study the past in preparation for the future. It stood as a monument to the nation's wealth and affluence, a symbol of their prosperity until it was destroyed by fire hundreds of years ago. The exact date and time are still unknown, though several theories abound.'

Papineau grimaced. 'The loss was catastrophic. Every record, every map, every drawing of the city of Alexandria was consumed by the blaze – as were details about the tomb and the golden hearse. Since the fire various clues and myths have surfaced, but historians have never been able to place them in the proper context.'

Cobb nodded in understanding. 'It doesn't matter if you know that the tomb was located next to the market if you have no idea where the market was. Is that it?'

'Exactly,' Jasmine said. 'We have bits and pieces about the city that we could string together into a very rough sketch of ancient Alexandria, but we have never had a primer: something that told us how to arrange the pieces.'

'Until now.'

'Until now,' she said excitedly. 'Your map may be the key to unlocking the entire history of Alexandria. The Roman occupation. The Persian rule. The Muslim conquest. The location of the tomb and more. There's no telling what your map might allow us to uncover. How soon until you can arrange for me to see it?'

Cobb shrugged. 'Oh, I don't think it will take that long.'

'Can you give me a number?' For her, the suspense was intolerable 'A week? A month? A year?'

Cobb rubbed his chin and pretended to do some math in his head. 'I don't know . . . maybe two minutes or so. Half that if I really hustle. How long does it take to run up and down a flight of stairs?'

Jasmine gasped even louder than before. 'You mean it's *here?*'

Cobb nodded. At the conclusion of their previous mission, he had pursued a mysterious IP address that had secretly monitored their secure transmissions from Eastern Europe. Hoping to learn more about Papineau's agenda, Cobb followed the signal to the Beau-Rivage hotel in Geneva, Switzerland where he intended to confront Papineau's silent partner – *if*, in fact, he had one.

Instead, Cobb quickly realized he had been duped.

The signal was nothing more than a digital breadcrumb, intentionally left so that Cobb would follow it to the five-star hotel where a private dinner had been arranged with one of the top historical experts in the world, a man named Petr Ulster.

Neither Cobb nor Ulster knew who had arranged their conversation – a nameless benefactor had paid their bills – but by the end of their meeting, Cobb and Ulster had bonded, and Ulster had entrusted Cobb with a copy of the ancient map.

'Where?' Jasmine demanded.

Cobb stood. 'It's upstairs in my duffel bag.'

5

While Cobb retrieved the map from his bedroom, the others waited in calm silence – all except for Jasmine, who cracked her knuckles and bounced her knees up and down in order to dispel her nervous energy.

'Relax. It's just a copy,' Sarah said.

Jasmine took the bait. '*Just a copy?* I understand it's *just a copy*, but it's a copy of something that I didn't know existed until a minute ago, and depending on its authenticity and accuracy, it may give us the inside track to one of the biggest archaeological finds of all time, not to mention millions of dollars for us and billions of dollars to Jean-Marc. So trust me: it's more than *just a copy*. It's *everything*.'

Sarah smiled. She wasn't teasing Jasmine to be mean; not that she hadn't done that in the past. She was pushing buttons because she enjoyed the fire that the new and improved Jasmine exhibited from time to time. Her words weren't meant to inflict pain; they were a subtle call to action. It was her way of reminding Jasmine that she was a lot tougher than she thought, that she should never be afraid to speak her mind when her views were challenged, and that she was a key member of the team.

Plus, it was a lot of fun to watch her freak out.

Sarah shrugged. 'Okay, okay. It's a *rare* copy. I get it.'

Garcia, who was oblivious to Sarah's true intentions, refused to make eye contact with her as he continued to assemble information on Alexandria. Ninety percent of his efforts were geared toward preparing research; the other ten percent was just to look busy. He prayed that neither woman would drag him into their argument. He was smart enough to realize that it was a no-win situation, so he kept his head down.

Cobb reentered the room a moment later. He was carrying a large cylinder that was fancier than the cardboard tubes commonly used to ship posters. This one was made of brushed metal, with a heavy leather shoulder strap connected to each end. While Jasmine held her breath, he took his seat and unscrewed the top cap of the case.

'Hector,' Cobb said, 'can you illuminate the tabletop?'

'How do you mean?'

'Can you make the surface bright like a drafting table?'

Garcia tapped on his keyboard, searching for the right command. When he found it, the top of the table began to glow. It was a clean, almost blinding sheen of white.

'Perfect,' Cobb said. With that, he removed the map from the canister and spread it across the table for everyone to see.

Against the gleaming tabletop, the dark lines of the map stood out like ink stains on a wedding dress. The ancient city was presented as a tangled web of intersecting lines and shapes, stretching south from the Mediterranean Sea to the northern edge of the Western Desert. The markings were so dense and overlapping that it was nearly impossible to determine where one stroke ended and the next began.

Despite her eager energy, Jasmine was more confused than captivated – and she wasn't alone. No one knew what to make of the sprawling mess in front of them.

McNutt furrowed his brow. 'What are we looking at?'

Cobb had anticipated their confusion because he had felt the exact same way before the document had been explained to him in Switzerland. 'That, my friends, is the entire history of Alexandria compiled into a single map. Every building that's ever been built or razed; every footpath, trail, road, and highway that's ever been laid; every well and every waterway that's ever snaked its way through the ancient city – all assembled into one map for our plundering pleasure.'

He took a step back and allowed them to get a closer look.

'Notice,' he said confidently, 'the labels were written in accordance with the era. They represent the people who controlled Alexandria during the time of construction. If it was built by the Egyptians, the label was written in Egyptian, and so on.'

Sarah tried to decipher the map, but it was no use. She spotted at least ten distinct languages, none of which was English. 'Jasmine, please tell me that you can make sense of this. Otherwise, this document is useless.'

'I can translate *some* of the map,' she explained. 'But I don't know anyone that could decipher these labels with a single glance. It's going to take some time.'

McNutt voiced his doubt. 'Forget the labels. Look at those lines. How is anyone supposed to follow that mess? It looks like Spider-Man took a shit on the table.'

Garcia laughed. 'I'm with Josh. I wouldn't even know where to begin.'

'Me neither,' Sarah admitted.

'Nor I,' Papineau added.

'Thankfully, I do,' Cobb said as he walked around the opposite side of the table and subtly moistened the tip of his thumb and index finger with his tongue. Then he grabbed the top corner of the map and gave it a slight twist. 'Like most problems in life, it's best to attack them one step at a time.'

The paper separated into multiple layers, revealing that the map was actually a collection of pages. Each sheet of translucent paper had been perfectly stacked on the sheet beneath it. When viewed together, the image was cluttered and difficult to comprehend, but the individual maps were much easier to understand.

Cobb flipped to the last page in the stack. 'The bottom map predates Alexander's arrival in Egypt – before the city of Alexandria came to exist.'

McNutt stared at the image. 'So . . . we're looking at a map of nothing?'

'Not nothing,' Jasmine assured him. 'Rhacotis.'

'Gesundheit.'

Jasmine smiled. 'I didn't sneeze, Josh. That was the name of the settlement before it was formalized as a city in 331 BC. Rhacotis dates back at least two thousand years *before* Alexander.'

McNutt nodded in understanding. 'Which means we can ignore it because Alexander wasn't dead yet.'

Sarah clapped sarcastically. 'Look at that, the monkey's learning.'

McNutt laughed and beat on his chest like a gorilla. 'Me smart monkey. Me take rock and beat Sarah in sleep as Pedro watch on fancy box.'

Garcia objected. 'My name isn't Pedro, and I don't watch Sarah when she sleeps! How many times do I have to tell you that?'

'That depends. When are you going to tell the truth?'

'I am telling the truth!' he assured the group.

Earlier, Cobb had cleared his throat to quiet the group. This time he felt the need to go a step further. He put two fingers in his mouth and unleashed a whistle so loud and shrill that Garcia was afraid the hi-tech table was going to shatter. He instinctively flung himself on the glass while the rest of the team covered their ears.

In their limited time together Cobb had never revealed this particular talent, so the team didn't know what to make of it. They simply stared at him with a combination of shock and awe; as if they had heard the voice of the devil himself.

'Now that I have your attention,' he growled as he glared at them in turn, 'I think it would be best if we stopped screwing around and focused on the mission at hand. We have a unique opportunity here to find something that's been lost for two thousand years, and I'll be damned if we're going to piss it away on my watch. Am I clear?'

The team nodded and lowered their eyes in shame.

'Good,' Cobb said with finality. He pointed at Jasmine, the only one who had stayed on task. 'Sorry about that. What were you saying about Rhacotis?'

She pointed at a section of the document. 'I'm glad the map starts in this particular era because Rhacotis – this shaded area on the northern coast – served a key function in the eventual design of Alexandria. The architect from Greece who planned the city, a man named Dinocrates, realized the importance of Rhacotis when he surveyed the terrain. Unlike many ports in the Nile Delta, Rhacotis was able to accommodate larger ships because of the depth of the harbor. So instead of tearing down Rhacotis and starting from scratch, he built the city around it. The locals were so appreciative, the area flourished and served as the Egyptian quarter of the city.'

'Good to know,' Cobb said as he grabbed the corner of the second page and flipped it over the first. As if by magic, the city doubled in size. 'Every layer represents a significant passage of time. Battles were fought, and land was won. With each new regime, a new layer was added to the map. This explains the destruction and construction of landmarks and the use of multiple languages.'

Garcia snapped to attention. 'I think I can help us with that.'

'How?' Jasmine wondered.

He reached out to grab the nearest corner of the map. Before touching it, he glanced at Cobb for permission. 'May I?'

'Of course,' Cobb replied.

Garcia pulled the top layer of the stack, separating it from the pile. He pushed it to the far corner of the hi-tech table. Next he took the second layer and arranged it beside the top layer. He continued pulling sheets from the pile until the whole table was covered with the various layers of the map.

Sarah stared at him. 'What in the world are you doing?'

'Just a second,' Garcia said as he hunched over his virtual workstation, typing furiously on the display. 'I promise it will be worth your while.'

The group watched in confused fascination as his fingers flew across the glass surface, the rapid-fire assault of his hands occasionally punctuated by a swipe or a distinct double tap of his keyboard. They had no idea what he was doing, but his agility and intense concentration were impressive nonetheless.

'Done!' he boasted with a final tap of a key.

'With what?' McNutt asked.

'With everything!'

Garcia pointed to the wall-sized video screen behind Papineau, which was now filled with a thumbnail image of every page of the map. Aligned along the left edge of the screen, the images were too small to be of any real use unless they were expanded to full size. For now, they served as a visual reference for the real focus of activity.

In the center of the screen, two windows displayed a flurry of movement. In the first, various sections of the map were being analyzed by an automated program designed to recognize letters within images. If one was found, it copied the letter to the second window where the program tried to identify the letter and language. Eventually words were formed, analyzed, and translated into English. With a touch of a button, Garcia could see the original letters, the language of origin, and even search for connections to other documents in the program's extensive database.

Jasmine gasped as she moved closer to the wall. She reached out and touched the ancient letters as they were projected on the screen. 'That's amazing. Simply amazing. If I had been forced to translate those maps by hand, it would have taken weeks. Yet you did it all in a matter of minutes. I can't thank you enough.'

Papineau nodded his approval. 'Well done. Well done indeed!'

Garcia beamed with pride.

Though impressed, Cobb was more pragmatic than the others. 'Where'd you get that? Did you design it yourself?'

'I wish,' Garcia admitted. 'I tweaked some things to get it to run more efficiently with our hardware, but the program itself came preloaded with the table. According to the manual, it was created by the Ulster Archives – some research facility in Sweden.'

'Switzerland,' stated Cobb, who had been unaware of the place before his dinner meeting with Ulster.

'Wherever,' Garcia said. 'The program didn't come with a title, so I gave it one of my own. I call it: *The Word Is Not Enough*.'

Sarah rolled her eyes. This was the second time Garcia had named something after a James Bond film. In their previous mission, they had used a program called *Goldfinder*. 'What's with you and 007?'

Garcia shrugged. 'I'm just a fan.'

'Me, too,' McNutt admitted. 'I mean, what's not to like? Fast cars, cool gadgets, and lots of loose women. Sounds like heaven to me.'

Garcia smiled knowingly. 'Josh, if you think *Bond*'s gadgets are cool, just you wait. You're going to love this . . .'

6

Garcia promised something cool – and he delivered.

The team watched in awe as the city of Alexandria rose from the tabletop like a ghostly apparition. An avid believer in the supernatural, McNutt slowly pushed away from the table, worried if he moved too quickly the poltergeist might attack him.

Garcia looked up from his keyboard and grinned. Only he knew how the illusion worked. 'The city is exactly to scale. Or rather, it's exactly what is represented on Jack's map. The computer can't tell the actual heights of the buildings, so those are approximated from the square footage of their bases and satellite imaging. If you give me more time, I can hack the city planner's office and make things perfect.'

The others remained silent as the city continued to rise, layer after projected layer. But instead of sprouting from the bottom, structures now materialized in a wave around the perimeter of the city as it sprawled farther and farther from the center.

Sarah waved her hand through the projection, searching for a reflective surface, but her hand passed through the image. 'How is this even possible?'

Garcia ignored her question. He was having too much fun blowing their minds. 'What you see is a reproduction of modern Alexandria. The city as it exists today.' He tapped a few buttons on his keyboard. 'Now if we overlay the previous map, we get something like this . . .'

Several structures disappeared as others took their places.

Garcia glanced at Cobb. 'If you'd like, I can keep going until we have every detail from every page of the map.'

Cobb nodded, his eyes never leaving the city.

Garcia entered a new command, and suddenly the holographic images intersected and overlapped in every conceivable way — similar to the chaos of earlier when they tried to view the document as a single map instead of separate maps. In many instances, whole buildings appeared to be consumed by larger ones like hungry nesting dolls.

Jasmine stared in disbelief. 'This is incredible!'

Sarah was more flummoxed than impressed, and she didn't appreciate the feeling. 'Seriously, how is this possible?'

Garcia shrugged, revealing nothing.

'Fine,' she snapped. 'I'll figure it out myself.'

He crossed his hands behind his head and smugly leaned back in his chair. 'Be my guest.'

Never one to pass on a challenge, Sarah stood for a better look. 'Under normal circumstances, light would need something to interrupt its path, like a screen or something. Otherwise it can't be seen by the naked eye.'

'True.'

She passed her hand through the image again, then watched Jasmine do the same on the opposite side of the table. 'But there's no screen here.'

'Nope.'

She leaned to the left and then to the right, hoping to learn more. 'For a truly three-dimensional hologram, you need something in the air — dust, water vapor, *something* — to reflect the light.' She rubbed her fingers together. 'But I can't feel anything.'

'If you could, you'd be the first.'

Cobb cleared his throat and tapped his watch.

Garcia got the hint and ended the game. He pointed to the air-conditioning vent above the table. 'This room uses specially formulated air. Its molecular composition is designed to reflect certain wavelengths of lights. When used in conjunction with the appropriate laser, you're able to do something like this.'

Cobb nodded knowingly. 'It's technology co-opted from the US military. The ability to project an image can be used in a variety of ways. For instance, it can fool the enemy into thinking our numbers are far greater than they actually are. In the not-too-distant future, we'll be able to create a battalion of fake soldiers out of thin air.'

'Correction,' Garcia said. 'Not out of thin air. Out of *thick* air.'

Cobb smiled. 'Duly noted.'

'Is it safe?' Jasmine wondered. 'We're not breathing in air loaded with lead or mercury or something like that, are we?'

Garcia shook his head. 'No, it's perfectly safe. It's a combination of—'

Papineau cut him off. 'I think your word is enough for now. The exact nature of the chemical elements is not important. If Hector says it's safe, it's safe.'

Jasmine nodded. 'If you say so.'

'Soooo,' echoed Sarah, who was still upset that she hadn't been given enough time to figure out the device, 'your toy is cool and all, but I don't see how it's going to help us find the tomb. I mean, a map is still a map – even if it's in 3-D.'

'Actually, it's a *lot* more than that.' Garcia extended his right arm with his hand facing up. Then he placed his left hand over his outstretched palm and slowly spread them apart. The movement, which looked like a gator's jaw opening, caused the layers of the holographic map to separate. Just as the paper map had been divided into sheets, the virtual map was now displayed as a stack of separate levels.

'Now watch this,' he bragged.

With a simple twitch of his finger, the program cycled through the layers of the map. Choosing one at random, he reached out and flipped his wrist to the side. As if by magic, the entire map began to spin on a center axis.

McNutt grumbled, still unwilling to approach the table as the ethereal map floated in front of him like a creature from *Ghostbusters*.

Meanwhile, Jasmine was ecstatic. 'Hector, this is amazing! Seeing the city presented like this provides so much more perspective.'

'How so?' Sarah asked.

'Within each layer there are noticeable developments, but the distinct layers appear to match perfectly with the changes that the city has undergone throughout the years. Hector, take us back to the bottom layer, please.'

Garcia did as he was told.

'The first layer represents the first three hundred years of the region. We know during that era the city was divided into five districts, or quarters, named after the first five letters of the Greek alphabet.' She pointed to the model. 'Look here and here. See how the city appears to be broken into five distinct regions. It's exactly what we would expect to find. Each subset of the populace had its preferred area, much like you'd find in cities today.'

'Flip to the next layer,' ordered Papineau, who approached the table. It was his way of not only urging Jasmine to continue but to see if her theory was correct.

Jasmine studied the map, looking for clues. 'Notice the difference? Now the borders between the regions have all but disappeared. The neighborhoods have been intertwined, a likely result of the newer Roman occupation and the conflict with the Ptolemies who sought to regain the land under their name. Please, keep going.'

Garcia flipped to the next map. The third level was almost incompatible with the previous version, as if the entire city had been razed and reconstructed.

Jasmine smiled, knowing that a complete transformation had taken place.

Papineau knew it too. Now convinced that Jasmine's theory was accurate, he urged her to continue her narration.

She happily obliged. 'Alexandria was nearly erased during the Kitos War. It was rebuilt under the direction of the Roman emperor Hadrian. His city stood until 365. On July the twenty-first of that year, the city was wiped clean again by the tsunami that Jean-Marc mentioned earlier. What wasn't destroyed by the flood – the so-called pagan temples – was torn down thirty years later when Christianity took hold of the city.'

Garcia turned to the next map.

'The Muslim conquest of Egypt changed the landscape yet again. It was the last major upheaval of control in Alexandria until the Ottoman reign of the fifteen hundreds. After that, the remaining redevelopment of the eighteen hundreds and nineteen hundreds was limited to localized damage inflicted during various battles and skirmishes.'

Garcia flipped back to the modern city as Jasmine finished her lecture.

'With these maps, we can trace the entire evolution of Alexandria from its inception to its current layout today.'

'And most importantly,' said Garcia, who was quite content working in the air-conditioned mansion, 'we don't even have to go to Egypt.'

Sarah rolled her eyes. 'I guess that means your table is going to magically find the treasure and beam it here like something from *Star Trek*?'

He rubbed his chin in thought. 'Maybe.'

'Now *that* would be cool!' McNutt blurted. It had taken a while, but he was finally warming up to the table. 'Where did you learn how to do all of that?'

'All of what?'

McNutt tried to replicate some of Garcia's hand gestures, but he looked like the town drunk trying to learn sign language. 'That wizard stuff.'

Garcia laughed. 'I was still working for the FBI when they introduced this system. It just so happens that they chose the Miami field office for the pilot program. That meant I was one of the first people in the entire bureau to get my hands on this technology. No pun intended.'

Garcia brought his palms together, thrust them into the hologram, and then pulled them apart like he was playing the accordion. In response the image expanded, revealing a level of detail that was truly phenomenal.

'I fell in love with the program almost immediately. I started putting it through its paces, seeing what it could really do, and it never let me down. But the bosses up the ladder couldn't figure it out. They were too set in their ways. They were convinced that corkboards and slideshows were better methods of processing information. Freaking dinosaurs, if you ask me.'

Jasmine mimicked his gestures. 'How does it work?'

Garcia pointed up. 'There are motion-capture cameras mounted in the ceiling that monitor your movements. The computer translates certain actions as specific requests. That information is conveyed to the various lasers that actually draw the map. They adjust the image accordingly.' He moved his hand like he was spinning a globe, causing the image to twist on its axis. 'It's very intuitive.'

Jasmine reached out and grabbed the map, bringing the hologram to an abrupt stop. She smiled like a kid who had just learned how to ride a bike.

Garcia beamed with pride. 'Ten years ago it was cutting-edge science reserved for government entities. Now they're using the same basic tech in video game consoles. Granted, they have more limitations than this, but the concepts are the same.'

Enjoying his moment in the spotlight, Garcia reached down and plucked a building from the map. Then he cocked his arm and threw it toward McNutt. 'Catch!'

Still trying to wrap his head around the technology, McNutt wasn't sure if the building would shatter on impact if he didn't catch the hologram, so he gave it his all and jumped high into the air – only to topple over his chair and crash to the ground.

The profanity that followed made Jasmine blush.

Meanwhile, Garcia yanked his hand back as if he were playing with a yo-yo. The flying building suddenly stopped in midair, reversed course, and headed back toward Garcia, who caught it and placed it back on the map with a huge grin on his face.

Sarah couldn't help but laugh.

McNutt continued to curse as he pulled himself back into his seat. It took him a moment to gather his senses. 'What happened?' Papineau answered drily. 'You missed.'

7

Cobb remained focused on the task at hand. He had to admit that the holographic map was far more impressive than the paper version. He hoped it would be more effective, too. 'How long will it take to analyze the layout of the city and come up with a list of possible locations for the tomb?'

Jasmine shook her head. 'First of all, let me be perfectly clear: there is almost no chance – zero – that Alexander's body is still buried in Alexandria. The area has been too well developed to hold out hope for a miracle like that. No, what we're looking for are clues as to where and when the tomb was moved.'

Cobb grimaced. 'You're one hundred percent sure that Alexander isn't there?'

'Well, no,' she admitted, 'I'm not a hundred percent sure about anything. But I can tell you this: people have been scouring the city for the last two thousand years, looking for Alexander. I choose to believe that if someone had credible evidence that he was still buried there, they would have found him by now.'

Cobb pointed at the hologram. 'But what about this? I thought this map *was* new evidence – something that no one else had at their disposal.'

'True,' she conceded, 'the map is a revelation. It offers tremendous insights into a place that was literally erased by time. With these new pieces of the puzzle, the things we could uncover about the ancient city are . . . well, they're limitless.'

'I understand that and I'm happy for you and historians around the world, but I'm not concerned about the full implications of the map. For now, all I need you to do is figure out what it tells us about Alexander. That's it. I simply need to know if the map will narrow down our list of possibilities; and if so, how long that process will take.'

'Okay. I can do that.'

Papineau cleared his throat at the head of the table.

Cobb glared at him. 'What?'

'If you're assigning tasks, does this mean that you've accepted my terms and will be leading the next mission?'

The team glanced at him, hopeful.

Cobb mulled it over. 'I'm in . . . for now.'

It was not the enthusiastic response that Papineau had been hoping for, but it was music to the squad's ears. They knew Cobb much better than Papineau did and he would not accept a mission that was doomed to fail; particularly one with so much at stake. As crazy as it sounded, if a levelheaded leader like Cobb believed that they could find Alexander's lost tomb, they knew it was more than possible.

They knew it was likely.

Instantly, a wave of energy surged through the team.

'Jasmine,' Cobb said, pulling their attention back to the matter at hand, 'can you have something for me by the end of the day?'

Jasmine grimaced and nodded at the exact same time. 'I can have *something* for you, yes. But it won't be everything. It might not even be close.'

'That's fine. All I need is a place to start. We can figure out the rest as we go.' He turned toward Garcia. 'Hector, I'm willing to bet that this program has a few more bells and whistles we haven't seen yet. Hopefully some of that can help Jasmine better understand what she's looking at. You'll show her what the technology can do?'

It was an order disguised as a question. Of everyone in the group, Cobb knew that Garcia had the most sensitive disposition. Appealing to his sense of importance was a small concession to keep him motivated.

'Absolutely,' Garcia replied. 'We've barely scratched the surface. You should see what this thing can do!'

'Another time,' Cobb said. 'Right now, I'll leave it up to you and Jasmine. She's the expert, but you're her Yoda. Walk her through everything.'

'My pleasure, it will be,' he croaked in Yoda's voice.

Cobb spun in his chair and stared across the table at McNutt. He could only smile as McNutt continually reached out in an attempt to grab the holographic images. He was thankful that the Marine was battle-tested, otherwise Papineau would have kicked him out of the unit as Section 8: *mentally unfit for service*.

Suddenly aware of Cobb's staring, McNutt snapped to attention. 'Yes, chief?'

'What do you know about Egypt?'

'It's in the Middle East. Does that answer your question?'

'No, but it's a start.'

'Control of the country is tenuous, at best. The national president has managed to piss off nearly everyone on both the Muslim and Christian sides of the aisle. In short, I think he's fighting for his political life – if not his actual life. Based on violence at recent protests, I'd say Egypt is on the verge of civil war.'

Cobb smiled, but not at the news. He found it amusing that McNutt, someone who seemingly viewed the world through cartoon eyes, was able to brief him on the political climate in the Middle East without any prep time, and yet a few minutes earlier he had just fallen over his chair in an attempt to catch a hologram.

'Take the rest of the day,' Cobb said to McNutt. 'Find out everything you can about the region: who's fighting who, where, and for what reasons. I want to know whom we can trust, if anyone, and whom we need to avoid at all costs. I also need a map of safe zones and restricted areas. Plus, I need a list of friendlies.'

'Friendlies?' McNutt said with a grin. 'Chief, I haven't been to that part of the world in years. And even when I was there, I was usually a thousand yards away from a target, laying low, waiting for an opportunity to strike. Establishing connections with the locals was a little above my pay grade.'

'Not to mention his abilities as a human being,' Sarah added.

McNutt laughed. 'See, she gets me. Yes, I'm adorable, and yes, women want to rip my pants off, but my sense of humor doesn't really translate to other cultures.'

'Doesn't translate to ours, either.'

'Exactly!' McNutt said. 'I'm not the guy you ask to make friends.'

Cobb conceded the point. 'Fine. Don't worry about the friendlies. But I want you to get me everything else by the end of the day. Understood?'

'Understood.'

'Good. I'm sure Garcia can set you up with whatever you need.'

On cue, Garcia pulled a laptop from a shelf in the corner and handed it to McNutt. 'It's already connected to our encrypted network. You have access to government and military databases, and just about anything else you can think of.'

'How about Google?' McNutt asked with a straight face.

Garcia chuckled. 'Yeah, it has Google.'

'Then we're all set,' McNutt replied. He grabbed the laptop and hurdled the small wall that separated the conference table from the more casual side of the room. He plopped onto a plush recliner, opened the laptop, and starting typing.

'He's like an obedient dog,' Sarah mused.

'You're right,' Cobb answered. 'When the time comes, he does exactly as he's been told. *Exactly*. No surprises. That's more than I can say for some people.'

'Am I too much for you to handle?' Sarah asked.

'I'm not sure. Let's go outside and find out.'

'Wait . . . What?'

'You and me, right now, out in the yard.'

'Hold up. You want to fight me?'

Cobb shrugged, as if to say he had nothing better to do.

'What about the mission prep?'

He scanned the room. 'Hector and Jasmine are looking into the map and the history of the city. McNutt is outlining our options for a visit. So unless you know something about Alexandria that you're not telling me, you can either stay here and play cards with Jean-Marc, or you can get some exercise with me in the yard. Your choice.'

She smiled. 'You're on.'

* * *

Sarah had started the day in blue jeans and a T-shirt but had traded the casual attire for something more athletic. Now she wore the type of outfit she preferred in the field: a form-fitting

57

black bodysuit that afforded an unrestricted range of motion and helped to conceal her covert movements. Although she looked the part of a cat burglar, she didn't view herself as one. Instead, she preferred 'retrieval specialist' to 'thief'.

For one reason or another, she hated that word.

Regardless of her title, the end result was the same.

She was still being paid to acquire items that didn't belong to her.

And she was very good at her job.

She circled Cobb like a hungry wolf. She was confident, but she knew her enemy could attack at any moment. She kept moving, searching for the right opportunity to strike. 'You really think this is the best use of our time?'

Cobb cracked his neck from side to side, then rolled his sleeves above his elbows. 'Do I think *what* is the best use of our time?'

'This,' she answered. 'Fighting.'

He shrugged. 'You're the only one who said anything about fighting. I just mentioned coming outside, and you took it as a personal challenge. Just like you always do. One of these days, we'll have to figure out why.'

'Wait. So what is this?'

'This is us having a conversation,' Cobb replied. 'Away from curious ears that might want to listen in if they thought we were up to something sneaky.'

He leaped forward and tried to sweep Sarah's leg with his own.

Sarah dodged the attack and threw a jab toward Cobb's midsection. 'You mean this is all just misdirection? You weren't really challenging me?'

Cobb deflected the punch and stepped back. 'Why would I

challenge you? I know what you can do in the field. I've seen you in action. I'll take McNutt in a gunfight, but in hand-to-hand combat, you're the one I want to watch my back.'

It was one of the highest compliments that Cobb could bestow upon her, and she knew it. She instantly swelled with pride. 'In that case, what do you need to talk about?'

'You've seen the video cameras recording our every move?' To emphasize his remark, he grabbed her arm and spun her tightly into his chest. It was meant to look like a modified bearhug/chokehold of some kind, but it actually allowed her to survey the entire yard as she twirled around.

'I count six,' she said as she tried to wiggle free. 'Three along the balcony and another three along the rear hedge.'

'What about inside?'

'Too many to count. Why?'

With her arms pinned to her sides, she kicked a leg toward the sky and hit Cobb in the face. Had she wanted to, she could have easily broken his nose. But since they were just putting on a show, she only hit him hard enough to make it look good.

Cobb released his grip and shoved her away. 'I want to know if there's anywhere private on these grounds. It seems that Papineau wants to watch our every move, and I need to know if he's got the whole place covered. If he doesn't, I want to know where our team can go to be alone. No cameras. No mics. Just us.'

'Countersurveillance,' she said. 'That's what you really want, isn't it? You want to watch him watch us.'

'We'll get to that later, but first, I need to know what he can and can't see. Can you handle that for me?'

'With pleasure.'

'If possible, I'd like you to do it before you leave for Egypt.'

She stopped circling. 'I'm leaving for Egypt?'

Cobb used the distraction to charge forward. Had he wanted to, he could have taken her out with a number of different moves, including an open-palmed strike to her nose that would have ruined her face forever. Instead, he opted to teach her a lesson by slapping the back of her head. 'Focus! Never let your guard down!'

She sneered at him. 'Screw you, Mr Miyagi.'

He ignored the *Karate Kid* reference. 'I'm serious. If this is going to work, I need you to stay focused at all times. Otherwise, we'll get into trouble.'

She returned to her fighting stance, looking for the opportunity to take him out. 'If what's going to work?'

'Our joint rekky to Egypt.'

She smiled. 'Hold on, are you asking me out?'

'Yes,' he said sarcastically, 'I'm taking you on a romantic getaway to war-torn Egypt because unstable governments are a huge turn-on for me.'

'No judgment. Whatever floats your boat.'

Cobb shook his head and circled to his right. 'You know damn well that I like checking out the scenery before I plan a mission, but considering the chaos in Egypt right now, I thought a second set of eyes might come in handy.'

'Makes sense to me. Should I bring lingerie, or do you prefer—'

'You know what? Forget it!' he said, blushing slightly. 'I'll take the trip alone. But while I'm gone, I'm leaving McNutt in charge of the team. I'm sure that will be a lot of fun for you. I can picture it now: a solid week of cleaning his guns while he's watching cartoons with the strippers he brought back from the club.'

She grimaced at the thought. 'So, when are we leaving for Egypt?'

Cobb nodded. 'Yeah. That's what I thought.'

'Seriously, when are we leaving?'

'I'll let you know. In the meantime, I need you to strangle me.'

'Jack, I'm not going to—'

'You know Papi's going to see this, and everyone heard you throw down the gauntlet. So we have three choices: I kick your ass, you kick mine, or we call it a tie.'

'I'll go with door number two.'

'I assumed as much. So here's what's going to happen. I'm going to attack, and you're going to—'

Sarah didn't wait for him to finish his instructions. Instead, she planted a foot on his knee and grabbed his shoulders. Then she swung her body around his like an acrobat, wrapped her arm around his throat, and leaned back with all of her weight.

The two of them fell to the ground.

As they did, she tightened her grip on his neck, her bicep squeezing his carotid artery like a python crushing its prey.

In a matter of seconds, he would be unconscious.

'Atta girl,' he said as he closed his eyes.

8

Built on the site of the Lighthouse of Alexandria, the Citadel of Qaitbay once represented the first line of defense against the invading forces that tried to conquer the city. But much like the ruins of the lighthouse itself, which were used as building materials for the massive stronghold, the citadel was forced to change with the times. No longer a military outpost, the restored fortress now houses a maritime museum on the outermost reaches of Alexandria's Eastern Harbor.

In most countries, this site would be a major attraction.

In Egypt, it was barely a footnote.

That spoke volumes about the area.

The entire region was filled with history.

Sarah stood near the main wall of the citadel and stared out across the bay. Behind her, the windswept waves of the Mediterranean Sea crashed against the break wall. In front of her, the city of Alexandria sprawled well beyond what she could see.

As the country's largest port, Alexandria hugs the northern coast of Egypt for nearly twenty miles and handles three-quarters of Egypt's foreign trade. Because of this, most of the development has occurred within two miles of the water. The long, narrow city is home to more than four million culturally diverse residents who have established some fifty distinct neighborhoods over six geographical regions.

Cobb and Sarah had only been in Egypt for a few days, but they had already visited many of the city's most recognized sites. They had started in the northeastern district, working their way south toward the Catacombs of Kom el Shoqafa – a massive, three-tiered burial chamber in the southernmost corner. They had kept to a tight schedule, familiarizing themselves with the layout of Alexandria, but there was still a lot of ground to cover before the team arrived.

In the military, this was known as a 'rekky'.

It was short for reconnaissance.

Cobb took in the view of the modern city. 'It doesn't look like a place that's seen nearly twenty-five hundred years of renovations, does it?'

Sarah didn't reply. She simply stood there, transfixed.

All it took was one glance, and Cobb understood her silence. 'How long has it been?'

She snapped out of her haze. 'How long has what been?'

'I've seen that stare before. That's not the look of someone who's establishing her thoughts for the first time. That's the look of someone who's remembering something. You've been here before. I'm simply asking how long ago.'

'Six years,' she said reluctantly. She turned to face him, her defenses on full display. 'And no, I don't want to talk about it.'

'Is it going to be a problem?'

'No,' she insisted.

'If you say so.'

Cobb didn't know everything about Sarah, but he knew

63

enough. She had been one of the Central Intelligence Agency's top assets. In light of her natural abilities – which were off the charts – she had received extensive training in the areas of infiltration and acquisitions. If she had been to Alexandria in her past life, there were two things he knew that no one would ever find: evidence of her visit, and the bodies she left behind.

To lower her defenses, he decided to change the conversation to a neutral subject. 'You'll never guess what was here before the citadel was constructed.'

Sarah gave him a funny look. 'What is this, a history lesson? If I wanted one of those, I'd call Jasmine.'

He smiled. 'I promise it's not a lecture. It's just something I read while we were walking the grounds. I thought it was interesting.'

She didn't know what to make of Cobb's sudden interest in playing tour guide. While he rarely gave her the icy stare that he often used with Papineau, he certainly hadn't earned a reputation for small talk. If this was his way of flirting, then he was clearly out of practice. 'No, Jack, I have no idea what used to be here.'

'Centuries ago, this was the site of the Lighthouse of Alexandria. It was a towering structure that stood nearly four hundred feet tall. At the top was a massive furnace, and its flames could be seen for more than fifty miles out to sea. It stood for nearly sixteen hundred years and was considered an absolute marvel of engineering. So much so that historians deemed it one of the Seven Wonders of the Ancient World.'

She glanced behind her and tried to imagine the lighthouse. It must have been a sight to behold for citizens and tourists alike. 'What happened to it? I imagine a four-hundred-foot pillar is pretty hard to dismantle.'

'Not for Mother Nature,' he said. 'A series of earthquakes destroyed the lighthouse at the turn of the fourteenth century. Some of the lighthouse was reused in the construction of the citadel, but most of it ended up at the bottom of the bay.' He stared into the blue waters of the harbor, then shifted his gaze to the city beyond. 'Two thousand years of history are buried out there. We just have to figure out where to start.'

Sarah remained quiet, deep in thought, for nearly a minute before she turned from Cobb and started to walk away. She made it all the way to the end of the stone platform before she cursed under her breath and walked back toward Cobb, who hadn't budged from his spot along the wall.

'Fine!' she blurted.

'Fine, what?'

'Fine, I'll fill you in.'

Cobb smiled. 'I thought you didn't want to talk about it.'

'I don't want to talk about it, but it's pretty obvious that you're going to torture me until I do.'

'Torture? I didn't think my story was *that* bad.'

'I'm not talking about your story. I'm talking about your no-pressure sales pitch. You know damn well that I worked in this region for several months; otherwise you wouldn't have invited me on this rekky. Yet in all this time, you haven't asked for any specifics. Not in Florida. Not on the plane. And not here. Why?'

'Because it's none of my business.'

'It isn't?'

He shook his head. 'Your work with the Agency is classified, right? Well, guess what: my past is filled with classified missions, too, and I'm sure as hell not going to tell you about them because it would violate the trust of others. I figure, if you can't trust your teammates, who can you trust?'

'Exactly!'

He stared at the waves as they made their way toward the shore. 'Then again, there are exceptions to every rule . . .'

'Such as?'

'For instance, if my past missions endangered the lives of my current team, then I would man up and tell you what you needed to know – even if I had to break the trust of others. Either that, or I would opt out of the mission entirely.'

'No, you wouldn't.'

'Yes, I would,' he assured her, 'because your safety – and the safety of our team – is my number one priority. Why do you think I flew halfway around the world? It certainly wasn't to eat hummus or to work on my tan. No, I hopped on a plane to figure out the path of least resistance to complete our mission. And just so you know, I brought you along because of your training, not because of your past.'

Cobb paused for effect. 'That being said, if you knew something about this city that you're keeping from me, I'd be more than upset – I'd be disappointed.'

'In that case, there's someone you need to meet.'

'A colleague?'

She shook her head. 'Not exactly.'

9

Sarah sat at the far end of the bar, alone, sipping what appeared to be her third vodka tonic. To the untrained eye, it was nothing more than a single woman getting a head start on a group of friends who were sure to arrive at any moment. But for those in the know, it was a specific set of protocols that had been established long ago.

She wasn't in this tavern because she liked the décor or because it was the easiest place to park. Sarah had sought out this particular place because it was a *gateway* – a monitored location where she could arrange a meeting with a local contact.

Or at least it used to be, many years ago.

After placing her order she had taken a seat on the farthest stool, the one closest to the back door. If she had been given anything other than club soda with a twist of lime, she would have known that the bartender was not aware of her request and the protocols had changed. That would have forced her to make contact through other means.

Fortunately, Sarah's drink was non-alcoholic.

Now all she had to do was wait.

After nearly an hour, she was tempted to leave because she had told Cobb, who was monitoring the tavern from across the street, that this rendezvous would take no more than thirty minutes, and she imagined his patience was wearing thin. They had agreed that her plan would never work if he sat next to her, but they had never discussed their window of opportunity.

She looked at her watch.

She knew that window was closing.

'Hey, sugar,' a voice said from behind. It was spoken in English, with the curious accent of someone who had been raised in the South but educated in New England.

Sarah turned and greeted her companion with a hug. 'Simon, it's about damn time. I was beginning to think you weren't going to show.'

'Great to see you, too,' he said with a laugh. 'I would've made it sooner, but it's not like I was sitting at home, waiting for you to show up after six years. No, I was out doing some sightseeing today – checking out the local sites like the Citadel of Qaitbay. Great place, interesting view.'

She groaned. 'How long have you known?'

He smiled. 'Three days.'

'You've been onto me the entire time?'

'Yep. You and your muscular friend. Is he your bodyguard?'

'Of course not! He's, um, an associate.'

'Is that a fancy word for *boyfriend*?'

'No!' she said. 'He's not my boyfriend. He's—'

Simon shook his head. 'Not here.'

She glanced around the room. 'Are you saying we aren't safe?'

'I'm saying a lot has changed since your last visit. You may not want to be seen with me in public.'

Sarah smiled. 'Oh, *now* I get it. You have a girlfriend.'

'No,' he said, blushing slightly, 'it's not that.'

She furrowed her brow. 'A wife?'

'Definitely not!'

'Then what?'

Before he had a chance to explain, a black sedan screeched to a halt in front of the bar. Two large men jumped from the car and stormed toward the front door. It was pretty obvious that they weren't there to drink.

Simon saw them through the window and cursed. Then he grabbed her arm and pulled her toward the rear exit. There was no time to explain his situation; not if they wanted to live. 'Like I said, a lot has changed. We gotta go . . . *now!*'

The thugs ran through the front door as Sarah and Simon fled out the back.

'There!' the first thug shouted in Arabic as he pointed toward their escape. The men gave chase, knocking over tables and chairs as they thundered through the saloon like a herd of buffalo.

Clearly frightened, Simon burst through the rear exit of the bar and sprinted down an alley that reeked of cat piss and garbage. Sarah matched him stride for stride.

'Where are we going?' she yelled.

'Just keep running,' he shouted.

The exit door flew open behind them as the first thug slammed into it. He was a bear of a man, with muscular arms and fists the size of melons. Remarkably, the second goon was even bigger, as if he had been fed steaks and steroids from the time of his hatching – because there was no way in hell anyone had given birth to him.

He was simply too damn big.

Simon reached the end of the alley and broke sharply to the right, down the busy street. Sarah followed suit, glancing over her shoulder to check out the thugs, who were blessed with less speed than size. Unfortunately, her joy was short-lived. Even on a dead run, she spotted something troubling: the black sedan from the bar was weaving through traffic and heading toward them at a high rate of speed.

'Shit!' she screamed as she struggled to grab her gun. It was tucked in her belt underneath her shirt. 'We have company!'

'More?' Simon wasn't happy with the news. He glanced back and saw the car. It was closing fast. 'Run faster, Sarah!'

'Screw you, Simon!'

At that moment, she was tempted to ditch Simon and cut her losses. After all, they were chasing him, not her, and the last thing she needed was to get entangled in someone else's mess. But a split second before she bailed, she heard the blare of a horn followed by a familiar voice.

'Sarah,' Cobb shouted, 'get in the damn car!'

She turned to see Cobb staring back at her from the driver's seat of the black sedan. The thugs had abandoned it in front of the bar, no more than twenty feet from Cobb's position across the street. With the keys inside and the motor running, stealing the car required less effort than hailing a cab.

Plus, there was no need to leave a tip.

Cobb slowed down just enough for her to open the rear passenger door. This time, it was Sarah who grabbed Simon by the arm. Diving into the back, she pulled him inside the car and on top of her. He reached back and pulled the door shut.

Meanwhile, Cobb casually checked the side mirror. He saw the goons emerge from the alley and scan the street for their prey.

They did not look happy.

'You're good,' said Cobb as the second thug punched a wall in anger. It didn't seem to faze him in the least. 'But stay low for another minute.'

Sarah nodded as she struggled to catch her breath.

Cobb remained quiet until he stopped at a red light several blocks away. Only then did he lean back and glance at the duo sprawled on the floor. 'Hey, Sarah?'

'Yeah, Jack.'

Cobb glared at her. 'Who's your friend?'

10

Cobb drove in awkward silence to the far side of town where he found a rough neighborhood to ditch the car. Until he knew more, the location satisfied his two most pressing concerns: it was far from the iron-fisted thugs, and it was nowhere near the hotel where he and Sarah were staying.

Before making his exit, he wiped the steering wheel and door handles clean of any fingerprints. Then he left the keys in the ignition and calmly walked away.

'Keep moving,' he told the others.

Stealing the car wasn't something Cobb had planned, but rather a necessary evil born of the situation. Now the best thing that could happen would be for someone else to notice the keys in the unlocked car and take it on a joyride of his own. The more distance he could get between themselves and a stolen vehicle, the better.

'Name's Simon, by the way.' He thrust his hand toward Cobb as they strolled toward a main road. 'Thanks for the help back there.'

'Sure,' Cobb said with a furtive glance.

Despite their time in the car, this was his first chance to size up the new addition. He was lean and wiry, a few inches shorter than Cobb and at least five years younger. His hair was closely cropped, and stubble covered his face. His look appeared to be one of convenience more than personal style. Nothing about him stood out. Not his size. Not his features. Not his attire. It was as if he had made every effort to blend in.

Knowing little else about him, Cobb turned to Sarah.

'Jack, this is Simon Dade,' she said. 'Simon, this is Jack—'

Cobb cut her off. 'Jack is good enough for now.'

Sarah understood Cobb's hesitation. He didn't know Dade, and until he did their relationship would remain casual, so first names were just fine with him.

She continued her explanation, hoping to allay some of Cobb's concerns. 'Jack, Simon is a CIA asset. He's what they call a "tour guide".'

'An asset, *not* an agent?'

'That's correct.'

'And what does a CIA tour guide do?' Cobb asked.

'Pretty much the same thing as an actual tour guide,' she replied, 'only he knows everything about the places that you'd want to avoid on vacation.'

Dade nodded. 'It's my job to know the city inside and out. Who's responsible for what, and where, and how? Think of me as your local "big brother". I can give you intel on every corner of Alexandria.'

Cobb glanced at him. 'Does that mean you have surveillance capabilities?'

Dade grinned. 'I might have access to a camera or two, sure. What are you trying to find out?'

'Nothing yet. I just want to know your limits.'

'Honestly? I'm not a very good cook. Other than that, I don't have many.'

Cobb considered the comment. This early on, he wasn't sure if he liked Dade's cockiness or hated it. 'When did you spot us?'

'The airport,' he answered.

'Bullshit,' Sarah said. 'No way you spotted us that early.'

'Wanna bet?' Dade pulled his phone from his pocket and found what he was looking for. He showed the picture to Sarah. 'You're very photogenic.'

The image showed Cobb and Sarah exiting their private plane from Florida. Chartered by Papineau under the name of a dummy corporation that was buried under four layers of paperwork, the private plane had delivered them to the Cairo International Airport, nearly three hours from their final destination.

The arrangement was intended to guarantee their anonymity. But it hadn't worked with the tour guide.

She glared at Dade. 'I wasn't listed on the passenger manifest, and we didn't fly into Alexandria. How did you . . .?'

He smiled cockily. 'In my line of work, it pays to have your bases covered. Alexandria. Cairo. I've got connections at all the private terminals and airfields in Egypt. The passengers of every flight are documented and sent to me and a few other associates. We get our information from mechanics in the hangars, controllers on the tarmac, even some of the pilots themselves. Anyone with access.'

'That has to be hundreds of flights a day,' Sarah replied.

'Try thousands,' Dade corrected. 'But trust me: the right picture to the right people is worth the effort.' He smiled. 'CIA checks don't bounce.'

It was a joke – the CIA would never risk a paper trail – but Sarah understood his point. A couple of hours spent scanning through photos each night was worth the government payday. The CIA was a lot of things, but it certainly wasn't bankrupt.

Cobb stopped and stared at Dade. 'I'd appreciate if you could keep us out of the Agency's spotlight. Considering what I did for you, I figure it's the least you can do.'

'No problem, Jack. Your secret's safe with me.'

'Glad to hear it.' Cobb turned and started to walk away. 'Nice meeting you, Mr Dade. Take care of yourself.'

Dade stared at Sarah for an explanation, but she had nothing to offer.

'Jack,' Dade called out. 'I can help you.'

'I'm not interested in your help,' he shouted back.

'Hey, *you* reached out to *me*, remember?'

Cobb spun around to address Dade. 'And then *I* came to *your* rescue when you brought your troubles with you. Or have you forgotten that?'

'What? Those two back there?' Dade waved it off. 'That was just a disagreement between friends. Nothing more. Besides, we could have easily outrun them. You just happened to be in the right place at the right time.'

'Maybe so,' Cobb snapped, 'but can you outrun gunfire? Next time you have a disagreement, make sure they're unarmed.'

Dade smiled, intrigued. He knew Cobb couldn't have seen the two men chasing him for more than a few seconds, yet he had still managed to pick out the silhouette of their pistols beneath their clothing. That was an impressive feat.

'Seriously, Jack. It was no big deal.'

'Listen,' Cobb said calmly, his voice as steady as his gaze, 'I already spend enough time looking over my own shoulder for trouble. I don't need to be looking over yours, wondering when Bigfoot and Biggerfoot will show up again.'

Dade raised his hand. 'I swear to you, I'll deal with them.

They won't be a problem. Just give me a chance to help. Tell me what you need to know.'

Cobb stepped closer. 'Why are you so interested in helping me? You don't owe me anything, and I'll be damned if I want to owe you anything. I saved your life, and in return, you're going to keep our whereabouts unknown. Or are you going to have a problem with that?'

'With all due respect, Jack, I'm not here for you – I'm here for *her*.' He nodded toward Sarah, who was quietly watching the scene unfold. 'The two of us go way back, and I owe her more than you can imagine. So please, tell me, what can I do to help?'

Cobb glanced at Sarah. It was up to her and her alone. She knew her history with Dade, and if she wanted to call in a favor, it was her decision to make.

Sarah nodded without hesitation.

'Okay,' Cobb said, 'we'll call on you when the time is right – but that moment isn't now. In the meantime, quit following us.'

'No problem.'

Cobb lowered his voice, so only Dade could hear it. 'I know you and Sarah have a past, but I'm a man who values his privacy. I can't stress that enough. Now that I know what you look like, you'll be on my radar from now on. And if I catch you snooping or lurking around, I won't hesitate to take you out. Understood?'

Dade nodded. 'Understood.'

'And trust me, I run a lot faster than the goons.'

Cobb didn't think Sarah would intentionally lead him astray, but he knew there were things she hadn't yet shared. He was willing to take her word that Dade was a CIA asset, but what aspects of Dade's life did he conveniently leave out of his résumé?

Cobb needed to know what Sarah knew.

And he needed to know now.

After parting ways with Dade, Cobb and Sarah had returned to their hotel. Initially, Cobb had considered booking rooms somewhere else, but he eventually decided against it. Dade had found them once before, and there was no reason to believe he couldn't do it again. Changing hotels would only tip off Dade that Cobb didn't trust him.

Cobb made his way to the window and pushed it open, allowing what little wind there was to circulate through the space. It still felt like summer in Egypt, and the unseasonably warm air was remarkably dry. The only relief came in the form of cooler sea breezes blowing in from the coast.

To his left, Cobb caught a glimpse of the Henan Palestine Hotel. It was picturesque, framed beautifully against the backdrop of the Mediterranean. Cobb thought about the air-conditioned rooms and the chilled bottles of water that no doubt waited in the miniature refrigerators. Just because he had spent more nights than he cared to remember with little more than military fatigues and a pile of leaves to make him comfortable didn't mean he couldn't appreciate the high-thread-count linens and down-filled pillows of a five-star establishment.

Next time, he promised himself.

For now they would make do with the no-star accommodations of the rundown hotel half a block from the Henan. Not that Cobb was complaining. The bed was clean. The neighborhood was quiet. And the door locked. Cobb understood that he and Sarah could have blended in with the crowd at any of the popular tourist hotels, but the last thing he wanted was an overly eager concierge keeping an eye on their every move.

Cobb preferred the kind of place where people minded their business.

He turned from the window and took a seat on the well-worn chair in the corner of the room. 'What else can you tell me about Simon?'

Sarah found a spot on the edge of the bed. 'What you really mean is, "Tell me everything about Simon Dade," right?'

'Yes, that's what I mean.'

'I've known Simon for roughly seven years,' Sarah said.

'Seven?' Cobb thought back to what Sarah had said earlier, remembering that it had been six years since she had last visited Alexandria.

'The operation we were running wasn't a hit-and-run. It went on for nearly a year.'

'What can you tell me about the op? I don't need to hear everything. Just the relevant points and how Simon was involved.'

'What do you know about sex-trafficking?'

Cobb groaned. From his time overseas, he was all too familiar with the horror stories. 'It usually starts with an abduction. Young girls are taken off the streets, and some are pulled right from their homes. After a steady diet of mind-numbing drugs, they are shipped across the world and put to work in brothels.'

'Or worse,' Sarah said. 'Many are sold at auction to the highest bidder. They spend the rest of their lives being victimized by the scum of the earth, men who feel their wealth gives them the authority to violate another human being with impunity.'

'How do you and Simon fit in?' Cobb asked.

'Egypt is a major hub in the sex trade. Girls pass through on their way to Europe, Asia, and most importantly – at least as far as the CIA was concerned – America. I was brought in for two reasons. First, we needed to figure out how the brokers were moving the girls in and out of the country and, as you know, borders are what I know best. Second, because of my youthful appearance, I could play a specific role: a sister or a friend searching for a missing girl from back home. You'd be amazed how many people will open their doors to an anxious family member. I was able to go places, hear things, and talk to people that other agents couldn't.'

Cobb was familiar with Sarah's undercover work, having seen her transformation in their previous mission. She had the ability to look any age from eighteen to forty.

She continued. 'We recruited Simon to help us determine where the traders were meeting next. He was a local expat who knew the landscape and seemed to have the right connections. Not a player, but someone with his ear to the tracks. As the point man, I was the one who reached out to Simon to bring him on board. Once I made contact, Simon literally walked me around the city. He gave me the guided tour of every place I needed to know and introduced me to everyone I needed to meet.'

'Hence the "tour guide" title,' Cobb said.

Sarah stood and started to pace. 'Other agents assured us that the brokers were gathering in Cairo, so that's where we concentrated our forces. Simon was the only one who kept insisting that the location was Alexandria. In the end, Simon was correct. Thirty-seven girls got sold here, and we were too late to stop it. We lost them all.'

She hung her head. 'When it was over, Simon collected the descriptions from all of his sources and gave us everything he could. He even convinced some of them to sit with forensic artists. They worked for hours, directing sketches from memory. They described accents, mannerisms, and anything else they noticed about the brokers.'

'Did it work?' Cobb asked.

'We tracked down five of the sellers and six of the buyers, all because of Simon's efforts. Eleven convictions because of him, yet he still feels indebted to me. He thinks if he had found something concrete about Alexandria instead of just rumors then we could have saved them all. To this day, he still feels responsible for the girls. He's been hoping to make it up to me ever since.'

'He's been hoping for more than that.'

Sarah looked at him quizzically. 'What do you mean?'

'Come on, Sarah, don't play dumb. You know damn well that Dade's interest isn't just professional. He's got a crush on you. Even I could see that, and I'm about as romantic as a hemorrhoid.'

'Nice visual,' she mocked.

Cobb stared at her, unwilling to let her off the hook.

'What do you want me to say? Of course I know that Simon

wants something more. But we aren't together, and we're never going to be together. It's just that when you go through something tragic like we did . . .'

Sarah didn't know the right words to finish her thought, but Cobb understood the sentiment. He knew that traumatic events could forge powerful connections.

'Sarah—'

He was cut off by the ringing of his cell phone.

'You get that,' she said. 'I'm going to step out for a bit.'

Cobb nodded. He could see the toll her story had taken and knew that she would never show her emotions in front of him. If she needed to scream, cry, or punch a wall until her knuckles bled, she would do it in the privacy of her own room.

Cobb waited until the door closed behind her before he answered the call from Florida. As far as he was concerned, the timing couldn't have been better. He had sent a simple text to Garcia during the trip back to the hotel that consisted of little more than Dade's name and a request to 'find everything'.

It wasn't meant as an insult to Sarah, who was able to provide personal details that wouldn't turn up in a field report. It was more to uncover what had happened to Dade since they had last worked together. Six years was a very long time – particularly in the cutthroat world of espionage. For Cobb to consider Dade as a potential asset, he needed a lot more than a personal reference. He needed a full workup, the type of deep background that could only be done by a computer hacker.

Thankfully, Cobb had one of those on his team.

'Simon Philip Dade,' Garcia began. 'Born and raised in Charleston, South Carolina. Normal middle-class childhood as far as I can tell. In fact, there's nothing noteworthy about his life until his parents died. That's when things get interesting.'

'How'd they die?' Cobb asked.

'A boating accident,' he replied. 'The honest-to-goodness kind, not the kind of "boating accident" we see in our line of work. His parents spent the night of their fifteenth anniversary on a forty-foot sloop, and there was an electrical fire in the engine compartment. The smoke overwhelmed them during the night. The Coast Guard found the vessel the following day.'

'That would certainly change a kid.'

'That, and the culture shock of being transplanted to a new city,' said Garcia as he scrolled through the information on his laptop. 'Dade moved from Charles*ton* to Charles*town*, as in Boston. His uncle took him in but only to get access to Simon's trust fund. Looks like the uncle wasn't exactly parent material – he was more like a drunken piece of shit – which meant Simon had to basically raise himself. His high school transcript has as many suspensions as it does recommendations. Most teachers considered Simon to be a brilliant student, but one who had trouble staying out of trouble.'

'What kind of trouble?'

'Shoplifting, vandalism, trespassing. The sort of thing you might expect from a teenager left to fend for himself. When he graduated, he enrolled at a local college. It lasted all of one semester. In January of his freshman year, he spent his winter break in Cairo as part of a school-subsidized trip. He never returned home.'

'What do you mean?'

'He just decided that he wanted to live in Egypt. The government over there granted him their version of an emergency visa until he could petition for citizenship. The school contacted the state department, and they agreed that he was eighteen and that he had filed all the necessary documentation. They had no authority to force him to return.'

Cobb shook his head. 'Something doesn't add up. Why would an American teenager with no ethnic connections to the Middle East want to move to the desert? London, I could understand. Same with Paris. But Egypt? That doesn't make sense to me.'

'Me neither.'

'Unless . . .'

'Unless what?'

'I wonder if there was a girl.'

Garcia studied the information on his screen. 'None that he married – I know that much. But I'll take a closer look, see if I can turn up a name or two.'

'In the meantime, any red flags?'

'Not really,' Garcia said. 'No arrests or citations. Not even a parking ticket. His tax records show him as the sole owner of a lucrative security and surveillance company. Apparently he's very good at what he does because he has clients throughout the city.'

'Well, that explains it.'

'Explains what?'

'How he kept tabs on us without us noticing. That was bugging the hell out of me. I thought maybe Sarah and I were getting rusty.'

'No sir, not rusty. He has cameras all over. He probably followed you without leaving his office.'

'If we needed to, could you tap them for me?'

Garcia laughed. 'Already have.'

Cobb smiled. He liked working with professionals: people with initiative, people he could count on. It made his job so much easier. 'Anything else?'

'Maybe,' Garcia said, unsure of himself. 'I hope I'm not stepping out of line by telling you this, but since you're overseas, I just thought you should know.'

'Know what?'

Garcia swallowed hard. 'McNutt's gone AWOL.'

12

Daytona Beach, Florida
(220 miles north of Fort Lauderdale)

Most dedicated bikers have a few 'must-see' events on their social calendar. The Sturgis Motorcycle Rally is usually one of them. It draws more than half a million riders to the Black Hills of North Dakota every year for a rowdy weekend of races, concerts, and parties. Another is the Rolling Thunder Run in Washington, D.C. It honors men and women of the armed forces who have been prisoners of war and those who have gone missing in action. Riders from all across the country descend upon the capital in a show of support for military personnel, both past and present.

Participants in these (and similar) rallies earn the right to wear a special patch associated with each event. Though it is nothing more than a simple piece of sewn cloth, it recognizes those who were willing to put in the time and miles. To bikers, they are symbols worn with pride, similar to military ribbons or medals.

McNutt had plenty of medals, but he preferred the patches. They looked cooler on his leather jacket.

The largest bike event in Florida is Daytona Bike Week. Early each spring, Daytona Beach is transformed into a haven for cabin-fevered riders from the north. McNutt had made the trip several times, but he had missed the most recent event. Fortunately for him, Daytona offers another opportunity for those who couldn't attend the main festival. Held every October, Biketoberfest is a second chance to enjoy bikes, beer, and camaraderie with like-minded souls.

Plus a chance to earn another patch.

Most of the bars off the main drag were virtually identical: narrow halls that started with a row of barstools and ended with a pool table. The only thing that changed was the clientele. A quick scan of the room was all McNutt needed to confirm that he had come to the right place. For all intents and purposes, the entire bar was one big reunion. Checking tattoos, McNutt saw representatives from every branch of the US military, as well as three members of the Royal Navy.

'Hey Jarhead, think fast!'

McNutt spun toward the familiar voice, knowing what would happen if his reactions were slow. As he turned, he spotted a pool ball flying at his chest and the smiling soldier who had launched it. Using his helmet as a basket, McNutt caught the speeding projectile then tossed the ball onto a nearby table.

Three younger Marines seated near McNutt stood to confront whoever was stupid enough to hurl an insult – and a pool ball – at one of their own. But two things stopped them in their tracks. The first was the size of the man himself. He looked like a weightlifter. Or a bulldog. Or a weightlifting bulldog. The kind of guy you didn't pick a fight with unless he spit on your mother . . . and even then you'd have to think about it.

The second thing they noticed, the one that quelled the argument completely, was the 'U.S.M.C.' T-shirt that he was wearing.

Coming from a fellow Marine, the name *Jarhead* was friendly banter rather than a sign of disrespect.

McNutt smiled as the others sat down. 'You'll have to do better than that.'

'Maybe next time,' the bulldog said as he waved his friend over to the table. He greeted him with an enthusiastic hug. 'Shit, man, I thought you were dead!'

'You're not that lucky,' McNutt replied. He motioned for the waitress to bring two more bottles of whatever it was that his friend was drinking.

'So, where the hell have you been hiding? Are you here for the festivities or to see me? Your message didn't really explain.'

'Sorry about that. I didn't want to get into it over the phone.'

'Didn't, or couldn't?'

'A little of both.'

The waitress delivered the next round, and each took a moment to enjoy a long, cold pull from his bottle as they stared at the waitress's ass. Somehow she had squeezed into a pair of shorts that would make a stripper blush, and they approved of her effort.

'As I was saying,' McNutt said with a laugh, 'I'm planning a trip to the Middle East and I needed a travel agent. You're the first person who came to mind.'

'I can understand why.'

Staff Sergeant James Tyson was a member of the United States Marine Corps' Force Reconnaissance Company. He and his men were the first wave of deployment into areas of enemy occupation. Their job was to gather all the relevant information – who was in command, what was their objective, what artillery did they have at their disposal, etc. – and relay that information back to their superiors.

'You in the mood to build some sand castles?' Tyson asked.

'The other way around,' McNutt said. 'I hear they have a lot of shit buried in Egypt, and I'm hoping to find some. You still know the area?'

Tyson nodded. 'The Middle East is my playground.'

'For now, I'm just interested in Egypt.'

'I'm sure you know about the instability.'

'Leaders can't please anyone well enough or long enough to gain a foothold. No matter what they do, someone sees it as a mistake.'

'Their constitution was dissolved a couple of years ago,' Tyson explained. 'It led to a political free-for-all. At last count, there were at least forty political parties in Egypt. More than forty different views of what is best for the country, each with its own candidate who believes he best represents the voice of the people. It's controlled lunacy.'

'But it's controlled?'

'Not really,' he said with a laugh. 'The hope is that the country will sort itself out and establish a power base that unifies the people – whether that unity comes from this president or the next, no one knows. But the Supreme Council of the Armed Forces is on standby in case things deteriorate. They've stepped in before. They won't hesitate to do it again. Not if the alternative is losing control of the country.'

'The Supreme Council?'

Tyson nodded. 'Twenty-one senior officials from various branches of the Egyptian military. They have the authority to overtake the reins of a failing government, not to mention the resources to ensure that their decisions are respected. Of course, that's just the urban areas. In the desert, there is no control.

There are only marauding nomads competing for whatever they can find . . . which is next to nothing. It's a brutal wasteland of sandstorms and scavengers. You get lost out there, and you're as good as dead.'

'Damn,' McNutt teased, 'you gotta be the worst travel agent ever. No wonder I'm your only client.'

Tyson grinned. 'Just telling it like it is.'

McNutt continued to joke. 'I'll take two tickets to the brutal wasteland, please. Are the sandstorms and scavengers included, or do I have to pay extra for that?'

'Fuck you,' Tyson laughed before taking another swig of beer. 'I try to hook you up with intel, and you rub it in my face. Kind of like that tranny rubbed it in—'

'Whoa! Whoa! Whoa!' shouted McNutt, who flushed with embarrassment. He glanced around the room to make sure no one had heard the comment. 'First of all, I was drunk. Secondly, I thought it was a chick. And most importantly, your dad was hot.'

Tyson spit out a mouthful of beer. 'Dude, that's *so* wrong.'

McNutt patted him on the back. 'Are you okay? Please tell me you're okay. If you can't breathe, I can call your father. I still have his number.'

Tyson wiped the tears from his eyes and the beer from his chin. He hadn't laughed like that in weeks. 'I'm glad you called, man. I really am. It's been way too long.'

McNutt nodded in agreement. 'Sorry about that, but you know how it is. When you're in the country, I'm not – and vice versa. How long you here?'

'Not very. How about you?'

'Pushing out soon.'

'To Egypt?'

'For starters. And you?'

'Same region, different zip code.'

'How close?'

'*Real* close.'

'Good to know.'

Tyson took a long swig of beer before he spoke again. 'Josh, I don't know what you're mixed up in, and the truth is I don't want to know. No, actually, I take that back. I *do* want to know – but I respect you enough not to ask.'

McNutt nodded. 'Same here.'

'That being said, I don't think you have a total grasp of the situation. I'm telling you: Egypt is rough. As bad as the deserts are, the cities might be worse.'

'How so?'

'Have you heard of the forty-niners?'

'The football team?'

'No, the *actual* forty-niners. The thousands of men and women who made their way to California in search of gold back in the eighteen hundreds.'

'Yeah, but – where are you going with this?'

Tyson continued. 'When the forty-niners came to California, they were at the mercy of those who came before them. What they found was that nearly everything required the payment of a toll. "You want to drink from my stream? That'll be a nickel." "You want to pass through my land? That'll be a nickel." Everywhere they looked, everything they did, they were being charged a fee.'

McNutt shook his head. 'I'm still lost. How does any of this relate to me?'

'That's what the cities are like in Egypt. It doesn't matter what you're talking about – legal or illegal; black market, white market, or gray market – there's always a fee. For everything. And if you don't pay, they make you pay.'

McNutt raised his hand and ordered another round. He'd stay here all night if he had to, buying drink after drink until he knew everything about Egypt.

'Who's they?' he asked.

Tyson explained. 'When the government went to hell, criminals saw a golden opportunity and seized control of the cities. And it's been like that ever since. "You want to build a refinery? Here's the toll." "You want to pave a new road? Here's the toll." Whoever controls the land sets the price of doing business in that particular neighborhood. And trust me, the fees are a lot more than a nickel.'

'How entrenched are they?'

Tyson laughed. 'They control everything in one way or another. Everything goes through them, or it doesn't go at all. Commerce. Tourism. Industry. You name it, they run it. Just like the mob in Jersey.'

'That bad, huh?'

He nodded. 'That shit you mentioned earlier – the stuff you're hoping to find? There better be a lot of it, because the withdrawal fees are going to cost you plenty.'

13

Garcia had already fulfilled his research duties for Cobb and had passed along the news about McNutt's desertion. Beyond that, he didn't have much to do.

To make himself useful, he approached Jasmine to see if she needed help. Of all the team members, he found her to be the least combative. And while he still preferred the company of computers to interactions with humans, he didn't really mind spending time with Jasmine. Besides, he still had a lot of gaps to fill before he completely understood what they were looking for, and he knew she could help with that.

'Are you getting the hang of the table?' he asked.

'Yes,' she replied. 'So far I've been able to rearrange the images and overlap them as I see fit, but I can't seem to figure out how to link the various layers.' She reached out and gently pushed the corner of the hologram, sending a layer of the map spinning. 'I can do that, but what if I wanted to spin the entire thing at once? What if I want it to act as one big piece, instead of several individual layers? Is that possible?'

'Sure.' Garcia tapped two adjacent points on two levels of the hologram and folded his hands together, interlocking his fingers as if he were about to pray. When he reached out and spun the lower level, the level above it now spun as well.

Jasmine shook her head as she duplicated the maneuver. 'That's so intuitive I should have thought of it myself.' She linked a few more layers together just for practice. 'What about notes? Is there a way to add notes to the map? That would make things a lot easier for me.'

Garcia extended two fingers and double-tapped on the display screen. 'You can add notes, add color, drop pins, calculate distances, and a few other bells and whistles. The entire toolbar incorporates a voice recognition system. Just tap on a section of interest, speak your note, and the computer will do the rest.'

He motioned for her to try.

She nodded and tapped on a tall Roman column in the middle of a large park. Built in 297 AD, the column towered above the plaza. 'Pompey's Pillar.'

A second later, the computer displayed the words POMPEY'S PILLAR on the screen. Garcia tapped the window again and the words immediately appeared on the map directly above the point of interest.

'Hector, that's fantastic!' She was so excited that she gave him a hug. 'Seriously, I can't thank you enough. This program will save me so much time.'

Garcia beamed with pride. 'Glad I could help.'

Papineau – who had a habit of coming and going as he saw fit, always without explanation – reentered the room as their hug was ending. 'Jasmine, what are you celebrating? Have you figured out where to start?'

'Start?' Garcia said. 'I thought the map was going to tell us where to *finish*.'

Papineau laughed him off. 'Unfortunately, no. It won't be that easy. There's no X that marks the spot. Instead, we must determine where to begin.'

'I thought we knew that already. We're going to start in Alexandria.' He glanced at them for confirmation. 'Right?'

'Yes, but where?'

Garcia stared at the map. He saw miles of roads, hundreds of buildings, and countless acres of underground catacombs. Finding one tomb in all of that seemed unlikely at best. 'Crap. This is going to be tougher than I thought: like trying to find a snowflake in an avalanche.'

'Hector, snowflakes would be easy by comparison. This is going to be substantially more difficult.'

Jasmine shrugged. 'Maybe, maybe not.'

Papineau lit up. 'You found something?'

'Nothing definitive, but . . .' Her tone was far from confident, as if she was still trying to convince herself of the possibility. 'Maybe.'

'Well, don't just stand there. Show us!'

Jasmine groaned, but did as she was told. She stripped away all of the more recent layers of the map, leaving only the oldest renditions. Then she enlarged the hologram, focusing on a depression in the center of the map. 'I know it looks like a hole in the ground, but I'm intrigued by the label. It's inscribed with the words "Donum Neptunus".'

Classically educated, Papineau didn't need a computer to translate the term. 'It's Latin. It means "The Gift of Neptune". What do you make of it?'

She sat in the nearest chair and rubbed her eyes, still trying to work through the theory in her head. 'There's an ancient story that I've heard many times before in a wide variety of ways that mentions a sacred well in the bowels of Alexandria. According to legend, if you believe these types of things, the

94

well was so magical that it played a major role in determining the fate of Egypt.'

'A water well?' Garcia asked. 'How did it do that?'

She explained. 'In 47 BC, Julius Caesar fought Ptolemy Theos Philopator for control of the city. There were two main battles. During the first, known as the Siege of Alexandria, Ptolemy's men flooded Caesar's freshwater reserves with seawater in an attempt to cause his surrender. To combat the sabotage, Caesar dug into the earth until he reached drinkable water. Caesar was then able to beat back Ptolemy's forces and eventually defeat him during the Battle of the Nile.'

Papineau nodded in understanding. 'Neptune was the Roman god of water. You think the Gift of Neptune is Caesar's Well.'

'I think it's possible.'

'Tell me more,' he ordered. 'Convince me.'

She smiled and accepted the challenge. 'Realizing the importance of a freshwater source, Caesar supposedly had the pit fortified with stone. He then surrounded that well with sturdy walls that were twice as thick as those of any other building – walls that were protected by an elite garrison of Roman guards. Legend has it that for the next seven hundred years, only priests were allowed to enter the temple that housed the well. It was seen as the only way to ensure the sanctity of the water source.'

'And after the seventh century?'

'Unfortunately, there's no mention of Caesar's Well after the Persian invasion in any of the books I've read. Then again, there's no official mention of the well *before* the Persian invasion, either. Like I said, this is just a legend. But . . .'

'But what?'

'But the Lost Throne was just a legend, and someone found that in Greece.'

Garcia stared at the map. 'So, assuming the rumors were true, and assuming that this "Donusm Neptunus" does refer to your mythical well, how does that help us?'

Jasmine connected the dots. 'Sometime around 200 AD, Emperor Septimius Severus had all evidence of Alexander's tomb taken into custody. And I mean *everything*. If a book contained so much as a mention of the tomb, it was confiscated by the Roman Empire. Next he ordered that the tomb itself be sealed forever.'

'What did he do with the evidence?' Garcia asked.

Papineau had never heard of the sacred well, but he knew the history of Emperor Severus. 'Some say he delivered it to the tomb before it was sealed. Some say he destroyed all the evidence in a giant fire. No one really knows for sure.'

Jasmine rose from her seat. 'That's just it. In the history of the world, how many things have been completely erased?'

Garcia scoffed at the question. 'How can we possibly know that? If it was completely erased, there'd be no evidence of its existence. And, obviously, if there was no evidence of its existence, then we would not be able to determine that it had been erased.'

Papineau chuckled at the analytical thought process of their computer whiz. 'Spoken like a true genius.'

Jasmine ignored Garcia's logic. 'Don't over-think it, Hector. What I mean is this: just because Severus tried to collect every scrap of evidence that pertained to the tomb doesn't make it possible. Do you really think anyone could accomplish something like that? Do you honestly believe he could find every trace of

Alexander's tomb in the world? Someone, somewhere had to hang on to something. A book. A drawing. A memory. Plus, if you know your history, there was one group in particular that secretly defied the emperor any chance they could – and they did it in plain sight.'

Papineau nodded. 'The priests.'

Garcia groaned in confusion. 'That doesn't make sense to me. Why would Roman priests defy the Roman emperor?'

Jasmine explained. 'In the time of Severus, Christianity had yet to be embraced by the Roman Empire. His religion had multiple gods. It would be another century before the people of the republic could openly worship the holy trinity. Until then, Christians were persecuted for their devotion to Jesus Christ. This would have put the Roman priests at great odds with the Roman emperor even as they continued to serve him. Severus believed that the very foundation of their belief system was a lie. And they, in turn, did not recognize the emperor as a member of the divine pantheon, as was the tradition of the day. Therefore, it actually makes perfect sense that the priests would defy the emperor.'

Garcia shrugged. 'If you say so.'

She continued. 'Severus allowed his son, Caracalla, to visit the tomb in 215 AD. That's the last official Roman sighting on record. But according to several Christian sources, the priests followed Caracalla to the tomb and documented its location. Furthermore, if the legend about Donum Neptunus is correct, it was also the priests who maintained the well for several centuries after the acceptance of Christianity. It's not inconceivable to think that we're talking about the same group of people.'

'And if we are?' Papineau asked.

She smiled. 'If you're trying to hide evidence of Alexander's tomb – evidence that could prove to be useful in your rebellion against the Empire – and you wanted to thumb your nose at the emperor at the exact same time, what better place to hide it than a heavily guarded, fortified building whose only visitors were fellow priests?'

Papineau laughed at the irony. 'If that's the case, the emperor's garrison would have been unknowingly helping the priests by protecting information about the tomb. How delicious!'

'Delicious, yes. But accurate? That remains to be seen. I won't know anything for sure until I examine the site.'

14

Cobb could have set up their command center in any section of the city, but after spending several days in Alexandria, he decided the coastal neighborhood of San Stefano was the perfect choice. Not only is San Stefano in the center of Alexandria's width, making it ideal for exploring the city, but it also caters to foreign travelers.

Thanks to the restaurants, hotels, and shopping centers, tourists flocked to the district like pigeons to a park. At almost any time of the day or night, men and women of every shape, size, and nationality crowded the streets. Here, no one would think twice about a gathering of three Caucasians, a Latino, an Asian, and a Frenchman.

Papineau stood on the deck of a seventy-foot, tri-level yacht that was tied into a slip just offshore. Though it didn't have the personal flourishes of the *Trésor de la Mer*, it was still an impressive craft. It included four staterooms, a gourmet galley, and three spacious lounges. Its massive freshwater reservoir and two hot-water tanks offered those on board the luxury of steam showers, while the satellite and state-of-the-art communications center connected them to television signals and the World Wide Web.

It had all the amenities of a hotel, plus the ability to relocate. It was the perfect base of operations.

McNutt was the first to join Papineau on deck. 'What time is it?' he asked as he groggily stretched his neck and looked out across the marina. 'Scratch that. Let's start with a better question: what *day* is it?'

He was only part joking. For him, the last seventy-two hours had been a whirlwind. No sooner had he arrived back in Fort Lauderdale from his Daytona Beach excursion than he was being told to pack for Egypt. The destination didn't matter for McNutt – he only had jeans and T-shirts, so his luggage would be the same regardless of where they were headed – but he had hoped for some time to recuperate, not only from his night of drinking, but also from the ride itself. His motorcycle was older than he was, and the worn seat was hard on his ass. And the twelve-hour plane ride certainly didn't help.

'It's Friday,' Papineau replied as he read the morning paper. 'And it's eight a.m. local time. I suppose that's zero eight hundred to you.'

McNutt yawned and reset his watch. They had lost twelve hours in transit, six hours in the time change, and another seven hours sleeping on the boat. Even with his military training, he still felt exhausted. Papineau could have told him that it was Christmas, and McNutt would have believed him. 'We have any coffee?'

'Right here.' Jasmine appeared from the galley deck below carrying a tray with a pot, cream, sugar, and six mugs. She looked around, noticing the absence of half of their team. 'Sarah and Jack aren't back yet?'

McNutt shrugged. He was still waking up.

'They're still surveying the city. I expect them soon,' Papineau said.

Of all the team members, Jasmine was the most eager to make the trip. Per Cobb's instruction, she had spent the last forty-eight hours researching her theory about the sacred well. He wasn't challenging her initial conclusion; he simply needed more information before he was willing to make a move. In his mind, there were still too many 'ifs' in her equation. In order to justify the risks of exploring the city, he needed more than rumor. He needed the *foundation* of the rumor.

It had taken a while, but Jasmine had found it.

Now she just needed to convince him.

McNutt grabbed a mug from the tray and poured himself a much-needed cup of coffee. 'I'd still be asleep if it weren't for Hector's snoring. Seriously, they should take that dude to a hospital.'

'Why? Do you think it's a medical condition?' Jasmine asked.

McNutt shook his head. 'I meant they could use him to wake coma patients. Hell, forget the hospital. Take him to the morgue and see if he can wake the dead.' He glanced at Papineau. 'You couldn't find a boat where we each had our own room?'

Papineau had taken the master suite for himself, leaving the others to determine their sleeping arrangements. Jasmine had claimed the largest of the three remaining rooms for her and Sarah, while Garcia and McNutt had taken the last double-occupancy berth in deference to Cobb. They might have been a motley crew, but he was still the leader. As such, he was given the quarters with a single bed.

The Frenchman sneered. 'How could I be so careless – placing an ex-Marine in a double room on a luxury yacht? I should be ashamed of myself, forcing you to live in such squalor. I am sure the American military always pampered you like a king. Nothing but opulent silk tents and clarets of fine wine in the tranquil dunes of Iraq.'

'And belly dancers. They liked to feed me grapes.'

Papineau rolled his eyes. 'In case you have forgotten, the reason we selected this marina is to hide in plain sight. The bigger the boat, the harder that is to do. You have been on the deck for less than five minutes. Tell me, which boats stick out?'

Without turning his head, McNutt detailed what he could remember. 'There's a jet-black double-wide across the dock, a triple-masted sailboat at the end of the pier, and a ridiculous monstrosity with a helipad anchored just offshore. It's gotta be one hundred and fifty feet long.'

'All bigger than our humble vessel,' Papincau said. 'We are surrounded by wealth and opulence – the toys of sheiks and royalty. And their prized possessions are designed to stand out. They wouldn't have splurged on them otherwise. Of course our goal is to blend in, so this yacht is the perfect choice.'

Cobb and Sarah suddenly appeared on deck. They had used a ladder from the dock to join the others.

'You are correct,' Cobb said as he grabbed a mug from the serving tray. 'But I don't think Josh noticed those particular boats because of their size.'

Papineau frowned. 'What do you mean?'

'Tell him, Josh.'

'Gladly,' McNutt said. 'The wax on the black hull creates a noticeable glare during the morning sun. The sails on the triple mast give me wind direction and approximate speed. And the big-boy acts as a breakwater for the waves. If he's here, the harbor is calm. If he leaves, there will be a lot more pitch and roll.'

'Glare? Wind direction? Pitch and roll?' None of it made sense to Jasmine. 'What in the world are you talking about?'

'Shooting conditions,' McNutt answered. 'Glare can hide your target. Wind can cause drift. Pitch and roll can throw off your aim.'

Cobb smiled. 'Once a sniper, always a sniper.'

Jasmine knew that she should probably be concerned about anyone whose first instinct was to gauge how to kill someone at any given moment, but she was oddly comforted by McNutt's awareness. Even in his sleep-deprived and jet-lagged state, his first thought was to consider his obstacles in protecting the group.

Somehow she felt safer with him around.

'So,' McNutt said to Sarah, who was standing behind him, 'how was your date with Simon? You're wearing the same clothes as last night, so I'm assuming you got lucky.'

She glared at him. 'First of all it wasn't a date. It was a night of surveillance. And if you must know, we all got lucky.'

'We did? Damn, I slept right through it. How was I?'

She grabbed his ear and twisted it hard. 'Stupid, like always.'

He rubbed his ear in agony. 'Ouch.'

Cobb clarified her statement for the others. 'What Sarah means by "lucky" is that no one in Alexandria has noticed us. Other than a minor issue with some local thugs, we seem to be off everybody's radar.'

'Are you sure?' Papineau asked.

'As sure as we can be.'

With Dade's help and surveillance equipment, they had spent the night monitoring the chatter throughout the city. They wanted to hear if anyone had mentioned a new boat in the marina; one carrying an odd mix of ethnicities. Fortunately, no one had noticed their arrival. If someone had, they would have moved their yacht to a different marina. The last thing they wanted while searching for treasure was attention of any kind.

Sarah looked around and noticed that Garcia was missing. 'Where's Hector?'

'Sleeping,' McNutt said, still rubbing his ear. 'That sound you hear isn't a passing motorboat. No, that's the chainsaw he calls a mouth.'

'Give him a break,' Jasmine said. 'He was up half the night putting together our command center. He needs his rest.'

'So do I,' McNutt grumbled. 'Do you honestly think the nerd carried in that equipment by himself? Why does he get to sleep in?'

Jasmine glanced at Cobb. 'If you want, I'll wake him.'

Cobb shook his head. 'Let him sleep. Besides, I want to hear from you before we do anything else. Did you find what you were looking for?'

'Yes and no,' she replied. 'There's quite a bit of evidence that Caesar's Well actually existed, but no proof that it held information about Alexander's tomb. However, there are accounts of an ancient temple that was built during that era. Furthermore, these accounts make it clear that the temple housed clerical records, and the records were kept and guarded by Roman priests.'

Cobb needed more. 'Go on.'

She continued. 'I found a Greek text by Aethlius that mentions the "humble place of divinity, where Arius would go to read the words of those most devoted to the calling". The temple was described as "an underground lair near holy water".'

Papineau signaled for her to stop. 'Arius?'

She nodded. 'Arius was a Libyan scholar who led a Christian congregation in Alexandria after the Roman acceptance of Christianity. He believed in the original power of God, and that all others who came after were subordinate to God, including God's own son. He agreed that both the father and son were divine, but he challenged the Christian priests to show evidence that Jesus and God should be held as equals. According to Aethlius, Arius met these priests and read their scripture "not in a house of worship", but rather "inside simple stone quarters near a hallowed pool". In my opinion, he's describing the temple that surrounded Caesar's Well.'

Cobb said nothing in response.

He simply sat there, contemplating the information.

Jasmine pressed on, hoping to erase all doubts.

'The Persian historian Ibn Rustah refers to the temple in the tenth century. His writings make note of a rock room, calling it "inconsequential, save for the clerics, who kept the annals of their city there". Later, Pope Theophilus of Alexandria, who was tasked with destroying all the pagan temples, spoke of a "solitary monolith" that should be revered. He called it a "vault of knowledge" that held the city's secrets, and said it would "bring understanding to the people of Alexandria for centuries to come".'

It wasn't like Jasmine to plead, but she was willing to try.

'Jack, please trust me on this one. I feel it in my gut.'

Cobb finally smiled. 'I do trust you. And I agree with you.'

She breathed a sigh of relief.

'Cancel your dinner plans. We're going in tonight.'

15

By midday, almost everyone in the group was well rested and well fed. Garcia had put in a full eight hours in his bunk, all the while breathing in deep, booming roars that didn't seem possible for a man of his size. Sarah had managed roughly half as much sleep, but it was more than adequate for her. She felt calm and focused, ready for the evening ahead. Even McNutt, who couldn't return to his room because of the noise, had found some peace and quiet on the foredeck. He had curled up in a lounge chair and enjoyed a morning nap while dreaming of belly dancers and grapes.

Cobb was the only one who hadn't slept. He had closed his eyes for a while, but his brain hadn't gotten the message. The mission was too close. In a few hours they would be entering the tunnels under Alexandria. They would have to work quickly and efficiently. He couldn't afford to sleep; not when the time could be better spent rehashing the details of everything he knew . . . and everything he didn't.

After a quick lunch of fruits and meats from the local market, everyone gathered in the makeshift command center that Garcia had pieced together on the boat. The radar room – a nook to the rear of the bridge – was usually used by the captain to plot their location and monitor their position. The radar system could display the harbors and other boats within an area of a hundred miles. Garcia had expanded the capabilities available in the small space by adding a multitude of electronics and computing hardware. With these upgrades, Garcia could not only chart a course, he could receive real-time audio and video updates from their destination – *any* destination, anywhere on earth. All he needed was someone on the other end to feed him information.

'Show me what you can do,' Cobb said.

Garcia entered a command into his computer, then turned a monitor so that everyone could see. The screen split into a grid, with each section showing what appeared to be live video footage. 'These are feeds from security cameras all around the city. As you can see, they don't cover every inch of public space, but if you get close enough to someone's house or their business, there's a good chance I can find you.'

'How do you have access to all of that?' Jasmine asked.

'Sarah's friend Simon. He was able to give me a list of all the frequencies being transmitted throughout the city. Most of this is actually coming from equipment he installed. The signals that aren't are coming from his competitors, but they have to share the information so there's no conflict. It took him less than five minutes to send me everything I needed.'

Papineau wasn't convinced. 'I imagine that only a handful of cameras operate on radio technology. The others would utilize cables, satellite feeds, or wireless signals. How are you able to tap into everything?'

Garcia smiled. 'It's all just numbers. Radio. Cable. Satellite. Wireless. Just different points on the electronic spectrum. You point the receiver at the right frequency, run the signal through a few filters, and *boom*, you get a picture.'

'It can't be that simple,' Papineau said.

Garcia was annoyed, even a bit insulted by Papineau's remark. 'Actually, there's nothing simple about the science. But I don't have the time or the patience to explain every little detail involved in the process. I went to school for the better part of a decade to learn how to do this, and then I spent years refining it in the field. So, despite my watered-down "Surveillance for Dummies" lecture, please don't question my expertise. If I say we'll get a picture, we'll get a picture.'

Papineau was so unaccustomed to backtalk from Garcia that he chose not to respond. Neither did the others, who sat there with their mouths agape.

Meanwhile, Cobb didn't have time to massage wounded egos. He pressed on, putting Garcia back on track. 'So, assuming there's a camera, you'll be able to see us.'

'Yes. Or you can take one with you.' Garcia entered a different command then picked up a flashlight. He swung the flashlight around the room, showing everyone that it was also a video camera linked directly to his computer. Whatever he aimed the lens at appeared in high definition on the monitor. 'Remember these?'

The group had used similar devices during their previous mission. They had worked precisely as intended: relaying information back to Garcia. All the while, no one outside of the team had known the gadgets' true capabilities.

To everyone else, they looked like ordinary flashlights.

'No need to reinvent the wheel,' Jasmine said.

Garcia nodded. 'Exactly. They worked before. They'll work again.'

Cobb noticed that this version was slightly larger. He took a second flashlight from the desktop, gauging the weight in his hand. 'These are a bit longer, a bit heavier than the ones we used last time.'

'You don't miss much, do you? You're right, these have been upgraded.'

'Upgraded how?' Cobb asked.

'For starters, I've embedded a memory card into the handle. Not only will you transmit, you'll also record.' He dropped a cloth over the lens of the flashlight. A moment later, the image on the monitor turned a pale shade of green. 'You also have night vision in this version. Press and hold the on/off button for five seconds, and it activates the infrared light. Even in pitch black, this captures everything. And it doesn't just help *me* see what's going on; you can use it, too.' Garcia unscrewed a cap at the butt of the handle, revealing a small viewfinder. He put the flashlight to his eye, holding it like a pirate would hold a spyglass. 'It might be a little awkward to navigate like this, but if you're trapped in the dark, this can get you out.'

Papineau took Garcia's flashlight and rolled it in his hands. 'You're sure that this can get a signal up through the ground? They're liable to be thirty, forty feet below the surface. Perhaps more.'

Garcia was getting tired of Papineau's challenges, but he kept his frustration in check. 'These were tested in Romanian caves. They transmitted a perfect signal through solid rock. Forty feet of sandstone and ancient sediment isn't going to be a problem. Between the flashlight cameras and the earpieces, we'll be in constant contact.' Garcia opened a small plastic case with miniature earplugs inside. These flesh-colored earpieces were communication devices that could be concealed inside the ear canal.

'Sounds good,' McNutt said as he reached into the case.

Garcia snapped the lid closed on his fingers. 'No, not you. You get something special.'

McNutt's role in the plan called for him to hide in plain sight, somewhere near the entrance to the tunnels. If anything went wrong for Cobb and Sarah, he was their backup. In the meantime, he had to blend in. That meant they couldn't risk someone noticing his earpiece; the last thing they needed was to raise suspicion.

Besides, Garcia had a new gadget in his bag of tricks.

This would be the perfect opportunity to test it.

Garcia raised a pair of tweezers that held a tiny sliver of thin, flexible plastic. 'It's been imprinted with all the necessary circuitry to both send and receive radio transmissions. And it would take a dentist to spot it.'

McNutt's face twisted in confusion. 'Why a dentist?'

'I'm going to anchor the film behind your molar, in the farthest corner of your mouth,' Garcia explained.

'Screw that,' McNutt said.

Papineau glared at him. 'You have an issue with this method?'

'I had a bad experience with a retainer once, so I'm not a fan of dental work.' McNutt laughed to himself. 'Then again, he could have told me that it would take a proctologist to find it, so I guess this is better by comparison.'

Garcia stepped toward McNutt as the others chuckled at the comment. He raised the tweezers, but McNutt cut him off before he could get anywhere close.

'Oh, hell no,' McNutt said. 'Not you. Let Jasmine do it. Her hands are smaller. You'll drop that thing down my throat, and it'll be seven years before we see it again.'

'That's gum,' Garcia replied.

'And this is plastic and, well, um, a bunch of other stuff that I don't want in my colon. Give Jasmine the damn tweezers, or I swear to God I'll bite your fingers off.'

Jasmine took the tweezers with the tiny device and set about installing it as Garcia explained how it would work.

'The microphone will pick up everything you say and transmit it across a secure frequency to the rest of us back here in the harbor. That much is fairly common technology. The real beauty of the implant is the way it uses your jawbone to project the incoming signals. It vibrates the fluid inside your head to amplify the sound. You, and only you, will be able to hear the voices. Anyone standing next to you will be completely oblivious to the conversation.'

'So I just talk normally?' McNutt asked as soon as Jasmine finished. 'Check one-two-three. Testing. One-two-three. Can you hear me, Papa Bear?'

Garcia stared at him. 'Of course I can hear you. I'm standing right here. Walk away or something so we can test it.'

McNutt did as he was told while Garcia put on his headset. He pushed the microphone in front of his mouth before he whispered, 'Can you hear me, Josh?'

'Yes!' McNutt shouted from across the room.

'Josh, just speak normally if you have to. But remember that your job tonight is to listen, not to talk . . . Okay?'

McNutt shouted again. 'Okay!'

Garcia winced from the sound in his ear. 'Josh, why are you screaming? I told you not to scream.'

'Why? Because you're freaking me out. It's like you're inside my head.'

'Technically, I *am* inside your head.'

McNutt froze in place. 'You can't hear my thoughts, can you?'

Garcia laughed, unsure if it was a joke. 'Why would anyone want to do that?'

16

The Fools of Alexander.

That's the derogatory name used by scholars to describe anyone who has wasted time searching for buried treasure in Alexandria. In a city of millions, it seems that everyone – not just historians and archaeologists, but also lawyers, waiters, and hobos – has a theory about Alexander the Great and the location of his golden tomb.

In most parts of the world, people buy lottery tickets.

In Alexandria, they buy shovels.

In recent years, digging has become an epidemic. Once the upper levels of the city had been thoroughly examined, the fools took to the sewers en masse, hoping to find a secret passageway into the ancient depths of the city. Most excavated without permits, often leaving common sense behind as they dug deeper, and deeper, and deeper.

Eventually, something had to give.

It didn't take an engineer to realize that the city's core was being compromised by the subterranean plague of treasure hunters, but the government brought in a team of experts to determine how bad it really was. The last thing officials wanted was for the city to fall again. The soldiers of Persia, Rome, and Turkey were one thing, but surely they could defend themselves against a horde of civilians with picks and shovels.

Once they had the proof they needed, the authorities ordered for all digging under Alexandria to cease immediately. In addition, all entrances and passageways that led to the ancient levels of the city were either sealed or locked. Signs posted in every corner of the city made it clear that the underground network of tunnels had been deemed off-limits to anyone but city workers and members of the Ministry of State for Antiquities – the final authority when dealing with anything related to the cultural heritage of Egypt. Only those who understood the structural consequences of digging and those trained in museum sciences were welcome in the ruins. Everyone else would have to be content with the officially sanctioned tours of the city's ancient tunnels.

Unfortunately, that wasn't good enough for Cobb.

And it would take more than a sign to keep him out.

* * *

It was a typical Friday night in a trendy part of town. The kind of place where locals and tourists gathered every weekend for food and entertainment.

Cobb and Sarah strolled down the block, as if they were early for dinner and had time to kill. Around them, the neighborhood was alive. Car horns were honking, music was playing, and pedestrians filled the sidewalks. As expected, the police presence was high, but they were concentrating on the streets, not the tunnels underneath.

'You ready?' Cobb whispered.

McNutt watched them through the window of the Internet café across the street. He had arrived a few minutes earlier with an empty bladder. He knew it would take at least four large coffees for nature to force him from his lookout. If he drank them slowly, it would be more than enough time for Sarah and Cobb to get what they needed.

'Ready,' he mumbled.

Garcia monitored all the chatter from the converted radio room on the boat. He was the digital maestro. Not only was he responsible for recording the video feeds, he also controlled who could talk to whom, and when. 'Remember guys, Josh is there to look and listen. The more he talks, the more this plan falls apart. Don't forget, he's sitting alone at a table. We don't need him talking to himself if it can be avoided.'

'Like he doesn't do that already,' Sarah teased.

'I heard that,' McNutt said.

Seated next to Garcia, Jasmine stared at a map of the ancient city on a next-generation computer screen. While it wasn't the same as the three-dimensional hologram, the software was still rendering an amazingly precise set of images. 'I've got all three of you on the map. The GPS units are relaying your location, loud and clear . . . Well, not *loud*. I mean, the units aren't beeping or anything because that would get annoying, but I can see where you are quite clearly. Well, not really *you*. Just dots on a screen.'

Garcia winced. 'For the love of God, what was that?'

'Sorry. I'm nervous.'

'Nervous, or drunk?'

'Nervous!' she assured him.

'Good, because we can't afford to have *two* drunks on the job.'

'I heard that, too!' McNutt growled.

Cobb had been hesitant about the global positioning trackers. He assumed that if Garcia could follow his movement, others might be able to home in on the signal as well. Not that anyone would. After all, they had no reason to believe that they were being followed. Still, Cobb wanted to stay off the radar, not announce where he was.

But Garcia had assured him that his security measures were sound: no one could hack the GPS signal without Garcia knowing it. And if someone tried, he could intercept the attack or shut down the signal before Cobb or Sarah's position could be traced.

Eventually, Cobb had decided that testing the accuracy of the map outweighed the risks. The odds of encountering the kind of elite hacker who could even identify a GPS signal – much less track it – were ten thousand to one, at best.

That is, if the technology even worked in the depths of the city.

They wouldn't know for sure until they tried it out.

Prior to the team's arrival in Alexandria, Cobb and Sarah had searched the district for non-traditional access points to the tunnel system and had found one in the subbasement of an apartment building. It had everything they were looking for: a wide grate to load equipment, ridiculously inadequate security, and virtual privacy.

Cobb cleared his throat. 'Sarah and I are walking up to the entrance now. We're in play in three . . . two . . . one . . .'

At zero, Sarah grabbed the doorknob and picked the lock faster than a senior citizen could turn a key. A second later, they were walking into the building.

'Impressive,' Cobb whispered.

'I know,' Sarah bragged.

They hustled down a flight of stairs and found themselves in a long hallway flanked by storage lockers for the residents. They quickly planted a small, wireless video camera above the lockers and made sure Garcia could see the feed. Then they made their way across the width of the building, silently hoping that none of the tenants was in sudden need of the spare lamps, battered suitcases, or rusted bicycles that cluttered the bins.

Fortunately, on this night, their path was clear.

When they reached the end of the hall, Sarah easily picked the lock on the boiler room door. They slipped inside and locked the door behind them.

'Holy shit,' she said as she turned on her flashlight and walked down the stairs. Steam hung in the air like a sauna.

'What's wrong?' Garcia demanded.

'It feels like Florida in here. Someone get me a towel.'

Cobb smiled as he planted a second camera just inside the door. Not only because her comment was accurate, but because he knew all of that steam needed somewhere to go – and that was why they were there.

The moisture drained into the ancient aqueducts below.

Cobb lifted the iron grate off the large drain in the floor. Sarah lowered herself into the hole first, bracing her body against the walls to control her descent into the tunnels below. Cobb followed her lead, easing the grate back into position as he did.

They dropped to the floor, one after another.

Both prepared for the worst, but they were alone in the darkness.

Cobb clicked on his flashlight and updated his team.

'We're in.'

* * *

Hundreds of miles away, a warning light flickered.

The moment the grate had been lifted, it had triggered the motion detectors that were actually embedded in the hollow iron. These tiny sensors could not only register vibration, their internal accelerometer could also calculate their orientation. The advanced technology could be used to determine if someone had merely stepped on the grate or if it had been removed entirely.

It was one of many security measures that had been placed throughout the cisterns.

The data collected from these devices was continuously fed to a remote system hidden amongst the rolling dunes of the Sahara where the signals were monitored by a massive computer that displayed real-time information from every corner of the underground labyrinth. If the lower levels of the city were breached in any way, the men who guarded them were instantly alerted.

No one got in or out without their knowledge.

It was the only way to protect their secrets.

With a simple text message, the personnel in the desert notified their contact in Alexandria of the impending threat. If further action was needed, it was his responsibility to ensure that appropriate measures were taken.

His men were always at the ready.

All they needed was a target.

17

The need for fresh water has always been a vital concern for the people of Alexandria. Most of Egypt is barren desert with few natural springs, and the ancient inhabitants of the city had no means of utilizing the salt water of the Mediterranean.

Fortunately, the Nile River has provided an inexhaustible source of drinkable water. With the help of man-made canals, the waters of the Nile were diverted into cisterns located throughout ancient Alexandria. There, the sediment slowly sank to the bottom, leaving clean, palatable water that could sustain the population.

The earliest cisterns were little more than square chambers cut into the sandstone, but when the Romans arrived in the second century BC, the simple stone pits were replaced by elaborate works of masonry. Before long, private reservoirs built of hand-fired bricks were the standard throughout Alexandria.

The following centuries brought a steady rise to the city's population, and with it came the need to move away from the shallow cisterns that could only serve a few families each. The newer cisterns near the outskirts of the city were designed with entire communities in mind. They consisted of a series of grand chambers that penetrated more than three stories into the earth. These cavities were reinforced with a honeycomb of massive stone pillars connected by elaborate marble arches. Much of the stone had been repurposed from the ruins of ancient buildings and temples, which gave the underground vaults a grandiose, almost majestic feel.

All told, the network of cisterns was a colossal undertaking that was unrivaled in its day – not only as a feat of engineering, but for the sheer beauty of its design. And yet thanks to the destructive nature of the Fools of Alexander, most of it was hidden from the general public.

Jasmine didn't know what she would see when the video from Cobb's and Sarah's flashlight cameras started to appear on her computer screen, but she wasn't expecting the system to be so impressive. 'Oh . . . my . . . God. It's amazing.'

Sarah had to agree: there was something awe-inspiring about the scene. Those who had constructed this vast system of water collection had done so with the same pride as those who had built the grandest of cathedrals. She found it hard to believe that something so majestic could be hidden away just below the surface of the city.

She looked at Cobb. 'What now?'

Cobb shrugged. 'Beats the hell out of me.'

She laughed at his honesty.

They swung their lights around the space and tried to solve the riddle. There were no walkways or stairs. And as far as they could tell, the only way to navigate across the cistern was to shimmy along the narrow arches, hugging the wide pillars that blocked their path. One slip, and they would fall thirty feet to the bedrock below.

'Any suggestions?' he asked.

'Maybe we can jump.'

'To where? The floor?'

'No. One level down.'

He grimaced and shined his light on the walkway below. It sat on top of a row of arches that sat on top of another row of arches that seemingly grew out of the floor itself. From this distance, there was no way to gauge the strength of the ancient stonework. It looked solid enough, but there was always a chance that the whole structure would simply collapse if they leaped to the arches below. Still, they needed to find a way down to the bottom level. That's where they would find the tunnels that once allowed water to flow from one chamber to the next. According to the map, the tunnels would grant them access to the entire network of cisterns and the foundation of the ancient city.

'Jasmine,' Cobb said via his earpiece. 'Do you see another way down? I don't want to test the strength of this stone if we don't have to . . . Jasmine, are you there?'

Transfixed by the images on the screen, she took a few seconds to snap out of her daze. 'Sorry about that. According to my research, there should be a ladder carved into the wall itself. Look at the base of the ledge you're standing on.'

As promised, he found a series of notches that descended to the floor below. Unfortunately, they were more worn than he had hoped, having eroded considerably over the centuries. Any shallower, and there would be no way for him to get a toehold.

He made a mental note to bring climbing gear on their next visit – if there was a next visit – because climbing thirty feet in both directions on the strength of his fingertips was a daunting prospect. He glanced at Sarah, wondering how she felt about the notches. 'You're the expert. What do you think?'

Sarah grinned and leaped off the ledge, catching herself on the first rung. From there she scurried down the wall like a gecko, as if her hands and feet could actually stick to the surface

of the rock. For her, the depth of the notches posed no challenge at all.

Cobb knew she had skills, but seeing her in action gave him
a new appreciation of her abilities. Unfortunately, it also served
as a tough act to follow.

She looked up at him from the safety of the chamber floor.
'Your turn.'

He grimaced with determination as he slid off the ledge. His
fingers strained and the toes of his boots dug into the rock, but
the wall held firm under his weight. Methodically he lowered
himself down the row of notches. His descent was nowhere as
graceful as Sarah's, but it was equally effective.

'That was fun,' he said at the bottom, though his tone
suggested it was anything but. He took a moment to catch his
breath. 'You find a passageway?'

'Nope. I found two.' She shined her light to the north, revealing
two entrances that stood side by side. 'Which one should we
take?'

Jasmine studied the map and relayed her thoughts. 'Actually,
I think they go to the same cistern. I think it's one tunnel that
was reinforced in the middle, cutting it in half.'

Cobb stepped toward the right as Sarah headed toward the
left.

She smiled. 'See you on the other side.'

'Yeah, that's not ominous at all.'

Fortunately, her prediction came true moments later when
they entered a cistern that looked remarkably similar to the one
they had just left. Same stone pillars. Same magnificent arches.
Same ominous sense that it might collapse at any moment. In
fact, the only noticeable difference was that the next set of

passageways was not ahead of them, but on opposite sides of the room: one to the left and one to the right.

Sarah shined her light at the first tunnel, then spun toward the second, then back to the first. 'Call me crazy, but I don't think these go to the same place.'

Cobb glanced at her. 'Thanks, Josh.'

Sarah laughed at the remark.

'I heard that,' McNutt grumbled in the café.

Jasmine's mood was not as playful. 'And neither one takes you in the right direction. You want to push north. Those tunnels take you east and west.'

Cobb motioned toward the east. 'No worries. We'll see where this goes, then we'll come back and explore the other one.'

Sarah glanced at him. 'Why not split up? We'll cover more ground that way.'

Cobb shook his head. 'I'm not worried about covering ground. I'm worried about covering each other. If we find trouble down here, we stand a better chance of dealing with it together.'

'Exactly what kind of trouble do you expect to find down here? Mole men? Sewer rats? Overgrown goldfish?'

He stood his ground. 'Whatever we find, we'll confront it *together*.'

She shrugged and followed him through the east tunnel.

18

Jasmine stared at the computer screen, conflicted by the video feeds of the underground water system. As a historian, every cistern was a work of art. They were glorious feats of engineering that she couldn't wait to see in person. She wanted to touch the stonework, to feel the texture on her fingers, to document it for future generations.

But as a navigator, the system was infuriating.

The tunnels never seemed to go in the direction that she wanted. Some chambers were built with east–west corridors; others went north–south. Furthermore, not all of the tunnels were built at the bottom of the cisterns. As the height and depth of the rooms continually changed, so did their path. Sometimes a second-level passageway in one cistern ended up on the third level of the next. This forced Cobb and Sarah to climb up and down ancient stone ladders as they made their way through the system.

Worse still, several tunnels led to dead ends. These sections, which had been blocked by cave-ins and/or safety fences, had forced Cobb and Sarah to double back and choose new routes on multiple occasions. It was fine with them – they understood the benefit of a thorough exploration, even if it meant retracing their steps – but Jasmine was discouraged by their progress. It seemed like every time they approached the possible location of Caesar's Well an obstacle got in their way.

After a while, she wondered if there was a reason why.

As they pushed deeper, they found fewer and fewer north-bound tunnels. They also noted that the width of each section was narrowing. In the beginning, there were five interconnected chambers, each an acre or more in area. The next grouping of cisterns was comprised of four chambers. The one north of that only had three. The system was funneling them toward a single destination.

Entering the last chamber, they knew something was different.

It wasn't the first time they had seen pools of water in the system. Runoff from the various drainage grates that dotted the ceiling had mixed with groundwater, settling in the low spots throughout the system. At times Cobb and Sarah had trudged through corridors that were filled above their ankles. The chambers themselves, however, were relatively dry, at least until now. Here it appeared that gravity had pulled the excess moisture from all the other chambers to the lowest area of the network.

This wasn't the shallow puddles of the other rooms.

This was substantial flooding.

Cobb shined his flashlight at the chamber. 'Are you getting this? It appears that the lowest level of the cistern is completely underwater.'

On the boat, Garcia checked the GPS readings. The units Cobb and Sarah were using weren't the standard consumer-grade models that anyone could buy off the shelf. They were high-end, military-issue devices that provided a lot more than coordinates.

Garcia nodded in understanding. 'According to the altimeter, you're now sixty feet below sea level. It's the deepest you've been so far.'

Cobb stared at the small lake at the base of the chamber and wondered how many millions of dollars had gone into the technology that had given him proof of what he had figured out on his own. 'Thanks. Keep me posted.'

'Will do, chief.'

Lurking in the shadows, Sarah stared at Cobb. The more she was around him, the more she admired his style. Instead of embarrassing Garcia and pointing out his analytical grasp of the obvious, Cobb had made him feel like a hero, as if he had contributed an important piece of information at a crucial time. It didn't take much – only four simple words – but she knew it would pay dividends in the days ahead.

Loyalty, after all, had to be earned.

Cobb turned and glanced at Sarah. If there had been more light, he might have seen her blushing. 'What are you doing back there?'

'Waiting.'

'For what?'

She shined her light in his eyes. 'For you.'

'For me?' he asked, confused.

'Yeah . . . to make a decision.'

'On?'

'Where to go next. And I suggest you hurry up because this place is falling down.'

To prove her point, she pointed her flashlight at the walls above, and he quickly noticed the poor condition of the chamber. While the other rooms gave the sense that they *could* fall at any moment, here it had actually started to happen. The stones in the pillars and the arch supports were cracked and crumbling. And there were chunks missing from the ceiling. They had no way of knowing if the damage had been caused naturally by floods, earthquakes, or drainage, or if it was the result of construction in the city above. One thing was certain: the years had taken their toll on this chamber.

An uneasy feeling twisted in Cobb's gut. He wasn't one for omens, but he had a bad feeling about this place. 'Let's keep moving.'

'Good idea,' she said.

But their choices were limited. They had just entered through the passageway from the south, and their only other option was at the far side of the cistern. Despite the danger, Jasmine urged them to head that way because the tunnel would take them closer to Caesar's Well. That is, if the city's blueprints were accurate.

Because of the treacherous footing, it took a few minutes to make their way down the path, over the water, around the crumbling stone pillars, and into the final passageway. The tunnel took them north through the foundation of the ancient city for another hundred feet or so before they were presented with a final challenge.

One that Jasmine didn't expect.

'What the hell is that?' she shrieked.

In the café, McNutt winced in wide-eyed pain as Jasmine's voice reverberated throughout his head. He would have gladly ripped out his own tooth if it meant avoiding another shout like that. He glanced around the room, searching for anyone with the look of an oral surgeon. 'Someone wanna tell me what's going on?'

'We can't go any further,' she answered.

'Why?' McNutt mumbled.

'We hit a wall,' Cobb explained.

It wasn't a figure of speech. The final tunnel was blocked by an actual wall. Not a pile of rubble with a safety fence, or an ancient wall made of stone.

This bastard was made of brick.

Cobb leaned into the barricade, then kicked it, hoping that he could force his way through. But it held firm, not giving an inch. 'It's solid.'

Jasmine hadn't even considered the wall's strength. She was more concerned about its substance. 'Why is it made of brick? Does it look new?'

Cobb pounded on it with the back of his hand. 'Not particularly. Don't get me wrong: it's much newer than the cisterns themselves, but this wall has been here a while. If I had to guess, I'd say it's older than I am.'

'No way,' Sarah teased, 'it can't be *that* old. They didn't have *tools* when you were a kid. They didn't have *fire*.'

'Ouch,' Cobb said.

'Nothing but caves, and clubs, and woolly mammoths.'

'Those suckers were tasty,' he said with a smile.

'Yum.'

He playfully pushed her away. 'Hector, can you—'

'Already on it,' Garcia blurted as he pounded away on his keyboard. Having already hacked the city planning office, he had access to everything on their system. He quickly scanned through page after page of construction logs, hoping to spot something that would help them determine the age of the brick wall. 'Hang on . . . here it is.'

The others listened as he summarized what he had found.

'There was a survey conducted to determine the structural integrity of the tunnel . . . engineers found evidence of erosion and other deficiencies . . . the decision was made to eliminate access to the deeper underground areas . . . sealed by means of a wall . . . *okay, right here:* a brick wall, constructed by the city engineers by mandate of the city council, approved on September the first, 1939, and erected immediately thereafter.'

Sarah had to laugh. 'So much for having a modern map. Then again, I guess anything less than a century old is modern by Egyptian standards.'

'September the first, 1939,' Garcia mumbled. 'Why do I know that date?'

Cobb answered as he glanced around the tunnel. 'You probably learned it at school. The invasion of Poland marked the start of World War Two.'

'Oh yeah. Hitler. I'm not a fan.'

Sarah glanced at Cobb. 'What are you looking for?'

He pointed toward the south. 'Back in the cisterns, remember the ductwork we saw in some of the rooms? I couldn't figure it out, but now I know what it was. Air vents.'

'Why?' Sarah asked.

'The war,' he explained. 'Someone realized that these giant chambers could protect them from air raids, so they added a ventilation system and turned this place into a giant bomb shelter. The vents would provide fresh air and eliminate carbon dioxide. Plus, they'd have fresh water from the cisterns.'

'That's ingenious,' Sarah admitted. 'There's enough space down here for hundreds of people. Maybe even thousands.'

Cobb nodded. 'Space is good. So why block off the rest of the system?'

Sarah kicked the brick wall. 'We're going to have to get through here to find out. Anyone have any ideas?'

McNutt coughed and cleared his throat.

Cobb smiled. 'That you, Josh?'

McNutt coughed again.

Sarah laughed. 'Hey hillbilly – you know you can just pull out your cell phone and pretend that you're talking to somebody. You know that, right?'

McNutt swore under his breath.

It was a thought that hadn't occurred to him.

19

'Bigfoot' was actually named Gaz Kamal. And 'Biggerfoot' was Farouk Tarek. Both of them were loyal soldiers, deputies in the service of the local district kingpin, a man known simply as Hassan. They had each spent several years of their lives behind the walls of Egypt's Tora Prison, and they had vowed never to go back.

It didn't mean they had abandoned a life of crime.

It only meant that death was preferable to incarceration.

Their boss dabbled in everything from the 'protection' of small businesses to the sale of exotic firearms. If it happened in his territory, Hassan owned a piece of the action. To ensure that no one operated in his area without paying the proper toll, Hassan had a network of informants to keep him abreast of local activities.

And his sources were everywhere.

Kamal and Tarek were enjoying dinner at one of their favorite restaurants when their cell phones began to vibrate in unison, notifying each of a new message. The day of the week or time of night didn't matter; as Hassan's enforcers they were always on duty. Protecting their boss, his interests, and his territory was a full-time assignment.

Glancing at his phone, Kamal saw a picture message from one of their most trusted scouts. Their platter of stuffed pigeons and couscous would have to wait. He clicked the icon and waited for the image to download, curious about the subject matter. He nearly jumped out of his chair when he saw the photo of Sarah.

'It's her,' Kamal said in Arabic. 'Dade's friend.'

Tarek glanced at the image. 'I'll get the car.'

Someone had recognized her from their description.

Better still, they now had a picture of their target.

* * *

Ten minutes later they were standing in the opulent foyer of their employer.

A spectacular mural depicting the Egyptian tale of the Treasure Thief wrapped around the entryway. It related the adventures of Horemheb, the master builder who had been called upon to construct an impenetrable vault for Pharaoh Ramscs III. Horemheb did as he was instructed, but left a hidden entrance so that his son might someday help himself to the treasure. Try as he might, the pharaoh could never catch the commoner who continually robbed his coffers. In the end, the son admitted his crime, but he had proven to be so brilliant in his deception that he had fallen into favor with the very king he had deceived.

It was the story of a criminal who was so skilled at his craft that the highest power in the land had no choice but to recognize his abilities and herald him as a hero.

Most people saw the tale through the eyes of the pharaoh: a powerful man who came to terms with his own limitations and was gracious enough to forgive and forget.

But Hassan identified with the thief who had outwitted a king.

Beyond the mural, two luxurious sitting rooms flanked a wide hallway trimmed in ebony and sandalwood – a corridor that led into the bowels of the mansion. Hassan had never been one to shy away from the finer things in life, even if the opulence might draw attention. He had built his empire from nothing, and he was determined to enjoy the spoils of war. His home reflected that philosophy.

Kamal and Tarek were still hungry, but now they wanted information, not poultry. They wanted to know more about the mysterious woman who had outrun them two days earlier. They wanted to know why she was in town, what connections she had, and who else had aided her escape. But before they could proceed with their investigation, they had to report to Hassan. His desire to know everything that happened in his territory even extended to the actions of his own men.

Gahiji Awad, Hassan's personal bodyguard, met them at the door. 'The timing of your call was fortunate. He's been waiting to hear from you.'

He turned and led them into the house.

Neither Kamal nor Tarek was particularly fond of Awad, not only for his arrogance, but also his skill set. Standing just over five and a half feet in height, the diminutive bodyguard should have presented little challenge in a fight. At least, that's what they had first believed. Despite his muscular frame, they dwarfed this tiny man by several inches and several pounds. They should have been able to crush his bones into powder.

But it would take more than brute force to defeat him.

The one and only time that Kamal and Tarek had physically challenged Awad, it had almost cost them their lives. Using a form of martial arts that the larger men had never thought possible, Awad had devastated them with a series of moves that bordered on superhuman. In the end, Kamal had three broken fingers, a dislocated hip, a separated shoulder, and three cracked vertebrae.

And he was the lucky one.

For weeks after the fight, Tarek couldn't pee standing up.

It was the last time they had confronted him.

Awad guided them to the rear wing of the property to Hassan's office. It was a magnificent space decorated with the finest Egyptian antiquities. Its warm, reddish hue was offset by the panoramic view of the harbor and the cool blue tint of the open sea beyond. Hassan stared at them from behind his desk. Between the parties, a sterling silver serving tray sat covered on the desktop, as if the news had interrupted his meal.

'Come . . . Sit.' The drawl of his Arabic was slow and pronounced. He waited for them to take a seat before he spoke again. 'You have news?'

Kamal nodded. 'We have a lead on the girl.'

'The girl you spoke of two nights ago?'

He nodded again. 'We described her to our sources on the street. They were given orders to notify us if they saw her. She was spotted this evening.'

Kamal took out his cell phone and handed it to Hassan so he could see the picture that had been sent. 'She is the same woman who ran from us in the bar. The woman who was speaking with Simon Dade.'

'What is her involvement with Dade?'

'We do not know. As you are aware, we have been unable to locate Dade these last few weeks. It appears he has gone into hiding. The recent encounter is as close as we have gotten. Again, our deepest apologies.'

'He hides from us, yet he emerged for this girl? Then *she* is someone worth knowing. Wouldn't you agree?'

'Yes,' they mumbled in unison.

Hassan smiled and leaned back in his seat. 'Gentlemen, you asked for this meeting, so tell me your thoughts: what does your instinct tell you? What do you make of her?'

Kamal and Tarek didn't know how to respond. In all the years they had worked for Hassan, he had never asked for their opinions on a subject. They were simply the muscle. Hassan was the brain. They fed him the information they had gathered, he dictated their actions, and they responded. They weren't accustomed to choices, and they certainly weren't called upon for their thoughts.

Tarek broke the silence after an awkward pause. 'We do not believe that she is a tourist.'

Hassan raised an eyebrow. 'That is all?'

Kamal sat up straight in his chair. If this was his chance to show his boss that he was capable of more than physical intimidation, he was going to make the most of it. 'As Farouk was saying, there is something *different* about her. She does not have the naïve look of a tourist. She carries herself confidently, like a professional.'

'A professional? Like a doctor?'

He shook his head. 'Like a criminal.'

It was an honest assessment, one that had come from years of observation. Alexandria might not be mentioned in the same breath as Caracas, Cape Town, or Juárez, but it still had its fair share of danger. Survival, particularly in their line of work, took a certain level of street smarts. Identifying the hustlers and con artists was an everyday chore, and those who couldn't were destined to become victims.

Kamal hadn't survived this long on his size alone.

He knew overlooking the girl would be a mistake.

Tarek joined in, warming to the opportunity to speak. 'Her meeting with Dade was not coincidence. They knew each other. She trusted him enough to run with him at the first sign of trouble. That is why we sent her description to our people. To determine who she is, and why she is here.'

Hassan nodded. 'Do you think she is cause for concern?'

'Concern?' Kamal echoed. 'Not at this time. But she *is* a person of interest. That is why we circulated her photo. We knew she could not hide forever.'

'Good,' Hassan replied. 'I want you to bring her to me. No more waiting. No more distractions. You are forgiven this time, but next time I might not be so charitable.'

Kamal and Tarek glanced at each other, confused. As far as they could tell, Hassan had agreed with everything they had said. So why was he threatening them?

Kamal was the one to voice it. 'Sir, have we done something wrong?'

Hassan glared at them. 'Do you actually think I didn't know where you were while this girl was roaming my city? You dare to indulge yourselves with fancy meals while this wildcard walks my streets, and you expect my gratitude for bringing me her *photo*? If not for your lackeys, you would still be searching for her. Now I see why you have yet to produce Simon Dade.'

'We thought—'

'Silence! I do not pay you to think!'

Kamal and Tarek could feel Awad circling behind them, like a shark in shallow water waiting to attack. They knew all he needed was permission.

Instead, Hassan smiled. 'But as I say, you are forgiven. In

fact, I've prepared a special treat for you, seeing as your meal was previously interrupted.'

Hassan lifted the sterling silver cover off the tray on his desktop. He revealed a Desert Eagle .50 caliber pistol, a gun so powerful that the resulting wound would be bigger than a grapefruit.

Next to the pistol lay two dead pigeons. Awad had broken their necks only minutes before Kamal and Tarek's arrival.

The birds were still warm. Their legs still quivering.

Hassan pushed the silver tray across his desk.

'Please, gentlemen, finish your meal.'

20

After returning to the yacht, the team watched footage of Sarah and Cobb's exploration for several hours. The film study may have seemed like overkill, but it served a purpose. Having searched the entire system, the only thing that stood out was the curious brick wall at the end of the final tunnel.

For some reason, it didn't seem to belong.

Garcia did some digging and explained what he had found. 'Jack's theory about the bomb shelter is dead-on. It was actually planned by the British military. They saw the tunnels as a way to protect the local population if the Germans decided to bomb Alexandria. The Egyptian government signed off on the plan, authorizing a sizeable project that was intended to transform the empty tunnels into shelters.'

'Transform them how?' Papineau asked.

'Where needed, they reinforced the stone with concrete to ensure that it wouldn't collapse. They lined the walls with wooden benches. And they installed a ventilation system to provide breathable air.'

'We didn't see any benches,' Sarah offered.

Garcia anticipated the comment. 'The benches have mostly been removed in the years since the war. The wood was needed in the ghettos. Some built with it. Some simply burned it. Either way, everyone turned a blind eye.'

Jasmine appreciated the information, but it didn't explain the brick wall. 'It still leaves us with one question: if the goal was to protect as many people as possible, why seal off part of the system? There's another cistern beyond the brick wall and several more tunnels. There would be room for hundreds of people. Why not use that space as well? Why put the barricade there? And how do we get past it?'

Silence hung in the air as everyone pondered the issues.

That is, until McNutt chimed in.

'I'm not great at math—'

'No shit,' Sarah said.

'But by my count, that was *four* questions, not one.' He double-checked his math on his fingers. 'Yep, *cinco*.'

Jasmine smiled. 'What's your point?'

'I have no idea how to answer the first three, but the fourth one is easy.' He broke into a wide grin. 'If you want to get through, I can get through.'

*   *   *

They weren't the only ones pondering new evidence. Kamal and Tarek had gone without sleep as well, having spent the night running down their only lead: the cell phone picture of the mysterious woman.

The photograph had been sent by an elderly shopkeeper at one of the businesses that they 'protected'. He, like many others, had heard of Kamal and Tarek's interest in the woman. Hoping to curry favor with the henchmen – the payments that he owed to them seemed to increase every week – the shopkeeper did what he could to find her.

Since his ailments prevented him from roaming the city, the shopkeeper had asked his grandson to keep an eye out for anyone matching Sarah's description. The grandson had then asked his friends for help, and one of those friends had snapped the picture of her down the street from the apartment building.

They didn't know where she was headed.

But if she returned, they would be ready.

*　*　*

There were pros and cons about returning to the tunnel so soon after their rekky.

On the plus side, it was still the weekend, which meant the streets would be filled with people of all shapes and sizes and the local authorities would be preoccupied with maintaining the general peace on the rowdiest day of the week.

On the other hand, if anyone had grown suspicious of Cobb and Sarah the night before, their reappearance might cause some alarm, especially since there would be more to notice on their return trip. This time they were bringing Jasmine, McNutt, and a wide assortment of equipment.

After sorting through all the possibilities, Cobb decided it was better to hit the tunnels while they were fresh in their minds than to sit on the yacht and wait.

The rest of the team agreed.

Papineau dropped them off in an alley near the apartment building before he returned to the yacht. Meanwhile, Garcia monitored the team's movement from his makeshift command center, using high-tech toys and surveillance videos.

Garcia tapped a few keys. 'Okay, boys and girls, I've got all of you up on my screen. That means your devices are transmitting . . . Can everyone hear my voice?'

'Yes,' said Jasmine.

'Hurry up,' urged Sarah.

'Who is this?' asked McNutt.

Cobb smiled. 'That's affirmative.'

Garcia checked his video screens. 'The street is clear in front of the building. The lobby is clear, too. Commence on your go.'

Cobb nodded at Sarah. 'Clear here. Moving in.'

To lessen their odds of detection, they traveled in pairs. Sarah and McNutt went first, followed by Cobb and Jasmine. Sarah picked the lock without breaking stride and continued down the hall toward the stairwell. McNutt slowed briefly, placing a piece of tape over the strike plate to prevent the lock from reengaging, before he caught up with Sarah. They continued toward the basement and the boiler room as Cobb and Jasmine arrived at the front door. Cobb opened the door like a gentleman while smoothly removing the tape from the frame. Jasmine walked through before he pulled the door shut behind him.

All in all, their breach had taken thirty-nine seconds.

One second less than they had expected.

Inside the boiler room, McNutt had no trouble removing the metal grate that led to the tunnels below. Sarah instinctively paused to listen for trouble. Hearing nothing but the steady hum of the boiler, she dropped into the system below and turned on her video flashlight.

'We're clear,' she said from the tunnel.

A minute later, the team was standing beside her.

'Now where?' Jasmine wondered.

No longer the navigator, she was relying on Garcia to guide them to the far end of the cisterns. Unfortunately, she knew it would take a lot of jumping and climbing to reach the brick wall – and *climbing* was not her forte. In fact, the last time she had climbed anything of significance was back in grade school, and that incident had resulted in a bloody lip when a classmate pulled her hair and she fell off a jungle gym.

Today, the stakes would be much higher.

And so would the obstacles.

As they approached the first cistern, Sarah pulled a thin climbing rope from her backpack and began tying it around Jasmine's waist. 'This will catch you if you fall. It's not the easiest climb down.'

'I'm going first?' Jasmine blurted.

Sarah smiled as she pulled the knot tight. 'No. I'm going down first to check the holds. If they're still solid, you'll come down next. If not, the guys will have to lower you with the rope.'

Before the others could argue, Sarah was off the edge and making her way toward the floor. Fifteen seconds later she was staring up at them. 'Jasmine, you're up.'

'Great,' she said in a tone that suggested otherwise. 'So, Jack, how do I do this? Do I just start climbing?'

Cobb smiled. 'Yep.'

'And if you happen to slip . . .' McNutt showed her the tight grip he had on the rope. 'I swear I've got ya.'

'You won't fall,' Cobb assured her. 'I did this yesterday in both directions, and the handholds are solid. Just have a little faith, and you'll be fine.'

Jasmine took a deep, calming breath, blew it out slowly, and then started her descent. Her pace was measured at first, but after she got a feel for the spacing of the slots, her speed picked up considerably for the rest of the climb.

McNutt went down next, followed by Cobb, who brought

the rope down with him. Once he reached the bottom, he quickly spooled the rope around his hand and elbow before he slipped it over his shoulder and nodded for Sarah to take the lead.

'This way,' she said.

The others followed as she led them through the twists and turns of the cistern system. Somehow she had memorized the maze and knew how to make it through without any guidance from Garcia – a feat that surprised everyone, including herself.

Although Jasmine had been amazed by the video footage of the tunnels, it was nothing like being there. In person, the underground cisterns were overwhelming.

'This stuff should be in a museum,' Jasmine said as she swept her flashlight across the space. 'It represents the breadth of the region's history.'

No one commented, so she continued.

She pointed to the base of a pillar. 'Look over there. That relief is influenced by the classical Greek style. But the arches in the last cistern were consistent with the angular, geometric design of Persia. The diversity down here is astounding. And it's so well preserved. It's amazing to think that by reusing pieces of ancient ruins they were actually protecting them. On the other hand, it's a shame that—'

Sarah spun around and shined her light in Jasmine's face.

'What's wrong?' Jasmine demanded.

'How should I know?' she said in a harsh whisper. 'There could be a herd of elephants charging toward us right now, and I wouldn't be able to hear them over your historical play-by-play.'

'Sorry. I'm just excited.'

Sarah softened her tone. 'Listen, we can discuss the finer points of architecture and what it means to mankind once we return to the boat. But right now, we have to focus on the mission at hand – and that's getting in and getting out.'

Jasmine nodded in understanding. She would continue to note the distinct features of each cistern, but she would keep the narration to herself.

While the women sorted out their differences and McNutt prayed for a wrestling match, Cobb took a more practical approach. At every turn, he marked their progress by applying invisible ink onto the tunnels themselves. The ink could not be seen with the naked eye, but under ultraviolet light it would glow like a neon sign. He hoped the precaution wouldn't be necessary, but he always prepared for the worst.

Always had, and always would.

It was just Cobb's way.

Unlike the rekky of the day before, this journey was destination-based. That meant Sarah wasted no time on sightseeing and led them directly to the brick wall. As she approached the far end of the tunnel, she checked in with Garcia to make sure that they were still within his range. 'You still there, Hector?'

'Copy that,' he said as he tested their GPS units and the video signals from their flashlight cameras. 'Tracking is good. Picture is clear. Four strong feeds, all recording.'

Sarah nodded toward McNutt. 'You're up.'

McNutt smiled in anticipation. 'It's about time I got to blow something up.'

The comment wasn't entirely accurate. He was actually going to reduce something to smithereens without explosives. He reached into a pocket of his cargo pants and pulled out a small tube no bigger than a penlight.

Jasmine stared at the device. 'What are you going to do with that?'

His smile widened. 'You know the spring-loaded batons that firemen use to puncture safety glass – the ones that drive a steel tip through the pane at high velocity to get out accident victims? Well, this kind of works in the same way, only instead of a steel tip, it uses a sonic pulse. And instead of shattering glass, it destroys cement, mortar . . . basically anything this side of solid rock.'

He glanced back at Cobb. 'You should see what this does to someone's face. Holy shit, it's *brutal*. Blood and teeth *everywhere*. It's like a hockey game.'

Jasmine grumbled, 'Wait a minute. No one said anything about collateral damage. Will it hurt any ruins on the other side of the wall?'

McNutt shook his head. 'Not a chance! The force will be localized on the target, just like a dentist's drill, at least in theory . . . I mean, I've never used this thing on an old wall before. For all I know, the tunnel might come crumbling down on top of us. In fact, the more I think about it, you guys better stand back, like, a hundred feet or so.'

Jasmine glanced at Cobb. 'Jack, is he serious?'

Cobb ignored her question. 'Come on, Josh. We're waiting.'

McNutt crouched and pressed the end of the device against the space between the bricks at the center of the wall. The group took a step back as he turned on the device, but it barely made a sound. And then it happened. As if by magic, the mortar between the bricks appeared to melt away. No messy fragmentation. No shards flying around the tunnel. One moment the wall was solid, and the next there was a gap in the center.

Eventually bricks started to fall to the ground like leaves from a dying tree.

Sarah stared in amazement. 'I want one.'

'Me too,' Jasmine admitted.

A minute later, McNutt examined the hole that he had opened in the wall. Then he shined his light through and saw nothing but empty space on the other side.

Just as they suspected, there was another tunnel.

And it appeared older than the others.

2 1

Jasmine groaned in disappointment. The other tunnels had opened into splendid halls, caverns of sturdy rock and meticulously placed stone that looked like works of art. But the latest tunnel had proven to be a gateway to something else entirely.

A monstrous pit of some kind.

Shining her flashlight through the gap in the wall, she studied the deep chasm that had swallowed the floor. The sinkhole had pulled the cistern into its gaping maw, causing the upper structures to tumble after it. What remained was a jumble of smashed columns and broken supports precariously stacked upon one another, with little more than a narrow ledge on the other side.

Sarah leaned in and surveyed the damage. 'Well, this explains why the tunnel was sealed. This is a disaster. Someone really did a number here.'

McNutt shook his head. 'No one did this on purpose. This wasn't man-made.'

'How can you be sure?' Jasmine asked.

'Let me clarify. If this was done intentionally, they did it the hard way. They dug a pit and let it fall, rather than planting some TNT and blowing it all to hell.'

Jasmine still wasn't satisfied. 'But how can you be sure?'

'Explosions leave telltale signs. The fire chars the walls. Chemical accelerants leave stains. Even the shockwave itself stamps a distinct pattern onto the scene. They're not always easy to spot, but they're there. If you know where to look.'

Cobb stared across the ravine. While the others were contemplating the damage and what had caused it, his attention was on what lay beyond. In the distance, he could see the outline of the far wall. He noticed immediately that the stonework was different from the walls and tunnels throughout the water system.

The blocks were wider and taller. Heavier.

The type of blocks you would use to fortify a temple.

Cobb looked at Sarah. 'Can you find a way across?'

'Across?' McNutt laughed. 'Through that? That'd be like playing the world's most dangerous version of Jenga. Only in this case, if the tower falls, you die.'

'I can make it,' Sarah replied confidently. She tied the rope around her waist and handed the other end to Cobb. She smiled playfully. 'You know . . . just in case.'

Cobb wrapped the rope around his forearm and anchored his boots in the dirt, ready to break her fall if the wreckage collapsed beneath her.

Sarah stepped cautiously onto the first fallen beam. She breathed a sigh of relief when it held firm. From there, she crossed the narrow surface toward a pillar that lay at an angle. It was pointed skyward like a circus cannon, leading to an arch that had fallen over and now sat balanced at the top of the heap of rubble. After carefully plotting her course, she shimmied up the pillar, mounted the fallen arch, and tiptoed over the apex.

Looking back, she realized she was halfway across.

There was no turning back now.

Sarah was able to pick her way down the other side of the pile of debris, carefully checking her footing with each step. She could feel the tangled mass sway, but she ignored the twinge of fear and kept moving forward. After pulling herself up over a sandstone support that blocked her path and sliding down a marble stanchion on the other side, all that stood between her and the ledge was a five-foot gap. She paused, steadying her nerves as she prepared for the final obstacle.

Three long strides and a leap later, she landed softly on the rocky ledge.

'Made it!' Sarah shouted. From her vantage point, she could barely see the others through the tangled web of wreckage.

Jasmine pumped her fist in the air with excitement.

Cobb smiled and put his arm around her shoulder. 'I'm glad to see that you're excited about this . . . because you're next.'

'What?' she shrieked.

He could see the enthusiasm drain from her face.

Sarah cupped her hands to her mouth and shouted instructions. 'Jasmine, listen to me. You can do this. Just follow the rope. It'll lead you right to me.'

Jasmine nodded, trying to psych herself up. 'I can do this.'

'Damn right you can,' Cobb said as he tied a rope around her waist and anchored it to the rope line. 'And I'll be holding on every step of the way.'

Surprisingly, she didn't need any further coaxing to start her journey. She slowly followed Sarah's lead, stepping onto the closest beam and trying to retrace the exact steps that Sarah had taken. When she reached the circus cannon pillar, her initial jitters had subsided. By the time she arrived at the top, her confidence was soaring. She could finally see Sarah on the other side. Not only was she climbing, she was actually enjoying it, or at the very least relishing the sense of accomplishment.

In another minute, she would reach the ledge.

In another month, she would tackle Mount Everest.

Unfortunately, things quickly took a turn for the worse.

As Jasmine started her descent toward the far ledge, she felt a tremor underneath her feet. It was followed by a loud, cracking sound that told her everything she needed to know about her immediate future.

'Something's wrong!' she screamed.

No sooner had the words left her lips than the first piece came tumbling down. The arch that lay across the pinnacle gave way, smashing pillars and other supports as it fell into the pit below. It set off a devastating chain reaction, causing the entire structure to shake violently as it began to crumble.

Cobb shouted: 'Jasmine, hang on!'

Meanwhile, Sarah braced herself on the other side.

As the stones fell out from under her, Jasmine was left dangling in the center of the void, enveloped by a cacophonous roar and a swirling cloud of dust. Adrenalin shot through her like lightning as she clamped down hard on the rope. For the next few seconds, it was the only thing that stood between her and certain death.

Though logic told him to pull, Cobb fought the urge until the air cleared for fear that he might inadvertently yank Sarah off the far ledge. He didn't want anyone falling into the chasm, much less two people. Fortunately, the horizontal tension on the rope told him there was still a chance that everyone would survive unscathed.

Once the dust settled, all that Cobb could see was Jasmine, the rope, and a black void below. The pile of rubble had completely disappeared into the hole.

McNutt called out to her. 'Jasmine, are you okay?'

'*Not okay! Definitely not okay!*'

'But you're alive?'

'*Of course I'm alive! I'm talking to you!*'

'Good point,' he conceded as he held on to Cobb. The rope was tied to Cobb, so McNutt's job was to keep him from falling forward. 'Can you make it back to us?'

Jasmine's mind raced faster than her heartbeat. She was in the middle of the chasm, where it would take just as much effort to go back as it would to press on. Going back meant returning to a tunnel system that they knew and a way out. Going forward meant the unknown possibilities of whatever they might find ahead.

She hadn't come this far to turn back now.

Besides, she wasn't about to abandon Sarah.

'Not a chance!' Jasmine shouted as she adjusted her grip. 'I'm not coming back. I'm going forward.'

McNutt wasn't sure how to respond. 'Um, okay.'

In the darkness ahead, Sarah couldn't help but smile. The old Jasmine – the one from their first mission – would have turned back and taken the easy way out. That is, if she had even attempted the climb to begin with. But the new-and-improved Jasmine was determined to see this through.

'Glad to hear it,' Sarah said. 'Just keep moving, hand over hand. Don't stop, and don't look down. You're more than halfway here.'

Jasmine did as she was told. She crept along the rope, pulling herself one arm's reach at a time, her feet sliding along behind her. On each end of the line, Sarah and Cobb pulled hard in an effort to reduce the slack.

The tighter the rope, the easier the climb.

Sarah's arms burned and her feet ached as she held fast, digging her boots into the rocky ledge. 'Almost there . . . Just a few more feet.'

Summoning every ounce of courage and every bit of strength, Jasmine powered through the remaining distance like a seasoned pro. Once she was absolutely sure that her body was over solid land, she uncrossed her feet and let them drop to the ledge. Then she let go of the rope and threw her arms around Sarah in triumph.

Sarah hugged her back. 'Great job. You're officially a woman. Welcome to the club.'

'Thanks,' said Jasmine as she fought back tears, partly from the dust, and partly from her joy. 'Thanks for holding on.'

McNutt unleashed a celebratory scream that echoed through the chamber. It was nearly as loud as the collapse itself. 'Ooooo-rah!'

But Cobb wasn't ready to celebrate. At least not yet.

Not with his team divided.

'Is there any way through?' he demanded.

'Hang on,' Sarah implored. 'We're still hugging.'

'Search now. Celebrate later.'

'Why? What's the rush?' McNutt wondered.

Cobb whispered, 'If they can't get through, we have to bring them back.'

'Fuck.'

'And if they *can* get through, we're going next.'

'Double fuck.' McNutt leaned forward and shined his flashlight into the darkness below. It was a long way down. 'I honestly don't know which one to root for.'

Cobb smiled. 'Me neither.'

'Okay,' Jasmine shouted, 'I think we found something.'

At the base of the wall, they noticed a stone block that appeared to have been crushed by the weight of the wall and the ravages of time. It was no longer solid. Instead, a spider web of cracks radiated out from its center. They could see where tiny pieces had already begun to shear off under the stress.

Sarah shouted across the void, 'Josh, throw me that sonic device of yours. I think we might be able to shatter the rest of the broken block. If it crumbles, maybe it'll open a gap to the other side. That is, if there is another side.'

'Screw that,' McNutt mumbled. 'I'm not throwing her anything. This boomstick is a military prototype. I had to blow an Army supply clerk to get my hands on it. We simply can't replace it.'

Cobb glared at him. 'Josh, throw her the damn stick.'

'But chief.'

'Either that, or climb over and use it yourself.'

His response was immediate. 'Hey, Sarah, catch!'

He flung the high-tech baton across the void, and she caught it with both hands. She handed the device to Jasmine, who was about to fire a sonic pulse into the stone wall when they heard a voice that had been uncharacteristically silent for several minutes.

Garcia cleared his throat. 'Guys, I don't mean to rush you, but you might want to pick up the pace a little bit.'

Cobb stared into his flashlight. He wanted his frustration to be visible on Garcia's video screen. 'Hector, we're kind of busy right now. What's the problem?'

His reply sent a chill down Cobb's spine.

'I think someone's looking for you.'

22

After Hassan's impassioned pep talk – punctuated with two dead pigeons – Kamal and Tarek were desperate to find Simon. To achieve their goal, they had distributed Sarah's picture to the far reaches of the city. Hundreds of people, from small-time, wannabe hustlers to legitimate businessmen who owed a weekly fee for protection, were looking for her. The thugs knew it was only a matter of time before she would be seen again.

They were intrigued when it happened in the same neighborhood.

They were alarmed when she was spotted with a team of her own.

Five minutes after the call, Kamal and Tarek were on their way to the apartment building. On Hassan's order, they were not to pursue her alone. They viewed the other two men as unnecessary, but neither dared to defy their boss.

Together, the four men searched the apartment complex. They checked every hallway, knocked on every door. Doors that were not answered were opened with picks. The ones that could not be picked were opened by force.

After thirty minutes, they had turned up nothing. Even worse, they believed the residents when they claimed they had not seen the woman or her team. Working alone, Kamal or Tarek could easily scare most people into confessing their deceit. When facing them together, lying seemed next to impossible.

And yet no one had seen her.

How in the hell did she vanish?

The street was covered. So was the back. They had even checked the roof; it offered nowhere to hide and no access to other rooftops. A four-story plunge to the pavement below would certainly draw attention – whether she survived or not.

They realized only one place had not been searched.

The basement.

* * *

Cobb froze in place. 'Hector, say that again.'

'I think someone's looking for you,' Garcia said.

'Explain,' he ordered. 'And be specific.'

So much had happened during the last several minutes that Garcia didn't know where to begin. During Cobb and Sarah's rekky, they had installed remote cameras in the basement hallway and the boiler room. This allowed Garcia to watch their backs while they were in the tunnel system. Tonight, he also had access to a video feed from a wireless camera that McNutt had planted across the street. Using those sources, he had been keeping his eye on the apartment building and the traffic outside.

Garcia studied the feeds on multiple screens. 'Thirty-three minutes ago, four men entered the building through the front door and went upstairs. They didn't do anything suspicious in the lobby, but you know that feeling you get when something doesn't quite add up? Well, that's the feeling I got when they arrived.'

'Is that all?'

'Of course not. I wouldn't bother you for something like that.'

'Then what's the problem?'

'Well,' he explained, 'three minutes ago one of the men

reappeared outside. He met a second carload of people and led them inside. I realize that could still be explained – after all it's a Saturday night and they might be on their way to a party or something – but instead of going upstairs to one of the apartments, all eight of them headed toward the basement. Right now six of them are rummaging through the storage lockers. The other two are trying to pick the lock on the boiler-room door.'

McNutt cursed. 'That's not good, chief.'

'No, it's not,' Cobb admitted.

As the lone civilian in the group, Jasmine remained optimistic. 'Maybe they're responding to vibrations from the cave-in. They could be looking for structural damage in the building's foundation. There's no way to know that they're looking for us.'

Sarah disagreed. 'Don't be naïve. Half were in the building *before* the collapse. Either they're psychic engineers, or they're looking for something else.'

'Hector, do you still have eyes on the grate?' Cobb wondered.

'Affirmative,' he replied. 'If they find the tunnel, I'll let you know.'

'By then it will be too late,' McNutt warned. He grabbed Cobb's arm to emphasize his point. 'What are we: two, maybe three klicks from the boiler room? And how many twists and turns are between them and us? If they're armed and get into the tunnels, we'll have no way of wrangling them – especially with their numbers.'

Cobb nodded in agreement. 'Ladies, I hate to abandon you at a time like this, but Josh and I need to tend to this mess before it becomes a problem. Meanwhile, I'd like you to keep moving forward if that's okay with you.'

'Of course it's okay,' Sarah joked. 'It's about time you men got off your butts and got your hands dirty. Us *ladies* can't do all the work.'

Cobb ignored the wisecrack. 'Hector, while we're gone, I need you to work your magic and keep us connected. I want to be able to reach them at all times.'

'No problem, Jack.'

'Good.' He glanced at McNutt. 'You ready?'

'Almost,' McNutt said. 'Before we go, I've got presents for everyone.'

He opened his backpack and pulled out a Smith & Wesson M1911 pistol. The weapon was considered a classic among US servicemen, many of whom preferred to carry it instead of newer models. This particular gun was custom-fitted with a suppressor, laser sight, and an extended clip for extra ammo.

McNutt handed the pistol to Cobb. 'This is for *you*.'

Next came matching Glock 19s. These handguns fit perfectly in Jasmine and Sarah's smaller, narrower hands, without compromising firepower.

'This is for *them*,' McNutt explained.

Then he pulled the last piece of artillery from his bag. The PM-84 Glauberyt was a Polish-made submachine gun that was renowned for its compact size and devastating punch. In close quarters like this, it was a wonderful choice.

McNutt smiled at it. 'And this is for *me*.'

Cobb could only laugh.

To deliver the Glock 19s, McNutt slipped the climbing rope through the trigger guards and raised his hands over his head. His improvised zip line sent the weapons sliding across the chasm. Once he was done, he tossed his end of the rope towards the women. 'Take the rope. We won't need it, but you might find a use for it.'

Sarah wound it in. 'Just so you know, I've got more gear on the boat. Harnesses, rigging, you name it. If all else fails, we can meet you back here and set up a transfer.'

'Won't be necessary,' Cobb assured her.

Garcia cleared his throat. 'Jack, you better get moving. These guys are after something, and they're running out of places to look. If they happen to find the grate, I'll lose track of them in the tunnels.'

'Relax,' Cobb ordered, 'we're leaving now.'

'Copy that,' Garcia said.

Cobb nodded at McNutt, who instantly sprinted toward the boiler room as if he had been shot out of a cannon. He had a flashlight in one hand, his submachine gun in the other, and a wide grin on his face. As a former Marine, he lived for moments like this – when he got to stare death in the eye, down the barrel of a gun.

Strangely, though, Cobb didn't move.

He simply stood in the tunnel, deep in thought.

Not because he had time to spare – because he certainly didn't – but because a sense of dread had washed over him like a downpour from a sudden storm. The feeling hit him so hard and so unexpectedly that he instantly had doubt about the orders he had given. It was so severe that he was tempted to stop McNutt and the women before they roamed too far so they could come up with an alternative plan of attack.

For a leader like Cobb, it was a horrible feeling.

There was no place for doubt in his world.

In fact, he had felt like this only once in his entire career: one time in thousands of missions.

Unfortunately, his gut had been right that day.

And many soldiers had died.

* * *

Sarah and Jasmine focused on the task at hand. Using their fingers, they dug away as many of the loose chips from the wall as they could. It amounted to more than an inch of stone. Still, they had no idea how thick the block was.

'Okay,' Jasmine said, 'time to use the wand.'

Sarah stepped away as Jasmine pressed the end of the baton against the rock and activated the sonic pulse. In an instant, the block cracked, but it didn't dissolve into the fine powder that they had seen with the mortar. Instead, it splintered into small, jagged pebbles.

Jasmine was thrilled. 'It worked!'

Sarah dove in with both hands, pushing away small piles of stones as she emptied the space the block once filled. On the third scoop, she felt a rush of cool air blow across her forearm. 'Did you feel that? It's hollow on the other side!'

She attacked with renewed vigor, tearing away fistfuls of debris as she widened the hole to almost two feet. 'It's going to be tight, but I think we can make it through.'

'I don't know,' Jasmine said as she crouched down for a better view. 'You can, for sure. I'm not so sure about me.'

Sarah checked her out; she was slight but curvy. 'Your butt?'

Jasmine nodded. 'Yep.'

'Too bad Josh isn't here. He'd offer to get behind you and push you through.'

Jasmine blushed. 'You're right. He would.'

At that point, they half expected to hear McNutt's voice in their ears, whispering something sexual and completely inappropriate as he sprinted away to save the day.

All things considered, they would have preferred that to Garcia, who chimed in with the update that they had all been dreading. 'Bad news everyone. They're in the boiler room, and they found the grate.'

23

Kamal and Tarek realized how ill prepared they were for a subterranean adventure as soon as they entered the water system. The only light in the first tunnel came from the boiler room above. Beyond its reach, the space was dark. Without the aid of lanterns, flares, or even flashlights, they were forced to rely on their cell phones.

They found the first cistern without difficulty. After all, it was a straight walk down a narrow tunnel – even a blind man could have found it. Sadly, the only thing separating them from a blind man was the soft glow of their phones, but that advantage disappeared as soon as they reached the cistern.

In the tunnel, their light was sufficient.

In the cistern, darkness ruled.

Their screens were like fireflies in a stadium.

The space was too large to light.

Thanks to the gloom, Kamal and Tarek overlooked the small notches that had been cut into the wall. From their perspective, their only option to reach the bottom was to leap from one level to the next. Without saying a word, they chose separate routes for their descent. Each knew that their combined heft would put the structure under considerable stress. By splitting up, they were able to cut that burden in half.

Still, each leg of their journey caused the supports to shake as their full weight dropped from the story above. Had they not separated, their combined force would have shifted the pillars so much that the entire structure would have come down. Instead, their split approach allowed the pillars to stay balanced, like fat kids on a seesaw.

Once they reached the bottom, Kamal took stock of the situation. There were two tunnels to explore, and his team had eight men. Even if he divided his forces, they would still have a fighting chance against the girl and her friends.

He shouted up to his men: 'Abed, stay there and guard the exit. No one gets in or out. The rest of you, come with me. We have a job to finish.'

*   *   *

Garcia was more worried than he had been in quite some time. What had started off as an 'easy' mission – if there was such a thing – had quickly gone to hell.

First, Jasmine had almost died in the cave-in.

Then the goons had arrived at the apartment building.

Now they were streaming into the tunnels with weapons drawn.

How could it possibly get any worse?

'Guys,' Garcia warned, 'I didn't get a great view of their guns, but it looked like they're packing some serious firepower.'

'Copy that,' Cobb whispered. 'I guess they're not engineers.'

A moment later, Cobb and McNutt heard an Arabic voice echoing through the tunnels. Even from a distance, they had heard it clearly. Suddenly they realized how easily their sounds could give them away. From that moment on, conversations would be conducted through whispers, hand gestures, and facial expressions.

Fortunately, the signal to kill was an easy one.

Unfortunately, Cobb wasn't ready to give that order.

After all, he was trespassing on government land. For all he knew, the gunmen could have been cops.

* * *

Jasmine looked at Sarah. 'What did he mean by "serious firepower"?'

Sarah shrugged. 'It means we should keep moving.'

'Please don't treat me like a kid. I know I'm new to the field, but how am I supposed to learn if you always keep me in the dark?'

'First of all, I'm not the one keeping you in the dark. The Ancient Egyptians are. They're the idiots who didn't put lights in here.'

Jasmine rolled her eyes. 'You know what I meant.'

'As for your question, who the hell knows? If his idea of "serious firepower" is anything like Josh's, they might have a tank back there. The point is I don't want to be around to find out. Do you?'

'I guess not.'

Garcia chimed in to clarify his remark. 'Relax, Jasmine, they do not have a tank in the tunnels. Guns? Yes. A tank? No.'

Jasmine didn't move. 'What about Jack and Josh? I know they have guns—'

'Trust me,' Sarah assured her, 'Jack and Josh will be fine. Whoever's following us will *need* a tank against those two.' She nodded toward the hole in the wall. 'Let's worry about our part. Focus on finding whatever it is that's down here to be found. After that, we can leave and so can the guys.'

Jasmine nodded her understanding and doubled her resolve. She slipped her arm into the hole, followed by her head. She rotated her shoulders, trying to find the angle that would allow her to pull herself through. Instead, she found herself stuck in the opening.

Sarah offered her guidance before panic could set in. 'Just breathe. The hard part is over. Your head is through. Just take your time.'

'Everything okay?' Cobb whispered.

'I think someone's having a baby,' McNutt replied.

Jasmine tried to laugh, but the stone restricted her breathing.

'Jasmine's stuck in the wall,' Garcia explained.

Sarah put an end to the nonsense. 'No one's stuck in the wall, and no one's having a baby. Jasmine just needs a minute.'

Embarrassed by the attention, Jasmine twisted and turned until she found the space to move her other shoulder through the opening. Thirty seconds and a gentle nudge from Sarah later, Jasmine pulled the rest of her body through the gap in the wall.

'Made it. Your turn.'

'No problem,' Sarah bragged.

Though she was taller than Jasmine, she had no difficulty getting through the wall. Her slender frame slid through the space with ease, courtesy of years of practice.

Jasmine didn't know whether to be impressed with Sarah's agility or disappointed in her own performance. Ultimately, she decided that being awed by Sarah was better than being down on herself. 'Good job.'

'Thanks,' said Sarah as she dusted herself off. 'Where to now?'

Jasmine smiled. 'I'll tell you later. We should keep moving.'

* * *

Kamal led three of the men down the left tunnel. Tarek took the others down the right tunnel. Moments later, they emerged on the other side.

They glanced at each other and smiled.

Maybe this wouldn't be as tough as they thought.

Maybe all of the tunnels would be this simple.

Unfortunately for them, they were wrong.

From that point forward, they were hopelessly lost. Everywhere they looked, the water system appeared the same. Their cell phones were partially to blame, but so was their lack of knowledge. After all, these men were soldiers, not scholars, and none of them knew anything about architecture. Heck, they barely knew the difference between Greece and Rome, let alone the distinguishing features of ancient columns.

They were paid to bully and intimidate, not to think.

Fanning out, the men quickly discovered the east–west passageways at the opposite ends of the room. Tarek took three of the men and led them to the west. The other two followed Kamal to the east.

From their perspective, they were in total control.

They had more numbers, more guns, and the element of surprise.

How tough could this be?

*   *   *

From the shadows at the top of the cistern, McNutt lowered his night scope when the last gunman had left the chamber. If he had been given permission, he could have gunned down the seven men and stopped the threat right there and then.

Unfortunately, he didn't have permission – and wouldn't get

it until they figured out who the gunmen were. As men of honor, they simply refused to slaughter cops or government officials who were merely doing their jobs.

McNutt turned to Cobb, who was hiding next to him in the darkness, and whispered the bad news. 'Sorry, chief, I still can't tell for sure.'

Cobb cursed. It wasn't the answer he had been hoping for. 'Best guess?'

'Criminals. Maybe soldiers.'

'Why do you say that?'

'Two are carrying assault rifles.'

'Really? What kind?'

'9A-91s.'

Cobb smiled. He was quite familiar with these. The Russian-made assault rifle is only slightly larger than a machine pistol, but it packs a lot of a punch in a small package. In close combat, the fully automatic weapon can rip an enemy to shreds in only a matter of seconds. 'I'll be damned.'

McNutt stared at him. 'You *will* be damned if they open fire with those. Thank God I only saw two. Otherwise, I'd be tempted to put money on the other guys.'

'You know,' Cobb whispered, 'I saw two of those guns before you arrived in the city. They were being used as concealed weapons.'

'Concealed? How do you conceal an assault rifle?'

'By being as big as a car.'

'Wait. You mean the guys who chased Sarah?'

Cobb nodded. 'One and the same.'

McNutt closed his eyes and played back the scene in his head. 'Now that you mention it, they appeared to be larger than the others, but I thought maybe it was an optical illusion. It's tough to gauge size from up here.'

'It has to be them. It has to be. Nothing else makes sense.'

'Wait. If it is them, what do they want?'

'I think they want Sarah.'

24

The bad feeling in Cobb's gut wouldn't go away.

Most of the gunmen had pushed past him, deeper into the network of cisterns. The only thing that stood between him and escape was a single guard who had been left to watch the exit. Cobb had no doubts that he and McNutt could outwit, outshoot, or outmaneuver one man in a matter of seconds.

Of course, that would mean abandoning Sarah and Jasmine. And they weren't going to do that.

The alternative was a deadly game of cat and mouse in the tunnels. While Cobb and McNutt had some tactical advantages – better equipment, better training, and better knowledge of the terrain – they were still outnumbered seven to two. Worse still, there was always a chance that the goons would call in reinforcements, who could level the playing field by bringing ropes, lights, and even bigger guns.

If that happened, Cobb and McNutt were screwed.

Worried about the women, Cobb tried to check in with them. 'Sarah, it's Jack. What's your status? Any luck with the wall?'

There was only silence on the other end.

'Sarah,' he repeated, 'have you made it through the—'

'They can't hear you,' Garcia blurted.

'Why not? Are they all right?'

'They're fine. At least I think they're fine.'

'What does that mean?'

Garcia explained. 'They made it through the wall okay, but that's the problem. Their new location was built differently than the cisterns. For some reason, the walls are blocking the transmission. They can't hear a word you're saying.'

Cobb knew that their flashlights included microphones. He hoped that a larger device meant a larger, more powerful transmitter. 'Can you hear them?'

'Nope,' Garcia replied. 'I can't see their video feed either. I lost them completely the moment they entered the new system.'

Cobb cursed under his breath.

'Sorry, Jack. I would have told you sooner, but I knew you and Josh had gone dark for a while. I didn't want to disturb you.'

'Well, I'm available now.'

Cobb and McNutt dropped from their perch and stared into different tunnels. Their night-vision optics revealed that the passageways were clear, but they knew their targets were out there somewhere. Years of training kicked in as they listened to Garcia in one ear while focusing the other on the path ahead.

'It's probably the stone,' Garcia guessed as he fiddled with his computer equipment. 'It's not an issue with the frequencies. I can assure you of *that*, because you're transmitting fine. But them? Their signals aren't getting through. It has to be the other tunnel. It has to be.'

Cobb nodded at McNutt, who ran off to find the enemy. It also gave Cobb a moment of privacy. 'Hector, I don't care why it's happening. I just want you to fix it.'

'But Jack, if it's the stone—'

'Listen,' he said a little too loudly for his own good. 'You told me communications wouldn't be a problem. You said that these devices were tested in Romanian caves, that they transmitted a signal through solid rock. And now you're telling me that they can't transmit through tunnels? Sorry, Hector, that simply won't cut it.'

Garcia remained silent for a few seconds. 'What do you want me to do?'

'You're the genius. Figure it out.'

* * *

Sarah had expected to see another chamber on the other side of the wall. If Jasmine's theory was correct, the temple built over Caesar's Well would have extended deep into the earth. It would have housed priests and scholars, not to mention the artifacts they had dedicated their lives to protecting. She didn't know whether to expect breathtaking opulence or humble simplicity, but she had envisioned a very large space.

Instead, they found themselves in a narrow, horizontal shaft barely eight feet in height. The cramped passageway did not lead upward, nor did it descend toward a source of fresh water. It simply ran parallel to the surface, like an ancient subway tunnel – although there were certainly no tracks to be found.

Sarah noticed a solid wall of rubble blocking the passageway to the left. There was no hope of escape in that direction, even with McNutt's sonic device. She could only guess as to whether the path had once led to a magnificent temple or to the fiery depths of hell because she hadn't examined this part of the temple on her rekky.

Sarah glanced at Jasmine. 'What is this place?'

Before answering, she took a moment to study her surroundings. The passageway was supported by a forest of pillars that were evenly staggered throughout the space. The effect eliminated any direct path and forced anyone navigating the depths to constantly twist and turn as they wove their way through the obstacles. It was clear that structural integrity was given priority over efficiency of travel.

Whoever built this tunnel built it to last through the ages.

She stepped closer to examine the craftsmanship. She could see that the columns were constructed from crushed rock and other fragments of stone, held together with a distinct mortar. She had seen the composition before.

'Oh my God,' Jasmine blurted. 'It's *opus caementicium.*'

'Opus what?'

'*Opus caementicium.*'

'English, please.'

Jasmine smiled. 'Sorry. It's Roman concrete.'

'And Roman concrete is . . .?'

'It's one of the most durable building materials ever discovered,' she explained. 'Today's concrete pales in comparison to the strength of what the Romans used. They combined water and a volcanic dust known as *pozzolana* and discovered that the mixture could withstand unbelievable stress for remarkable lengths of time. Have you ever wondered why buildings like the Pantheon and the Colosseum are still standing? Roman concrete is the answer. And from the look of things, these columns are even older.'

By the first century AD, it had become custom for Roman architects to cover the concrete base of a structure with a layer of fired-clay bricks. This not only protected the concrete from the elements, it was also considered to be more aesthetically pleasing. The absence of an outer layer of brick meant that these columns were probably built more than two thousand years ago.

Jasmine couldn't hide her fascination. 'Do you realize that these pillars predate Jesus Christ? They've outlasted the rise and fall of empires and dynasties. They've withstood two millennia of constant strain, and they're still standing strong.'

Sarah didn't have the same sense of wonderment. To her eyes, there was nothing overly impressive about the construction. Once age was taken out of the equation, they looked like normal concrete pillars. 'The columns were built to last, and they lasted. To that I say: good job, Romans!'

'It's more than a good job. It's an amazing job.'

'You're right. I'm underselling it. I'm simply *thrilled* that this tunnel is still standing two thousand years later. Otherwise, we would be forced to turn back.'

'Exactly.'

Sarah pointed forward. 'Speaking of which, let's keep moving. I hear there are some *really* old sidewalks up ahead that I've been dying to see.'

*   *   *

Kamal checked his watch and began to worry.

He had found three passageways leading from the second cistern, branching out in all directions. He had split the two men with him and ordered them to investigate separate tunnels. Kamal would check out the third tunnel, then they would all meet back at the cistern so that he could determine their next move.

They were supposed to regroup after five minutes.

That was ten minutes ago, and neither of Kamal's men had returned.

Unable to call his colleagues, Kamal turned off the light on his phone. He hoped that the darkness would allow him to see the others returning, led by the glow of their own screens.

Instead, all he saw was black.

He tapped a button on his phone and his screen sprang to life, allowing him to see a few feet in front of him. Refusing to waste any more time, Kamal chose a direction and continued his journey forward.

* * *

As Cobb roamed through the tunnels, a plan sprang to mind – one that had worked for him before during night combat. 'Josh, do you have an extra flashlight?'

'Affirmative,' McNutt whispered.

'Good. I want you to leave it in the middle of the path.'

McNutt needed to hear the order again, just to be sure. He crouched in a corner and put his finger to his ear. 'Please repeat. I think I misheard you.'

'You didn't mishear me,' Cobb assured him. 'I want you to leave the light where someone will see it. Repeat, I want them to find the light.'

McNutt didn't know what Cobb had up his sleeve, but he was eager to find out. He took the spare light from his backpack and dropped it to the ground. He knew the rugged plastic casing would keep the bulb from breaking, and he wanted the scene to look as authentic as possible. A pristine flashlight carefully set in the middle of the path would look staged. But a scuffed light would hint at an accidental drop.

If the enemy was properly trained, they would know the difference.

'Okay, chief. I did what you asked. Now what?'

'Hide and watch.'

McNutt climbed to the uppermost pillars where he found a nice spot to wait. From there he stared at the flashlight through his rifle's scope, using the night-vision optics to see. It wasn't long before one of the thugs came into view.

At first, the Egyptian didn't know what to make of the discovery. He circled it cautiously, as if it were a grenade that could blow at any moment. Finally, he reached down and grabbed the flashlight.

He rolled it over in his hands, examining it.

After concluding that it was, in fact, an ordinary flashlight, he tentatively pressed the switch to activate the light.

He grinned when it didn't blow up.

Like most people when they get a new, shiny toy, his first thought was to show it off to his friends. He wanted to prove to them that they weren't chasing a ghost. The woman was somewhere out there – and she was running scared.

So scared, she had dropped her flashlight.

Without so much as a cursory glance around the room, the goon raced back through the tunnels in search of his comrades, the flashlight guiding his way.

This left McNutt more confused than normal. 'Jack, I'm not sure if your plan worked. The guy took the light and ran off, but I don't know what—'

Just then, three gunshots echoed from the adjacent chamber. The blasts were so loud and so close that McNutt instinctively ducked for cover.

A few seconds passed before he heard anything else.

This time, it was the sound of Cobb's voice in his ear.

'The plan worked.'

25

Cobb had assumed that the gunmen were operating under the rule of 'shoot first, ask questions later', but he had to be sure. He could defend himself against people determined to kill him – in fact, he was quite good at that – but he didn't want to take any lives unless it was absolutely necessary. The challenge was how to determine their intentions without putting himself or McNutt in harm's way.

Turns out, all he needed was a flashlight.

Tarek had heard someone approaching. He could distinguish the heavy panting of a man, but he couldn't discern the direction of the sound. Then he saw the light: literally. The shimmer of a flashlight had made the hair on Tarek's neck stand on end. He knew his men had only their cell phones to help find their way.

When the flashlight emerged from the tunnel, Tarek opened fire on the person carrying it. He was shot on sight. No mercy. No hesitation.

Cobb now had the proof he needed.

These men weren't there to talk.

*   *   *

Cobb listened as the other men hurried through the tunnels, trying to find their way back to the scene of the gunfire. He could hear them scurrying along the stone floor and splashing through the standing water like overgrown sewer rats. More importantly, he could hear the frantic confusion in their rush to find out what they had missed. Cobb needed a way to stir the hornet's nest of emotion gathering inside them. He needed a way to pluck their nerves, to turn curiosity into panic.

'Now,' Cobb whispered.

On his order, both he and McNutt fired volleys of gunfire into the air. They alternated shots, listening as the booming explosions reverberated throughout the water system. The cacophony masked the fact that they were only two men. The echoes made it sound like an entire platoon was engaged in a firefight.

And his deception worked.

Once they stopped firing, random blasts continued throughout the water system. Obviously the enemy had panicked and had started to take wild shots in the darkness even though Cobb and McNutt were tucked safely in another part of the tunnels.

Cobb smiled, realizing that their job had just gotten easier.

* * *

Confused by the gunfire, two of the goons had accidentally fired on one another.

As one man entered a cistern, another reacted by shooting him twice. The first round caught him in the leg. The second tore into his gut. This error was compounded when the wounded man fired back and struck the first shooter in the face.

Kamal, who was standing ten feet away in the darkness, watched it unfold. He saw the first gunman's head explode as the other man crumpled to the floor.

Worried that he might get shot in the confusion, Kamal raised his weapon and aimed it at the wounded man as he identified himself in the dark. It didn't take the bright lights of an emergency room to know that his injuries were severe. The muscle of his leg was shredded, and dark blood seeped from the opening in his stomach.

Sensing the wounded man's fate and unwilling to leave him behind, Kamal opted to speed things along. 'I am sorry, my friend.'

Then Kamal silenced him forever.

*　　*　　*

Cobb studied the henchman. Unlike his companions, the gunman hadn't charged foolishly toward the sounds of battle. Instead, he had crouched low, waiting for the enemy to come to him.

He wouldn't have to wait long.

Cobb looked down upon the unsuspecting goon from the third level of stonework. The stacked pillars that supported the spacious room had served another purpose: allowing Cobb to shimmy his way upward. Beyond the reach of the cell phone lights, Cobb walked across the myriad of sturdy stone arches, readying his attack.

Cobb stalked his prey from above, like a panther looking down from a tree. Besides his angle of attack, Cobb had another distinct advantage: he could see his target with the night vision feature of his flashlight, but his target was blind. In an effort to surprise the next person to enter the room, the thug had turned off the light from his cell phone.

Cobb took position directly above the goon and silently dropped to the ground. Before his foe could scream or even comprehend what was happening, the battle was over. Cobb plunged his knife through his opponent's trachea with surgical precision. With a quick twist of the wrist, Cobb had separated his airway and severed his spinal column. Even if his brain had fired off one last message, a final order to resist or fight back, the message would never have reached his trigger finger.

'One down,' Cobb whispered.

Garcia drew a slash on his notepad. It was up to him to keep track of enemy personnel in the tunnel, or lack thereof. 'Copy that. One confirmed.'

* * *

McNutt was confused by the broadcast. Something was definitely wrong. Either he had missed an earlier transmission, or Cobb had just radioed in bad intelligence.

No way, he thought. *Cobb doesn't make mistakes.*

Then again, the evidence was hard to dispute.

'You mean *two* down,' McNutt replied.

'Negative,' Cobb shot back. 'One down. Repeat. *One down.*'

McNutt frowned. He looked at the gunman lying at his feet and kicked him gently to see if he was alive. It was obvious that he wasn't since he was lying in a puddle of blood and his guts were spilling out. 'Chief, I'm standing over your handiwork. Dark hair, about six feet tall, incision from his crotch to his chest. Sound familiar?'

'*Negative,*' Cobb replied. 'Not mine.'

Even if Cobb was the joking type – which he wasn't – the tone of his voice told McNutt that he wasn't fooling around.

'Well, it's certainly not mine,' McNutt assured them. 'I would have remembered this one because this guy was gutted. What about Sarah?'

'Not hers, either,' Garcia said. 'She's still off the grid.'

'Then whose is it?'

Cobb gave it some thought. 'Either they're killing each other, or . . .'

Or there are more people down here than them and us.

'Guys,' Cobb whispered, 'I don't think we're alone. I think there's an interloper in the tunnels.'

McNutt froze in place. 'Fuck me. Is that like an alligator?'

'No! A third team. I think there's a third team in the tunnels. Us, the gunmen, and someone else.'

'Cowboys, Indians, *and* aliens?'

'Yes! Three separate entities.'

The newcomers – murderous assassins who had been dispatched to protect the tunnels at all costs – did not play favorites. The motion detector in the iron grate and the infrared cameras hidden in the crevices of the ceiling had signaled two groups of trespassers, and the assassins were there to ensure that no one survived.

McNutt cursed under his breath. Initially, the discovery of the dead gunman had been a blessing, but now that he understood the full scope of the situation – that there was a knife-wielding third party lurking in the tunnels – he realized that the killer might still be nearby. He quickly raised his scope in order to survey the room, a split second before the attack began. He only caught a glimpse of the man, dressed in black like a ninja, before the blade struck him. The glancing blow sliced through his arm like a razor.

Ignoring the pain, McNutt kept the gun pressed tightly to his shoulder as he followed the track of his attacker.

Both spun toward each other, determined to inflict a fatal wound.

It was McNutt who found his mark first.

He squeezed the trigger of his Glauberyt and watched as the hail of bullets pierced the swordsman's chest. Blood splattered on the wall as the body dropped to the ground. McNutt relaxed his grip and stood there in silence, thankful for his quick reflexes.

But it wasn't over.

His senses now fueled by adrenalin, McNutt heard footsteps scurrying across the beams behind him. He turned again, his weapon raised, his instincts still intact.

The last thing McNutt expected was a circus performance, but that's what it looked like to him. Three new arrivals leaped about the upper levels of the cistern with acrobatic moves that were as graceful as they were astonishing. While he and Cobb had been forced to climb the columns using brute strength and an iron grip, McNutt watched as the gymnastic mercenaries propelled themselves upwards by springing off the columns and landing on the arch above. They used momentum to defy gravity, all while keeping a firm grasp on their blades.

They moved about the room like monkeys.

But they were circling like sharks.

'Jack, we've got company. At least three more men.'

McNutt took aim and fired. The rounds missed the assassins and smashed into the ceiling, showering him with bits of rubble. He fired again, and bullets ricocheted in every direction as more pieces of the stone cavern were dislodged.

He cursed under his breath and tried to spot them in the darkness. In all of his years of combat, he had never seen anyone move like that.

If his life hadn't been in danger, he would have been impressed. Instead, this new breed of enemy only strengthened his resolve.

Bear down! You're a fucking Marine!

The moment for subtlety had passed.

It was time to unleash hell.

26

McNutt aimed his gun at the monkey men and unleashed a torrent of gunfire. He swung his Glauberyt from side to side, spraying the cistern above like a sprinkler.

The invading force had no choice but to take cover. An unsuspecting target was one thing, but this was something else entirely. Having been spotted, they now faced the full fury of a submachine gun and decided to hide behind the pillars.

McNutt reloaded, determined to continue the onslaught. He slammed the magazine into place, chambered a round, and pulled the trigger.

Instead of a hail of bullets, a single shot cut through the darkness.

McNutt released the trigger, then squeezed again.

But nothing happened.

'No,' he muttered. 'No, no, no, no, no!'

With danger lurking, he felt along the side of the Glauberyt, searching for the source of the problem like a blind man reading Braille. His scope – his source of sight in the darkness – was no use to him, as it was securely mounted to the gun itself.

It took a few seconds, but he eventually figured it out.

Typically, the force of a discharged round would initiate a chain of events that would cycle a fresh round into the chamber. But in this case the bolt, the mechanism that drives the shell from the magazine to the chamber, was jammed.

Which meant the Glauberyt couldn't fire.

Like most Marines, McNutt could fieldstrip and reassemble a gun with his eyes closed. He could do it in the dark, upside down, and underwater, using only his sense of touch and his absolute knowledge of the weapon to guide him. Having been through all of those scenarios in the past, the prospect of fixing his rifle wasn't daunting.

Unfortunately, it would take more time than he had.

With few choices left, he decided to taunt his opponents, hoping it would buy him a few extra minutes. That is, if the enemy even spoke English.

McNutt stared at the darkness above and shouted, 'Come and get me, monkey men! I've got night optics and a submachine gun! I live for shit like this! As far as I'm concerned, we can play all day!'

He punctuated his threat by making monkey sounds.

A second later, he lowered his voice to a whisper. 'Guys, I'm screwed. My gun is jammed, and the monkey men are ready to attack.'

'Did you say *monkey men*?' Garcia asked.

McNutt ignored the question. 'What was I thinking? Why did I pick a Polish gun? When's the last time they won a war? Shit, *have* they won a war?'

'I repeat, did you say *monkey men*?'

'Yes, Tito, I said *monkey men*. Now answer my goddamned question!'

'What question is that?' Garcia shouted back.

'Have the Polacks ever won a war?'

'I honestly don't know!'

'Quit shouting at me! The monkey men can hear you!'

183

'For the love of God, what is a monkey man?'

Cobb had heard enough. 'Josh, how can I help?'

McNutt instantly calmed down. 'Do you have a gun that works?'

'Yes.'

'Cool. Then I'm coming to you.'

From his time in the service, McNutt knew that there was no dishonor in running – especially when it was authorized by his commanding officer. Cobb was out there, somewhere, waiting to help.

Now all he had to do was find him.

'Tell me where you're hiding and I'll bring the monkeys with me.'

'Copy that,' Cobb said. 'Hector, a little help.'

Garcia, who was keeping track of his team's positions, knew the shortest way through the maze. 'Take the first tunnel on your left, and I'll guide you from there.'

'Thanks,' said McNutt as he sprinted toward the left. 'Be ready, chief. I'll be coming in fast with multiple bogeys on my tail.'

'No worries, Josh. I'm ready right now.'

*　　*　　*

In all of her studies, Jasmine had never seen anything like it.

She wished she could take it with her, but that was unrealistic, if not entirely impossible, because she was staring at a very long wall that had been chiseled and polished with great care in the depths of the temple. Located less than a hundred yards from the reinforced tunnel, the wall was covered with a series of ancient carvings.

She was stunned by their discovery. 'Hector, are you getting this?'

There was no reply.

She waved her hand in front of the flashlight, hoping to draw Garcia's attention – assuming he was still watching.

Again, there was no reply.

'I think we've lost our connection,' Jasmine said.

In Sarah's previous life in the CIA, agents didn't break radio silence unless it was absolutely essential. Most of the time, she was on her own in the field. Having someone chattering in her ear was still a new concept to her, which was why she hadn't noticed Garcia's absence until that very moment.

Jasmine stared at the images. 'We have to preserve this.'

Sarah agreed with the sentiment, but she also realized the impracticality of Jasmine's request. 'We can't take the whole wall. It's, like, a hundred meters long.'

It wasn't an exaggeration. The carvings extended as far as her eye could see. They covered the entire wall, from ceiling to floor, like an ancient, colorless mural.

Jasmine slowly swept the beam of her flashlight across every inch of the surface, documenting their discovery with the video camera. They couldn't take the wall, but at least she could study the recording later.

Meanwhile, Sarah was less concerned about capturing the images for posterity and more concerned with how the carvings could help their mission. She wondered what the markings meant. 'Jasmine, can you read any of this?'

Jasmine studied the wall, using what symbols she could translate to piece together the story that they were trying to tell. 'It's pictography. It spells out the history of the city.' She pointed to the first frame on the wall. 'It all starts here.'

Sarah could see the outline of Alexandria's coast. Tiny waves had been etched into the stone, representing the waters of the Mediterranean. But no distinguishing features were carved into the area that represented the land. Instead, there was an image of a single man: a giant, with the horns of a ram protruding from his head.

'That's a depiction of Alexander,' Jasmine explained. 'The horns symbolize the belief that he was the divine son of Amun. The fact that he is surrounded by empty space indicates that there was nothing in Alexandria before the appearance of the god-king. That's not entirely accurate, but you can understand why a culture based on the reverence of one man would choose to start their history with his arrival.'

The next frame depicted the same outline of Alexandria, only now a series of squares had been added throughout the city. Cut amongst these squares were figures of tiny people, living their lives in a golden age.

She continued, 'Under the watchful gaze of Alexander, the city flourished. Homes were built, and a great many people lived happily in this land.'

She walked along the wall, summarizing her interpretation of the events portrayed in the carvings and recording everything that she saw. The upside-down image of the horned man meant the death of Alexander. The transition toward Roman influence was conveyed in the form of a giant wolf.

'It's probably a rendition of the Capitoline Wolf,' Jasmine said. 'Legend holds that the city of Rome was founded by twin brothers, Romulus and Remus. They had been abandoned at birth and were raised by a she-wolf.'

Jasmine paused, carefully studying the next image.

Her lips slowly curled into a smile.

Sarah stared at the symbol. 'What is it?'

Jasmine traced the outline with her finger. 'Three cobras. The trio of Uraei. This was the personal symbol of Cleopatra.'

Sarah understood Jasmine's reaction. Cleopatra was the last pharaoh of Ancient Egypt. As queen, she was believed to be the living manifestation of the goddess Isis. She was beloved by her people and revered by her peers. In an era ruled by men, Cleopatra's reign proved that there was no such thing as the weaker sex.

As Jasmine marveled at the scene of Cleopatra, Sarah moved further down the line. Though she lacked Jasmine's training, she was still able to decipher some of the images. She recognized the Christian cross and the papal seal, indicating the rise of Christianity. She understood the scenes of battle, though she had no way of knowing that they represented the Kitos War, when the Romans targeted the local Jewish population.

But there was one picture that she could not interpret.

She called for help. 'Jasmine, come look at this.'

Jasmine rushed over and immediately understood the emblems portrayed in the image. Not only that, she was excited by their significance.

'It's the destruction of the library,' she explained as she pointed to the long, rectangular block drawn with columns on all sides. There was a split carved through the center of the block, as if it had been broken in half.

Jasmine beamed. 'If this is accurate, we now know when it was destroyed.'

'How can you tell that from the picture? I don't see any dates.'

'There aren't any dates, but we can infer from the context.'

Jasmine pointed to an image of a man with rays of sunlight

radiating from his head. 'This is the symbol of Sol Invictus, the Roman sun god. It was adopted by the Emperor Aurelian during his reign as an expression of his belief that Sol alone held divinity over all others in the pantheon. In an effort to assert Roman dominance in Alexandria, Aurelian destroyed the city's Royal Quarter in a great fire.'

Sarah understood the implications of such an act. 'A fire that also consumed the Library of Alexandria.'

Jasmine nodded. 'There has never been any sense of certainty when it came to the history of the library. Rumors place its destruction at any one of a number of instances. But this would appear to give us a specific occurrence. If Aurelian did in fact destroy the library, then we know it fell sometime around 270 AD.'

Sarah understood Jasmine's excitement. 'That question has been haunting historians for centuries, and I saw it before anyone else. How cool is that?'

As Sarah patted herself on the back, Jasmine moved on to the final frame of the pictograph. The news about the Library of Alexandria was certainly fascinating, but in her mind it was overshadowed by the final piece of information.

This was the clue they were looking for.

A revelation about Alexander's tomb.

27

Jasmine deciphered the final images in silence, completely immersed in the message. It was a new insight that would have far-reaching implications – both for the history of Alexandria and the future of their mission.

After what seemed like an hour, Sarah couldn't wait any longer. 'So, what are we looking at?'

There was no reply.

'Jasmine?'

'Sorry,' she said as she snapped out of her trance. 'I just got a little caught up in everything. This is unbelievable.'

To Sarah, it was little more than rough sketches and symbols she couldn't translate in the slightest. All she knew was that they had just determined the fate of the Library of Alexandria – something that no one had been able to do in modern history. Given that frame of reference, she was ready to believe almost anything from the last section of the pictograph. She simply needed Jasmine to explain it to her.

'What's unbelievable?' she demanded.

'These markings,' said Jasmine as she circled her finger around three of the carvings on the wall. 'These symbols represent the Roman Parcae – the female personification of destiny. The spindle represents Nona, the maiden. She spun the thread of life from her distaff onto her spindle. The scroll is Decima, the matron. She determined the length of each thread with her measuring rod. The shears is Morta, the crone. When the thread had reached its end, it was Morta who cut it. Together they embody the Fates. According to Roman mythology, they controlled the destiny of mankind.'

'Believe it or not, I'm familiar with the Fates.'

'Really?'

Sarah nodded. 'What can I say? I'm a fan of powerful women. I could've sworn they had different names, though.'

'Actually, different cultures used different names to represent similar myths. If you learned the myths in school, you probably learned the Greek version. Instead of the Parcae, they were known as the Moirai.'

'Yes. That's what I was thinking: the Moirai.'

'That's what I figured. Their names were Clotho, Lachesis, and Atropos, and they were mentioned in Homeric poems, in Plato's *Republic*, and even Hesiod's *Theogony*. Centuries later and thousands of miles away, the Norse had their own version of the Fates. They were called Urðr, Verðandi, and Skuld.'

'And how does it help us?'

'It doesn't. I was just showing off.'

Sarah laughed, happy to see Jasmine in her element.

'Anyway,' she said as she directed Sarah's attention back to the pictograph. Starting with the Fates, she traced the path of an arrow toward the etching of an ominous cube. 'This represents Pandora's box. When opened, it released Moros, the spirit of doom.'

Below the cube were images of people forming a line from the city to a waiting ship at the shoreline. They were carrying a large block above their heads, and in that block lay the horned man. Their path was the very same tunnel Jasmine and Sarah were standing in.

Jasmine continued. 'They thought the end was coming. They used this tunnel to escape the city. The boat was there to take them to safety.'

Sarah shook her head. 'Okay, back up. One: why would they think the city was doomed? And two: why go through all the effort of building this tunnel when they could have just walked *across* the city, not under it?'

Jasmine was ready with an answer. 'The concept of prophecy was rife in the culture of the ancient Romans – and remember, that's what this was, even though Alexandria was in Egypt. Not only did they believe that all events resulted from the will of the gods, but they also believed that the gods spoke their will through human mediums. These oracles were said to justify and admonish the deeds of man by conveying the gods' approval or displeasure with their actions.'

Sarah wanted to make sure she understood things correctly. 'You're saying that these prophets were able to channel divine messages and relay them to the people, and that the people would in turn live their lives in accordance with the message?'

Jasmine nodded. 'They would *rigorously* adhere to the words of the prophets. It would have been as if the god or goddess had spoken to them directly. So if the Fates, or Moros, or any other deity had sent a message letting them know that the city was in jeopardy, they would not have challenged it. They would have made the necessary preparations to save what they could.'

Before Jasmine could answer the second half of the previous line of questioning, Sarah added another query. 'But the city didn't vanish, so why didn't the people eventually get the idea that the gods were wrong?'

Jasmine smiled. 'No one said anything about vanishing. This

only implies a belief that the city was doomed. And it was.' She pointed to the far edge of the pictograph. Instead of a straight line, the border was drawn as a series of tall waves.

Suddenly, things made sense to Sarah as she recalled Papineau's video presentation during their initial mission briefing. 'The tsunami.'

'Yes,' Jasmine said as she touched the waves, 'the tsunami.'

On July 21, 365 AD, a magnitude eight earthquake rocked the Greek island of Crete, triggering a tsunami that devastated Alexandria. The surging water crushed buildings, flattened districts, and killed tens of thousands of people. It was the worst disaster in the history of the city and the greatest Egyptian tragedy since the biblical plagues.

Sarah pointed at the wall. 'And you're saying they knew it was coming?'

'I'm not saying it. The symbols are saying it. That's why they left.'

'Then why take the effort to build a tunnel? Why the elaborate evacuation?'

'They weren't evacuating. They were smuggling.'

'Smuggling? Smuggling what?'

Jasmine took a few steps back and shined her light on the horned man portrayed earlier in the pictograph. She moved the beam back, focusing on the large block carried by those in the tunnel. Finally, she stepped forward again and pressed her finger against the depiction of a waiting ship.

Sarah now realized what she had missed.

The hull of the ship was emblazoned with the head of a ram.

'I'll be damned. They moved Alexander's tomb.'

*　　*　　*

McNutt had lost his bearings. Running through a maze of tunnels was hard on his sense of direction. Throw in a team of sword-wielding monkey men tracking him in the darkness, and he prayed that he wasn't running in circles.

'Hector, where the hell am I going?'

Garcia had been monitoring his location and was able to guide him through the passageways. 'Keep going straight for another fifty feet. When you get to the next chamber, jump down one level and go to your left.'

McNutt never broke stride. There wasn't time. He had seen the men chasing him, and if they were as fast as they were agile, he knew he was in trouble. He ran across the tops of the narrow arches with purpose.

'Through the tunnel straight ahead of you,' Garcia continued. 'Then up two levels and cross to your right. Two more chambers.'

This was followed by Cobb's reassurance that things were about to get a whole lot better. 'Keep moving, McNutt. I'll be waiting.'

Jumping down to lower levels was easy; climbing up was the greater challenge. When McNutt ascended, he was blind. He needed both hands to pull himself upward. Only after reaching the higher beam could he grab his flashlight and reestablish his vision.

'Take the tunnel to your right. You're almost there,' Garcia said.

McNutt burst into the empty chamber where he paused, briefly, and surveyed his surroundings. He saw the reflection of his flashlight on the pool of water below and realized that he was in the flooded cistern – the final intact chamber. From there, it was either backtrack into the swarm of assassins or press ahead toward the void.

Regrettably, he didn't like his choices.

Even worse, there was no sign of Cobb.

'Jack!' McNutt shouted.

He didn't get the reply he was hoping for.

Suddenly, the three men who had been following him charged into the cistern. They were no more than twenty feet behind him, and they were closing fast.

McNutt swore he could hear them snarling like wolverines. They were ravenous, bloodthirsty creatures, driven by the thrill of the hunt.

He bolted for the final tunnel, hoping to use their aggression against them.

They don't know about the sinkhole.

They won't be expecting it.

* * *

Cobb heard his name as McNutt sprinted past him in the flooded cistern, but he wasn't able to respond. He was far too busy holding his breath.

The tip of his gun emerged from the black water like a periscope, waiting for the enemy to cross his path – *literally* cross his path because he was hiding next to the only bridge that connected the entrance to the cistern and the exit on the far wall.

Cobb's lungs began to burn, but he remained hidden.

His trigger finger quivered in anticipation.

A moment later, the assassins burst into the chamber. They spotted McNutt up ahead and continued their chase, realizing that he had only one avenue of escape. They were so intent on catching him that they failed to consider the possibility of an ambush.

The mistake cost them their lives.

Cobb rose from the depths like a leviathan. With fire in his lungs and ice in his veins, he calmly zeroed in on his targets.

Three shots boomed in the cistern.

Three splashes soon followed.

Each marked a watery grave.

28

Now it was Sarah's turn to stare at the wall in disbelief. If Jasmine's interpretation was correct, they knew *how*, *when*, and *why* Alexander's tomb had left the city.

Someone had smuggled it out without anyone knowing.

Sarah then studied the multitude of supports that kept the tunnel's roof from caving in. The level of reinforcement made a lot more sense now that she understood the true purpose of the tunnel. It was built to transport the world's most precious cargo.

Jasmine continued her explanation. 'I'm not trying to make light of the situation or overlook the number of lives that were lost, but the smugglers couldn't have hoped for a better tragedy. A tsunami was the perfect cover.'

'What do you mean by that?'

'First,' she said, 'the ground started to rumble as the aftershocks reached the Egyptian coast. It didn't have the impact of a full-blown earthquake, but the tremors would have been enough to get everyone's attention.'

Sarah smiled, knowing what was to come: another one of Jasmine's history lessons. But unlike most of her previous tales, Sarah was actually looking forward to it.

Jasmine did not disappoint. 'You have to understand the setting. The religious views of the Roman Empire were in disarray. Emperor Constantine had pushed toward Christianity, but there were still a great many people who resisted the conversion. Chief among them was Emperor Julian, one of Constantine's successors. In fact, in the era preceding the tsunami, Julian made every effort to renew the polytheistic belief system. He quickly replaced the so-called corrupt administration that Constantine had left behind and vowed to return the empire to the glory it once knew. After Julian's death, his successors once again stressed Christian ideals, but there were many in the general public who were firmly rooted in the old beliefs.'

Sarah understood her point. 'Those who believed in the pantheon of Roman gods would have seen the earthquake as a sign of divine intervention. They would have believed that the gods were angered by the adoption of Christianity, and the earthquake was proof of the gods' displeasure. Maybe even a warning of things to come.'

'Exactly,' Jasmine replied. 'And after the gods grabbed their attention by shaking the earth, they proved their glorious power by drawing back the waters of the sea. It's said that creatures and ships alike were stranded in the muck as the water receded all along the coast. Then as thousands gathered to marvel at the sight, the gods buried them all with a surge of water large enough to flood the desert.'

'Like Moses and the Red Sea,' Sarah offered.

'In the wake of the tragedy, no one really cared about Alexander's tomb. There were more important things to worry about, like fresh water and food. Furthermore, the disappearance of the body could be attributed to the flood. No one – not even the emperor himself – could challenge the assertion that the tomb was buried under rubble somewhere in the city or swept out to sea entirely. Besides, those in power had to worry about reconstructing the city and tempering the religious turmoil. They might eventually get around to locating Alexander's body, but it was certainly a low priority.'

Sarah still had questions. 'Okay, I'm with you so far. But who are *they*? Who was responsible for shipping Alexander's tomb out of the city?'

Jasmine shrugged. 'I wish I knew. As much as I would love to give you a definitive answer, I'll need to dig into this a lot more if there's any hope of getting concrete answers. There are experts who have a lot more experience in this type of thing than I do. We might need to reach out to them, maybe even bring a couple down here to look at this and see it for them-selves. I'm just not sure—'

Sarah cut her off. 'Jasmine, don't be foolish. We can't bring anyone down here to look at the wall. You know damn well Papi won't allow it. There's simply too much at stake to trust outsiders.'

'Like Simon?'

Sarah glared at her. 'What's that supposed to mean?'

Jasmine took a step back, surprised by the sudden hostility. 'Nothing.'

'Bullshit,' she hissed. 'It meant something or you wouldn't have said it. Tell me what you meant, or I'll really be pissed.'

'It's just, well,' she stammered as she struggled to find the words. 'I know you reached out to Simon when you first arrived in Egypt, and from what I heard, it didn't turn out too well. Weren't you chased by some gunmen?'

'This isn't my fault!'

'Wait. What are you talking about?' It took a few seconds for Jasmine to connect the dots. 'Sarah, I wasn't implying that you had anything to do with the guys in the tunnels. Honest to God, I wasn't. I have no idea why they're here.'

'Listen,' Sarah said icily, 'take your pictures and collect whatever evidence you need because we won't be coming back anytime soon. And be quick about it.'

'And you?'

'I'm going to check out the rest of the tunnel. I want to see where it goes.'

* * *

McNutt helped Cobb from the water as each pondered their next move.

'How many have you spotted?' Cobb demanded.

'No idea,' McNutt admitted. 'I haven't had time to count because I've been running for my life. Speaking of which, who the hell is chasing us?'

Before Cobb could reply, a blood-curdling wail echoed through the chamber.

'And what the hell was that?' McNutt added.

Cobb didn't like surprises. If someone was still out there searching for them, he preferred to bring the fight to them, not the other way around. 'Let's find out.'

'Let's not,' McNutt said. 'My weapon is fucked.'

Cobb growled and handed him his gun. 'Here.'

'Screw that. I'm not taking your gun.'

'Why not? You gave it to me in the first place.'

'True, but . . .'

He forced it into McNutt's hand. 'Take the gun and follow me. That's an order.'

McNutt nodded. 'Yes, sir.'

Cobb sprinted from the flooded cistern to the adjacent

chamber where he effortlessly jumped to the floor below. Much as it pained him to admit it, he knew that McNutt was the better shot, so giving up his gun had been an easy decision to make. As the team leader, his job was to help his team succeed, and the best way to do that was to give them the tools they required. It didn't matter to Cobb that he was temporarily defenseless, save for his years of training. What mattered was his team's success.

Up ahead in the darkness, Cobb spotted someone lying face down in a shallow pool of blood. Before McNutt could join him on the floor, he signaled for him to stay where he was and provide cover from an elevated position.

McNutt dropped to his knee and raised his gun.

Cobb approached the victim cautiously, unsure if it was a trap. As he got closer, he noted the size of the body. This wasn't an ordinary man. This was a giant; most likely one of the gunmen who had chased Sarah and Simon from the tavern.

If not, then they had stumbled across a Yeti.

Cobb crouched low and pressed a finger to the victim's neck, checking for any signs of life. There were none. Shaking his head to inform McNutt that the man was dead, Cobb rolled the body over onto its back. The first thing he noticed was the assault rifle that had been pinned underneath the man's sizeable frame. The second thing Cobb noticed were the entrails that spilled out of the hole in the man's torso.

Though the cut to the stomach appeared to have been the fatal blow, it wasn't the only wound. Deep lacerations covered the brute's face and torso. Chunks of flesh hung from his arms. Three fingers and his nose had been completely cleaved from his body, and his left leg had been repeatedly sliced to the bone.

Cobb knew torture when he saw it.

This was something more.

They had toyed with him.

*   *   *

Kamal had also heard the scream. The low, terrified howl reached every corner of the water system. Kamal had already seen what had become of the others in his crew. The two that had mistakenly shot each other had been lucky in comparison to the other three he had discovered – those who had met their fate at the tip of a blade.

He didn't need to witness the execution to know who it was.

The cries of agony were all he needed.

Tarek was dead.

As he struggled to climb the ramshackle pillars back up toward the boiler room, Kamal's mind raced. This was a catastrophe. Not only had he failed to recover the woman, he had somehow managed to lose six men including his best friend in the process.

Hassan would have his head on a platter.

Kamal reasoned that killing everyone was a better option than returning with news that the woman was still on the loose. Now all he needed was a way to make that happen.

The city's water main was his salvation.

The wide conduit ran along the ceiling of the first chamber before disappearing into the infrastructure above. Nearly a third of the city was serviced through this one channel delivering thousands of gallons of water every minute of the day.

Rupturing one pipe would flood the entire network.

It would also prevent the woman's escape.

Kamal smiled at the thought.

29

During the cistern's conversion into a bomb shelter, the water main had been tapped for those who might be forced to take refuge underground. Valves had been installed that would divert the flow of water into the cistern, providing a source of hydration and a means to bathe. The pipes that once channeled the water to the floor far below had long since been removed, but the old valves were still in place.

Shards of metal and rust flew in all directions as Kamal emptied his clip into the antiquated plumbing. He couldn't destroy it completely, but he could damage it.

His bullets created multiple leaks.

The leaks became a lengthy crack.

And the pressure tore the crack apart.

A torrent of water gushed from the pipe, showering everything in the room. But it still wasn't enough for Kamal. To ensure that anyone in the network of tunnels would be unable to exit through the apartment building, he braced his legs against the nearest arch and pushed it with all of his might. The stone quivered against the stress of the giant's strength, which was fueled by adrenalin and rage.

He pushed, and pushed, and pushed some more.

Until the ancient arch gave way.

Then he gazed at the wreckage and said a prayer for his friend.

* * *

McNutt jumped down from the arch above and stared at the body of the monstrous thug. Without saying a word, he calmly handed the pistol back to Cobb. He then stepped forward and retrieved the assault rifle from the pile of guts on the floor. Wiping away the thick film of gore that coated the weapon, McNutt's eyes gleamed with joy.

'Happy now?' Cobb asked.

'Very,' McNutt answered.

'Good. Let's keep moving.'

'Right behind you.'

As Cobb crept through the tunnels in silence, he followed the markings on the walls that he had left earlier. Because of his foresight, there was no need for Garcia to guide them through the system. This allowed Cobb and McNutt to focus their attention on the sounds of the underground network instead of directions.

Hearing a noise, Cobb suddenly froze.

He crouched into a defensive stance and listened.

McNutt nearly tripped over him as he stepped backwards through the darkness, covering their rear. He turned to see why Cobb had stopped and was met with the sight of Cobb's closed fist. In the military, the signal meant to stop immediately.

No movement. No questions. No sound.

Cobb slowly opened his fist and tapped his finger to his ear.

There was something out there, and Cobb could hear it.

Both men peered into the darkness, searching for the source of the sound.

In the end, they felt it before they saw it.

'The tunnel's flooding,' Cobb said as he stood.

McNutt did the same. He looked down and saw wet circles

on his pants legs, the result of kneeling on the floor. He was pretty sure he hadn't pissed himself, so he agreed with Cobb's assessment. 'I think you're right.'

The surprises didn't end with the flooding.

With the water slowly rising around their feet, an eerie glow sprang to life across the ceiling. Unfortunately, the light was nestled on top of the arches – too far away for Cobb and McNutt to see from the bottom of the cistern. Like indirect lighting, they could see the glow but not the source.

'What the hell is that?' Cobb demanded.

'You can see it, too?'

'Of course I can see it!'

'Thank God! I thought I was seeing things again.'

Cobb growled in annoyance. 'Cover me.'

With McNutt standing guard, Cobb tucked his pistol into his waistband. Then he used the carved slots in the wall to climb up to the next level. Once he was on top of the bottom arch, he pulled out his gun and called down to McNutt. 'Your turn.'

'Coming, chief.'

From that point on, they alternated their climbs until they could determine the source of the light – one man covering the other as they made their way from the bottom of the cistern to the very top. With unknown forces still in the tunnels, Cobb and McNutt couldn't risk lowering their weapons at the same time because that would leave them defenseless.

Unfortunately, when they reached the ceiling and saw what they were facing, they realized that their guns couldn't protect them at all. Instead, they simply stared at the sources of the light as the horror of their discovery crept in.

'Holy fuck,' McNutt said in awe.

Multiple packs of explosives had been attached to the highest arches. Not one or two packs, but more than a dozen, spread out in all directions in the cistern. Each pack included a booster charge – a detonator that would trigger a much bigger blast – and a digital timer. It was these timers that cast the eerie glow.

Cobb glanced at the closest one.

4:48 . . . 4:47 . . . 4:46 . . . and counting.

Though McNutt was the expert, Cobb had enough experience with explosives to understand the gravity of the situation. He shined his light on the nearest bomb pack and could see the telltale red coloring of Semtex. The explosive would, at the very least, bring the whole room down on itself. Given the amount of Semtex spread across the ceiling, the more likely result would be a massive, smoldering crater that would devastate anything and anyone above the cistern.

In that moment, dozens of questions flooded Cobb's mind.

How long had the explosives been there?

Had they been placed prior to his rekky the night before, or had his rekky led to the placement of the bombs?

If his rekky forced their hand, what were they trying to hide?

Was it information about Alexander's tomb, or were the tunnels being used for criminal activities such as break-ins or drug running?

Ultimately, Cobb knew this wasn't the time or place to worry about any of those things. At that moment, the only thing that mattered was a single, crucial question that would determine their fate.

He glanced at McNutt. 'Can you defuse them?'

McNutt shook his head. 'No time.'

*   *   *

There were no more pictographs in the final tunnel. The walls were bare and roughly hewn, without carvings or decorations of any kind. The only thing Sarah found as she pushed deeper into the passageway was a number of steps leading up toward the surface. Appearing in pairs, the steps created tiers rather than stairs. A few of the paired steps were only a few paces apart, but others required a longer walk between them.

Sarah hadn't bothered to keep track of how many steps she had taken, but she knew she had to be getting close to the surface.

She scanned the farthest reaches of her light, searching for an exit.

A few minutes into her exploration, Sarah caught the glint of her flashlight's beam as it reflected off the floor of a large cavern. Stranger still, it almost seemed like the shimmery floor was swaying back and forth inside the tunnel. Intrigued by the phenomenon, she jogged forward and found she wasn't looking at the floor at all.

She was staring at a pool of water.

The walls of the tunnel widened, rising high above the grotto. The natural cave was encircled by massive pylons that supported the rotunda above – all constructed from the same Roman concrete described by Jasmine earlier. Sarah raised her flashlight and could see where the dome had been smoothed and polished. She traced her light across the curved ceiling, then back down the opposite wall to the water's edge.

Amazingly, the movement of the floor wasn't an illusion at all. It was actually the ebb and flow of water as tiny waves were pushed into the cave and then sucked back out again. To her, it was a welcome sign. The ever-changing volume meant the pool was fed by the sea. And if it was, they could swim their way to safety.

Sarah breathed a sigh of relief.

Things were finally going their way.

Not only had they survived the collapse of the stone archway, but they had found evidence about the tomb and the library. As long as Cobb and McNutt handled the goons – and she was confident they would because they could handle just about anything – then this day had turned out better than she had hoped.

But her tranquility didn't last long.

Confusion set in the moment she turned to her left and spotted an object that didn't belong in an ancient chamber forgotten by time.

There, in the corner, was a plastic cylinder.

Not a remnant of the past, but a product of today.

Cursing softly, she plucked it from the ground and examined it in the beam of her flashlight. Unfortunately, one glance confirmed her fears.

It was a glow stick.

A fluorescent glow stick.

That meant she and Jasmine weren't the first ones there.

'Son of a bitch!' she cursed as she flung it against the wall. Then she picked it up and was ready to throw it again.

'Sarah?' said a crackling voice. After being out of range for several minutes, she was finally close enough to the surface to make contact. 'Is that you?'

She put her hand to her ear. 'Hector? Where have you been?'

'Trying to find you!'

'You're not going to believe this, but I found a tunnel that leads to the sea.'

'Then use it!' he shouted. 'Use it now!'

Sarah froze. 'What do you mean? I don't know where it goes, and Jasmine's still back in—'

'Sarah, shut up and listen to me! You guys need to leave, like, right freaking now. You've got less than three minutes to evacuate. Jack and Josh found a bunch of explosives. The whole network is going to blow, and when it does—'

His voice cut off as she turned and ran.

Not toward the sea, but toward Jasmine.

30

Although there were crucial questions that needed answering, Sarah would worry about them later. For now, her lone aim was saving Jasmine.

Her stomach churned as she ran deeper and deeper into the depths of the city. By the time she had reached the bottom of the steps, she knew something was seriously wrong. She should have seen the flicker of Jasmine's flashlight; instead, she saw only darkness.

'Jasmine,' she screamed, 'we need to go!'

The tone of her voice made it clear.

They needed to leave *now*.

'Jasmine!' she screamed louder. 'The tunnels are going to explode!'

Once again, no response.

With adrenalin surging, Sarah sprinted through the tunnel until she reached the stone pictograph that Jasmine was supposed to be documenting for the sake of the mission. But instead of finding Jasmine, she spotted two things that filled her with dread: a broken flashlight, and enough explosives to bring down a building.

Sarah couldn't believe what she was seeing. Several of the Roman pillars had been rigged with Semtex, right there in plain sight. She could actually see the wires of the detonators and the compact payloads. Unfortunately, none of that mattered. She had been taught how to plant bombs, not defuse them.

The planned destruction didn't end with the pillars. The entire pictograph had been covered in thick foam. To the untrained eye, it looked like whipped cream, but Sarah had seen it before and knew that eating it would be a horrible mistake. Known as Lexfoam, *liquid explosive foam* was a combustible compound that could be sprayed onto any surface and, once it hardened, it was nearly impossible to remove.

Like cement with a powerful kick.

Sarah glanced at one of the timers and cursed.

The countdown was forcing her hand.

She wanted to search longer. For Jasmine. For the bombers. For more clues about the tomb. But none of that was possible, not anymore.

Not if she wanted to survive.

As much as it pained her, she knew what she had to do.

She grabbed Jasmine's flashlight and ran for her life.

* * *

Cobb and McNutt charged through the tunnels. They weren't sure how many men still remained in the underground chambers – if any – but they didn't have the time to be cautious. They acknowledged the possibility that any turn might lead to a hostile encounter, but if they were trapped in the tunnels when the bombs detonated, neither would survive.

With each chamber, the scale of the impending catastrophe grew larger. They could see the faint light of timers dotting the ceilings of every room. The damage wouldn't be limited to a single building; it would consume an entire city block.

Cobb still didn't know when the explosives had been placed.

It could have been months since the bombs were hidden on top of the uppermost arches, far from the prying eyes of security guards or government workers who inspected the tunnels below, or it could have been during the last few hours. The packs were portable, Semtex was extremely stable, and timers could be turned on at any time with a remote device.

Common sense led him to believe that their presence in the cisterns had prompted the activation of the devices, but ultimately he knew it didn't matter. The bombs would go off soon, no matter when they had been placed.

'What's the latest on Sarah?'

Garcia answered. 'She hasn't come back from getting Jasmine.'

It wasn't the news Cobb had hoped for, but he had to stay focused. Sarah and Jasmine could take care of themselves. There were others who had no idea of the carnage about to erupt beneath their feet. He wanted to help them.

'Hector, contact emergency services. Hack into the system, do whatever you have to do. There have to be hundreds of people up there.'

'You want me to evacuate the buildings?'

'There's no time for that,' Cobb insisted. 'Tell them to send ambulances, fire trucks, and anyone with paramedic training to the neighborhood above.'

His message was clear: they couldn't prevent the tragedy, but they could jumpstart the rescue efforts.

Garcia checked the GPS trackers. He could see that Cobb and McNutt had finally made it to the tunnels leading to the first cistern. A few moments more, and they could climb their way to the boiler room.

'The next chamber is the exit,' Garcia informed them. 'The

boiler room is clear. You've got an unobstructed path to the street.'

As they emerged from the final tunnel, Cobb and McNutt panned their flashlights upward, revealing the 'unobstructed path' to the exit.

Garcia had spoken too soon.

The cistern was a death trap.

Water poured from the broken pipe near the ceiling, dousing everything and making every surface slippery to the touch. The arch nearest the boiler room had been toppled, and chunks of broken stone crashed down from above, pried loose by the force of the gushing water.

McNutt raced over to the chiseled ladder on the far side of the room. He reached for the first handhold, but the cascading water prevented a solid grip. He tried again, but it was no use. The ancient grooves were too slick. The ladder was useless.

They attempted to pull themselves up to the next level, just as they had in all the other cisterns. Only this time they were pelted by torrents of water and hammered by falling chunks of debris. Their muscles burned and their fingers ached as they tried to claw their way upward.

Through it all, they could hear Garcia shouting above the clamor of rushing water. 'Thirty seconds! Get out of there!'

Cobb realized the futility of their effort. The downpour was too great an obstacle to overcome; and even if they could reach the top, someone had destroyed their access to the ledge. There was no way to make it out in time, and Cobb knew it.

McNutt knew it, too, but he wasn't about to give up. He

frantically struggled against the unyielding force of the water. If he was going to die, he would go out fighting – like he had been taught in the Marines.

Fortunately, Cobb had a different idea.

One that didn't involve dying.

* * *

When Sarah reached the water's edge she offered a final update, hopeful that her message would get through to someone on her team.

'If anyone can hear me, Jasmine is missing. I looked for her as long as I could, but I can't wait anymore. I'm going to swim for it. I have no idea where I'll surface, but I sure would appreciate a ride. With luck you can follow my GPS.'

With that, she took two huge breaths and plunged into the underwater passageway. She pulled herself through the water with powerful strokes, kicking like her life depended on it – which, in this case, it did.

Her flashlight died quickly, and she found herself submerged in darkness. But she refused to panic. Instead, she blocked out the creeping fear of death and convinced herself that if she kept her course and held her breath, she would survive.

Moments later, her faith was rewarded.

She could see a faint light in the distance like a beacon, guiding her to safety. Her strength was waning, but she knew she could make it if she kept fighting.

Starving for oxygen, her vision narrowed. Her lungs burned, desperate for her next breath. But the light grew brighter with every stroke. The open sea was right there in front of her; all she had to do was reach out and grab it.

As the tunnel bent upward, Sarah grabbed the jagged rocks

of the fissure and pulled herself in the direction of the surface above. By then, she had nothing left to give.

Only her own buoyancy could save her.

Her eyes rolled back into their sockets as she finally broke the surface, but her chest heaved as she instinctively gulped for air. It had never tasted so sweet.

She was alone, disoriented, and struggling to keep herself afloat.

But she was still alive.

For now.

31

The roar of flooding water echoed through the chamber. It was loud enough to drown out any conversation between Cobb and McNutt. Rather than compete for his attention, Cobb simply grabbed him by the belt and pulled him toward the farthest corner of the room. McNutt stumbled a bit but followed Cobb's lead. He didn't know what his friend had in mind, but it had to be better than their current predicament.

If not, they would soon be dead.

When the cisterns were converted to bomb shelters at the start of World War II, whole levels of the system were reinforced with concrete. The result was a series of long alleys that could be used for protection. The accommodations weren't luxurious – they offered little more than fresh air, safe water, and wooden benches – but they were better than nothing.

Many residents of the city knew what lay beneath their feet. Stories were passed down through family members, wartime tales that described the threat of air raids and the proposed exodus into the tunnels. The older generation was proud of their government's efforts to save its people. They were comforted by the massive corridors that would protect them from an aerial assault, even if they hadn't seen them in person.

Luckily, Cobb had.

He had spotted the reinforced hallways during his rekky. He had also found smaller, hidden spaces that could house only a handful of people. These compartments were not designed to save everyone, only to protect a precious few. Cobb knew the first rule of tactical defense was to ensure the safety of those in authority, so he assumed that these spaces would have been built to withstand a direct hit.

In a time of war, their country would depend on it.

Today, Cobb and McNutt would test its strength.

They ran to a narrow section of the wall where the ancient stone had been replaced by modern cement. Peering through a crack no wider than his head, McNutt could see a small, open space beyond the cement barrier. He knew if they could crawl inside that they might be able to weather the explosion.

Together, they set about expanding the entrance.

Shards of cement flew as they hammered away, using their weapons as tools. After a few quick blows, a larger chunk of the wall gave way. Cobb and McNutt were able to slither through the opening as the final seconds ticked down.

Three . . . two . . . one . . . BOOM!

For an instant, they could feel the detonation before they could hear it. The air rushed past them as the explosion sucked in more life-sustaining fuel. As experienced soldiers, they knew the sudden change in air pressure caused by the blast could literally pulverize their internal organs, so they opened their mouths to counter the impending shockwave.

And they covered their ears to block out the deafening roar.

Then they closed their eyes and prayed.

There was nothing else to do.

* * *

Earthquakes were fairly common in Alexandria. Over the centuries, the city had been hit with its fair share of seismic activity;

everything from slight tremors to catastrophic events. Given this history, few people on the street panicked when they heard the rumbling sound rising from the earth.

They had no reason to believe that their lives were in danger and assumed it would pass rather quickly.

This time, they were dead wrong.

Throughout the vast network of cisterns, the Semtex obliterated the uppermost arches. Shards of rubble rained down from the heights of each chamber. The air was heavy with smoke and particles of pulverized rock. The ceiling of every room was charred, scorched by the heat of the explosion and not by an actual fire.

Semtex had been chosen for a particular reason. Unlike pyrotechnic compositions such as Thermite – which can burn at more than forty-five hundred degrees Fahrenheit – Semtex doesn't create a raging inferno. The Semtex charges were designed to instantaneously demolish the stone supports at the upper level of the cisterns.

The bombs weren't meant to burn the pillars.

They were meant to destroy them.

The initial blast was over in an instant, but the damage was far from done. The destruction had been focused on key structural points that were essential to the integrity of the cistern. Once the arches crumbled, the pillars quickly gave way. Without the stanchions the ceiling was not able to support itself, and it collapsed under its own weight. The cumulative burden of the ceiling and the upper level was simply too much for the lower supports to bear, and they were crushed under the load.

It was known as the pancake effect.

And it was quite effective.

This controlled, vertical shaft of destruction used the force of the collapsing upper levels to wipe out everything in its path. The explosions just triggered the process; gravity did most of the work. For city engineers, it was the preferred method of destruction when dealing with large buildings in a crowded metropolis. When done correctly, there was no damage outside the blast radius but total destruction within.

That was bad news for the city of Alexandria.

And the neighborhood above the cisterns.

With nothing to support them, whole buildings began to sway like timbers in a swirling breeze. A moment later, they started to sink into the earth.

The roar of collapsing homes, offices, and restaurants was accompanied by the screams of those trapped within. Onlookers stared in awe as the ground ruptured and split, pulling helpless victims into its gaping maw. The deep canyons below the surface swallowed everything and everyone above.

Glass shattered as the buildings broke. Fires raged as sparks from electrical lines ignited gas leaks and fuel spills. The scent of death filled the air.

Five minutes earlier, the city block had been thriving.

Now it was a scene from the apocalypse.

* * *

Sarah heard the rumble of the explosions and felt the shockwave that funneled through the flooded passageway before dissipating in the water beneath her feet. Now she stared in horror at the carnage just beyond the coast.

Smoke billowed into the sky. The wind swept clouds of dust and noxious fumes in all directions. During her years with the CIA, Sarah had seen plenty of people die. She had even played a role in some of those deaths. But this was different.

Her targets had been criminals.

These victims were innocent.

If all the cisterns had been rigged like Garcia had described, she knew the destruction would be widespread and the casualties would be severe. The body count would reach well into the hundreds, if not thousands, and her friends were most likely dead. After all, how could they possibly survive a blast that brought down a city block?

To her, none of it made sense.

Who would do something like this?

Was this because of Alexander's tomb?

Or did we stumble onto something else?

As she pondered the questions in the back of her mind, she spit water from her mouth and tried to talk. 'Hector . . . can you hear me?'

She tapped her earpiece, hoping that her message got through. 'Hector . . . if you read me . . . I'm float—'

She never got the chance to finish her thought.

One moment she was fine, the next she was being pulled under by the surging water, which was dragging her back to the opening of the tunnel. The explosions had pushed the air from the underground system, and the sea rushed in to take its place. As huge bubbles forced their way to the surface, the tunnel continued to gurgle, toying with Sarah as she bobbed in the choppy surf above.

She choked on mouthfuls of seawater as she gasped for air, trying to stay afloat as if the hand of Neptune pulled her from below. In her struggles, she somehow spotted an approaching boat, but the undertow wouldn't allow her to call out for help. The most she could do was flail her arms wildly in the hope of drawing attention.

As the final pocket of air was expelled from the tunnel, the current pulled her deeper into the void. Exhausted from the swim and without a full breath of air, she knew she wouldn't last much longer. Her vision blurred, either from lack of oxygen or the increasing depth – she didn't know which. Not that it really mattered, because neither was a positive development in the middle of the sea.

The last thing she saw was a silhouette.

Then her whole world went black.

32

Cobb slowly opened his eyes. The concussive force of the explosion had thrown him against the wall of the bunker. That much he remembered. The painful dizziness and the trickle of warmth he felt rolling down his face told him that his head had taken the brunt of the impact – and that the stone had proven harder than his skull. The dull pain in his side let him know he had bruised at least a couple of ribs in the fall.

His head throbbed and his breathing was labored.

But he was still alive.

'Josh,' he called out, 'are you okay?'

If there was a reply, Cobb couldn't hear it. The buzzing in his ears blocked out nearly all the ambient noise. The only things he could detect were the crackles and pops from his earpiece. They might have been voices. They might have been static. They might have been a figment of his imagination.

In his current state, he couldn't tell the difference.

Cobb groped for his flashlight in the darkness. It had been knocked from his hand in the blast, and he was blind without it. He would worry about escaping later. Right now, he needed to know if McNutt was still alive.

Thankfully, he saw a sign of life.

Because of the dust and smoke, it didn't look like a beam of light. Instead, it looked like a radioactive cloud had swallowed the room because the entire chamber started to glow. As Cobb stumbled toward the source of the light, the ringing in his ears began to fade. For the first time, he could hear his friend calling out to him.

'Answer me, chief! Say something!' McNutt hollered.

'I'm fine! Just banged my head a bit,' he shouted back.

Neither realized that they were actually yelling.

McNutt stepped closer and shined his light on Cobb. He could see the laceration on his head, but there was no point in mentioning it. He didn't have stitches to close the wound or even a pad of gauze to stop the bleeding. Cobb was walking and talking, so McNutt hoped the only real damage was a splitting headache.

'Good,' McNutt said. 'Let's get the hell out of here.'

McNutt's optimism was a bit premature. For all they knew, they were now trapped below a hundred tons of dirt and debris. If the damage were even half of that amount, it would take a fleet of excavators to find them, and they would have used up their oxygen long before the arrival of a rescue party.

'Hector, can you hear me?' Cobb waited a few seconds before he tried again. He knew the odds were slim, but he had to try. 'Hector? Sarah? Jasmine?'

'Anything?' McNutt asked.

'Nope. I think the blast fried the circuitry.'

'Same with mine. I couldn't even hear your transmission.'

'That means we're on our own.'

McNutt shrugged. 'I've been on my own since high school.'

Cobb forced a smile. 'You went to high school?'

McNutt laughed. 'More than one.'

Ignoring their odds, they inspected the entrance to the bunker and saw that the concrete had shattered. What was once a hole was now a stack of rubble blocking their path. Fortunately, it wasn't solid. They could see through to the other side.

McNutt pushed his way into the cistern and got the first glimpse of the destruction. The thunderous vibrations of the bombs had shaken many of the pillars out of position. The ancient supports were precarious *before* the explosion. Now they stood like a house of cards – one wrong move and the whole structure would come tumbling down.

McNutt was thankful that the water main had dried up. The chamber was still soaked, but they wouldn't have to fight a waterfall on their climb. It was the first good thing that had happened to them in quite some time.

Blood dripped from McNutt's arm and Cobb's head as they slowly made their way up the wreckage toward the surface. As they climbed higher, their reserves got lower.

But still, they pressed on.

They were battered and bruised, but they weren't broken.

The same could not be said for the city above.

Their hearing had improved greatly by the time they saw daylight, but it was a mixed blessing. For the first time, they could hear the cacophony of horrors radiating down from the street. Sirens. Screams. The sounds of panic and fear.

Human instinct told them to run away.

Their training told them to charge forward.

* * *

Seawater poured from Sarah's lungs as she vomited uncontrollably. She rolled onto her side, trying to purge the fluid that had nearly killed her. Nothing around her mattered: not the boat, not the two men hovering near her. Not Alexander's tomb or the loss of her colleagues. For the moment, her singular goal was to just keep breathing.

When her coughing finally subsided, she rolled back over to face her saviors. Only then did she recognize that it was Papineau standing over her. He was still wearing his customary shirt and tie, but now the tailored ensemble was dripping wet.

Sarah couldn't believe her eyes. 'Papi?'

Papineau smiled warmly. 'How are you feeling?'

It was a look she had never seen before. 'I'm fine. Thanks to you.'

'I merely recovered your body,' Papineau explained. 'Hector is the real hero. You weren't breathing when we first pulled you aboard. He was the one who brought you back to life.'

Sarah turned to see Garcia crouched on the other side of the boat. He was nearly panting as he dealt with the residual adrenalin coursing through his system. In spite of their previous adventure, he was still adjusting to real-world emergencies. He was much more comfortable dealing with things from behind his desk.

There, he could always reboot the system and start again.

In the field, things weren't always as simple.

Sarah stared at him with decidedly mixed feelings. She was thankful that he had saved her life but knew he would never let her forget it.

Garcia smiled at her. 'Don't worry. Your breath was fine.'

Sarah nodded her thanks and tried to stand, but found that her legs were still too shaky to support her weight, especially in a rocking boat.

Papineau caught her as she collapsed. 'Easy, Sarah. Take a moment to rest.'

Sarah had been a part of recovery missions in the past. They were often physically demanding, that much she knew, but they were nothing like this. Her perspective had changed. Rescuing someone was tiring. But *being* rescued was exhausting.

Still, there were questions that couldn't wait.

'What about the guys? Did they make it out?'

Garcia shrugged. 'We lost them.'

Sarah took the news like a sucker punch.

Sensing her misinterpretation, Papineau jumped in to clarify the situation. 'What he means is that we lost their signals.'

Sarah stared at Garcia, annoyed by his poor choice of words.

Garcia quickly realized his mistake. 'Oh, God. I didn't mean it like that. They're not dead – at least, we don't know that for sure. We just lost tracking and communications. When the bombs detonated, it must have damaged their electronics.'

This time, his words struck a different chord.

'When the comms went out,' she said, struggling to find the right words. 'When we entered the second tunnel and we couldn't hear you, could you still hear us?'

Papineau waved off her question. 'Sarah—'

'Could you still see the video feeds from our cameras?'

Papineau again tried to silence her. 'Please, you need to—'

This time it was Garcia who cut him off. 'We lost the live feed, but that doesn't mean we lost the footage. If you were still using the flashlight camera, it was still recording. There's internal memory, a micro-drive that stores the video files.'

'How much footage will it hold?' she asked.

Garcia shrugged. 'Something like a thousand hours, why?'

Papineau shook his head in frustration. Their attention

shouldn't be on the treasure; it should be on the things that really mattered.

Sarah fished both the flashlights from the cargo pockets of her pants and presented them to Garcia.

'We found something,' she explained. 'A wall with carvings all across it. It's a pictograph that explains what happened to the library and why Alexander's tomb was moved. I remember some of the details, but these should show us everything.'

* * *

Cobb and McNutt climbed out of the wreckage and into a nightmare.

The streets were lined with victims of the tragedy. Those who made it out of their homes and offices before the buildings collapsed now watched in horror as their neighbors suffered. Paramedics tended to the injured. Firemen rushed to contain the flames. Police officers struggled to keep the gawking crowd at bay.

It would have been easy for Cobb and McNutt to flee the chaos and return to the relative safety of the yacht to have their minor wounds tended to. After all, they were still dazed from the blast and grieving for the friends they assumed were dead and/or buried under so much rubble that there was no way they could reach them, but leaving the scene would have gone against everything that they stood for.

One trip into the burning rubble quickly became two, and then five, and then ten. Time and time again they shuttled the wounded from the smoldering wreckage to the waiting medical personnel. Cobb knew that many of the victims had fatal injuries. Still, those not mutilated or burned beyond recognition deserved a chance to survive, and both he and McNutt were determined to give them that opportunity.

Eventually, there was nothing left to be done. The twisted pile of debris was too unsteady to climb on, and the growing fire had become too hot to withstand. Continuing their effort would only put more lives at risk – including their own.

They had saved everyone that they could.

Now it was time to find the bombers.

33

Cobb's tank was empty. So was McNutt's. They had started the day on a magnificent yacht, and now they leaned against a battered fire truck. Their muscles ached and their wounds throbbed as they tried to make sense of everything that had happened.

The cisterns were destroyed, the tunnels were buried, and hundreds were killed or injured – all at the hands of a mysterious foe that had surfaced with violent intent. Sarah and Jasmine were presumed dead since they had last been seen heading toward the epicenter of the blast, and they couldn't reach Garcia to confirm anything.

All in all, it was a horrible day.

The worst they could remember.

Despite the carnage, McNutt forced himself to take stock of his surroundings. Everywhere he turned, all he saw was chaos. Burning buildings. Sobbing onlookers. Emergency vehicles of every shape and color, along with dozens of crews attempting to handle the situation. After a while, it all started to blend together into one continuous vista of death and destruction . . . until he saw something that stood out.

McNutt rubbed his eyes in disbelief, convinced that the smoke was playing tricks on him. And yet the man's appearance didn't change. He had seen him less than an hour earlier in the cistern.

McNutt nudged Cobb to get his attention. 'Jack, it's one of them.'

'One of who?'

'One of the guys from the tunnels. The goddamn monkey men.'

'Where?'

'At your three o'clock.'

Cobb zeroed in on the triage area, scanning for anything that looked familiar. Only one man stood out. 'Black pants, black tunic, dark skin.'

'That's him.'

'You're sure?'

'Almost positive.'

Cobb nodded in understanding. McNutt didn't recognize his face, but the man was wearing the same clothes as the other men in the cistern.

Plus, he was acting strangely.

With nothing else to go on, they stood back and watched as he worked his way through the tent that had been set up on the edge of the blast site. The victims, both dead and alive, had been spread out in rows so that the doctors could quickly work their way through the masses. Many of the dead had been covered with sheets, towels, or scraps of clothes, and he took the time to uncover every last one.

Cobb and McNutt understood his intentions.

He was searching for someone.

Maybe one of his own. Maybe one of his targets.

Either way, it showed remarkable dedication to his cause.

And his boldness filled Cobb with rage.

Once the man had finished his search, he broke away from the makeshift hospital and made his way toward the periphery of the madness. Determined to get answers, Cobb knew they needed to act fast. They simply couldn't let a lead like that walk away. Despite the crowd, Cobb sensed their opportunity and decided to take him down.

'Nice and slow,' he whispered to McNutt. 'We don't want to spook him.'

'Slow, I can promise. But *nice* is out of the question.'

Cobb took a course to intercept the man while McNutt trailed from a safe distance. No discussion was needed; both knew how to proceed. They had been taught well by the US military. They knew how to coordinate their actions and predict each other's moves. The entire time they scanned the crowd for trouble without making themselves known. They walked casually but quickly, confident but not defiant.

They simply looked like they belonged.

Meanwhile, the bomber was the exact opposite.

He strode purposefully through the chaos. Not strolling or running but somewhere in between, as if he were trying to do some light cardio in the middle of a warzone. As he walked, the man shook his head back and forth to someone in the crowd.

The movement was subtle, but Cobb noticed it. Looking ahead, he spotted an ambulance parked fifty feet away. A second man stood next to an empty gurney behind the vehicle. He looked the part of a medic – the uniform, the comfortable shoes, the sterile gloves – but the anger on his face gave him away.

This was a man who *took* lives, not a man who saved them.

Cobb lowered his head and tried not to be spotted, but he was a large white man in an Egyptian city. It wasn't easy to hide. Eventually the medic saw Cobb's approach and knew their cover had been blown. He slapped the side of the ambulance, shouting instructions to the driver in Arabic. A moment later the engine roared to life as the medic opened the rear doors and climbed into the back of the van.

For an instant, Cobb was tempted to raise his gun and fire.

But all of that changed when he saw the cargo inside.

Somehow, someway, Jasmine was in there.

Obviously he was thrilled that she wasn't buried under a million pounds of rubble like he had feared, and yet her appearance was mystifying.

When did they grab her?

Why did they grab her?

And how did they smuggle her out before the blast?

The last time he had seen her was in the depths of the tunnels, more than a block away. She and Sarah were heading off to investigate the Roman temple; now Jasmine was lying on a tilted gurney, as if she were watching TV. Her hands and feet were bound to the railings with plastic straps. Heavy tape covered her mouth. Her unblinking eyes were frozen open, but Cobb couldn't tell the reason why.

Maybe she was drugged. Maybe she was dead.

Until he knew for sure, he couldn't risk a shot.

Cobb, McNutt, and their initial target all broke for the ambulance at the same time. The medic in the van kicked the empty gurney into Cobb's path, slowing him down just enough for the first assassin to get inside. He dove into the rear compartment as the medic slammed the doors shut behind him.

Tires squealed as the ambulance sped off.

Bile burned the back of Cobb's throat as he sprinted after the vehicle. His frustration had been growing throughout the day, but seeing Jasmine had pushed him over the edge. Though he prided himself on his calm demeanor, rage began to fuel his actions. It was a consuming, blinding hatred of those responsible for the day's tragedies.

In his mind, justice wasn't enough.

They needed to be punished.

* * *

The layout of Alexandria has changed very little in the last two thousand years. Though much of the city has been destroyed and rebuilt numerous times, the architects retained the original design of north–south and east–west streets whenever possible.

Obviously, the grid has grown over time and the roads have been vastly improved, but the only considerable difference between the ancient and modern layouts was a handful of major thoroughfares that linked Alexandria to the rest of Egypt. Had the explosion taken place in the suburbs, the ambulance would have had an easy escape route. On the outskirts of town, wide surface streets offered quick access to the larger arteries that connected the various districts around the city. Once the ambulance reached the highway, Jasmine and her kidnappers would have disappeared.

But in the city, things were more complicated.

Though contemporary in appearance – McDonald's and Starbucks sightings were commonplace – the older section of the city was surrounded by the classical, narrow streets of Alexandria's past. There were no medians or bike lanes. Even the buses were forced to fight their way through traffic, just like everyone else. It was a striking juxtaposition: the progress of modern buildings nestled in an ancient city.

Unlike the tragedy of 9/11 when millions of citizens fled New York and stayed away for days, people in the Middle East were more accustomed to bombings. As crazy as it seemed, the streets were clogged in both directions with a mixture of locals fleeing the scene and people who wanted to see the damage for themselves.

Both groups slowed the bombers' escape.

Cobb watched as the ambulance's lights began to flash and its siren began to wail. Normally that would be enough to clear a path through traffic, but not on a day like today. There was simply nowhere for the other cars to go.

When the ambulance ran out of road, it bounced over the curb and sped down the sidewalk. Surprised pedestrians jumped from the path of the careening van before it suddenly veered back onto the asphalt. A moment later it changed direction again – this time disappearing around a street corner to the left.

Despite their anger and their fitness, Cobb and McNutt knew there was no way for them to keep up with a speeding ambulance, not on foot. Their desperate desire to retrieve Jasmine would keep them going until they dropped; but they *would* drop.

They needed something faster. Something mechanical.

Something that didn't feel fatigue.

Fortunately, scooters were quite popular in Egypt.

The nimble motorbikes allowed riders to dart in and out of traffic and down narrow alleyways where cars weren't allowed to travel. What they lacked in top-end speed, they made up for in agility. In the congestion of the older neighborhoods, they were a remarkably efficient means of transportation.

Plus, they were pretty easy to steal.

McNutt eyed the closest rider and braced for impact. This wasn't the time for negotiations. This was a time for action. McNutt charged toward the rider like a jouster without a horse. Or a lance. At the very last moment, he threw his arms out in front of him and tackled the rider to the ground as his scooter toppled, then slid, to a crashing halt.

McNutt hopped to his feet and reached out his hand.

Lying bruised and battered on the pavement, the dazed rider stared up at McNutt and was ready to curse him out in a dialect that McNutt wouldn't have understood anyway, but the moment he saw the rage in McNutt's eyes, he knew any complaints on his part would most likely lead to a severe beating – or worse.

He quickly changed his approach. 'Take it, my friend. The scooter is yours.'

'No thanks,' McNutt said as Cobb lifted the bike from the ground and quickly sped off toward the ambulance. 'I'll take the next one.'

34

As luck would have it, a passing rider stopped at the crash site to see if the first biker was injured from his fall. Unbeknownst to him, this random act of kindness might have saved his life. Of course, it probably didn't seem very fortunate when McNutt pulled out his gun and stole the Vespa in the middle of the street, but at the very least it prevented him from being tackled from his speeding scooter.

'Sorry,' McNutt apologized, 'I need it more than you.'

Then he grabbed the handlebars and sped off toward Cobb.

They followed the path of the ambulance, jumping the curb and speeding down the sidewalk. When they reached the end of the block, they slowed and frantically searched the street for any sign of the ambulance. It should have been easy to track – the ambulance was not only painted in bright orange and green, it also had flashing lights and a blaring siren – yet the vehicle was nowhere in sight.

McNutt's stomach rolled at the thought of losing Jasmine. Cobb's blood boiled at the idea of her kidnappers surviving the night without suffering intense pain.

Both developments were simply unacceptable.

Fortunately, their fears were a bit premature.

Cobb spotted the ambulance in front of a large truck. 'There!'

The ambulance swung wide and swerved through an intersection, running through a red light as the oncoming cars screeched to a halt. From its acceleration, it appeared that the driver had found some room to move.

McNutt gunned the throttle, launching the mini-bike toward the crossing. It was the same approach they had used when tracking their target at the blast site: McNutt would follow the ambulance directly while Cobb looked for a way to get ahead of it. Following McNutt's lead, Cobb did his part, tearing off in the same direction as the van.

Cobb zipped in and out of his lane, dodging slower cars and oncoming traffic as he tried to keep pace with the ambulance. The unrelenting stream of cars on both sides of the centerline forced him to focus on the road ahead. As the spaces between the vehicles grew tighter, Cobb knew he needed more room to operate.

He found it on the sidewalk.

Terrified pedestrians jumped out of his way as Cobb motored down the footpath. Building after building whizzed past as he sped through the city. The alleyways and cross streets offered fleeting glimpses of his target, but he needed to narrow the gap.

Cobb ducked low to lessen the drag and tried to squeeze every last bit of power from the small motor. From his rekky earlier in the week, he knew the upcoming parking garage provided his best opportunity to close the distance between himself and the kidnappers. It was a risky move, but their time was running out. If the ambulance made it to the highway system, there was no way that they could keep up.

Not on tiny scooters.

McNutt chased the van on the main street as Cobb swerved left and steered his bike up the entrance ramp of the massive structure. At the top of the incline, he cut diagonally across the garage's uppermost level. Had it been earlier in the day, the spaces would have been filled with cars, but at this hour the floor was virtually empty.

With no traffic to slow him, Cobb pulled in front of the ambulance. Unfortunately, his view was over the side of a building, looking down to the pavement below.

Under normal circumstances, Cobb never would have risked a shot. The streets were full of innocent bystanders, and Jasmine was inside a speeding vehicle. And yet he sensed that this was his best opportunity to stop the van in the city.

It was a risky move, but one he opted to make.

Cobb steadied his aim, knowing that it should have been McNutt taking the shot. When it came to weapons, Cobb was highly skilled, but he wasn't on McNutt's level. Cobb knew all the variables – speeding vehicles, uneven pavement, varying elevations, wind, even temperature – but precisely compensating for their effects was a different matter. The calculations involved were staggering.

Unfortunately, McNutt was more than a block behind.

Cobb alone had the tactical advantage.

He took a deep breath then squeezed his trigger several times.

His first shot missed wide, but the windshield of the ambulance exploded on the second. The van lurched to the side, veering across the street through oncoming traffic. Other motorists were forced to take evasive action as the van swerved in front of them. The booming gunshots were followed by the sounds of brakes screeching and cars slamming into each other, one after the next. The groans of metal shearing against metal were accented by high-pitched cracks of shattering windows.

Cobb had hit the ambulance, but he had failed to stop it.

Worse, he had inadvertently created even more destruction.

He watched in horror as the day's injury count grew in the massive pileup. Only McNutt's quick reflexes saved him from becoming a casualty of the aftermath. As it was, he was merely immobilized, hemmed in by wreckage.

But the ambulance pressed on.

As Cobb reloaded, the driver pushed the accelerator to the floor and steered the ambulance down a narrow one-way alley. A moment later he turned sharply and the van disappeared behind the buildings one block over.

Cobb cursed as he gunned his scooter and looked for an exit.

By the time he reached street level, Cobb feared the worst. Five seconds can make all the difference in a chase. Thirty seconds was an eternity. The time had allowed McNutt to extricate himself from the traffic jam, but it had also put them at an even greater disadvantage. There was simply no way of knowing what had happened when they lost sight of the ambulance. As they sped down the one-way alley, Cobb knew they needed a break if they hoped to pick up the trail.

Ironically, their break *was* a trail.

At the end of the alley, they found torn chunks of rubber. Just beyond that, a scorched line had been burned onto the pavement. It started near the alleyway and haphazardly meandered down the street into the distance.

Cobb had seen similar markings before. He knew the rubber was a tire that had been torn from its wheel and that the ambulance was now riding on a rim. It was the grinding of metal on asphalt that had left the scarring. The zigzag pattern in the road meant the driver had never experienced losing a tire and was having trouble with the lack of stability.

More importantly, it meant they could follow the kidnappers.

Cobb and McNutt tore down the street in pursuit, their eyes pinned to the trail that led the way. Like the spark at the end of a fuse, they would inevitably reach the end. And when they did, they expected fireworks.

Not only had the missing tire made the ambulance hard to drive, but it had severely limited its speed. Only a few blocks from where they had first picked up the trail, they found the disabled vehicle stranded in the roadway.

Cobb and McNutt dismounted their bikes and approached on foot, using parked cars, garbage cans, and lampposts as cover. Neither liked the situation as they sensed they were charging into an ambush, but each accepted it was a chance that they had to take if they hoped to get to Jasmine and the bombers before the police arrived.

'Cover me,' Cobb said as they ducked behind an SUV less than twenty feet from the ambulance. 'If they rigged the van to blow, you'll be safer here.'

'Screw safe,' McNutt growled. 'I want blood.'

'You can get it from *here*. Now cover me.'

'Yes, sir.'

Cobb took a deep breath and sprinted toward the ambulance, ready to return fire, but there was no sign of the man in black, the medic, or the driver. Still, he knew he wasn't out of danger. There were a thousand different ways for the bombers to rig the rear doors. He realized any action he took from here on in might be his last.

Still, he had to know.

He carefully pulled the latch, hoping that the next sound he heard was a simple click rather than the deafening roar of a bomb followed by the singing of angels.

Instead the door swung open, revealing nothing.

The ambulance was empty.

35

Garcia was relieved to be back on the yacht. He had viewed his time on the speedboat as a necessary evil. Not only did it take him away from the gadgets and gizmos of his command center – the only things that helped him feel connected to the world – he simply wasn't comfortable on the open water.

Never had been, never would be.

It wasn't just because moisture was the mortal enemy of electronics. It had far deeper roots than that. His uneasiness had developed long before he had written his first lines of code. Even as a young boy, swimming in anything but a shallow pool had felt unsafe, no matter what his parents said to comfort him. He knew when he was out of his element, and he preferred the constant steadiness of the land to the uncertainty of the sea.

He had swallowed his fear to rescue Sarah.

But not enough to actually dive in the water.

Thankfully, Papineau had jumped in and saved the day.

Garcia was deeply troubled by his indecision but he didn't have time to worry about it now. The only thing that mattered was his current task.

His search would start with the video footage recorded on Jasmine's hard drive. That is, if he could salvage what was left of it. To speed the drying process, he took apart Jasmine's and Sarah's flashlights and spread out the waterlogged parts on a lint-free pad on his desk. To aid the recovery process, he dipped the memory cards in a vat of fresh water before he placed them in a natural desiccant to pull moisture from the circuitry.

'How's it going?' Papineau asked as he entered the room, freshly showered and wearing a different suit than before – one that wasn't wet. He glanced over Garcia's shoulder and tried to figure out what he was doing. 'Is that rice?'

'Yep,' Garcia said as he placed the last few components in a paper bag and added several cups of uncooked rice. 'I would have preferred packets of silicon dioxide – it's a gel that sucks up moisture like a sponge and has a lot less dust than grain – but time is the most important factor when rescuing data. The clock was ticking, so I had to act fast.'

'Let me guess,' Papineau said as he considered the scene. 'You didn't anticipate a need for silica packets, but we had rice in the pantry.'

'Exactly.'

'And the vat?'

'Filled with your finest spring water.' He pointed to several empty bottles in a nearby bin. 'I used the liquid to bathe the parts before I started the drying process. Otherwise, the salt crystals from the seawater would have messed with the circuitry.'

Papineau shook his head. He had authorized an unlimited budget for the best equipment that money could buy, and Garcia was retrieving key data with rice and water. 'What do you think: can you undo the damage?'

Garcia nodded. 'Once the water's been sucked away, the drive from Sarah's flashlight should give us something to work with. There might be a few bad sectors that were damaged beyond repair, but I'm fairly confident we'll be okay.'

'And Jasmine's?'

'Yeah, well, that's a different story. Her flashlight was basically destroyed. The drive didn't just get wet, it got smashed. That means there's a far greater chance that her data will be unrecoverable. We'll have to wait and see.'

'Keep me posted.'

'And you?'

Papineau arched an eyebrow. 'What do you mean?'

Garcia pointed to the row of small monitors that he had set up for Papineau. It allowed him to watch several satellite feeds of the various international news networks simultaneously. 'Anything on the blast?'

Papineau nodded. 'The explosion is being covered around the world, as I expected. The BBC and CNN are withholding their speculation until they see a report from Nile TV here in Egypt, and that won't happen until Nile gets a preliminary finding from the Deputy Minister of Special Police. Al Jazeera is calling it a natural disaster. The Chinese are saying it's an act of terrorism. And the North Korean government has labeled it proof that the Egyptians now have a tactical nuclear device.'

Garcia shook his head and laughed. 'That they used against their own people? That doesn't make any sense.'

'I mention North Korea, and you expect the story to make sense?'

'Well, I—'

Garcia stopped abruptly and stared at the video feed from the security camera that he had installed on an outside rail. The camera pointed down the dock, allowing him to see anyone approaching the boat from shore. In this case, he spotted two battered men as they opened the gate and made their way toward the yacht. They were covered in so much filth and blood that they were virtually unrecognizable.

'What's wrong?' Papineau demanded.

Garcia glanced at him, then back at the screen. 'I'm not sure if anything's wrong. Two men are coming this way, but . . .'

'But what?'

'I think . . .' Garcia didn't want to create false hope until he knew for sure, so he waited to make his pronouncement until the last possible moment. 'Oh my God! It's Jack and Josh! They're here – and alive!'

'They're here?'

'And alive!'

Garcia and Papineau rushed down the stairs and met Cobb and McNutt in the galley below. Both soldiers were exhausted and covered in grime.

Garcia wanted to hug them both, but he sensed they weren't in the mood so he kept his distance and said the only thing he could think of: 'Welcome back.'

McNutt nodded his appreciation as Cobb rummaged through the refrigerator for two bottles of water. He tossed the first to McNutt and chugged the second himself.

When his thirst had been quenched, Cobb finally spoke. 'We lost Jasmine. She's been taken by the bombers.'

'Taken?' Papineau blurted. 'Why would they take Jasmine?'

'I don't know,' Cobb admitted. 'But they had plenty of opportunities to kill her and they didn't. In fact, they did the exact opposite. They saved her life by taking her.'

Garcia stared at him. 'Jack, you keep saying *they*. Who are *they*?'

Cobb shrugged and handed his cell phone to Garcia. 'I was hoping you could tell me.'

'Pictures?' Garcia asked.

Cobb nodded as he tipped back another bottle of water.

'We documented as much as we could,' McNutt explained. 'They used an ambulance to get away from the blast. It was empty by the time we caught up to it. You should find enough to give you a make and model, as well as images of the plates and the vehicle identification number. Unfortunately, we couldn't stick around. We only had a few seconds before the police arrived.'

Papineau grimaced. 'The police? Do they know about Jasmine?'

'I doubt it. I don't see how they could,' McNutt answered.

He breathed a sigh of relief. 'Good. Let's keep it that way. Meanwhile, I'll reach out to some of my contacts and try to get a sense of things. If they're after money, I'll do everything I can to negotiate her release.'

Cobb nodded but said nothing.

'In the meantime, what else can you tell me?'

Cobb wasn't in the mood to talk, but he knew he had to fill in the rest of his team so they could get to work. 'There were maybe a dozen guys. All dressed in black, all armed with blades. They were experienced and well trained. They knew exactly what they were doing. They got in and out of the cisterns without us noticing. They eliminated everyone they encountered, and they erased their presence with a series of explosives.'

'Except for the ambulance,' Garcia blurted. He could see that Cobb and McNutt had been through hell, and he was trying to boost their spirits. 'It's a good place to start.'

Papineau stroked his chin in thought. 'Back up for a moment.

You said they eliminated everyone that they found in the tunnels? You mean they *weren't* working in tandem with the men from the boiler room?'

'Working with them?' McNutt laughed at the suggestion. 'Not a chance. They sliced those bastards like deli meat. No way they were playing on the same team.'

Cobb glanced at Papineau and could see the wheels turning in his head. The news was more than unexpected; it was baffling. Cobb was oddly comforted by Papineau's confusion. Cobb didn't like secrets on his team, and it appeared that the Frenchman didn't know any more about the men in the tunnel than he did.

Cobb would dig into the matter later on, but for now, there were more important things to worry about. 'What about Sarah?'

Papineau lowered his voice to a whisper. 'She's resting.'

'Are you positive?' McNutt demanded.

'Yes. I'm sure.'

McNutt took a deep breath and tried to contain his emotions. Given his presumption that Sarah had been crushed in the explosion, McNutt was certain that Papineau was doing his best to soften the confirmation of her death. It never occurred to him to take the news literally. 'Has anyone called her family?'

'Of course not. Why would we do that?' Garcia wondered.

'Why?' McNutt growled, as his face turned bright red. 'Because that's what you do when someone's *resting* – you notify their next of kin!'

Earlier it had been Garcia's poor choice of words that had led to Sarah's confusion. This time fault fell on Papineau's shoulders. Garcia was so thrilled to have company in the team's doghouse that he started to laugh uncontrollably.

Which, of course, made McNutt even angrier.

'And now you're laughing! You cold, heartless, son of a bitch! What the hell is wrong with you? This isn't a video game! We can't just hit the restart button and bring Sarah back from the dead.'

'Dead?' Papineau bristled at the suggestion. 'Sarah isn't dead. She's asleep in her berth. Who said anything about her being dead?'

'You did! You said she was resting! I thought you meant: RIP.'

Despite the tragedy of the day, or maybe because of it, Papineau started to laugh as well. 'Josh, you're a Marine, not a two-year-old. If someone dies, I'll say they died. I won't say they're resting – and I won't say they're living on a farm upstate.'

'Whoa! Whoa! Whoa!' McNutt blurted as he struggled to make sense of things. 'You're telling me that Sarah is *alive*, but my dog is *dead*?'

'Your dog?' Papineau asked.

McNutt nodded glumly. 'My parents sent him upstate when I was seven. Despicable people, those two. Obviously a pair of liars.'

'Sorry to be the bearer of bad news.'

McNutt shrugged. 'Oh well, at least Sarah's alive.'

'Wow,' Sarah said as she appeared in the ship's kitchen from a back hallway, 'try not to sound so glum when you say that.'

McNutt's face filled with joy as he sprinted across the room and lifted her in a giant bear hug. 'Oh my God! I'm so happy to see you! And you smell so clean!'

Sarah appreciated the affection, but she could have done without the hug and the layer of filth that now covered her clothes. 'Josh, put me down.'

But McNutt didn't stop. He simply swung her back and forth

like the clapper inside a bell. 'Seriously, you smell *really* good. I'm tempted to lick your face like Sparky used to do.'

'Don't you dare! Josh, put – me – down! Now!'

McNutt laughed as he lowered her to the floor.

Sarah took a step back and dusted herself off before she truly studied Cobb and McNutt. At that moment, she realized that nearly drowning might have been the easy way out because the guys looked like they had finished their shifts at a coalmine before they had decided to run a marathon through Chernobyl.

Their clothes were grimy and stained with sweat. Dried blood covered McNutt's arm and matted Cobb's hair. Their hands had been scraped raw when they dug through the shattered rock, and their eyes were bloodshot from the smoke of the burning crater.

All in all, she had seen healthier-looking zombies.

Sarah pushed her freshly washed hair over her ears and smiled. 'I guess they buried the lead about getting me out in time. Sorry about that.'

Cobb shrugged, his eyes locked on hers. 'I wasn't worried. I knew you'd make it.'

Sarah blushed slightly. 'I knew you'd make it, too.'

36

Cobb needed three things: a shower, a sandwich, and a summary of what had happened to Sarah and Jasmine in the tunnel.

At that moment, the shower would have to wait.

McNutt tore into the pantry as Cobb rummaged through the fridge for life-sustaining fuel. Neither had eaten since that morning – an eternity with the stress and workloads of their day – and they were willing to make a meal out of almost anything. Fortunately, they wouldn't have to rough it. The kitchen was well stocked with meats and cheeses, a variety of breads, and an assortment of fruits and vegetables.

The meal did more than satisfy their hunger. It also gave Sarah a chance to fill them in on everything that had happened between the arrival of the gunmen, which was when the team separated, and her escape through the sea tunnel. She spent a few minutes describing Papineau and Garcia's heroic rescue before Cobb asked her to concentrate on the evidence that they had discovered inside the temple.

'Jasmine called it a pictograph,' Sarah explained as she drew tiny symbols on a paper napkin to illustrate. 'Carvings on a wall that represented events from the city's past.'

McNutt whistled. 'That's a lot of history. How big was the freaking wall?'

Sarah shook her head. 'It wasn't a complete history. More like a highlight reel. It included depictions of various wars, those who came to power, that sort of thing. It even explained what happened to the Library of Alexandria.'

She paused, allowing Cobb and McNutt to ponder that last bit of information. Although they understood the basic implications of her statement, it was Papineau who clarified the importance of such a discovery.

'The pictograph may not rewrite history – because rumors about the library have existed for years – but it will unquestionably bring it into focus. Where there once was doubt, we now have certainty,' he said.

'Great,' McNutt said as he picked fig seeds from his teeth with a toothpick. 'But how's that going to help us?'

'The wall also describes the history of Alexander's tomb.'

Cobb perked up. 'Is that true?'

Sarah nodded. 'The carvings started with the arrival of Alexander and the creation of his city, and they ended with his body being smuggled out of Alexandria just before a massive flood leveled everything.'

Cobb thought back to Papineau's original briefing in Florida. It had included a video simulation of a catastrophic tsunami in 365 AD. 'The earthquake in Crete?'

'Good memory,' said Sarah, who was surprised that Cobb was still upright let alone functional. 'According to Jasmine, an oracle warned the priests that a natural disaster was on the verge of destroying the city. The prophecy gave them enough time to smuggle Alexander's tomb to safety.'

Cobb grimaced. 'A prophecy, huh?'

'Look,' she admitted, 'I don't know about the prophecy part, either, but it doesn't matter what we believe. People back then lived for that shit. And if the almighty oracle told them that their city was on the verge of a horrible tragedy, I'm pretty sure they would have dug up Alexander and carried his skeleton to somewhere safe.'

Cobb was intrigued by the possibilities, but not enough to distract him from what mattered most – and that was Jasmine. With that in mind, he needed to figure out who had the most to gain by destroying the pictograph and the cisterns.

'Sarah,' he said, 'did you find anything else down there? Were there any signs that someone had been there recently?'

'You mean apart from the Semtex and the explosive foam?'

Cobb smiled. It had taken a while, but he was actually starting to appreciate her biting sense of humor. 'Yes, Sarah, other than the bombs.'

'Maybe,' she replied. 'I found a used glow stick at the seaside end of the tunnel. I have no idea if the bombers dropped it, or if it was sitting there for five years.'

'Did you take it?'

She laughed at the absurdity of the question. 'Of course I took it. Like you even have to ask. I would have taken the wall, too, if I didn't have to swim.'

His smile widened. The glow stick was exactly the kind of clue he was hoping for. Torches were impossible to trace, and flashlights were so commonplace that tracking them was almost irrelevant, but the glow stick gave him hope. The technology was relatively new, dating back only forty years or so, and there was only a handful of manufacturers.

'Josh,' Cobb said as he assembled a plan of attack in his head. The clock was ticking, and they needed to get to work. 'How are you feeling?'

McNutt sucked on his toothpick. 'Kind of bloated – how about you?'

'I mean, are you able to work?'

He sat up straighter. 'Yes, sir.'

'Good. I want you to find out everything you can about the explosives. Who deals in Semtex and Lexfoam in this part of the world? What would it take to get the amount that was needed for this job? I want you to plan the mission in your head and give me all the angles. Your flashlight should have recorded plenty of close-ups of the bomb packs and detonators, so have Hector pull the files if you need a visual reference.'

McNutt's eyes lit up. He loved the thought of planning an explosion; even the one that had almost killed him. 'I'm on it, chief.'

Cobb spun to face his computer whiz. 'Hector, you're going to be quite busy the next few days, so crack open a Red Bull, Mountain Dew, or whatever geniuses like to drink. I need to know everything there is to know about that glow stick. Make, model, country of origin, retail distributors – all of it.'

'No problem.'

'How long until you know about the flashlight drives?'

'Tomorrow morning at the earliest.'

'Why so long?' Cobb demanded.

'The worst thing you can do to a wet circuit is to power it up. That's why I took the batteries out right away. Even the smallest surge can fry a drive.'

Cobb trusted his judgment. 'Don't rush the process, but don't take all week, either. We need this sooner rather than later.'

Garcia nodded. 'Understood.'

'And Hector, as soon as the footage is ready, I want you to find Sarah. She can walk you through all the symbols that Jasmine explained to her. Cross-reference her interpretations with whatever expert analysis you can find online – without actually talking to anyone. We need to keep this as quiet as possible.'

'No worries. I hate talking to people.'

'And they hate talking to you,' Sarah added.

Garcia grumbled under his breath. 'I can't believe I saved your life. What was I thinking?'

'Probably: look! An unconscious female! Here's my chance to make out with her before she wakes up!'

McNutt laughed. So did the others.

The only one who didn't laugh was Garcia.

Sarah turned to Cobb. 'And what about me?'

Cobb answered, 'We're going to comb through every other video that we shot. I want to know how these bastards got in and out of the cisterns. You can't open a manhole and drop in a few hundred pounds of explosives without being seen. We spent two days down there. I want to know what we missed.'

Sarah nodded in understanding. They had detected very few entry points during their rekky, and none offered the access required to deliver their supplies. That meant they had overlooked something. 'Alright. I'll meet you in the lounge – *after* you've showered.'

'Not before?' he teased.

'*After*,' she stressed again. 'Definitely *after*.'

Cobb smiled and turned his attention to Papineau, who had been uncharacteristically quiet during the briefing. 'Jean-Marc, I'd like you to—'

Papineau cut him. 'Sorry, Jack. I have my own leads to pursue.'

Cobb frowned. 'Such as?'

'I have colleagues who might be able to help us in a great number of ways. The explosives, the glow stick, the translation of the pictograph – I can cover all aspects of the investigation, but I can't do it from here. My connections must be made in person.'

'If you say so,' Cobb grunted.

When it came to Papineau, the rest of the team had grown somewhat accustomed to his eccentricities. They knew he was a curious creature who flitted in and out of their lives like a distant relative who only surfaced when the moment fit his needs. Occasionally he brought gifts and sometimes he offered guidance, but other than that, he played things so close to the vest that his agenda was practically indistinguishable from the fabric itself.

For Cobb, that was a major problem. He still knew far too little about the man who had presented them with such a captivating offer. He had entered into their arrangement with a hearty level of distrust, and thus far Papineau's actions and behavior had only served to provoke Cobb's suspicions.

'Can you at least tell us where you're going?' Cobb asked.

'The Orient,' Papineau lied. 'Which already says too much.'

His point was abundantly clear.

He wasn't going to provide a straight answer.

As tempted as Cobb was to call him on his bullshit – and he was *very* tempted after the long day he'd had – he ultimately decided to shrug it off. In his mind, it wasn't the time or place to create disharmony on his team.

Not with so much at stake.

Instead, he decided to bring the team together.

Cobb cleared his throat. 'As you know, I'm not one for making speeches, but I want to remind each of you that we're working toward a common goal here. We might be approaching it from different angles, but it's still a common goal. So if you find anything – and I do mean *anything* – that may help one of your teammates in his or her search, then I want you to voice it immediately. Not later, not tomorrow, and certainly not next week. I want you to speak up as soon as you possibly can because one of our friends is in danger and it's up to us to bring her home.'

37

Kamal stared at the lavish home of Hassan and swallowed hard. Of the eight men who had been sent after Sarah, only Kamal and the lookout he had assigned to the boiler room had survived the cisterns. Despite the staggering amount of bloodshed that occurred in the tunnels, both men realized that their biggest threat still lay ahead.

They had yet to face their boss.

Nothing that day had gone as Kamal had intended. Tarek and five others were dead, and their target had eluded them. Worse still, an entire city block of Hassan's territory had been utterly demolished, and Kamal had no idea who was responsible.

He would be punished for his failures.

He was sure of that.

For a fleeting instant, Kamal considered running away. He wondered how far he could get before dawn and how long it would be before Hassan placed a bounty on his head. In the end, it didn't matter. Hassan *would* demand blood, and there were few places Kamal could hide for any length of time. He was way too large and too well known to hide anywhere in Egypt, and if Hassan turned the whole underworld against him with a promise of riches, he would have to leave the hemisphere.

No, running away wouldn't solve his problems; it would only make them worse.

So he climbed the stairs to meet his fate.

Hassan's bodyguard Awad answered the door. He smiled wide when he saw Kamal and the other henchman on the porch. It wasn't a friendly greeting. It was excitement over what was to come. Awad didn't want to miss Kamal's explanation of what had happened in the city – or the consequences that would follow.

Without saying a word, Awad led them into the house.

As Kamal passed the foyer mural, he glanced at the image of the treasure thief who had found mercy through admitting his crimes. When his trusted servant had wronged him, Pharaoh Ramses had granted the misguided craftsman a reprieve. Kamal wondered if Hassan would be so forgiving or if he would live up to his fiery reputation.

Kamal would find out soon enough.

As he stepped into Hassan's office, his eye was drawn to the center of his boss's desk. The gleaming Desert Eagle .50 was still there, loaded and ready to be fired.

Hassan looked up at him from across the room. His eyes were fiery with rage. The veins in his neck bulged, as if ready to erupt. 'Sit down.'

The words were growled more than they were spoken.

Kamal and the lookout did as they were told. They dared not speak until spoken to, but as the silence drew out, they began to second-guess their decision. Finally, after the quietest minute of their lives, Hassan vented his anger.

'A whole city block – *gone*! Police and soldiers everywhere! The eyes of the world upon us! Do you realize how much this will cost me?'

The loss of life was of little interest to Hassan. He was more concerned with the financial considerations of the tragedy. It was hard to collect from dead tenants.

Hassan slammed his fist down onto his desk. 'I gave you and your boyfriend six men to find the girl! More than enough to bring her back to me! Instead, you destroy my city and return with nothing. At best, your actions are incompetent. At worst, they reek of defiance. Is that what this is, a mutiny?'

Kamal knew Hassan was addressing him and only him. Hassan had given him the responsibility to find Dade's friend, and he alone was to answer for the calamity. Unfortunately, the lookout – who had never met Hassan before today – ignored the chain of command and charged in with a defense of their actions.

'I swear, it was not our fault,' he pleaded. 'We did everything we could. There were others protecting the girl. At least—'

All it took was a glance from Hassan for his bodyguard to spring into action. Awad grabbed the unsuspecting lookout from behind, forced his head back, and pried his jaw open. Before the lookout could say a word, Awad pulled a small stiletto from his belt and severed the lookout's tongue from the base of his mouth. Not wanting to spill any blood in Hassan's meticulous office, Awad left the meaty hunk of muscle in the victim's mouth and then pulled his forearm under the lookout's chin, forcing his jaw shut.

Hassan barely blinked. 'Don't say another word.'

The henchman struggled for breath as Awad kept his grip tight. It wasn't the chokehold that was cutting off his air; it was the lifeless tongue in his mouth and the blood draining down his throat. As his lungs began to fill, he strained against the grasp of the muscular bodyguard, slowly but surely drowning in his own bodily fluids.

Despite the distraction, Hassan continued his questioning. 'Is this true? There was someone protecting the girl?'

They were the most unsettling questions Kamal had ever heard. Not because of the words themselves, but because of the coldness of the man asking them. Hassan carried on like there was nothing else happening – as if they were alone in his office and there wasn't a man fighting for his life in the chair next to Kamal. Even more chilling, the tortured agony seemed to have a calming effect on Hassan.

Kamal nodded. 'She was not alone. Two of our men were shot. The others were disemboweled. There is simply no way she could have killed that many men in that many places in that short a time. Not by herself. Only a demon could do such a thing.'

There was something about his description that gave Hassan a moment of pause. Kamal could see the concern on his face. Hassan's eyes shifted uneasily, as if the destruction of his city made perfect sense. His lip curled in thought.

Hassan glanced at Awad as he spoke. 'Did you see these other forces?'

Kamal didn't know what was going on, but he knew better than to delay his response. 'No. I only saw the bodies they left behind.'

'Do you believe that they survived the explosion?'

Kamal couldn't see how anyone could have survived the blast, but he also didn't believe it was a suicide mission. It stood to reason that those who triggered the explosion were well clear of the area before it went off.

Kamal swallowed hard. 'I do.'

Hassan rocked back in his chair. He said nothing as he contemplated his next move. After a few moments of silence, he leaned forward and delivered his order. 'Find them. The girl and her guardians. Bring them to me, dead or alive.'

'Yes, sir. Of course, sir.'

'Take whomever you need, whatever you need. But do not fail me again.'

Kamal nodded. 'I won't, sir. I promise.'

'Now leave me,' he said with a wave of his hand. Then he turned his gaze to the lifeless body in the other chair. 'And take him with you.'

*   *   *

The forward lounge of the yacht was designed for entertainment. It included a well-stocked bar and a selection of comfortable couches and chairs from which the passengers could take in the scenery. A semicircle of floor-to-ceiling windows offered sweeping views of the sea or the current port of call. When there was little to see – moonless nights on the open ocean can result in a stunningly blank panorama – the space could be converted into a de facto theater room. With the touch of a button, a massive flat-screen television could be dropped from a hidden compartment in the ceiling.

Like everything else on the boat, the design was meticulous.

No expense was spared.

While it would be several more hours before Garcia could determine if there was any recoverable data on Jasmine and Sarah's flashlights, he had been able to access the footage from the other hard drives immediately. As Cobb lowered the screen in order to view the recordings that he and McNutt had made in the tunnels, Sarah stared vacantly through the glass walls. It was a look Cobb had seen before.

He didn't need to ask her what was wrong.

He already knew what she was thinking.

'Now's as good a time as any, don't you think?'

It took Sarah a moment to realize that Cobb had spoken at all, much less that he had been addressing her. She turned from the vista of the marina and the open water beyond and saw Cobb linking one of Garcia's laptops to the colossal monitor.

'I'm sorry. What was that?'

Cobb glanced over his shoulder. 'I said, we might as well talk about it now.'

Sarah furrowed her brow. 'Talk about what?'

'What do you think?'

Sarah knew there was no use in playing coy. Cobb had a way of knowing exactly what was on her mind. It was a connection she had never experienced before; and one she didn't yet know how to handle.

She nodded knowingly. 'You're talking about Simon.'

Cobb said nothing. He merely waited for her to continue.

She pursed her lips. 'Trust me, I've been thinking about it all night, and I honestly don't know what to say. Why would the goons who chased Simon follow us into the tunnels?' She shook her head. 'I don't believe that Simon set us up. Why would he do that? We've got nothing to do with this place. We're not on anyone's shit list.'

'You're right,' Cobb said. 'We have nothing to do with this place, but *you* do.'

Sarah flinched. 'You think they were coming after *me*?'

He shrugged. 'Maybe, maybe not. But if they hadn't been chasing us, we would have had a much better chance of noticing the bombers. Instead, we were so preoccupied with the Bigfoot twins that we lost Jasmine in the chaos.'

He let the idea sink in.

Sarah often projected a 'me against the world' attitude, but

Cobb saw through her tough exterior. He knew the thought of putting other lives at risk would get to her. It was an ember that would slowly smolder in her consciousness.

When the time was right, she would know how to use it.

38

Monday, November 3
Castillo, California
(22 miles north of San Diego)

Papineau felt exhausted after the intercontinental flight, a combination of the distance he had traveled and the anxiety he felt anytime he was summoned to California. Though he liked the weather and loved the wine, this was one of his least favorite places on earth.

And all because of one man.

Papineau drove to the edge of his employer's estate and placed his palm on the security scanner mounted next to the driveway. Once his identity was confirmed, he heard the click of the lock, followed by the whir of the electric motor as it reeled in the barricade. Ten seconds later the obstacle had all but vanished, neatly tucked away behind the stone wall that encircled the property.

Once past the gate, which shut behind him with a loud *thunk*, Papineau drove up the long, winding driveway through the seemingly laser-manicured landscape of the scenic estate. He left the window open so the breeze from the Pacific Ocean could reach him. It was strange how it smelled different from the Atlantic. Much fresher, he knew, because of the cleansing Santa Ana winds that blew through the property.

As usual, Papineau found himself holding his breath when the car neared the crest of the drive. Rising into view was his employer's principal residence – a reinforced castle that looked as if it were erupting from the hilltop itself. It was rooted there, looking both ancient and modern, affording a clear view for miles in every direction.

The smooth asphalt road gave way to painstakingly installed cobblestones that massaged the car's tires rather than jolting them. Papineau parked alongside the Koenigsegg, McLaren, Pagani, and Bugatti sports cars, which were lined up face-out along the curved drive. They were an intimidating sight – like a steel quartet of multi-million-dollar predators, ready to attack the scenic bluffs of southern California.

Papineau emerged from his rented town car and took a moment to admire the blue water of the Pacific as the gentle breeze cooled his face. Given the altitude and location, the air was still temperate, even in the autumn days of November. The only clouds were wispy, white ones, and the sky vied with the sea for the more pleasing blue.

As he approached the entrance, the most visually stunning woman he had ever seen opened the door. He smiled as he gazed upon her exquisite Brazilian features. Her deep, dark eyes seemed to twinkle in the sunlight. Her raven hair shimmered. Her toned, five-foot, nine-inch frame, the symmetry of her face, her seductive grin: it was all perfect. Papineau had seen men completely lose themselves at the mere sight of her.

'Good morning, Isabella,' he said.

'Good morning, monsieur,' she replied softly. She stared longingly at the world beyond the doorway, as if she had just been given a glimpse of something she could never have again.

Papineau walked by her, saddened, as the door swung shut behind him. He had seen her change from a lively and curious young woman into the broken hostess that she was now. Her beauty hadn't faded, but it was merely a shell.

Her husband had drained the life from her, as he had his previous three wives. He had never laid a hand on her in anger, but he had defeated her spirit just the same. He was not cruel, but he was unyielding. His intensity, his energy, his precise demands – and also his impetuous, vague requests – made this the castle of an ogre, not a king.

Remarkably, the house had more spirit than the woman who called it home. It had been built from deeply hued cuts of granites, quarried from all across the country and shipped at tremendous expense. The artwork that hung from its walls was tasteful yet bold, as was the handcrafted furniture that littered the rooms. Staggered skylights across the breadth of the ceiling allowed natural light to flood every corner of the structure.

Papineau glanced stealthily behind him. Isabella was gone, as if she had never existed. The Frenchman proceeded to the heavy oak door of what the owner laughingly called his study. In actuality, it was the largest room in the house. It stood nearly three stories high and was designed to be the envy of the world's greatest designers and architects – not to mention other billionaires.

The outer walls were lined with custom bookcases that extended from the floor to the rafters, all filled with hundreds of volumes covering every era of literature. Each piece in the collection was a first edition – including the Gutenberg Bible – and none of them was less than a treasured specimen. The space was dotted with heavy tables that were covered with maps, parchments, books, and charting instruments. The research spanned the length of recorded history and considered every corner of the world. It was clear that an extensive search was underway, though the exact target of these efforts was a closely guarded secret.

Beyond the tables was a ten-foot-wide, circular slab of redwood that had been transformed into a sprawling desk. Its rough bark edges indicated that it had been shaved from the end of a massive timber. A chair in the center, accessed through a channel cut into the far side of the wood, allowed for nearly three hundred and sixty degrees of usable surface, nearly all of which was covered in documents.

Standing next to the desk was Papineau's employer.

A man named Maurice Copeland.

It was clear from his open-necked, cotton shirt and faded blue jeans that Copeland preferred comfort to fashion. Understandably so, as there was no one in his life that he felt the need to impress.

In his world, he was the alpha – the apex of the food chain.

He stared at Papineau with an expression that would pass for puzzlement in most men. In his case, the look signified annoyance.

'You ever hear of Sam Langford?' Copeland asked out of the blue.

'No, I haven't,' Papineau replied as he took a seat.

'He was the most feared fighter in the first two decades of the twentieth century,' Copeland explained. 'They called him "the Boston Terror". He was short, maybe five foot-seven, but he had long arms like a pair of untailored sleeves.'

Just like you, Papineau thought.

'He was ahead of his time,' Copeland continued, his voice

matching his bulldog face. 'He could fight inside, he could fight outside. He could fight lightweight, he could fight heavyweight. And once he hit you, you stayed hit. None of this "shake it off" crap. You couldn't hurt him either. *If* you somehow managed to land a shot, he just kept on coming like nothing happened. That guy was a freak of nature.'

Papineau was used to these lectures. If there was one thing Copeland loved as much as beautiful things, it was boxing. One look at him revealed that. Copeland had the crushed, altered features and hunkered-down bearing of a pugilist.

A hardheaded brawler, not a fancy-foot jabber.

His nose had been broken at least four times. His ears were just shy of being cauliflowered. His cheekbones looked flattened and weren't quite the same height. And his knuckles had been split to the point that his gnarled hands looked more like clubs.

Copeland had often said that he had fought his way out of the Bronx in New York City. He had started his battle in the ring, but he quickly realized that the managers made all the money. So he took the fight to them. When he discovered that managers kicked their payments up the ladder to the promoters, Copeland went after them as well. He kept fighting his way higher and higher, until there was no one left to challenge.

His early struggles had given him a glimpse of how the world worked. Business was like boxing: it wasn't the biggest guy, or the toughest guy, or even the smartest guy who won. In the end, it all came down to who wanted it more. Getting your hands dirty was inevitable; it was just part of the game.

Copeland balled his fists and threw a few jabs from behind his desk, ducking and weaving as he did. 'Langford fought almost four hundred times in twenty years. Towards the end of it, he was nearly blind and a shell of his former self, but he kept fighting until he couldn't see at all. Eventually, someone made the decision for him. Someone had the balls to sit him down and tell him that he was done.'

Papineau swallowed hard.

He suddenly grasped the metaphor.

Copeland was talking about him.

39

Nearly a decade earlier, Papineau had been a rising star in high society, a man positioning himself for greatness. He had already found success as an antiquities broker, and the wheeling and dealing had made him a wealthy man. Not super rich, but in the neighborhood. Looking for more, Papineau had used his money to consolidate several businesses in Europe, hoping to build an empire.

Copeland – a major player in his own right – admired him and appreciated his skills, but he sensed that the feeling wasn't mutual. He gave Papineau a single chance to prove his respect: an olive branch in the form of a partnership. When word returned that Papineau had not only refused his offer but had actually laughed at it, Copeland was outraged.

The insult stung, but his response would hurt much worse.

Copeland initiated a hostile takeover.

By the time Copeland was done, Papineau was all but ruined. His businesses had been picked clean, leaving him with little more than the suit on his back and a sullied reputation. It had taken Copeland less than a year to destroy everything that the Frenchman had spent his life creating, and all because of a slight.

Like so many others, Papineau had underestimated Copeland because of his battered appearance and his rough upbringing. It was a mistake he wouldn't make again. When the victor graciously offered him a middling position in his organization, Papineau took it, hoping to learn how Copeland had gotten the better of him and how to get revenge.

That was nine years ago.

Nine long years.

And he still hadn't found a weakness to exploit.

Copeland glared at him from behind his desk. 'Tell me, Jean-Marc, has our relationship run its course?'

'No, sir,' Papineau said with just the right amount of vigor. 'I don't believe we're finished. There's still plenty of work to be done.'

'I agree. But perhaps you're not the right man for the job.'

'Sir, I'm not quite sure what I've done—'

'What you've done?' he asked incredulously. '*What you've done* is increase our risk a thousand fold. *What you've done* has jeopardized our entire operation. *What you've done* has drawn the attention of every media outlet across the globe!'

He tossed a newspaper across the desk as he continued his rant. 'I read about your exploits on the front page of the local paper. It was right next to the weather report.' He rehashed the news in a mocking tone. 'Hmm, it's going to be eighty and clear tomorrow, and oh look, Jean-Marc and his band of idiots blew up half of Alexandria!'

Papineau could sense that this was just the beginning of Copeland's tirade, so he kept his mouth shut and prepared for the worst.

His boss did not disappoint.

'I have given you everything that you asked for. Not once have I questioned your requests. Guns, cars, houses, yachts – whatever it is that allows you to get the job done. All I ask in return is that you keep your team out of the spotlight. These people should know better than to destroy ancient layers of a city. Or, at the very least, they should have had the good sense to wait until after we've found what we're looking for!'

Copeland took a deep breath to control his anger.

'So,' he continued, 'since you put this team of misfits together, please enlighten me. What the hell were they thinking?'

Papineau defended his team. 'We had *nothing* to do with the explosion.'

Copeland looked at him curiously. 'You weren't exploring under the city?'

'Yes, we were there, but we weren't alone.'

Copeland considered the possibilities. 'The syndicates controlling Alexandria are fiercely protective of their territory. You should have been aware of that.'

'We were,' Papineau assured him, 'but this was something different. When we searched the tunnels, we found the bodies of several local thugs. They had been sliced to pieces, and my team had nothing to do with it. The explosion wasn't the result of a turf war. It was an attempt to make sure no one ever went down there again.'

Copeland pondered what he had been told. He couldn't care less about the bombs or the people who were killed in the neighborhood above; he was only interested in *why* the mysterious men had felt the need to bury the tunnels.

He leaned closer. 'What did you find beneath the streets?'

'A pictograph in a subterranean temple and a secret tunnel that led to the water. One of the walls was covered in carvings. We haven't studied the symbols yet because the digital files were damaged in the chaos, but we believe that they illustrate the evacuation of Alexander's tomb sometime in the fourth century.'

Copeland's face lit up. 'Evacuation to where?'

'We don't know. That's where the story ends.'

'Surely Ms Park has a theory. What does she say on the subject?'

'What does she have to say? Nothing! Absolutely nothing!'

Copeland raised an eyebrow. 'Why not?'

'Because the bombers abducted her.'

'Well, that sucks,' Copeland said with a laugh. 'I was wondering what got your knickers in a twist, and now I know.'

'Yes, now you know.'

Copeland stared at him. 'I have to admit, I'm not used to seeing so much backbone from you . . . I'm still trying to decide if I like it.'

'You're about to see more.'

'I can't wait.'

'In my opinion, Jasmine's abduction was completely avoidable. If my team had been properly prepared, none of this would have happened.'

'I completely agree.'

'No, I don't think you do.'

'Wait,' Copeland said. 'You're blaming me for this?'

Papineau glared at him but said nothing.

Copeland laughed. 'Don't stop now. Speak your mind.'

Papineau took a deep breath and considered what to do. Even though he had been given permission to speak freely, he was hesitant to voice his concerns. Still, he knew that mistakes had been made, and he couldn't afford to have them pinned on him. 'It would be easier for me to run my team without any more of your surprises.'

'Which surprises are you referring to?'

'Cobb introduced a map into the equation. Based on the details he provided, I have to assume that your efforts led to its acquisition from the Ulster Archives.'

Copeland nodded. 'Of course.'

'Where did they get it? And why was I left out of its procurement?'

Copeland leaned back in his chair. 'I'm a very busy man, Jean-Marc. I can't keep you in the loop on *everything*. Where would I find the time? As for the Archives, the map was sent to them by Dr Manjani a few months ago.'

Papineau gasped in disbelief. He knew that a group of archaeologists had gone missing in April and that their trip to Egypt had been led by a notable scholar named Cyril Manjani. But he was also aware that their camp had been found abandoned and that the entire team was presumed dead. Not one member had been heard from since.

Now Copeland was telling him that Manjani had survived.

Papineau didn't know where to begin.

'He's alive? How did he survive? And where has he been?' He shook his hands in the air, waving off his previous questions. There were more important things to consider. 'What is the connection between Manjani and Alexandria? I thought his expedition was lost in the desert.'

'Dr Manjani shares our interests. He was searching for the tomb of Alexander the Great, just like we are. As for the desert, I have no idea what led him there. I only know that he didn't find any answers buried in the sand. Given his failure, I was hoping your team could see something in his map that he himself had missed.'

Papineau needed more. 'You said he escaped. Escaped from what? What *did* he find in the desert?'

'I think it's more a case of what found him,' Copeland explained. 'He claims his team was slaughtered in the night. After that, he went into hiding, but not before sending the map to the Ulster Archives. From what I understand, he knows the curator.'

'Slaughtered?' Papineau growled. 'His team was slaughtered while looking for Alexander's tomb – the same thing that *my* team is looking for – and you chose not to tell me about it?'

Copeland's stare suddenly grew cold. 'Check your tone, Jean-Marc. They are not *your* team. They're *my* team. It's *my* money that they're spending and *my* money that they're trying to earn. You'd best remember your place!'

Papineau lowered his voice but continued to make his point. 'If there was a chance that we were walking into danger, you should have—'

Copeland cut him off. '*Danger?* Did you say *danger?* This isn't the Boy Scouts. We're not after merit badges. We're after treasure. Of course there's *danger.* I wouldn't be paying them millions of dollars if there wasn't *danger.*'

Papineau remained silent. He knew Copeland wasn't finished.

'If the attack in the desert is related to the attack under the city, I cannot be held responsible. No one could have known that one would lead to the other. After all, the two incidents took place hundreds of miles apart. Besides, that Marine of yours requested enough firepower to invade a small country. You're telling me that he couldn't defend himself against some local thugs?'

Papineau shook his head. 'The men who rigged the bombs were not local thugs. They were something more. I don't know what exactly, but something.'

'Well, find out!' Copeland demanded. 'I want answers, not problems.'

'Of course.'

Copeland stood, signaling the end of their conversation. 'In the meantime, if you need either of the missing historians to understand the symbols on the wall, you have my permission to search for Ms Park or Dr Manjani. However, if you can figure out the message on your own or you know of another expert who can step in and fill their void then their recovery is a total waste of time.'

He glared at Papineau to emphasize his final point. 'As you know, the only thing that matters to me is the tomb.'

40

Jasmine woke to the sharp burn of vomit as it bubbled from her stomach.

The tickle at the back of her throat was the only warning of the nasty fluid that would soon follow. It was all she could do to turn her head before she retched, her system trying to rid itself of the potent chemicals that had kept her unconscious for the last few hours. Her arms trembled and her body heaved as she purged until there was nothing left. She rolled onto her back, exhausted from the involuntary efforts.

Only then did she manage to open her eyes.

Though her thoughts were still fuzzy, she could immediately tell that she was no longer under the city. The tunnels had been dark and damp, the floors and walls made of gray stone and concrete. But this room – wherever it was – was bright and dry. Sunlight streamed in through small slits in the wall near the ceiling, illuminating the dirt floor and the rough, reddish-tan bricks that surrounded her. The small room was completely barren, with only a small break in the wall leading to a hallway beyond.

She closed her eyes again, trying to piece together anything that might help her determine how or where she had been moved. She remembered being attacked and struggling to resist, then succumbing to an overwhelming sensation of sleep. Her nausea and clouded mind told her that she hadn't simply given up; she had been drugged – though the initial dose hadn't knocked her out completely.

She remembered being jostled about in the back of a van and being pinned to the floor by one of her assailants. At some point they had abandoned the vehicle, she knew, because someone had pulled her from the cargo area and tossed her limp body over his shoulder. She recalled fleeting visions of a cramped bazaar and glimpses of alarmed faces as she was carried through the frenzied crowd. But no one intervened and no one seemed to care, as if this sort of thing was common in Alexandria.

But that wasn't the case at all.

In her semi-lucid state, Jasmine had actually missed the explosion. She had no way of knowing that the frantic patrons had much bigger things to worry about than a woman being toted through the masses.

For all they knew, she was being rescued, not kidnapped.

The bazaar had not only given her assailants cover from the satellites that were circling overhead, it had also camouflaged their escape on the ground. Their efforts blended in with the panicked retreat of the customers and shopkeepers. In the confusion, Jasmine had been whisked away from the city and delivered to the rendezvous point. After which, her kidnappers were relieved of duty.

Their job was to grab her.

Others would handle her interrogation.

Still reeling from the drugs and nausea, it took Jasmine several minutes to notice that her socks and shoes had been removed, leaving her feet bare. Not only that, her wrists had been bound by heavy metal cuffs connected by a long chain that ran through an eyebolt securely anchored into the floor. The shackles would allow her to stand, but her movement about the room would be restricted to a five-foot circle.

Jasmine could feel the sweat beading down her face as she pawed frantically at the sturdy clamps that encircled her wrists. As the severity of her situation continued to set in, panic and the sweltering heat of the room kept her from catching her breath. Perspiration soaked her skin and clothes as she desperately tried to slip her hands from their steel restraints. The moisture allowed the metal to slide an inch or two, but it wasn't nearly enough for Jasmine to escape. Each time she tried to pull her arms free, she succeeded only in chafing her skin even more.

When her efforts began to draw blood, she knew it was time to give up.

She would have to find another way.

Jasmine took a deep breath and steadied herself as best she could. She knew she could get through this. She just needed to keep calm and work through the situation, as with any other problem that she had overcome in recent months.

This self-confidence had not been present a year ago. Back then, real-world dangers would have left her paralyzed with fear. Despite working for a newspaper as a translator, her talents lay in research and language skills, not fieldwork. Of all the members of the team, she was the least suited for their missions.

But she had worked hard to narrow the gap.

She knew she could never possess the skills the others had honed over their years of service in the military, FBI, and CIA, but she was determined to eliminate any concern that she was holding them back. When Cobb had instructed her to learn the art of self-defense, she had immersed herself in the training. Day after day, session after session, she had studied the techniques of her sensei, building her skills until the movements became second nature.

To keep pace with the others, she had broadened her development to include lessons in other areas. Garcia had taught her advanced computer skills, and McNutt had been more than eager to help with weapons training. He took her through a crash course in everything from sub-compact pistols to shoulder-mounted rocket launchers. And yet it was Sarah's tutelage that would prove to be the most important.

As part of her 'survival training', Sarah had taught Jasmine a few tricks of the trade. She had started with the basics, explaining how best to blend into a crowd and hide in plain sight, then worked her way up to more complicated endeavors such as avoiding surveillance cameras and circumventing standard security measures such as window alarms and motion detectors.

At Jasmine's urging, Sarah had even taught her how to pick locks.

Now, as Jasmine studied the manacles that bound her hands, she could sense her fortune changing. She had yet to master the art of tumbler locks like those found in homes and cars, but handcuffs were a different story. Since handcuffs were designed so that a single key could open many models and sizes, the lock was much simpler. All she needed was something sturdy and small enough to trip the internal mechanism.

Jasmine scoured the floor for something that could be used as a makeshift lock pick. Seeing only dust and dirt, she checked the pockets of her pants. Then she ran her fingers through her hair, hoping against all logic that she would find a random bobby pin, even though she seldom wore them. Unsurprisingly, there were none to be found.

Then the answer suddenly came to her.

In an instant she had unfastened her belt and pulled it from the loops around her waist. She rolled the buckle in her hands, pondering its use. The prong of the clasp was skinny and stiff, with a slight curve at the end. As far as improvised tools were concerned, this was as good as it got.

Jasmine was confident that she could make it work.

She slipped the bent end of the prong into one of the cuffs and slowly rotated the pick around the edge of the keyhole, searching for resistance. Normally, the single bit of the barrel key would release the bite of the receiver, but the belt buckle would work just as well. All she had to do was find the right pressure point.

As she felt the prong catch on something, she adjusted the angle of entry and pressed hard. With a simple *click* the rounded steel popped loose from her wrist, its well-oiled hinge releasing her from its grasp. Jasmine smiled as she repeated the process on the second cuff. A few seconds later, it too popped open with the same satisfying *click*.

Jasmine beamed as she tossed the cuffs to the floor. She had freed herself. Yes, the confidence and the skills had been imparted by her teammates, but they weren't around to see her through. She had done this all on her own, without anyone there to help.

She swelled with pride but kept her emotions in check.

Just because her hands were free didn't mean that she was.

Jasmine silently rose to her feet. Her first steps were clumsy, but her coordination began to return as she walked to the gap in the wall that led to the hallway. There she listened for any signs of her captors. Hearing nothing, she peeked around the corner to the other side. She could see an adjacent room, only slightly larger than the space where she had been held.

But it too was empty.

With nothing else to investigate, she crept toward the wooden door at the far end of the adjoining room. She pressed her ear to the warm wood and hoped to hear something – *anything* – that would help her pinpoint her location.

Instead, there was only silence.

Testing the handle, she was surprised to find the door unlocked. Combined with the empty rooms, Jasmine could only reach one conclusion: whoever was guarding her was waiting just beyond the door.

She looked down, wondering how far and how fast her bare feet could carry her. She breathed deeply, summoning her courage and clearing the last few cobwebs from her mind. Once she stepped through the door, she wouldn't stop sprinting until she had reached safety. To survive, she only needed to outrun her captors.

Jasmine nodded to herself.

It was now or never.

41

Under the cover of darkness, Cobb piloted their yacht into the Mediterranean Sea. He knew that the devastation in Alexandria would draw the attention of the world media. Even worse, every nation with reconnaissance satellites under their control would have them focused on the region, looking for anything suspicious. Many of these satellites had sophisticated optics capable of reading the numbers off license plates from two hundred miles above the ground. Tracking something as large as a human would be easy.

All they needed was a target.

Cobb was determined to avoid the cameras circling overhead. He knew that every harbor and marina would be scrutinized, with the identity of each boat being compared to the registry from its home country. Vessels flying foreign flags would be of particular interest to the Egyptian government. As a port city, Alexandria's coastal waters offered the same access to terrorists as they did to tourists, and even though no one would be looking for his team specifically, most of them were listed in military databases.

He knew any of their faces could trigger a red flag.

Spotting all of them together would be cause for alarm.

So they opted for international waters.

He was by no means at ease, but at least he knew that no one could take them by surprise. They could see ten miles in every direction, and the radar could warn them of approaching aircraft and other ships before they even came into view. The move had cut off their access to the city, but it had also cut off the city's access to them. And until they figured out their next step, the isolation was worth the inconvenience.

Once the yacht was anchored, Cobb headed below deck to the forward lounge. He brought a tray of snacks with him. His team had been working non-stop and he sensed that they needed a break. 'Any luck?'

Sarah looked up from her stack of notes, her expression conveying her frustration before she even spoke. 'Not yet. But I'm still looking.'

Cobb nodded and set the tray of food on one of the tables. Other than a few bathroom breaks, she hadn't left the room in over a day. She had spent most of her time studying the video footage that Garcia had pulled from Cobb and McNutt's flashlights, with an emphasis on the mysterious men from the tunnels. She studied their clothes, their movements, their methods, and every other noticeable detail, hoping to match their wardrobe or tactics to other known forces in the Middle East and beyond.

So far, she had come up empty.

'Here,' Cobb said as he tossed her an orange. 'Eat something.'

She nodded her appreciation. 'Thanks.'

A moment later, McNutt bounded into the room. His bulging eyes, disheveled hair, and breathlessness told the others that he too hadn't gotten much rest. It was also clear that a massive dose of caffeine was now pushing him through the fatigue.

Cobb stared at him, concerned. 'Are you okay?'

'I smell food,' McNutt shot back. He lunged for the tray and grabbed a sandwich that Cobb had actually made for himself. A look of pure pleasure spread across McNutt's face as he stuffed it into his mouth. 'Oh, man, this is good. What is this?'

'Mine,' Cobb said.

McNutt wiped his mouth with his forearm. 'Well, you did a *wonderful* job. It's really, really good. Do I taste mustard?'

Sarah shook her head in disgust. 'You know, there's a whole pantry of things to eat. Not to mention a stocked refrigerator. You don't need to barge in here and take ours.'

McNutt took his next bite. 'I didn't come for the food. That was just a bonus. I came here because I think I can help you.'

She eyed him suspiciously. 'Help me with what?'

He plopped down on the couch across from Sarah. 'I've got a lead on the explosives. Well, kind of . . . I mean, maybe.'

She didn't have time for games. 'What the hell does that mean?'

Cobb had faith in McNutt's abilities, but he understood Sarah's frustration. The Marine's delivery needed some work. 'Josh, what are you talking about?'

McNutt could sense their annoyance. This wasn't the time to be ambiguous. Too much was at stake. 'I can almost guarantee that the Semtex was made in the Czech Republic, at a company called Explosia.'

'*Explosia?*' she scoffed. 'You're making that up.'

'I swear I'm not,' he assured her as he continued to eat. 'That's the actual name of the company. It's located in Semtín, a suburb of Pardubice in the Czech Republic. They invented the compound in Semtín – that's where Semtex gets its name – and they're still the world's leading manufacturer of the stuff. They make at least a half-dozen different varieties, and there's no shortage of buyers.'

Cobb knew that explosives were often marked with unique

chemical or powdered metal tags that labeled specific batches. These *taggants*, as they were called, were like encoded messages that identified the origin and purchaser of the material. If they could determine the taggant, then all they needed was the manufacturer's paperwork. They could simply compare the marker that had been detected to the entries on their master list, and that would give them the name of the buyer.

Cobb cursed himself for not taking a sample of the compound when he had a chance. 'If we can get you a forensic report, can you trace the signature?'

'Probably not,' McNutt answered. 'But that's okay. We don't need to go through all of that.'

'Why can't you trace it?' Sarah asked.

'And why don't we need that information?' Cobb added.

McNutt answered Sarah's question first. 'You probably won't get a trace because taggants weren't mandatory in Semtex until recently. And even then, the regulations only apply to *new* Semtex. There are still warehouses full of older, unmarked Semtex that has yet to be sold.'

He turned toward Cobb. 'The reason it doesn't matter is because the explosive is only part of the equation.'

Cobb didn't understand. 'How so?'

'Well, when I learned that you can't trace Semtex, I looked for something else that might help us.' He opened the folder he had brought with him and held up a picture of a detonator attached to a bomb pack. 'And I found this.'

Cobb recognized the image. It was a close-up shot of the timer used to synchronize the explosions in the cisterns.

McNutt didn't wait for questions. 'It may look like an ordinary digital counter, but it's not. It's one of a kind. It's made in Tunisia by a company named Mecanav. They make ships, of all things. This sucker actually belongs in the instrument panel of a high-end marine display.'

Sarah tried to connect the dots. 'I don't get it. Why is a Tunisian boat timer being used to detonate explosives?'

McNutt smiled. 'Convenience.'

He pulled out a map of Northern Africa and pointed at the small country of Tunisia, which sat at the tip of the northern coast. He ran his finger south into Libya.

'Remember Muammar al-Gaddafi – the whack job who ruled Libya for, like, forty years? Under his leadership, Libya became Explosia's biggest and most-important client. The Semtex that they received was technically the property of the Libyan Army, but most of it ended up on the black market.'

Cobb needed specifics. 'How much are we talking about?'

'A scary amount,' McNutt replied. 'At least seven hundred tons. And that might be a conservative estimate. Some experts put that figure at well over a thousand.'

Cobb groaned. For Sarah's benefit, he put the number into perspective. 'Remember the Lockerbie bombing in 1988? A few ounces took out an entire airplane.'

Sarah was familiar with the incident in Scotland, having studied it extensively during her training with the CIA. She knew about the damage not only to the plane, but also to the two hundred and fifty-nine people who had lost their lives.

McNutt didn't let her linger on the past. 'Libya is a hotbed for the Semtex market, but it doesn't have the manufacturing base to supply the rest of the components needed to construct a bomb. The nearest source of reliable electronics is Tunisia, their neighbor to the north. Namely: Mecanav. Entire truckloads of these timers have disappeared as they made their way from the company's assembly plant to the shipyards. They almost always turn up on the streets of Tripoli or Benghazi.'

McNutt tapped the picture of the timer to reinforce his next point. 'Forget about the tomb, this is where the real money is. You could buy an entire boat for the same price that just a few of these timers go for on the black market.'

Cobb finally had the whole picture. It might have taken McNutt a few minutes to get there, but it was worth the wait. The Libyan border was less than three hundred and fifty miles from Alexandria – close enough for a team to get in and out in less than a day. It meant that they could narrow their investigation.

'Sarah—'

She cut him off. 'I can limit the parameters of my search. I'll focus on groups operating out of Libya, specifically those who have a track record with explosives.'

'Well-financed groups,' Cobb added. 'If the timers are that expensive, there's got to be some big money supporting their efforts. The way they blanketed the whole network of cisterns, they certainly weren't worried about the cost.'

Sarah grabbed the laptop she had been using to pull up research material and attacked it with renewed vigor.

Though it was only a minor breakthrough, Cobb felt the need to compliment McNutt. 'Nice job, Marine. Well worth the price of a sandwich.'

McNutt smiled and burped. 'Thanks, chief.'

42

Garcia raced down from the command center as Cobb and McNutt talked and Sarah pounded away on her keyboard. 'Do you mind if I interrupt?'

Sarah shouted, 'Yes!' as Cobb said, 'No.'

Cobb grinned. 'Did you find something?'

Garcia tossed him the used glow stick. 'I found the distributor.'

Cobb rolled the plastic cylinder in his hand. 'Let me guess: Libya?'

Garcia, unaware of the conversation that had prompted the response, was temporarily confused. He knew that Cobb wasn't prone to wild shots in the dark, but the comment seemed to be coming out of nowhere. 'Um, no. Not Libya.'

Sarah chimed in. 'Tunisia?'

McNutt couldn't resist. 'The Czech Republic?'

Garcia didn't know what was happening, but the expressions on their faces told him that they weren't joking. 'No and no. It was sold in Greece.'

'Greece?' Cobb echoed. 'Are they available in other countries?'

Garcia shook his head. 'Nope. They're manufactured in Piraeus, Greece, and the company only sells them domestically. No exports at all for tax reasons.'

Sarah cursed under her breath. 'Back to square one.'

Annoyed that someone had ruined his moment, McNutt hurled the rest of his sandwich at Garcia. 'Thanks a lot, Fernando.'

Garcia tried to catch it, but the sandwich separated in mid-flight, sending chunks of bread, cheese, and mustard-covered meat at him like shrapnel from a fragmentation grenade. All he could really do was try to protect his face.

'What the heck?' he screamed as he surveyed the damage to his vintage T-shirt. 'That was totally uncalled for.'

'And so was your update!' McNutt shouted back.

Cobb ignored their bickering and tried to make sense of the new development. Everything he had just learned about the nautical timers and the Semtex pointed to a force operating out of Libya. They hadn't yet determined if the men were affiliated with a larger group or if they were hired mercenaries, but their location was a good lead.

A lead that Garcia had just thrown into doubt.

Given the magnitude of the setback, Cobb needed more. 'How sure are you that the glow sticks came from Greece?'

'I'm ninety-nine percent positive,' Garcia replied as he peeled a slice of salami off of his chest. He knew better than to offer anything higher. In his world, nothing was an ironclad certainty. There was always a margin of error.

'But *not* one hundred?' Cobb asked.

Garcia sensed that Cobb wouldn't let it rest until he heard exactly how he had reached his conclusion. Unfortunately for Garcia, that meant their conversation was about to go in a very strange direction. 'Have you ever been to a rave?'

The typing stopped as Sarah cocked her head to the side. She honestly didn't know which was more amusing: Garcia's question or Cobb's reaction.

'A rave?' Cobb repeated.

The mere thought of it made McNutt laugh. 'Oh sure, Jack's

a regular on the rave scene. Trip-hop, acid house, reggae dub – he's into all that shit.'

Cobb had no idea what McNutt was talking about. It was like he was suddenly speaking in a foreign language. All Cobb knew about raves was what he had seen on television. 'You mean the all-night dance parties where blitzed teenagers act like zombies? No, Hector, I can't say that I have.'

'I'm not advocating the lifestyle,' Garcia said defensively. 'I just needed to know if you were familiar with the concept.'

'Yes, I know what they are. Why?'

Garcia knew he needed to make his point quickly before Cobb shut down the conversation. Still, he felt a little background information would help his cause.

'Raves,' he explained, 'started out as a way for kids to blow off steam. The physical exertion of a dance marathon was just innocent stress relief. The problem was that some people didn't know when to quit. When a few hours of dancing wasn't enough, they turned to pharmaceutical alternatives to help them mellow out or to keep the party going. Ecstasy, Crystal Meth, Special K, GHB – it was all being passed around like candy. These kids would wind up naked in the hospital, with absolutely no recollection of how they got there.'

McNutt sighed. 'God, I miss the nineties.'

Cobb smiled. 'So it was a great time for drug dealers. What's the point?'

Garcia continued. 'Besides drugs, the other common element at most raves was an abundance of glow sticks. People would attach them to their clothing or wave them through the air. I'm talking about maybe a thousand people all drawing shapes in the darkness. It's pretty cool when you see it sober. In a drug-fueled haze, the effect is mind-blowing.' He paused briefly. 'Or so I've heard.'

'Go on.'

Garcia looked back at Cobb. 'The only people who appreciated the light show more than the inebriated masses were the authorities. Particularly the DEA.'

Cobb scrunched his face in confusion. He couldn't figure out why the Drug Enforcement Agency had an interest in plastic lights. 'Why's that?'

'The biggest raves were thrown by the biggest narcotics distributors. Why waste time selling single hits on the street when they could sell five thousand hits overnight? The DEA knew that the problem was only getting bigger, but the nature of the enterprise left very few clues. These parties would be announced only an hour or two before they started, and all they left behind were overdose victims. Them, and a trampled field or filthy warehouse full of spent glow sticks.'

Cobb finally made the connection. 'Somewhere along the line, an agent got the idea to check the serial numbers of the glow sticks. If they could determine the manufacturer, they could track where the shipment had been delivered. And if they knew the point of sale, they could get the name of the buyer.'

Garcia nodded. 'You don't just walk in and buy ten thousand glow sticks off the shelf. You have to order them in advance, to make sure they're available on rave night. The party favors led the authorities to the masterminds. They've been keeping a logbook on every glow stick manufacturer ever since. They can tell every product, where it was made, by whom, and where it was delivered.'

He pointed to the plastic tube in Cobb's hand. 'Which is why

I can tell that this glow stick was made and sold in Greece. I'm sure of it.'

'Okay,' Cobb said, 'I'm convinced. The glow stick is from Greece, not Libya. We'll adjust our theories accordingly. Anything else?'

'Yes,' he said as he grabbed a paper towel from the sink and tried to clean the mustard from his T-shirt, 'I was finally able to salvage some of the footage from Jasmine's flashlight. Not everything, of course, but a pretty good chunk of it. We'll be able to access it soon.'

'How soon?' Sarah demanded.

He glanced at his watch. 'Another minute or two. I'm currently uploading the video to our network server. Once the process is done, we'll be able to view the footage on our televisions, our laptops, and even our phones. As long as you're on our encrypted network, you'll have access to the file.'

Cobb nodded his appreciation. Though they were working toward a common goal, each of them was focused on a different part of the investigation. Once the briefing was over, they could view the footage whenever and wherever they liked, without getting in each other's way or fighting over the remote control.

But that was later.

In the meantime, they would view the video together.

As a team.

43

Garcia tapped a few buttons on his digital tablet. A moment later, the footage from Jasmine's flashlight was streaming to the television.

Cobb, McNutt, and Sarah watched as he sped through the first portion of the video. They had been with Jasmine when she first entered the cisterns, and there was nothing in those images that they hadn't seen before. They were much more interested in what her flashlight had recorded after she crawled through the wall.

When Jasmine reached the reinforced tunnel on the screen, Garcia allowed the video to play at normal speed. The footage wasn't as smooth as the others. It was a rough, choppy assembly of the segments that Garcia was able to save. It looked more like an aged 8mm movie than a modern digital film.

But it met their basic needs.

Sarah saw glimpses of the pictograph. 'Those are the carvings we found.'

Jasmine's narration played over the images. Like the video, portions of the audio had been mangled as well. Her voice sounded as though it were coming from the wrong side of a bad telephone connection.

'I tried to double-check her comments; at least, the ones I could decipher,' Garcia said. 'But I had no luck at all.'

'Why not?' Cobb wondered.

'Because my keyboard has *letters*, not ancient Egyptian *symbols*. Try as I might, I couldn't figure out a way to type in "a face with horns next to a squiggly line".'

Eventually, the final panel of the pictograph came into view. They could see the depiction of the tunnel, the waiting boats, and the symbol of Alexander the Great. They listened to the brief exchange between Sarah and Jasmine that they had heard previously on Sarah's footage and watched as Sarah disappeared into the tunnel.

Once she was gone, Jasmine retraced her steps to the beginning of the wall. She scanned every inch of it, making sure to capture the images for posterity.

To her, it was the opportunity of a lifetime.

When she reached the final panel for a second time, the image froze on the screen. At first, Cobb and the others assumed that it was another glitch in her hard drive, but that wasn't the case at all. Garcia had stopped the video on purpose.

'Guys,' he warned, 'the rest is . . . it's hard to watch.'

Cobb nodded in understanding. 'Maybe so, but we need to see it.'

Garcia swallowed hard and restarted the footage.

On screen, Jasmine didn't have time to notice anything suspicious. There were no investigations of unknown noises, no calling out to mysterious shadows. One moment she was focused on the wall, and the next she was fighting off an attack.

At first glance, there was little to be gleaned from the frantic images on the screen. The footage showed little more than a panicked blur of movement as she reckoned with an unknown intruder. The muffled screams and agonized groans confirmed that she had been taken by force, and the haunting calm of her sudden silence left them wondering how badly she was injured when she was finally subdued.

A moment later, the video stopped abruptly.

Several seconds passed before anyone said a word.

'That's it,' Garcia whispered. 'There's nothing left to see.'

McNutt shook his head. 'Play it again.'

'No, don't,' Sarah pleaded, still feeling guilty for losing her teammate. 'We know what happened. I don't need to hear it again.'

But McNutt was insistent. 'Play it again. I think I saw something.'

Cobb knew better than to challenge a sniper on what he had or hadn't seen. 'Hector, you heard the man. Play it again.'

McNutt walked closer to the screen. 'Go to the part at the very end, right before the footage stops.'

Garcia rewound the video and played it again.

McNutt stepped even closer. 'Again.'

Garcia played it one more time.

'Again,' he demanded. 'This time in slow motion.'

Garcia adjusted the playback settings, and the footage ticked by slowly. Halfway through the segment, McNutt's hand shot forward and he pointed at the screen.

'Freeze it!' he shouted with glee. 'I told you I saw something!'

Garcia and the others leaned in, trying to see why McNutt was so excited. But all they could make out were patches of light and dark on the screen.

'Where?' Sarah asked.

McNutt pointed to the center of the screen. 'Right *there*.'

Cobb glanced at the blob of pixels, then at Sarah, who was scrunching her face in total confusion, then over to a squinting

Garcia. It was quite obvious that none of them was having any luck with the image. 'Josh, what are we trying to see?'

'A monkey man,' he said proudly.

Sarah rolled her eyes at the assertion. 'Monkey *shit*, maybe. But not—'

'I'm telling you, there's someone there!'

McNutt growled in frustration as he rumbled over to the corner of the lounge that she had been using as a workstation. He snatched a black marker off the table and rumbled back to the monitor. Then he drew directly onto the television with heavy black ink.

'Not the screen!' Garcia shouted a moment too late.

'Look here,' McNutt said as he outlined the blob. 'This is his *head* . . . This is his *neck* . . . And these are his *shoulders* . . . So all of you can suck it.'

He reinforced his point by circling the dark blob several times.

This time it was Sarah who glanced at Cobb for a second opinion. 'Am I the only one who can't see this guy? Because I'll be honest: I'm horrible at those Magic Eye puzzles. I stare and I stare, but I never can see the dog in the funny hat.'

'I *always* find the dog, but I can't see the guy,' Cobb admitted.

McNutt groaned as he looked around the room for art supplies. 'Does anyone have crayons or a bucket of paint?'

'Wait!' Garcia blurted. The mere thought of it made him nauseous. 'Before you do anything irreversible, let me try some digital magic. If we're lucky, I might be able to filter out some of the diffusion.'

'Speak in English,' McNutt demanded.

'I was,' Garcia assured him as he tapped on his tablet. 'I would have tried this earlier if our source material was a little bit clearer, but due to the missing sectors, I'm honestly not sure what my formatting palette will do to the image. It might make it better; it might make it worse.'

A few seconds later, they got their answer.

The borders of the image suddenly sharpened.

Sarah looked on in amazement. 'I'll be damned. The hillbilly was right.'

Cobb nodded. He could finally see it too.

A head. A neck. And a set of shoulders.

McNutt smiled in victory.

And then he suddenly stopped.

Instead of gloating, he leaned in and studied the pixels even closer, so close his nose was nearly touching the man on the screen. Then he backed away, spit on his hand, and tried to wipe the magic marker off the man's neck. The mixture of saliva and ink on the high-end television made Garcia start to dry-heave, but McNutt ignored the gagging and continued with the task at hand, much to the amusement of Sarah and Cobb.

'What are you doing?' Sarah asked.

'I see something else,' McNutt said.

She rolled her eyes. 'No, you don't.'

'Yes, I do,' he assured her as he kept spitting and wiping.

'Josh,' Cobb asked, 'what do you see?'

'Some kind of mark. Maybe a tattoo. Maybe a scar. I can't really tell because some idiot wrote on the screen. But it's definitely something funky.'

'Define *funky*.'

McNutt stepped back and pointed at the image. 'See for yourself.'

Cobb studied the unusual marking. It consisted of two

concentric circles supported by a pair of pillars that narrowed from their base. Unfortunately, it was a symbol that he had never seen before. 'Anyone know what it is?'

Sarah cocked her head to the side, wondering what to make of the image that was now clearly visible on the screen. 'It's too shiny to be a tattoo. I think it's a brand – like the ones they get in fraternities.'

'I meant the shape itself,' Cobb said.

'Oh,' she said as she looked closer. 'The outline reminds me of an old-fashioned keyhole. The kind that used skeleton keys.'

'I can see that,' Cobb admitted, although his gut sensed that wasn't right. It seemed more abstract. 'Hector? What about you?'

'Me?' Garcia said meekly. He slowly peeked to see if saliva was still visible on the screen. Once he realized it had been wiped away, he was able to focus on the image. 'I don't know. Maybe some sort of hieroglyph, like the ones from the wall. I can try to check it, but like I said, I don't know how to do that without sending it to an historian.'

His words hung in uncomfortable silence as the same thought entered their minds.

If Jasmine were here, she would know.

44

Jasmine opened the door of the hut and ran forward until she saw that there was nowhere to run to. There were no streets, no roads, no buildings, and no one waiting for her on the other side of the door. The scene was empty, without any signs of life, as if she had been dropped in the middle of nowhere and left to die. Confused by the development, her determined sprint quickly slowed to a perplexed, meandering stagger.

In every direction, all she could see was desert.

The sand scorched her feet as she tried to make sense of things. She knew that she couldn't continue walking much longer . . . at least not like this. Though the temperatures in the desert had dropped from the extremes of the summer, she would still need something to protect her feet. Now that she knew what she was facing, she needed to rethink her plan. Begrudgingly, she turned around and made her way back toward the relative safety of the simple hut.

Driven by curiosity, she paused only briefly at the doorway before walking around the corner of the building, enduring the scalding terrain under her feet for a few moments more as she investigated. Hoping that the rear of the structure would somehow offer some form of encouragement, what she saw had the exact opposite effect. Instead of salvation, she found faint tire tracks that led off into the distance.

She strained to see something on the horizon – anything that would signal civilization – but there was nothing to be found. No matter which direction she looked, the endless sea of sand stretched out in front of her. Under different circumstances, she would have found beauty in the unbroken vista of rolling dunes and piercing blue sky. But at that moment, she was struck by the horror of her predicament.

Jasmine didn't like her options. The men who had taken her would surely return to the shelter at some point in time, and although they had kept her alive so far, she really didn't want to be around to find out why they had abducted her. She knew she had the element of surprise on her side, but she doubted her ability to defend herself against a group of armed men. Besides, she had never taken a life. If it came to that, she wasn't sure if she could bring herself to do it.

On the other hand, she was well aware of the desert's ability to kill. It showed no mercy, especially to those who ventured into the void without the proper supplies: basics like water, sunscreen, and shoes. In her mind, they were all mandatory provisions to even consider such a journey, and yet after giving it some thought, the desert seemed to be a much better alternative than waiting for her abductors to return.

Who knew what they had in store for her?

Whatever it was, it certainly wasn't good.

To protect her feet on her desperate journey, she tore the sleeves from her shirt and fashioned them into crude moccasins. She knew her arms would fry under the intense rays of the sun, but at least her soles wouldn't blister. She could keep walking with sunburned shoulders; she couldn't stand on seared feet.

With her makeshift shoes, Jasmine was ready to head off into the unknown. She reasoned that the tire tracks led toward the nearest settlement, but she also knew that following that route would increase the risk of meeting her kidnappers. As such, she opted for the opposite direction, hoping it would lead her into the trading routes of desert travelers. It was a calculated risk, but one she was willing to take.

* * *

Jasmine walked for what seemed like days, but it was actually only a single afternoon. The relentless sun robbed her of hydration and energy, but she never lost hope. Even as each step grew more and more difficult, she continued to press on.

She told herself that if she wore through her sleeves-turned-shoes, she could rip strips from her shirt. When those were reduced to tatters, she would tear cloth from her pants. She would cross the desert in her underwear if she had to, but she would not give up.

She assured herself of that.

As she glanced at the sun, she noted that it would soon dip low enough to touch the horizon. She didn't know how long she had been walking, only that she had been traveling north the entire time. The setting sun to her left had told her that some time ago. Back then, she had hoped she might be able to reach the thoroughfares that ran along the coast if she did not encounter someone on her walk, but now she feared she would find neither. At its current rate of descent, she would only have the sun for another hour or so. Darkness would bring relief from the heat, but it would also signal the coming of a long, hard night in the open desert.

Even if she survived until dawn, she wasn't sure she could do this for another day.

Not without food, water, or divine intervention.

Her spirit waning, she took a moment to survey her surroundings in hopes of finding shelter for the night. Instead, she found something better. There in the distance, outlined against the setting sun, were three men on camelback. Mustering her last reserves of strength, Jasmine screamed at the top of her lungs. When the trio stopped, she waved her hands wildly above her head, hoping that the erratic pattern would draw their attention.

A moment later, she watched as the three travelers turned their camels and began racing toward her. Assuming they weren't figments of her imagination, they would reach her in a matter of minutes. And if they were real, Jasmine would be saved.

She was exhausted, but she had made it.

She dropped to her knees and wept.

* * *

The first man to reach Jasmine leaped from his camel and landed beside her with a soft thud. Without saying a word, he lifted her chin and pressed his canteen against her cracked lips. The liquid was gritty and brackish, but she swallowed without complaint.

She knew the water would save her life.

Once her thirst had been quenched, her savior pulled back the canteen and smiled. For a brief moment, Jasmine was struck by his teeth – or rather, the lack thereof. His mouth was almost completely empty.

'Is good?' he asked, hoping that she understood his English. She nodded and smiled back. 'Very good. Thank you.'

He smiled even wider. Then, for the benefit of the other riders, he spoke to them in their native language.

Jasmine listened intently, trying to decipher the sounds. After a few sentences, she was almost certain that he was speaking in a Berber language common throughout North Africa. She wasn't fluent in the dialect, but she could understand and speak enough to join in the conversation. She knew they were wondering if she could be moved.

'I'm okay,' she offered in their native tongue. 'I can walk.'

The others froze in surprise as their faces fell slack. Their response made it clear that they had never met an outsider who could understand their words. To them, it was as if she had somehow read their minds.

'I can speak a little,' she explained. 'My name is Jasmine.'

The man beamed and pointed to his chest. 'I speak, too,' he replied in the same broken English he had used before. 'I am Izri.' He stood, then helped Jasmine to her feet. 'You are lost?'

Jasmine shook her head. 'No. I was taken.'

She repeated the phrase in Berber to ensure that she had made herself clear. The concerned look on their faces told her that they understood. 'There is a house in the middle of the desert. I was held there.'

'Who?' Izri asked. 'Who take you?'

'I don't know,' she answered. 'I never saw them. But they took me in Alexandria and brought me here.'

Izri's eyes narrowed in confusion. 'Why they bring you here?'

'I don't know. I don't even know where "here" is.'

'You are in the desert.'

Jasmine smiled at the obvious insight and cut right to the point. 'I hate to trouble you, but can you take me to a phone? I need to call my friends. They must be worried sick.'

Izri smiled and nodded. 'Yes,' he said proudly. 'We can take you tomorrow. But tonight, you must rest.'

45

It had been more than forty-eight hours since Jasmine's abduction, and the uncertainty of her disappearance was beginning to take its toll on the team.

They needed to know who had taken her.

Or where. Or why.

So far, all they had to go on were the carvings of the pictograph and a single image of scarred flesh. At this rate, their investigation might stretch on for weeks, which was a guaranteed death sentence. Cobb knew they needed more, and they needed it now.

He turned toward Sarah. 'It's time to call Simon.'

She nodded in agreement. 'Maybe he can tell us about the brand. If we're lucky, it's part of a gang initiation for a local crew.'

Cobb shook his head. 'We're not telling him about the brand. And we're not telling him about the Semtex or the glow stick. That's all need-to-know, and right now, he doesn't qualify. Understood?'

'If you say so,' she replied tersely. 'But if we're not telling him about the things we've found, how are we going to use him?'

'We'll talk about it on the ride in.'

'Fine,' she said. 'I'll make the arrangements.'

Garcia pulled out a satellite phone and handed it to Sarah. 'Use this. It's encrypted and untraceable.'

As Sarah left the room to make the call, Cobb gave McNutt his marching orders. 'Reach out to your connections in North Africa. I mean everyone – civilian, military, and *other*. In fact, start with the others.'

McNutt knew that Cobb was referring to ex-soldiers and former members of the intelligence community who had come to embrace the shadier side of international relations. Contrary to what most people believed, not all conflicts could be boiled down to black and white. There's always a gray area in between. For those with the right connections, this gray area can be a great place to make a lot of money.

'I'll hit up every friendly mercenary this side of the Ganges,' McNutt replied. 'What am I trying to find out?'

'Find out who stands to gain from the explosion. Who bene-fits politically and economically? Get whatever you can: names, goals, bases of operations. You know the drill. If you have assets in the city, use them. Trade what we can confirm about the bombing for information about what might happen next – just don't let anyone know how we know what we know.'

'And if they need proof that I'm not making this up?'

'Use the footage we shot in the tunnels. Send them screen captures of the bombs if you have to. Just make sure they think that you got the pictures from someone else. I don't want anything being traced back to us.'

McNutt nodded enthusiastically.

'Be careful,' Cobb added. 'With the explosion so fresh, gath-ering intelligence on anything right now is going to be messy. Stay off the radar. And I mean way, way off.'

McNutt looked at Garcia and held out his hand. 'You have another one of those encrypted phones?'

'In the command center. There should be another one sitting on the chart table.'

McNutt looked back at Cobb as he backpedaled out of the room. 'I'll be above deck if you need me.'

As the only one left, Garcia was anxious to do his part. 'Jack, how can I help?'

'I need you to work on that symbol. We need to know if it's just a random piece of art or if it has a specific meaning. Check body art forums, image databases, and so on. Call Tom Hanks if that's what it takes. I saw him work this shit out in a movie. Just find out what that design means. Okay?'

Garcia smiled at Cobb's attempt at humor. 'Okay.'

'Hector, one more thing. If you figure out what it means, don't tell anyone but me. Not Jean-Marc, not Josh, and not Sarah. You tell me, and only me.' He paused. His look told Garcia that he wasn't joking. 'Nod if you follow what I'm saying.'

Garcia nodded slowly.

'Good.'

'Jack, I need to ask one more thing.'

'Go ahead.'

'Josh mentioned "friendly mercenaries". I've never heard that term before. Is that a real thing?'

Cobb smiled. 'It must be. You're looking at one.'

* * *

Cobb dropped the throttle and listened to the roar of the twin Mercury outboard motors. At a combined six hundred horse-power, the thrust of the engines sent the skiff rocketing across the water. Cobb stood at the helm and let the warm sea air wash over him.

He glanced at Sarah. 'What's wrong?'

It was hard for her to grasp that she had been in the speedboat before. Nothing looked familiar. She didn't recognize a single thing from her last ride. Of course, the last time she had ridden mainly on the floor, covered in her own foamy vomit and still reeling from the explosion. On this trip, her vantage point was considerably different.

'Nothing,' she answered. 'I'm just thinking about Garcia's mouth.'

He looked at her with a mix of surprise and confusion. 'Is there something you want to tell me?'

She laughed. 'Actually, it's the other way around. There's something you need to tell me.'

'What's that?'

'What good does it do to tell Simon only part of what we've learned? Why not give him the whole picture?'

Cobb nodded. He knew he owed her an explanation. 'I'm not saying we won't eventually get there, but we need to know a few more things before that happens. This conversation isn't about *telling* him anything. It's about asking what he already knows.'

'Knows about what?'

Cobb reached into his cargo pocket and pulled out an envelope. He handed it to Sarah without saying a word. She eagerly opened it and rifled through the photos inside.

'Garcia pulled those images from my flashlight,' he explained.

She could identify the man in the picture, but only because Cobb had already informed her of his presence in the tunnels. Otherwise, she never would have recognized the man who had chased her from the tavern. His face was that badly disfigured.

'Damn,' she said as she studied the image. 'They sliced him

up, then left him to die. This wasn't quick, and it was meant to be painful.'

'Yes,' Cobb agreed.

'So why was he tortured?'

'Better question – why was *he* following *us*?'

Sarah read between the lines.

This was why they were meeting with Dade.

'Let me see if I got this straight,' she said, trying to put the pieces together in her mind. 'The goons were following me because of Simon?'

Cobb shrugged but said nothing.

'Why would they think that I could lead them to Simon? Just because we met for a drink doesn't mean we were working together.'

'Well, it doesn't mean that you *weren't* working together,' he replied. 'Think about it. All they saw was you and Simon running away. It leaves a lot to the imagination.'

'Yeah, but—'

'Unless . . .'

'Unless what?'

'What makes you think that *we* were leading *them* to Simon? Given everything I know, I'd say there's a much better chance that Simon led *them* to *us*.'

Sarah stared at him. 'I don't believe that for a second.'

And yet Cobb could see the uncertainty welling up inside her. Her nostrils flared. Her breathing grew heavy. Her eyes flickered with the first hints of rage. Which was exactly what he was hoping for. If their meeting with Dade was going to work, he didn't want her to be protective of her longtime asset.

He needed her to be aggressive.

He needed her to be angry.

'Simon wouldn't do that,' she muttered. Her insistence was meant to convince herself more than Cobb. 'He'd never put me at risk.'

Her sense of betrayal was now on full alert. She couldn't imagine that Dade had set her up, but the possibility was hard to ignore.

Why did the goons follow us into the tunnels?

Was it to find Simon?

Or on behalf of Simon?

Suddenly, she was filled with doubt.

Cobb turned his head and fought the urge to smile.

This was the Sarah that he needed for their meeting.

The one determined to get the truth.

46

El Agami, Egypt
(17 miles west of Alexandria)

Simon Dade trudged through the white sand, searching the faces in the conservatively dressed crowd. Though many of the beaches on the Mediterranean were private, owned and monitored by the resorts that dotted the coast, El Agami beach was open to the public and governed by local law, which meant women were forced to adhere to the strict standards of dress common in this part of the world.

That meant more burkas than bikinis.

And less skin than an Amish wedding.

Dade shielded his eyes from the glare of the sun as he scanned in both directions. Sarah had told him to meet her there at 1 p.m. He checked his watch and noted that it was already a quarter after. It wasn't like Sarah to be late.

He was ready to loop back toward the buildings that lined the shore when his phone started to vibrate. He glanced down and saw a blocked number.

He lifted the phone to his ear. 'Sarah?'

'Simon,' she replied.

He smiled at the sound of her voice. 'I've been walking up and down the strand for fifteen minutes. Can you see me?'

'Of course I can see you.'

He spun in a circle, still searching. 'Where are you?'

'Stop spinning,' she demanded. 'Look out into the Med.'

Dade did as he was told. He could see dozens of boats bobbing in the waves, everything from kayaks to catamarans. In the center of them all was a speedboat, with Sarah standing on the bow.

He grinned at the sight. 'Where do you want to pick me up?'

'Right here. I know you know how to swim.'

Before Dade could reply, she disconnected the call.

He knew from her tone she wasn't joking.

Dade pulled off his shirt and wrapped it around his phone. For a moment he contemplated leaving them both on the shore, but the information stored in the device was too precious to be left behind. He would rather lose the names and numbers to water damage than risk them falling into the wrong hands.

He held his polo above the waves as he waded into the sea.

* * *

Cobb waited for Dade to pull himself onboard before he started the engines and steered the boat into open water, putting some distance between themselves and the surrounding vessels. Dade unwrapped his phone from his shirt and smiled. The bundle had been splashed a few times, but his phone appeared to be fine.

He looked up at Sarah. 'You know, there are easier ways to get me out of my clothes. You could've just asked.'

It was an attempt at humor.

It didn't work.

Sarah snatched the phone from his hand and flung it overboard.

Dade was so surprised he didn't know how to react. 'What the hell?'

She didn't smile. 'I had to make sure you were clean.'

He glanced at Cobb, then back at Sarah. 'Clean? Is that why you put me through all of that – because you think I'm wearing a wire?'

Sarah ignored the query. She was there to ask questions, not answer them. 'Who were the two men that chased us through the city?'

'The two men? Do you mean last week?'

'Of course I mean last week. Why, do you get chased through the city a lot?'

'Not a lot,' he joked, 'but—'

'Who are they?' she demanded.

'Trust me,' he said, trying to keep his cool, 'they have nothing to do with either one of you. It's just a little problem I'm having.'

'Really? They have nothing to do with us, huh?' Spittle flew from her mouth as she vented her frustration. 'If that's the case, how do you explain this?'

She grabbed the photo of Tarek and thrust it toward Dade, narrowly missing his face by inches. He forced a smile and took a step back to focus on the image. Then she watched his eyes widen in fascination as he studied the mutilated corpse of the goon. In the photo, Tarek looked like he had been dropped into a food processor.

'I've seen him look better,' Dade admitted.

Then, as he took the time to think things through, his cool demeanor started to melt in the hot Egyptian sun. First he looked at the photo, then he glanced over at Cobb, who stared at him without a hint of amusement on his face, then back to the picture of his adversary. As he did, beads of sweat pooled on his upper lip.

Suddenly, he realized how far they were from shore.

'Wait,' Dade demanded. 'How did you get this? Did you . . .?'

Sarah let the question linger. If he was willing to believe that she or Cobb had killed the goon, she wasn't going to correct him.

At least not yet.

'That's not important,' she said as she handed the photo to Cobb. 'Right now, you need to explain what you've gotten us into.'

'Me?'

'Yeah, you.' She was tired of Dade's evasive responses. She needed answers, and she was willing to do whatever was necessary to get them.

She lifted her shirt and pulled her Glock 19 from her waistband. 'The only thing that connects him to me is *you*. So you see my problem – if someone sent him after me, there's only one person it could be.'

Dade fell silent again.

To drive home her impatience, she aimed the gun at Dade. 'Simon, I swear to God I'm not bluffing. One more chance before I get pissed: what the hell is going on?'

Dade took a deep breath. 'His name is Farouk Tarek. He works – I mean, *worked* – for a local gangster named Hassan. Trust me, Hassan is bad news. He thinks he's the King of Alexandria, and everyone else is his pawn.'

'Including you?' she asked.

Dade closed his eyes and slicked back his wet hair. 'Yeah, I used to work for him. I didn't like it, but he gave me no choice.'

'Doing what?' she asked.

'I was his security consultant. Not personal security, mind

you. I wasn't willing to protect that bastard. I simply showed him how to get past everyone else's security. I explained the blind spots, the workarounds, everything he needed to avoid detection.'

'What was he targeting?'

'Banks, businesses, ritzy homes – anywhere that might have hoards of cash or valuables.' Dade glanced away. 'You have to understand: it was my only way out of a bad situation. When you owe money to the wrong people, they don't just tax you, they *own* you. You do whatever they want, or you don't wake up in the morning.'

'And Hassan is the wrong person to owe?'

Dade nodded. 'One of the worst. But he gave me a choice: he'd forgive my debt in exchange for doing what I'm good at. I figured most of the stuff was insured anyway, and a clean in-and-out is much better than a messy smash-and-grab. I know they weren't victimless crimes, but at least my way kept people from getting hurt.'

'Except it didn't, right?' She had been around enough criminals in her life to know that something invariably went wrong. 'Tell me what happened.'

Dade glanced away again. 'There was this Saudi sheik. He had a big, extravagant house with minimal security. We knew that he and his bodyguards were leaving the country for a few days, so we timed our break-in for the first night. I figured we'd clean him out in a couple of hours, and he'd never know what hit him.'

'Let me guess: he left a guard behind.'

'Worse,' Dade answered. 'When the goons broke in, they found three housekeepers and a gardener. Normally they would have been staying in the servants' quarters out back, but I guess they decided to pamper themselves in the mansion for a couple of days while the sheik was away. They weren't a threat, but Hassan's men didn't hesitate. They just gunned them down and started packing up the loot.'

'And?' she demanded.

'And what?'

'What does that have to do with me?'

'A week after the massacre, the police received a recording from a security camera mounted outside the property. It showed two men – both employees of Hassan – pulling up to the house in a van and leaving a couple of hours later. It wasn't enough to get Hassan arrested, but it was enough to rattle his cage.'

Sarah worked out the rest on her own. 'It was you, wasn't it? You sent the video to the police. You couldn't let them get away with murder, and you thought the heat it brought would force Hassan to stop.'

'That's what I'd hoped,' Dade admitted. 'But somehow he figured out that I had set him up, and I've been running from him ever since.'

Sarah lowered her weapon. 'You went from being one of his biggest assets to being his biggest liability. That's why he sent the goons to kill you.'

Dade shook his head. 'Killing isn't enough for them. They could have done that to me on the street. No, Hassan wants to catch me alive so he can watch me suffer.'

47

Dade couldn't stop thinking about the image of Tarek. It would stay with him for quite some time. 'What happened to the other one?'

'The other one?' Sarah asked.

'The other goon that chased us. Trust me, Tarek was too dumb to work alone. If he was tracking you to get to me, you can bet that Kamal was there, too.'

'Kamal who?'

'Gaz Kamal,' Dade replied. 'He's the uglier, meaner half of the demonic duo.'

'He was there,' Cobb assured him. Although he had promised Sarah that she could run the interrogation, he sensed that the conversation was headed in the wrong direction. This was his subtle way to get things back on track. 'We saw Kamal in the tunnels with six of his men. Seven if you count Tarek.'

'Wait. What tunnels?' Dade asked.

Sarah answered. 'The tunnels beneath the city.'

Dade's eyes nearly bulged from their sockets. 'Wait a goddamn minute! That was *you*? The explosion was *you*? What in the hell were you thinking? Do you know how many innocent people were killed in the—'

'Simon,' she shouted to cut him off, 'you know damn well that I would never blow up a city. And neither would Jack. We did everything in our power to stop it.'

'Wait,' Dade said as he tried to fit the pieces in his head, 'are you saying that Kamal and Tarek planted the bombs? Why would they do that? That was Hassan's territory. Do you know how much money he's going to lose from the blast?'

Sarah shook her head. 'It wasn't them, either.'

'Then I'm *really* confused.' Dade clasped his hand behind his head and squeezed the back of his neck. 'If it wasn't *them* and it wasn't *you*, who the hell was it?'

Sarah tried to explain. 'Kamal and Tarek followed us into the tunnels, but someone else followed them. Whoever those guys were, they weren't messing around. We know they slaughtered at least four of Kamal's crew, including Tarek himself. They also rigged the tunnels with explosives and collapsed the city block.'

Dade considered the information. He chose to focus on the part of the equation that affected him directly. 'Do you know if Kamal escaped?'

Sarah nodded. 'He made it out of the tunnels before the bombs detonated. He might have been swallowed in the rubble, but we have to assume that he's still alive.'

'Great,' he said sarcastically. 'Glad to hear it.'

'Believe it or not, it is good news for you,' Cobb offered.

Dade stared at him. 'How do you figure?'

'At least you know what he looks like. I can't say the same about the bombers.'

Dade shrugged. 'What does it really matter? It's not like you'll be sticking around to deal with them.'

'Of course we will,' she said defiantly.

'No, you won't,' Dade argued. 'We have to get you out of the city as soon as possible. In fact, we need to get you out of the country. I don't know what you've stumbled into, but it's only going to get worse. Kamal and Hassan will be out for blood, and it's pretty clear that the other guys don't give a damn about collateral damage. They were willing to blow up a huge chunk of the city, and I'd be willing to bet that they're looking for you right now.'

'Simon,' she said, 'you're not following. We *can't* leave the city because the mystery men took a member of our team. We're not going anywhere until we get her back. And you're going to help us.'

'Sarah, I just told you – I'm on the outside looking in. Kamal wants me dead. Hassan wants me tortured. And I have absolutely no idea why anyone would want to blow up a city block. Simply put, I don't know who you're looking for.'

'Listen,' she shouted, 'you kept me in the dark about Hassan and his goons. Everything that happened after that – the uninvited guests, the explosion in the city, the disappearance of my friend – it all traces back to your mistake.'

She leaned in closer and whispered in a threatening tone, 'You might not know who we're looking for, but you're damn well going to find out. It's time to start atoning for your sins, or else I'll shoot you myself and feed your body to the sharks.'

Cobb watched as a look of panic washed over Dade. His tanned face grew pale. His dark eyes glazed over. His mouth hung open in fear. Cobb had no idea what Sarah had whispered, but it sure as hell was effective.

Dade stammered, 'I don't even know where to begin.'

'We do,' Cobb said. 'You can start by looking into the ambulance that the bombers used to escape. We tried to chase it, but it got away from us in the chaos. By the time we caught up to it, the kidnappers were gone and so was our colleague.'

'Does your colleague have a name?'

'Of course she does,' Cobb said, 'but I'll be damned if I'm going to tell it to you. So far, you've proven to be the least reliable asset I've ever worked with. Prove your worth, then we'll see if we can trust you with her name.'

Although Dade had plenty of reasons to help their cause, Cobb figured it couldn't hurt to mention that they were looking for a woman. After all, it was the guilt Dade felt from losing a bunch of young girls to the sex trade business that had made him feel indebted to Sarah to begin with, so Cobb decided to use the fact to his advantage.

'What do you know about the ambulance?' Dade asked.

Cobb showed him a picture of the vehicle on his phone. 'Standard issue Volkswagen for Egyptian Emergency Services.'

Dade was familiar with it. 'Probably stolen in the chaos after the explosion.'

'I'm not so sure,' Cobb explained. 'The driver was wearing a paramedic's uniform, and his partner was calmly looking through the victims. I could be wrong, but I think they had this planned in advance. Maybe not the kidnapping, but at least the idea to use an ambulance to evacuate injured colleagues from the scene.'

Sarah reached into her bag and handed a street map to Dade. It traced the route of Cobb and McNutt's pursuit through the city. 'We need you to reach out to every source you have. Start with those along these streets. Find out if anyone saw anything in the last few days. Maybe someone caught a glimpse of the vehicle or recognized a face. And if you have any clients with surveillance cameras along the route, pull that footage whether they want you to or not. Don't take no for an answer.'

Dade nodded in understanding.

'Seriously,' she stressed, 'I don't care if you have to burn every bridge you've built in this city to get the information that we need. This is a matter of life or death.'

'I get it,' Dade assured her. 'I'll start checking right away. Or at least I could have if you hadn't hurled my phone into the Mediterranean.'

'When did I do that?' she asked innocently.

Though it had appeared as if she had tossed his phone into the water, she had actually palmed the device and had thrown a burner phone instead. The sleight of hand not only grabbed Dade's attention, it had given Cobb the opportunity to hack into his phone.

Using a program that Garcia had given to him before they left, Cobb had secretly copied the phone's contents – contacts, pictures, texts, and so on – without ever touching the device. Before terminating the wireless connection, Cobb had also inserted a next-generation GPS virus into his phone. Even a surveillance expert like Dade would never notice the tracker because it wasn't an actual bug. It was merely a line of code that would force his phone to send out a continuous signal for Garcia to follow.

'Here you go,' she said as she handed the phone to Dade. 'I know how much you depend on this thing. It would have been cruel to throw it into the sea.'

Dade grinned at the turn of events. 'You sneaky devil! That's the Sarah I remember from six years ago. I'm glad she's still in there, somewhere, under that rough exterior.'

Sarah laughed as she squeezed his shoulder. 'Don't worry, Simon. I'm the same ol' Sarah from back in the day. Always have been, always will be.'

'Glad to hear it!'

She leaned in closer and whispered, 'But here's the thing. The sweet girl that you remember is the *fake* Sarah. The *real* Sarah is the angry one.'

'If you say so.'

She dug her nails into his skin. 'Oh, I *do* say so. And if you fuck me on this, Kamal and Hassan will be the least of your problems. Understood?'

'Understood,' he said as he took a step back. 'Take me back to shore, and I'll get started right away. I promise.'

Cobb shook his head. 'Not quite yet. Before we go anywhere, I need you to do me a favor. You're not going to like it, but you're going to do it anyway. After all, my life was endangered in the tunnels, too.'

Sarah didn't know where Cobb was headed, but she knew that Dade didn't really have a choice. Cobb wasn't asking; that much was clear.

'How can I help?' Dade replied.

'I need you to personally introduce me to one of your contacts.'

'Sure. Which one?'

'Your pal Hassan.'

Dade laughed. 'You're kidding, right?'

Cobb stared at him. 'Do I look like I'm kidding?'

'Please don't take this the wrong way, but fuck you, Jack! It's *not* gonna happen! The guy wants me dead!'

'And I'm offering you a way to get back on his good side,' Cobb assured him. 'Take me to see Hassan, and I promise that you'll survive the meeting.'

48

Citadel of Qaitbay
Alexandria's Eastern Harbor

Dade had asked for a day to arrange a meeting with Hassan.

Cobb had given him an hour.

The way Cobb saw it, he held the better cards and wanted to play them right away. He already knew that Hassan wanted Dade, and he imagined that the crime lord would also be interested in information regarding the men who had destroyed his territory.

Cobb could offer both.

Without time to scout for a new location, Cobb chose a place that he knew well, a building that he and Sarah had explored during their initial rekky of the city.

It was a landmark that every local could find.

Even a hardened criminal like Hassan.

The Citadel of Qaitbay was once an imposing fortress guarding the waters of Alexandria's Eastern Harbor. Seemingly modeled after an English castle, the towering stronghold provided distant views of approaching invaders. Its thick limestone walls – accentuated by red granite salvaged from the site's previous occupant, the famed Lighthouse of Alexandria – were designed to withstand the fiercest attacks. It was a defensive stalwart, having protected the city for more than four and a half centuries.

Even though the citadel is now meant more for tourists than soldiers, it still evokes a sense of awe. McNutt whistled as he walked along the courtyard that led to the building's front entrance. The wide enclosure was paved with massive slabs of concrete flanked by lush, green grass. Trees encircled the lawn, and square patches of landscaping served as a contrast to the built-in stone benches that lined the main walkways.

'Didn't Robin Hood rescue Maid Marian from this thing?' he asked as he strolled with a backpack filled with ammo around the grounds. 'I'm pretty sure he did.'

Garcia, who heard the comment on his headphones, was too preoccupied to laugh. He wasn't particularly fond of working in the field – not because he was scared of confrontation, but because he didn't like exposing his electronic arsenal to the elements.

McNutt wasn't sure what to make of his silence. 'Is this thing on?'

'Sorry,' Garcia said. 'I'm dealing with some serious glare here.'

'Relax, Hector. It's called sunlight. I know you don't see a lot of it in your mom's basement, but it can't hurt you.'

'Actually, it can,' Garcia replied from one of the stone benches. 'You need a high SPF to protect you, or you're just asking for trouble.'

McNutt instinctively patted the assault rifle that he had tucked under his jacket. 'If I find trouble, I've got something a little better than sunscreen to protect me.'

'I hope you're not referring to your intelligence.'

'Of course not. Don't be stupid.'

At Cobb's insistence, the two of them had arrived early, using the yacht's inflatable Zodiac to reach the harbor before the others. Cobb didn't want anyone, including Dade, to know that McNutt and Garcia were a part of his team, or else they would lose the element of surprise. To increase their chances of success, they tapped into the citadel's surveillance system, which allowed Garcia to monitor the entire building from his laptop while McNutt surveyed the building on foot.

As always, Cobb's team would be linked by comms.

'Approaching the fort,' Cobb whispered as he walked a few paces ahead of Sarah and Dade toward the citadel's front court-yard. 'Can you hear me?'

'Audio confirmed,' Garcia said as he tapped on his keyboard. 'And let Sarah know that she's good to go. I can hear her talking.'

'Will do.' Cobb gave her a subtle nod before he turned his attention to McNutt. 'Josh, how are we looking?'

'Not too bad,' McNutt said from up ahead. As point man, he would enter the citadel before the others in case Hassan was setting up a trap. 'I've counted five goons so far, and all of them were obvious. Even Hector spotted them.'

Garcia frowned but didn't comment.

'What about Hassan?' Cobb asked.

'He's here – *somewhere*. He showed up about ten minutes ago and went straight inside. Where are you supposed to meet him?'

'No idea,' Cobb admitted. 'Since we picked the place, he got to choose the room. I was kind of hoping Hector could tell us where he is.'

Garcia chimed in. 'I had him for a while, but this building is really big and really old. There are blind spots all over the place. Whoever put in this system should be shot.'

'He's not the one I'm worried about getting shot,' Cobb admitted.

Garcia kept his eyes glued to the computer screen. 'With that in mind, I see a potential problem inside the front door. Your giant friend is waiting by the entrance.'

'Kamal?' Cobb asked.

'Yep,' McNutt said as he walked past the giant and casually glanced around the lobby as if he was a lost tourist trying to get his bearings. 'Don't worry. I got him. He's kind of hard to miss. If he makes a move, I'll take him out.'

'Glad to hear it.' Cobb turned around and glanced at Sarah. Even though she had been talking to Dade the entire time, mostly to distract him, she had been half-listening to Cobb's conversation with the others. She gave him a subtle nod to let him know that she was aware of Kamal. 'Okay, we're coming in.'

'Still clear,' McNutt assured him.

But just to be safe, he fingered his trigger.

Cobb entered first, followed by Dade, then Sarah. Unlike the others, Dade wasn't prepared for the sudden appearance of Kamal, who clogged the lobby with his looming presence. Standing by the castle gate, he seemed more like an ogre than a man.

Dade could almost feel the brute's hot breath on his face.

And Kamal did little to hide his anger.

For a moment, Dade was worried that Kamal would ignore the others and simply shoot him right there on the steps.

Instead, he motioned for them to follow him.

As they moved deeper inside, Cobb marveled at the stonework and the ingenuity of the building's design. A central column opened to the sky, with the rooms of the structure built around it. Grated windows on every level allowed for quick communication between the floors. These openings meant that anything shouted from the roof could be heard all the way to the ground – saving valuable seconds in the event of an invasion.

Up ahead, Cobb could see a strange green light radiating from one of the rooms. His mind flashed back to the timers of the bomb packs, and the eerie glow that they had given off in the darkness of the tunnels. The thought reaffirmed why they were here: they had to find out who was responsible for Jasmine's abduction.

Even if it meant meeting the devil himself.

'This is where I lost Hassan,' Garcia announced, as he tapped away on his keyboard. 'There are no cameras beyond the door.'

'And no way to circle ahead,' McNutt said.

Just then, Kamal stopped short of the room.

He turned, then motioned for the others to continue.

McNutt, who was lingering in a nearby hallway, was concerned. 'Chief, we have no eyes in that room. Repeat. We have no eyes in that room. It might be a trap.'

But Cobb knew better. And so did Sarah.

They had been there before.

The first thing Cobb noticed when he peeked inside was the filtered green light cast by the wall-mounted lamps. It was simply unavoidable; the whole room was bathed in green. From his previous trip, he knew that green was a traditional color of the Islamic faith. He also knew that this wasn't just a random room in the castle.

This was a mosque – a sacred place of worship.

And standing in the center was Hassan.

The divine symbolism was not lost on Cobb. He knew that Hassan's intentions were far from holy. In fact, they were a desecration. He had brought them to this room to make one thing clear – that their fate was his to determine.

But Cobb didn't quite see it that way.

Before Hassan could utter a word, Cobb refused to enter the room. 'Not in here. It isn't appropriate.'

It wasn't a demand. It wasn't a request. It was a clear statement of fact. There was no way that he was going to conduct business in a holy room.

No matter what.

Hassan, who was used to getting his way, reacted poorly to the situation. He shouted something in Arabic that neither Cobb nor Sarah could understand.

Suddenly, Kamal moved to block Cobb's retreat into the corridor. He was several inches taller and several inches wider than Cobb. He stared down at him with rage in his eyes. 'You stay.'

Cobb looked up at Kamal. 'We're not meeting in here. Not in this room.'

Hassan shouted again in Arabic.

Kamal translated. 'You have a problem with Islam?'

Cobb turned and faced Hassan. 'No. But the things we must discuss are not meant for these walls. Your faith preaches forgiveness. I'm here for vengeance.'

Hassan smiled and switched to English. 'As am I.'

Dade's heart pounded in his chest as Hassan walked toward them. The Egyptian joined Cobb at the mosque's entrance where he took a moment to slip on his shoes. In truth, that was another reason that Cobb had refused to enter the room. He knew it was customary to remove one's shoes before entering a mosque, and he didn't want to face a possible gunfight in his bare feet.

He had learned that from *Die Hard*.

Hassan stared at Cobb, sizing him up. 'Shall we walk?'

Cobb nodded in agreement.

They walked side by side through a long, arched corridor that connected the front and back halves of the building. Sarah, Dade, and Kamal trailed behind, eyeing each other cautiously like warring nations during a ceasefire.

Hassan opened the conversation. 'You have news about the explosion?'

'I do,' Cobb replied. He knew there was no reason to string him along. The purpose of this meeting was simple: he would offer everything he knew about the bombing in exchange for anything Hassan knew about the bombers. 'They used Semtex, most likely from the Libyan black market.'

'How can you be so sure?'

'The bomb pack was crafted from a Tunisian timer. My sources tell me that fits with a configuration popular among Libyan suppliers.'

'Your sources? Who are you?'

'American. Former military. That tells you enough.'

Hassan laughed. As he climbed a flight of steps to the second level, he waved his arms and glanced around the stairwell. 'This whole building was constructed before your Columbus even discovered America. What are you doing in Egypt?'

'I'm looking for my colleague.'

His tone made it clear that he had no interest in discussing their original mission. The only thing that mattered was Jasmine. 'The men who took her are the same men who blew up your territory. I believe that puts us on the same side of the equation.'

Hassan grinned. 'The enemy of my enemy is my friend, yes?'

49

Cobb shook his head. He didn't want there to be any miscommunication with the crime lord. 'Let's not kid ourselves. You and I are not friends – and we're never going to be friends. Let's just say we have a common interest.'

Hassan shrugged. He didn't care about semantics; he was more concerned with Cobb's ulterior motives. *Something* had brought the Americans to his city, but he didn't know what it was. 'And all you want is the woman?'

'No,' Cobb assured him, 'I also want to punish the men who took her. If you have any objections, please speak now because later will be too late.'

Hassan shook his head. 'I have none. As you have said, these men have wronged me as well. I wish to see them punished for all they have done.'

'Then tell me everything. This is your city, and you know the players. If you have any clue about what we're up against, let me know. In exchange, I'll hunt them down, and everyone gets what they want.'

* * *

One of the many traits that distinguished Garcia from the rest of the team was the way he saw patterns in seemingly random events. His photographic memory allowed him to match things that he had already seen with whatever new data was presented to him. It was an innate ability that had driven him into mathematics, then computers, then eventually the FBI.

Using his laptop, Garcia watched Cobb's conversation with Hassan as they moved from hallways to stairwells and back again. Eventually, something bothered him.

'Josh, do me a favor and slow down a bit.'

McNutt did as told. 'Problem?'

'I think Hassan has a shadow.'

'No shit,' he laughed. 'So far I've counted six.'

'And you've pointed out all of them.'

'What's your point?'

'I think I found number seven.'

McNutt decided to hear him out. 'Fine. Who?'

Garcia stared at the image on his screen. 'The short, bald guy with the sunglasses. He's been circling the others, but they have yet to cross paths. That's an unlikely coincidence. He's intentionally avoiding a run-in, yet he's staying close enough to strike if Hassan needs him.'

McNutt glanced at the man in question. While his shaved head gave him a slightly intimidating quality, he was barely five and a half feet tall. Furthermore, he was thin and willowy – hardly the bodyguard type.

'Are you sure the sun's not getting to you?'

'Just humor me,' Garcia said. 'Don't lose track of him.'

'I'll try, but that may be tough.'

'Why?'

'That guy is a shrimp.'

* * *

Cobb had detected six shadows as well. These men thought they had gone unnoticed, but each had been betrayed by their actions.

Glances that lasted too long. A pace that was too fast or too slow. Feigned interest in the smallest of details.

Cobb noticed them all.

They might as well have worn little nametags that read: HELLO, MY NAME IS: GOON.

But it wasn't a surprise to Cobb. He knew that Hassan would bring a lot of protection. A man of his stature had more than just Kamal, Tarek, and the other tunnel rats on his payroll. That much was certain.

As they exited the lower floors of the citadel and stepped out onto the expansive terrace, Cobb pressed Hassan for details. 'Given the damage that I saw, there were at least a dozen men in the tunnels – some to set the charges, and the rest to clear their way. These weren't amateurs. They knew exactly what they were doing.'

'Did you see them?'

'Only the dead ones,' Cobb admitted. 'They could see like owls and climb like monkeys – like some sort of olive-skinned ninjas.'

'What about their clothes?'

'They wore black pants and black tunics. And their weapon of choice was a unique blade that I've never seen before. Does any of that sound familiar?'

Hassan did not answer. He simply leaned against the outer wall of the citadel and stared out across the water. His lungs filled with sea air as he closed his eyes, allowing the afternoon sun to warm his face.

Sensing reluctance, Cobb issued an ultimatum. 'I'm starting to lose my patience here. I've given you details about the explosives and the men, but I've received nothing in return. Either tell me what you know, or we're leaving with Dade.'

Hassan opened his eyes and looked back at Cobb. 'This blade – the one you weren't familiar with – it was part-saber, part-scimitar?'

'Yes,' he replied. 'It had elements of both. What is it?'

'It is known as a *khopesh*.' Hassan nodded in understanding as he turned back toward the sea. 'You are describing the Muharib.'

* * *

Garcia opened a second window on his laptop and ran a search for *Muharib*.

Meanwhile, he kept a watchful eye on the bald visitor.

'Hey Josh,' he said as he scanned the information on his screen. 'Lex Luthor is about to exit onto the far side of the roof. I think everyone would feel a lot better if you put yourself between him and the conversation.'

'*Not* everyone,' McNutt scoffed. 'Do I look like a human shield?'

Garcia ignored the question. 'Jack, my searches for "Muharib" all circle back to the Arabic word "hirabah". It means "unlawful warfare". Sorry, but that's all I've got.'

* * *

Cobb grinned at the irony. The person on his team with the best chance of knowing anything about the Muharib was the one that they had taken. 'Go on.'

'You are a soldier. Are there limitations as to those you will fight?'

Cobb shook his head. 'I took an oath to defend my country from any foe, foreign or domestic.'

Hassan laughed. 'I am not asking about geographical constraints. I am questioning your moral limitations. In times of conflict, do you believe that every resident of a rival land is your enemy? Must the blood of innocents be spilled as well?'

Cobb hated the insinuation. 'Of course not. It goes against everything that I stand for; and everything my country stands for.'

'And yet, some would argue that is why your country fails. Some would say that the only way to truly defeat an enemy is to wipe their people from the planet. In order to win, you must leave no one behind – for the innocent may someday be corrupted.'

Cobb wanted to disagree but wasn't given the chance.

Hassan cut him off. 'This philosophy is the way of the Muharib.'

Cobb was all too familiar with the strategy. It was the driving force behind the ethnic cleansing he had seen throughout Africa and Eastern Europe. Millions of men, women, and children had been murdered simply for living in areas that were connected to religions or ethnicities that the ruling class had deemed intolerable.

'What are the Muharib trying to destroy?'

'Anything that threatens their way of life – and that is the problem.' Hassan pointed north, then swept his hand westward as he continued to speak. 'The legend of the Muharib extends from Damascus to Marrakesh. No one knows where they truly came from. No one knows their ways. And no one knows their secrets. For countless generations, they have been feared as the shadow men of the Sahara. They have killed thousands, with little rhyme or reason to their actions.'

Cobb was skeptical. The desert that Hassan was describing was larger than the lower forty-eight states. If a single group had laid claim to that much territory, surely someone in the intelligence community would have heard about it. Even in light of the harsh terrain of the Sahara, it seemed unlikely – if not impossible – that a powerful group could hide in it for hundreds of years.

'Why should I believe that they are anything but an urban legend: boogeymen created to keep children from the desert?'

Hassan laughed. He reached down and picked up a small sliver of rock that had broken from the parapet. He used it to draw upon the wall, defacing the ancient citadel as if it were his personal chalkboard.

His body blocked his artwork as he spoke. 'I am sure that many felt the same way at first, but a thousand years of slaughtered innocents has a way of convincing most skeptics. Inhuman agility. Nocturnal vision. Ruthless efficiency. And always – *always* – the blade. Tell me, did they bear the mark?'

Hassan moved to reveal his work.

For the first time, Cobb could see the symbol on the wall.

The etching was crude, but its design was unmistakable.

It was the same as the scar that McNutt had noticed earlier.

Hassan knew that his question had hit home. 'The mark is burned into their skin. It is a symbol of their permanent devotion to their cause. Few who have fought the Muharib have ever lived to speak of it. Fewer still have sought them out.'

Cobb had heard enough. He had the information that he had come for, now he needed to use it. It meant using every available resource. 'One last thing. I need Simon.'

'Need him – but why? What use do you have for a traitor? He will only betray you the first chance he gets.'

Cobb lowered his voice. 'He *is* a bit of weasel, isn't he?'

Hassan laughed. 'Yes, he is.'

'Still, he serves a purpose. He knows his way around the city, and he understands the way the game is played. For this to work, he needs to know – scratch that, *I* need to know – that you're not going to take him out during the game.'

'And when this is over?'

Cobb shrugged. 'If Simon leads us to the Muharib, he gets his freedom.'

'And if he doesn't?'

'You can feed him to your giant.'

Hassan glanced at Dade and laughed. 'You may have him on one condition: Kamal goes with him at all times.'

'Done.'

Dade and Kamal stared at each another in disbelief, but neither had the courage to stop it.

Hassan turned toward Kamal. 'Keep him alive, for now.'

Kamal reluctantly nodded.

Sarah leaned in and whispered to Dade: 'See! I told you every-thing would be alright. Not only did we save your life, we got you the best bodyguard in town.'

* * *

Cobb smiled at the latest development as he left the meeting. It hadn't been his idea, but he almost wished it had been. Partnering Kamal with Dade had taken the thug out of the equation or, at the very least, had made him a known variable.

Keeping track of Dade meant keeping track of Kamal.

And vice versa.

Better still, the presence of Kamal guaranteed the coopera-tion of the underbelly of the city. If people refused to answer Dade's questions, Kamal was there to talk some sense into them. And if that didn't work, he could always beat it out of them.

* * *

As Hassan stared at the sea, he sensed that Awad was behind him. 'Are they gone?'

Awad nodded. 'Gaz took Simon in his car. The others left by boat.'

'How many?'

'Four, including the two that you met. They were covered by a scruffy man dressed as a traveler and a Latino with a computer. They heard and saw everything.'

'Including you?'

'Yes.'

Hassan smiled. 'So they know what they're doing. That's good to hear. Hopefully we'll get some answers without losing additional men.'

'Sir?'

Based on Kamal's description of the slaughter in the tunnels, Hassan had suspected the ancient warriors. 'They have met the Muharib, just as I feared.'

'In Alexandria? I thought the Muharib were desert dwellers. Why would they come to the city?'

Hassan shrugged. 'That's what we need to find out.'

50

The battered Jeep bounced across the sand, jostling the driver and his passenger as they sped toward the remote hut.

Under normal circumstances, the interrogation of a prisoner would have been conducted slowly and methodically. It would have lasted for days, perhaps even weeks, until they were certain that their subject had given up every last detail.

A moment of pain can weaken anyone's spirit.

But prolonged suffering will shatter even the most hardened of wills.

Unfortunately, things had not gone as expected in Alexandria. At least two of the Americans had escaped the destruction of the cisterns. To make matters worse, the duo had witnessed the abduction of their colleague and had chased the bombers.

The men could no longer afford to let the interrogation drag out.

They needed answers, and they needed them now.

Their intensity grew with each passing mile.

* * *

As the camels plodded through the desert, Jasmine's frustration continued to mount. Seated behind Izri atop the lead animal, she wanted to thrust her heels together and spur the beasts to sprint for all they were worth, but she resisted the urge. She knew this was the pace of life in the Sahara. Here, slow and steady wins the race. Perhaps nowhere else on earth was the proverb more accurate.

Despite her impatience, Jasmine had to acknowledge that their sluggish pace might actually be for the best. She considered the very real possibility that it was safer to keep moving than to stop. Presumably, the ideal places for camps and settlements were known throughout the desert, giving her captors a good place to start looking once they realized that she was missing. While she was appreciative of the Berbers' rescue efforts, she wondered if they were inadvertently leading her back into the hands of the enemy.

Jasmine leaned forward and spoke to Izri. 'Please tell me about your village.'

Izri smiled at her improving familiarity with his language and laughed at her description of their community. 'It is too much to say that we are a village. We are simply a collection of travelers. We move where we must, when we must, as we have done for generations.'

'But is there a place you call home?' Jasmine asked.

Izri spread his arms wide. 'The whole of the Sahara is our place.' He glanced over his shoulder at Jasmine. '*This* is our home.'

*   *   *

As the Jeep pulled up to the rear of the hut, the men did not notice the disturbed sand near the base of the building. Even if they had, they would have assumed it had been caused by the transport team there earlier. The possibility of their captive's escape would never have crossed their mind. It wasn't until they reached the front of the building that they knew something was wrong.

On most days, the desert breeze quickly erases any and all trails through the sand. Footprints and tire tracks alike are routinely swept away by the gusting winds, leaving nothing but a vast, blank canvas. Without these signs, it is nearly impossible to track someone's movement through the barren terrain.

Unfortunately for Jasmine, the air that day was unusually still.

Standing at the front door, the men stared in surprised horror at the line of smooth indentations that led off into the distance. They could plainly see that these were not the prints of their comrades' boots, nor were there multiple sets of tracks. This was the trail of a single hiker – one who had been forced to fashion her own footwear.

They rushed inside, hoping against all reason that they were mistaken, that the captive was still secured to the floor in the far room. Instead, their worst fears were realized.

The woman was gone.

Only the shackles remained.

Normally they were the ones who caused panic in their victims, not the other way around. Now it was their turn to face fear. Even though they had yet to take possession of the American, they knew they would be held responsible for her disappearance.

The punishment would be swift and severe.

Their superiors would not tolerate incompetence.

They had to retrieve her before anyone knew she was missing.

*   *   *

As the sun vanished beneath the horizon, Jasmine still could not see the camp, but she had faith that her rescuers knew their way.

'Is it much farther?' she asked.

Izri shook his head. 'Perhaps another hour. Two at most.'

Jasmine noticed that none of the men wore watches or carried timepieces of any kind. She understood that the position of the sun could be used to track the hours during the day, but she wondered how the nomads kept time in the darkness. Ultimately, she let the concern pass. It didn't matter how long it took to reach their destination, only that they got there. Instead, she asked another question that had been puzzling her.

'How do you know English?'

Izri smiled. 'My grandfather teach it to my father. My father teach it to me. Someday, I teach it to my son.'

'You have children?'

'Yes. I have—'

His answer was cut short by the shouts of the man bringing up the rear.

Turning to see what had drawn his interest, Jasmine saw him pointing toward a small cloud of dust in the distance. Looking closer, she saw that it wasn't a natural phenomenon, it was a vehicle: a World War II-era Jeep. She was amazed that such a relic was still operational, especially in the harsh environment of the desert.

As the other two men dismounted to await the newcomers, Jasmine leaned close and whispered to Izri, 'Do you know who it is?'

Izri smiled. 'No, but it is not uncommon to meet other travelers. Paths cross all the time. The desert may be vast, but the people who live here are much closer than you may think. There is no need for concern. The Sahara is a friendly place.'

To reinforce his point, Izri turned his camel around and maneuvered it so that they would be the first to greet the new arrivals. He even raised his hand and offered a friendly wave. To his surprise, the Jeep showed no signs of slowing.

By the time he realized his mistake, it was too late.

The passenger in the Jeep rose from his seat and swung mightily toward his target. In a flash, the cold steel of his blade sliced through the camel's neck, cleanly severing its head and killing it instantly. The one-ton animal dropped to the ground, pinning both Izri's and Jasmine's legs under its body as it crashed to the sand.

Izri's companions reached for the archaic rifles that they had tucked in their saddles, but the proximity of the Jeep had startled their camels. It was impossible to retrieve their weapons from the backs of the flailing beasts that were trying to run away. The swordsmen slashed at the men mercilessly, spilling their guts and cleaving muscle from bone. Though Izri's friends survived the initial attack, they wouldn't last long.

The driver stopped the Jeep and jumped out with his partner close behind. With a quick thrust, the swordsmen drove their weapons deep into the chests of their victims. Their actions were as coordinated as they were brutal, as if there were some sort of hideous choreography in play. Spines snapped and lungs deflated as the blades were pushed through the defenseless prey, leaving only heaps of lifeless flesh.

Jasmine stared in horror, wondering if she was next.

Instead, the men turned their attention to Izri.

As the assassins closed in, Jasmine strained against the carcass. The sand had prevented her leg from being shattered by the animal's bulk, but it wasn't loose enough to allow her to pull free. Try as she might to wiggle out, she was trapped under the fallen camel. No matter how far she stretched, Izri's rifle lay just beyond her reach.

Izri stared at the men hovering over him. He raised his arms in defense and begged for mercy, the desperation in his voice clearly understood in any language. He knew they had won. He only wished that his life be spared.

In response, the larger of the men grabbed Izri's hair and yanked his head backwards. With a simple swipe of his blade, the man split Izri's throat in two. Releasing his grasp, he screamed in triumph as the life literally drained from the nomad's face.

Jasmine felt her stomach heave as she turned her head, unwilling to watch the horror of his death. A moment later, she felt the quick pinch of a needle piercing her shoulder, followed by a warm sensation as her vision grew hazy and her mind began to swirl.

The last thing she saw was Izri's lifeless eyes staring up at the heavens.

After that, there was only darkness.

51

Despite the powerful engines on the speedboat, Cobb and Sarah were soundly beaten back to the yacht. This had more to do with McNutt's driving than Cobb's. Having noticed Garcia's dislike of the sea, McNutt had pushed the low-horsepower motor of the inflatable raft to its absolute limit while hitting every swell that he could possibly find.

Eventually, two things happened, neither of which was unexpected.

One, Garcia puked all over the raft; and two, by the time the Zodiac had reached its destination, the outboard motor was smoking more than Cheech & Chong.

Cobb and Sarah noted both upon their return.

As they made their way toward the galley to ask what had happened, they heard not only McNutt and Garcia, but a third voice as well. It was an accent that they hadn't expected, but one that they recognized immediately.

McNutt was the first to see them coming. 'Look who we found.'

Papineau turned to face them. 'I hear you've been busy.'

It was clear that he wasn't in the mood for small talk. His mind was occupied with the business at hand, and he wanted to know what they had been doing in his absence. But there was something about his aloofness that rubbed Sarah the wrong way. He had been gone for forty-eight hours – doing

God knows what while they were risking their lives for one of their teammates – and he didn't even have the decency to say hello.

'It's great to see you, too,' she said sarcastically. 'Did you bring us any souvenirs from the Orient? I hear it's lovely there this time of year.'

Papineau stared at her but said nothing. He had more than enough reasons to find Jasmine and bring her back safely, but he was adding another one to the list. Sarah had been a firecracker from the very beginning, but it seemed the dislike that Cobb and McNutt felt for him was rubbing off on her. Selfishly, he needed Jasmine to balance the sense of civility – or least provide an alternate target for Sarah's snide remarks.

Cobb smiled at the exchange. 'Yes, we had a meeting with a resource that might be able to help us out. How much did they tell you?'

'Only the basics,' McNutt assured him. 'We mentioned Hassan and the citadel, but nothing else. We were waiting for you to explain the rest.'

Papineau didn't give him the chance. 'You call that man a *resource*? What were you thinking? Aziz Zawarhi Hassan is not a resource – he's a *criminal*!'

Cobb grimaced. 'I guess you've heard of him—'

'Of course I've heard of him! Did you really think I would bring you to a city without knowing whom and what to avoid? We all have our own ways of prepping a mission. You have your rekkys, and I have the INTERPOL watch-list. Don't you get it? We're trying to stay clear of any unnecessary encounters with the police, yet you go off and do business with a well-known crime lord. Explain it to me, Jack, because it sounds like you've lost your mind.'

Cobb couldn't remember seeing Papineau so animated. He wondered if the irritability was merely a symptom of jet lag, or if something had happened during his trip. Either way, he was fairly confident that Papineau wouldn't give him a straight answer, so he avoided the topic completely and opted to charge ahead.

'Are you finished?' Cobb asked calmly.

Papineau fumed at being talked down to; he'd had enough of that with Copeland in California, but instead of lashing out he bit his lip in silence.

'Yes,' Cobb admitted, 'I reached out to Hassan. And yes, he is a criminal. But no, I haven't lost my mind – I used it. The men we're looking for aren't angels. They don't spend their days thinking up ways to make the world a better place. They're killers, just like Hassan. If we have any chance of getting close to them, we needed access to that world. Hassan gets us in. And Simon Dade helps us navigate through it.'

Papineau's eyes bulged in frustration. 'Dade? Why are we messing around with him? Hasn't he caused us enough trouble already?'

Sarah couldn't help herself. She felt obligated to defend Dade – or at the very least, her decision to recommend him. 'Without Simon, we'd have never made the connection with Hassan. He might have gotten us into this mess, but he's doing what he can to get us out.'

Papineau shook his head in frustration. 'The mess in the tunnel had nothing to do with Hassan. It had everything to do with *us*.'

'What are you talking about?' she argued. 'Hassan's goons were followed into the tunnels, and we all got caught up in something that—'

'No we didn't!' he shouted, much to their dismay. From

the looks on their faces, Papineau quickly realized that his message had come out a lot harsher than he had intended, so he took a deep breath and started again in a much softer tone. 'No, Sarah, we didn't. We didn't get caught up in a turf war between Hassan and his enemies. His goons weren't followed, *we* were. The slaughter in the tunnels was designed to stop *our* search.'

Sarah stared. 'What do you mean?'

He took another deep breath. 'Seven months ago, a group of archaeologists disappeared in the Sahara while on a search similar to our own.'

Before anyone could react, Cobb held up his hand demanding silence. He wanted to know where Papineau was going with this information *before* they mentioned what they had learned about the Muharib.

'Where did this happen?' Cobb demanded.

'Two hundred miles southwest of Cairo,' Papineau said. 'Near some godforsaken village that doesn't even have a name.'

Cobb knew there was more to come. 'Go on.'

Papineau continued, eager to share the details he had put together during his return flight. 'The group consisted of eleven people: ten graduate students and the team leader, a Greek professor named Cyril Manjani. He financed the entire expedition on his own.'

Cobb rubbed his chin in thought. Knowing little about archaeological digs, he wondered if self-financing was common. 'An expedition for what?'

'According to my source, Manjani was obsessed with ancient kings. He had spent his entire academic career mapping the discovered tombs and theorizing as to where the others could still be found. He used to drone on and on about Akhenaten, Smenkhkare, and other missing pharaohs, convinced that he would someday find them.'

'Did he mention Alexander?' Sarah asked.

Papineau shook his head. 'Not that we know of, but any scholar in that field would be well aware of the mystery surrounding Alexander's tomb.'

McNutt didn't care about theories or assumptions. He wanted facts. 'What happened to the team?'

Papineau grimaced. 'That's where things get interesting. A month after their arrival, two representatives from the Ministry of State for Antiquities were dispatched to check up on the endeavor. They were to verify the activities of Manjani's team and to ensure that all the rules and regulations of the ministry were being followed. But when they arrived, they found little more than an abandoned site. Not ransacked or ravaged – *abandoned*. Their tents and other equipment were undisturbed. Their supply of fresh water was untouched. But there wasn't a soul to be seen.'

'That's it? They just disappeared?' McNutt demanded.

'Officially, yes. The area had been hit by a series of sandstorms, and the authorities speculate that the group got confused and simply walked off into the desert. Apparently such things are fairly common in the Sahara. People get turned around, and they simply vanish. The windswept sands literally rip them to pieces or bury them alive. Either way, survivors are seldom found.'

Cobb was waiting for the other half of the explanation; the important half, as far as he was concerned. 'What about unofficially?'

'Six months ago, one of his friends swears that he received a phone call from a man that sounded a lot like Manjani. The connection was bad, and the caller was rambling, but he remembers the man saying something about demons that simply appeared in the night. Manjani – if it was Manjani – said that he watched his team get barbarically slaughtered. He said they were dragged from their tents and then cut to pieces. And when the bloodbath was over, the demons disappeared.'

Sarah looked at Cobb. 'Who does that sound like?'

Cobb nodded in agreement. 'Does your source believe Manjani is still alive?'

'He does,' Papineau replied. 'But he has no idea where he's hiding.'

Cobb looked at Garcia. 'Hector, add that to your to-do list. I can't imagine he'd be stupid enough to use his real identity if he's trying to stay lost, but check it out anyway. Credit cards, cell phones – you know the drill.'

Garcia was already taking notes on his tablet. 'Where should I start?'

'When they're in trouble, most people run to what they know best. Start with Greece, then work your way out from there.'

McNutt furrowed his brow. 'Jack, I'm not following. Shouldn't we be focusing our efforts on the Muharib? How does a missing professor help us find Jasmine?'

Papineau was confused as well. 'I'm sorry. The Muharib?'

Cobb answered McNutt first. 'Honestly, Josh, I'm not sure how he fits into this mess, but my gut tells me that he does.'

McNutt nodded. 'That's good enough for me.'

Papineau didn't like being ignored. 'Again, who are the Muharib?'

Cobb turned and faced him. 'If my hunch is correct, they're the demons that killed Manjani's team and kidnapped Jasmine.'

52

There is a simple tenet that has been drilled into United States Marines for as long as anyone can remember.

Improvise. Adapt. Overcome.

Cobb was Army, not USMC, but he believed in their mantra all the same.

In their struggle to recover Jasmine, it seemed that every hour brought new details needing to be factored into his plan. As the minutes ticked by, he knew the odds of finding her alive fell less and less in their favor, but he wouldn't give up.

Cobb turned to Papineau for additional information about Manjani. 'Can you show me where his team was last seen?'

'Certainly,' he said, 'but I'm not sure what good that will do. There's nothing to see there and no one to talk to. All traces of their expedition have been taken down or swept away.'

'And yet I'd still like to know where he disappeared.'

Papineau nodded. 'Yes, of course, how silly of me. I have a map in my luggage. I'll get it for you immediately.'

Sarah waited for Papineau to leave before she took a seat next to Cobb. 'Jack, in regards to Manjani, I think I know someone who can help our cause.'

'Oh?'

She nodded confidently. 'If there are any stories floating around about him, this is the guy who would know. I'm telling you, he'll be able to separate all the bullshit rumors from those worth pursuing. Not only that, he's one of the best I've ever seen at tracking down digital information. If it's out there, he can find it. I'm talking Garcia-level skills in his realm of expertise.'

Cobb smiled 'Don't take this the wrong way, but I think I'll pass. Given your track record with assets, I'm more comfortable with the real Garcia doing the digging for us instead of Hector 2.0.'

Sarah refused to budge. 'Do you know how the CIA finds people?'

'Very slowly,' he teased.

'Jack, I'm being serious.'

Cobb sighed. He had a lot to do, but he could see the determination on her face. She wasn't going to accept his decision without a fight. 'I assume you send agents out into the field to track down your targets.'

'Wrong,' she assured him. 'There aren't enough spies in the world to track everyone who needs to be watched. Think about it: there are seven billion people on the planet, and a few thousand spooks to watch over them. That's a serious lack of manpower.'

'And a serious misrepresentation of the facts. I mean, the CIA doesn't need to keep tabs on all seven billion, now do they?'

Sarah just stared at him.

'C'mon,' Cobb laughed, 'you're not saying—'

'All I'm saying is that when it comes to finding targets, spies don't pick up the trail on their own. It's the bloodhounds that lead us in the right direction.'

'Sarah, I'm not following. What bloodhounds?'

'Like I said, the CIA only employs a few thousand people.

That means they have to outsource a lot of the legwork. When the Agency needs to find a target, they turn to specialists who have spent their entire lives hunting for people. These guys are known as bloodhounds – or hounds, for short. And trust me, they don't care who you're looking for or what you do to the target once it's found. All that matters is that you meet their price.'

'How is that any different than Simon?'

'Simon was a local asset. We used him because he was part of the neighborhood. He's good-looking and sociable, which meant he could blend in with the crowd. He didn't have to *become* one of them; he already *was* one of them. For an asset like Simon, that's the biggest risk. Connecting to your environment means you start to personally identify with the community around you. It's easy to lose perspective. And when something goes wrong, it can tear you apart.'

'You're talking about the girls in the slave ring.'

She nodded. 'All I can tell you is that before that, he never would have worked with a man like Hassan. I think the experience six years ago broke his spirit. He saw evil win, and he felt it always would.'

'If you can't beat 'em, join 'em?'

'Something like that,' she said. 'But that's not my point. Bloodhounds aren't burdened by the emotions that other assets have. They aren't tasked with fitting into a community, and they aren't concerned with making friends. They're loners driven by one thing and one thing only: the almighty dollar.'

'So you're recommending that we reach out to an obsessed sociopath who doesn't play nice with others?'

She didn't laugh. 'Jack, I know this source, and I'm telling you he can help. After we missed our shot at the sex slavery auction, we used him to find the bastards involved. To offset the impact of an opportunity lost, the director was willing to break the bank for information. This guy accomplished more in a week than our agents could have found in a year. He's pricey, but he's worth every penny.'

She lowered her voice to a whisper. 'Listen, we have the money, but we don't have the time. Jasmine is out there right now, praying that we're doing everything in our power to find her. This guy can help. Trust me on that. And even if I'm wrong, shouldn't we at least give it a shot? Don't we owe her that much?'

Improvise. Adapt. Overcome.

Cobb turned to Garcia. 'Hector, change of plans. Forget about Manjani for now. Focus your efforts on Jasmine and the Muharib – nothing else. You should have all of Simon's surveillance footage from the city by later tonight. I need you to work through every frame. The camera doesn't lie, so find out how the kidnappers disappeared.'

Papineau, who had gone to his room to fetch a map, returned and handed it to Cobb. 'I marked the location of Manjani's expedition, as you requested.'

Cobb looked into Papineau's bleary eyes. He could see that he was running on fumes. 'Jean-Marc, why don't you get some sleep? You look exhausted. Hector will wake you in a few hours and fill you in on everything he's learned about the Muharib. Until then, you're not going to do us any good in your current state.'

Papineau nodded. 'You're probably right. And Jack – sorry about before. My behavior was totally unprofessional.'

'Compared to whose? McNutt's?' Cobb said with a laugh. 'No

need to apologize for emotions. Stress gets the best of all of us from time to time. It lets us know you care.'

McNutt hustled over at the sound of his name. 'Did you call me, chief?'

'I didn't, but I was about to.'

'Wait,' he said, confused. 'I heard my name before you said it? How cool is that? I wonder if the blast made me psychic?'

'I see your point,' Papineau said as he excused himself from the conversation. 'There's no way I was worse than that.'

Cobb smiled. 'Anything new on the Semtex?'

'Nope,' McNutt answered.

'In that case, I'm giving you a new assignment. I know we've got a clear line of sight in all directions on the water, but it doesn't mean I feel safe. I need you to make sure we can defend ourselves. Keep an eye on the radar, and make sure Hector and Jean-Marc know how to use whatever arsenal you've brought aboard. I don't want the boat getting overrun just because we don't know where to find the missiles.'

McNutt leaned in. 'How do you know about the missiles?'

'How? Because they're in a crate marked "missiles".'

'Oops. My bad.'

'Anyway, please make sure the ship is secure.'

'Aye-aye, skipper.'

McNutt turned and headed for the door. He was halfway there when he stopped and turned back. 'What about the two of you?'

Cobb glanced at Sarah, then McNutt. 'What do you mean?'

'You asked me to train Hector and Jean-Marc on our arsenal. Does that mean you're leaving me alone with them?'

'Maybe.'

'Is this because of the bloodhound?'

'Maybe,' Cobb repeated. 'If he can help.'

'Chief,' he said timidly, 'may I speak freely on the subject?'

Cobb raised his eyebrows. 'You may.'

'I'm confused about something. If this hound is so damn good at finding people, why do we care about Manjani? Why don't we hire him to find Jasmine?'

Although Sarah loved making fun of McNutt for his near-constant state of confusion, this was one of the rare times when it was justified. 'May I?'

Cobb nodded. 'Be my guest.'

'Josh,' she explained, 'it's a completely different kind of search. In Jasmine's case, she's been *taken*. That means looking at surveillance tapes for the smallest of clues, and trying to figure out who targeted her and why. Meanwhile, Manjani is *hiding*. He's trying to stay off the grid, but there's always a chance that he slipped up and made a mistake. We need someone who can find the digital footprints that he's left behind and verify any rumors. With all due respect to Hector, we need someone with a vast network of contacts and a proven track record of success.'

McNutt nodded in understanding. 'When you put it like that, it makes perfect sense.'

'Thank you,' she said.

'Can I ask you one more question?'

'Sure.'

'Is your contact Bryan Mills?'

Sarah laughed. She had recently seen the movie *Taken* and knew 'Bryan Mills' was the name of the character played by Liam Neeson. 'Unfortunately, no, but my asset is also blessed with a very particular set of skills.'

McNutt grinned. 'Awesome.'

Meanwhile, Cobb was completely lost by the reference. 'While you two chat about Bryan Mills – whoever the hell that is – I've got a source of my own to call. And trust me, *he* possesses a very particular set of skills as well.'

53

*Küsendorf, Switzerland
(82 miles southeast of Bern)*

In less than a minute, Petr Ulster would have his answer. Every action he had taken thus far had been leading to this moment. Soon he would know if the meticulous planning and preparation had ultimately led to success – or if he was doomed to fail yet again.

Like an expectant father in the waiting room, he leaned closer to the window, desperately searching for the slightest sign that everything was okay. He knew to keep his distance, but the anticipation was almost more than he could stand. Sweat dripped down the sides of his face as he stared at the clock, watching the seconds tick down.

Finally, the buzzer sounded.

The moment of truth had arrived.

Ulster lowered the oven door and peered inside. So far, everything was perfect. He slowly wrapped his gloved hands around the tiny crock, careful not to dip his fingers into the scalding liquid below. He held his breath as he gently lifted the bowl from the water. And then, without warning, his miniature soufflé collapsed.

Ulster sighed in frustration.

He dropped the bowl back into the water bath of the baking dish and yanked the entire assembly from the oven. As he turned toward the island of his expansive kitchen, he realized that he was quickly running out of space.

The counters were littered with soufflés in various states of disrepair. What had started early that morning as a craving for a tangy lemon treat had quickly turned into a culinary challenge of epic proportions. When he had run out of lemons, Ulster had switched to salmon as it was then his fourth hour of battle and a savory lunch seemed more appropriate. As night fell, he had switched yet again, this time preferring the fine Swiss chocolate of his homeland.

Yet no matter how hard he tried, the soufflés would not stand.

An entire day of laboring, and he had yet to taste victory.

Ulster laughed at the sight, knowing that he had a busy night ahead of him if he were to have the kitchen cleaned by the time his personal chef returned from his day off.

As he switched off his oven and conceded defeat, he felt the vibration of his cell phone from somewhere deep inside the pocket of his apron. Twisting to retrieve it, his sizeable girth strained against the tightly wrapped fabric. He suddenly felt as if he were bound by the casing of his favorite Polish sausage.

When he finally reached his phone, Ulster was surprised by the blocked number on his caller ID. His private line was unlisted, and he had taken great pains to guard against its dissemination. With that in mind, he decided to play a hunch.

'Jonathon?' he guessed.

'No, this is Jack Cobb. We met in Geneva about a month ago.'

'Of course! We had dinner at the Beau-Rivage.' Some people

used mnemonic devices to recall people and places, but Ulster remembered meals. 'You had just returned from the mountains, if memory serves. Something about a train?'

'Yeah,' Cobb grunted. 'Something like that.'

As far as he knew, it was more than anyone had learned about his previous adventure. Given the purpose of his call, he was encouraged by Ulster's knowledge but slightly disturbed by his insight. He wondered where Ulster had acquired his information because it certainly hadn't been from him.

Then again, their entire relationship had been rooted in mystery. Neither of them was fully aware of the circumstances that had led to their initial conversation – a mysterious benefactor had made the arrangements – but both were willing to play along because both benefited from the relationship. Cobb had access to one of the top historians in the world, and Ulster liked to talk about history even more than he liked to eat and drink.

And that was saying something.

'So, Jack, to what do I owe this honor?'

'You said to give you a call if I ever need help, and the truth is that I've run into some trouble here in Egypt.'

'Alexandria!' Ulster blurted. He suddenly remembered that Cobb had been tasked with exploring the Egyptian city. He didn't know what Cobb was looking for – after all, Cobb didn't even know what he was looking for when he was given the map – but one thing was certain: cleaning the kitchen could wait. 'How stupid of me! Please forgive my momentary lapse of memory. It's been a very stressful day.'

'I know the feeling.'

'I bet you do,' conceded Ulster, who had watched coverage of the bombing on the news. 'The Egyptian authorities have yet to release a statement, but off the record they're downplaying the event. Do they really believe that people will accept their inane story about earthquakes and ruptured gas lines? I have seen my fair share of explosions in recent years, and it's clear to me that this incident was *not* caused by seismic activity.'

'You got that right.'

Ulster lowered his voice to a whisper, as if he were about to deliver privileged information. 'Jack, if you're in trouble, I *know* people. Just tell me what you need, and I will make the call. My friends are former military, and trust me when I say that they're very good at what they do.'

'*I'm* former military,' Cobb argued, half insulted by the comment. 'I appreciate the offer, but I've got that angle covered. The help I'm looking for is more academic in nature. I was hoping you could lend me a hand.'

Though he hardly looked the part in his dirty apron, Ulster was the director of the Ulster Archives, a facility that housed the most extensive private collection of documents and antiquities in the world. Founded in the Alps by Petr's grandfather, the Archives had grown from a small assortment of artifacts – smuggled from Austria to Switzerland in coal cars in advance of the Nazi occupation – to what it was today. Though its early success could be attributed to his ancestors, Petr was directly responsible for its recent additions including a magnificent haul from Mexico.

'Certainly!' Ulster boomed. 'How can I be of service?'

'My team came across something that we're not quite sure how to interpret. I was hoping you could give me your thoughts.'

'Jack,' he said tentatively, 'I'd be happy to help with your project, but I think it's important for you to know that I am not a certified Egyptologist. Yes, I admit that I am somewhat versed in all manners of history – after all, it is a job requirement – but the detailed knowledge that you're looking for should probably come from someone on your own team. That last thing I want to do is to step on anyone's toes.'

Cobb grimaced. 'That's part of the problem. Our historian has gone missing. I have some of the footage she recorded before she disappeared, and I'm asking you to take a look at it. Do you have access to the Internet?'

'Yes, of course. Just give me one moment.'

Ulster removed his apron and tossed it to the ground as he hustled from the kitchen to his nearby office. He activated the hands-free feature on his cell phone as he sank into the over-stuffed, high-back office chair in front of his computer. Then he grabbed the mouse and waited for further instructions. 'Okay, I'm ready. Now what?'

'Look at your e-mail. You should see a message from James Bond. Open it, and click on the link.'

'Look at that,' Ulster laughed. 'I got an e-mail from James Bond!'

'Sorry about that. My computer guy is kind of obsessed.'

Garcia had known that the team would need the camera footage available to them at all times, even when they weren't in range of the boat's wireless network. Rather than load the files onto each of their phones, Garcia had made the data available on a secure website that he had created. The information was streamed from his server, which was encrypted with so much security that it would take even the best hackers weeks to work their way through. Access to the site was normally limited to their personal devices, but Garcia had programmed a temporary password to allow partial access to the system.

Ulster was given the code, and he punched it in.

A moment later, he was scrolling through images.

'These are spectacular,' Ulster blurted.

'So I've been told. But what do they mean?'

54

Cobb had spoken to Ulster on one previous occasion, and he had quickly learned that Ulster had the ability (and the desire) to talk about anything and everything under the sun. So he was more than a little surprised by the silence on the other end of the line.

'Are you still there?' Cobb wondered.

But Ulster didn't respond. He was far too focused on the images on his computer screen to hear that question or any other that Cobb had asked.

'Petr!' Cobb shouted.

'Hmmm, errr, what? Did you say something?'

'I've been saying a lot of somethings, but you've been ignoring me for the past five minutes. If you keep it up, I'm going to shut down your access to the website.'

Ulster flushed with embarrassment. 'Sorry, Jack. I truly am. Sometimes I'm like a horse with blinders: I only focus on what's in front of me. That is particularly true when history is involved, and let me assure you: this *is* history.'

'In what way?'

'In every way!' he said excitedly. 'Hieroglyphs like this simply do not exist in the modern world. The clarity. The depth. It's as if these were carved only yesterday. These symbols are utterly remarkable. Where did you find them?'

'On a wall in the ancient cistern level of the city.'

'Amazing. All this time and they were just waiting there, hidden under everyone's feet. Tell me, is the wall recoverable in a single slab? Or will your team remove it in sections?'

'Recoverable?' Cobb blurted. It suddenly dawned on him that Ulster hadn't connected the dots on his own. 'Petr, listen to me. There's no more wall. There are no more symbols. They don't exist anymore. The bombs destroyed everything.'

Ulster's heart sank. 'Why would someone destroy something like this?'

Cobb rolled his neck. 'Petr, that's why I'm calling you. Our historian was in the middle of examining the wall when she was taken by the bombers. Without her, we don't know what to make of this or why she was taken. I was hoping you could help.'

Now that Ulster understood what was being asked of him, and what was truly at stake, he took a long, hard look at the images. He started with the one that he felt had the most significance. 'This glyph of the horned man symbolizes Alexander the Great. The protrusions are meant to evoke comparisons to Amun-Ra, the head of the Egyptian pantheon. Alexander considered himself the divine progeny of the creator.'

'Go on,' Cobb said.

Ulster clicked forward on the website. 'The rectangular blocks and papyrus reeds represent the foundation of Alexandria. As you may have noticed, trees are scarce in that region. But the annual flooding of the Nile delivered a bounty of mud that could be formed into sun-dried bricks. These were used to create their homes.'

Cobb nodded, satisfied with Ulster's translations. Now that he had seen the historian's abilities firsthand, he was willing to give him one more piece of the puzzle: the brand on the bomber's neck.

'This brings us to image three,' Ulster said as he geared up for his next lecture. 'If you take a closer look at the overlapping triangles, you will notice—'

'Let me cut you off right there.'

Ulster paused. 'Am I going too fast?'

'Definitely not,' Cobb assured him. 'I simply wanted to get your thoughts on a specific image. One that we *need* to keep confidential.'

Ulster nodded in understanding. 'Yes, of course. You can count on me. Though I am a bit loquacious at times, I do it within the bounds of secrecy.'

'Glad to hear it. Please check your e-mail again.'

Ulster did as he was told and opened the new message with a photo of the brand. Even though the symbol was much darker than all of the others, he recognized it immediately. 'Where did you get this? Did it come from the wall?'

'No,' Cobb replied. 'This symbol wasn't carved into stone; it was burned onto flesh. You're looking at the back of a man.'

'Oh my heavens! Then the legends are true!'

'Legends? What legends?'

If Ulster had a weakness other than food and spirits it was his tendency to ramble. Even the simplest of questions were often addressed with long-winded monologues that encompassed much more than was asked. It wasn't arrogance – he had no intention of touting his knowledge or belittling others – he simply felt that some inquiries were worthy of a comprehensive presentation.

Unfortunately for Cobb, this was one of those times.

Ulster took a deep breath. 'As you probably know, the Sahara is one of the most treacherous places on planet Earth. No fewer than seven distinct deserts encompass more than three hundred and fifty thousand square miles, with virtually no water at all. And it has been that way since the Neolithic Era.'

'Did you say *Neolithic?*' Cobb grunted in annoyance. He simply didn't have time for the history of Africa. 'Fast forward please.'

'Yes, of course,' Ulster said, racking his brain for the best place to restart. 'In 525 BC, a Persian army of more than fifty thousand men was ordered to lay siege upon the Oasis of Siwa in western Egypt. Not a single soldier arrived at their destination. How is it possible that *no one* – not a single soul in fifty thousand – survived a direct march across Egypt? Are you telling me that the sun and sand ravaged an army that was well stocked with food, water, and supplies? Or were there other forces involved?'

Cobb jumped in. 'Petr, I'm sorry, but I have no idea what you're talking about. What does any of this have to do with the brand?'

'I was just getting to that,' he assured him. 'As far back as the Persian Empire, there have been stories about the Sahara and the people who defended it. Warriors who could overwhelm any army. Warriors who bore *this* mark. Nowadays, it's probably hard to fathom why someone would still worship an ancient deity like Amun-Ra, but ancient religions – Christianity, Islam, and so on – are still widely practiced throughout the world. As a general rule, the more isolated a community, the more fervent their culture.'

'Meaning?'

'Isolation breeds *purity*. Purity breeds *devotion*. Devotion breeds *fanaticism.* And based on everything I've seen, the bombing in Alexandria was the work of fanatics.'

'No need to tell me.'

Ulster flushed with embarrassment. 'Yes, of course. I didn't mean to suggest that I know more about the devastation than you. I mean, you were *there* in the rubble, and I was *here* on my sofa, and—'

'Petr, relax. I wasn't insulted by your statement. In fact, I found it insightful. I've been trying to wrap my head around the extreme nature of the blast ever since I left the tunnels, and now it makes perfect sense. These men weren't just protecting symbols on a wall; they were protecting their way of life.'

'Exactly,' Ulster said.

'It also explains the other attack.'

'Which attack is that?'

Cobb filled him in. 'We think these warriors were involved in the slaughter of an archaeological team near the Bahariya Oasis. We also have reason to believe that the expedition leader survived the attack. If so, we're hoping that he has information about the men who took our historian.'

Ulster nodded. 'You're referring to Cyril Manjani.'

'Wait! You know about the Manjani expedition?'

'You could say that and a whole lot more. The truth is I actually *know* the man himself. And so do you, on some level. After all, what is a man but his life's work?'

Cobb was certain that he had never met Manjani, and all of that other nonsense about a man's work went directly over his head. 'Honest to God, I have no idea what you're talking about. Absolutely none. Please explain it.'

Ulster nodded. 'The map of Alexandria I gave to you in Geneva?'

'What about it?'

'It's *his* map. *He* found it on *his* expedition.'

The words hit Cobb like a sucker punch, so much so that his brain kept interrupting one thought with the next as he tried to piece everything together.

If Manjani knew—

Then that must mean—

And Jasmine found—

Then the symbols might—

After several seconds of utter confusion, Cobb eventually settled on a single question. 'How did you get the map?'

'How?' Ulster said with a chuckle. 'By opening my mail! Believe it or not, Cyril sent it to me here at the Archives. At first I thought it was some kind of sick joke – after all, I thought he had perished in the attack at the Bahariya Oasis – but once I saw the level of detail, I realized that it wasn't a prank. It couldn't be. It was authentic.'

'But why? If the map was so valuable, why would he give it away?'

Ulster shrugged. 'I don't know for sure, but I'd imagine it had to do with the tragic outcome of his expedition. At least that's what I gathered from his note.'

'What note? You didn't say anything about a note!'

'I didn't?' He laughed at himself. 'Sorry about that. Like I said, sometimes I live my life with blinders, and when I get too involved in one thing, I tend to forget—'

'Petr! Do you still have it?'

'Yes! As a matter of fact, I do. Hang on, I'll read it to you.'

Ulster rummaged through the piles of research strewn about his desk until he found the note that he was looking for. Although the message was written in Ancient Greek, he translated it flawlessly. 'My dearest Petr, it is with great shame that I send you this map. I hope you may someday finish what I have started. Sadly, I dare not risk my life again to find what I sought. Forever grateful, Cyril Manjani.'

Cobb shook his head, trying to fit the pieces of the puzzle together in his mind. Some things made perfect sense. After the slaughter of his team, Manjani was too scared to use the map that he had discovered during his expedition, so he had sent it to the Ulster Archives, a facility that encouraged the sharing of knowledge in the academic community, with the hope that someone else would continue the search for the tomb.

And yet other things made no sense at all: particularly Ulster's motivation for giving the map to Cobb in the first place. If it was as rare and valuable as Jasmine had claimed, why did Ulster give it to someone he had only just met?

'Petr,' Cobb said, 'I hate to put you on the spot like this because I know how much you value confidentiality – ironically, I wouldn't be talking to you if you didn't – but I need to ask you a straightforward question that requires a straightforward answer. Otherwise, I'm not quite sure we can continue our chats.'

'You want to know why I gave you a copy of the map.'

Cobb nodded. 'Exactly.'

'You're right,' Ulster assured him, 'I value confidentiality more than most. After all, my grandfather would have been shot by the Nazis if not for the silence of a great number of people who smuggled our family library out of Austria. Not only would the Archives never have existed, but neither would I.'

'I realize that, which is why—'

Ulster cut him off. 'That being said, I fully understand your need for answers, so I'm willing to speak in hypotheticals. How much do you actually know about the Archives?'

'Only what you've told me and what I've read online.'

'Then you know that the main goal of the Archives is not to hoard artifacts. Instead, it strives to bridge the schism that exists between scholars and collectors. In order to gain admittance to the facility, a visitor must bring something of value, such as an ancient artifact or unpublished research that might be useful to others. In return, we provide access to some of the finest relics in the world. On rare occasions, we allow objects to be loaned out to people who are unable to make it to Küsendorf, but in those cases, we require something extra special as collateral.' Ulster smiled. 'And if they donate something *extraordinary*, I'm willing to personally deliver the item they requested.'

Cobb read between the lines. Obviously the nameless bene-factor who had set up his initial meeting with Ulster had donated something substantial because the Archives were willing to loan out a copy of a map that very few people even knew existed. 'Hypothetically, can you give me an example of extraordinary?'

Ulster smiled even wider. 'Oh, I don't know – perhaps detailed information about a missing train and photographic evidence of everything that was recovered. Something like that would generate a lot of goodwill, don't you think?'

55

Forty-five hundred years ago, the newly constructed Great Pyramid of Giza was revered as the final resting place of the pharaoh Khufu. Only the most noble of visitors were permitted entrance into the sacred grounds. It was an honor reserved for royalty.

Today, anyone can tour the ancient structure.

All it takes is a ticket.

Tourists come from far and wide to stand in the shadows of the Giza pyramids and to marvel at the Great Sphinx. To most, they are simply remnants of a bygone era whose only significance is their ability to withstand the rigors of time. Only a precious few see them for what they really are: monuments to honor fallen gods.

Though she had been to Egypt on several occasions, Sarah had never seen the pyramids in person. Her perception of the area was based entirely on what she had seen on postcards and in movies. It was quickly apparent that these promotional images had been shot from strategic angles at ideal moments in time because the reality of the scene in front of her was almost startling in contrast.

She had always pictured the pyramids as secluded temples with miles of barren desert separating them from any form of civilization. She quickly realized that the urban sprawl from nearby Cairo had overwhelmed the once quaint village of Giza – which was now the second largest suburb in the world with more than two and a half million people – and this unexpected growth had forced a collision between the ancient and modern worlds. As ridiculous as it sounds, it was now possible to tour the Great Pyramid of Giza, an architectural masterpiece that was hailed as one of the Seven Wonders of the Ancient World, and then walk across the street for dinner at Pizza Hut.

Sarah was fascinated – and disappointed – by the dichotomy. 'This is unbelievable. It's not at all like I thought it would be.'

Cobb shrugged but wasn't surprised. 'They put a Starbucks in China's Forbidden City. Why should this be any different?'

Sarah stood near the base of the Great Pyramid and lifted her gaze toward the sky, taking in the towering peak that stood more than 450 feet above her. 'It's not *just* the Pizza Hut. It's . . . I mean, look at this thing! It's crumbling as I speak!'

Sadly, her description was accurate. The smooth casing that originally blanketed the sides of the pyramid had been torn off centuries ago. In 1356, Sultan An-Nasir Nasir-ad-Din al-Hasan ordered that the polished limestone exterior be used to build mosques in Cairo, and the removal of the pyramid's outer layer had left it vulnerable ever since.

Exposed to the desert winds, the stone had become cracked and broken. Chunks of rock had fallen from the massive two-ton slabs that lined the sides, littering the ground with boulders of various sizes. The flat, pristine slopes were now jagged and stepped. It had taken centuries, but the elements had ravaged the surface of the pyramids.

The condition of the ruins, everything from the crumbling façade of the pyramids to the missing nose on the Great Sphinx, made Cobb reconsider what they had discovered underneath Alexandria. If the Giza Plateau had been allowed to fall into such disrepair, what did it say about the tunnel they had found? It seemed that the pictograph on the underground wall had been cared for in a way that the Great Pyramid had not.

But why?

And by whom?

Cobb would have to ponder those questions later. At the moment, he needed to focus on the task at hand. 'You're sure your friend will meet us here?'

Sarah nodded. 'He'll show – despite the warning.'

The US State Department had recently issued an alert to avoid the most popular tourist spots in Egypt. It wasn't that Americans were being targeted, per se, but US officials weren't entirely comfortable with the bombing in Alexandria and the mobs of demonstrators expressing their displeasure over the current political climate. It would only take a tiny spark to set off a full-blown revolution, and the last thing the American embassy needed was a group of sightseers getting caught up in the civil unrest – with the whole world watching on CNN.

Cobb scanned the plaza as a busload of tourists made their way into the grounds. 'And you're sure you'll recognize him after all these years?'

'Trust me, I'll know him. He always looks dapper.'

'Dapper?'

She smiled and nodded. 'See what I mean?'

Cobb turned and followed her gaze. He saw a well-groomed man looking back at them, his broad smile accentuated by a canary yellow bow tie and matching suspenders.

'Subtle,' Cobb whispered.

Sarah shuffled aside as the group passed, leaving one man standing in front of her. 'Seymour, you never disappoint.'

The man beamed. 'Thank you, my dear. I do make an effort.'

She turned to Cobb. 'Jack, this is Seymour Duggan. He's the best bloodhound I've ever worked with and a genuinely good guy.'

Seymour thanked her for the compliment by doffing an imaginary cap before he extended his hand toward Cobb. 'Pleased to meet you. I hope I can help.'

'Me, too,' Cobb said, but he was doubtful.

At first blush, Seymour looked more like an accountant than a CIA asset. Skinny and balding, his diminutive frame was covered by an impeccable linen suit. His loud tie matched both his suspenders and the handkerchief that he was using to dab his brow. There was also the matter of his accent, which was definitely non-American.

'Kiwi?' Cobb asked.

'Guilty as charged,' Seymour said. 'Born and raised in Christchurch, on the eastern side of the island. Have you ever been?'

'No,' he admitted. 'The closest I've been is Australia.'

'Scared of hobbits, are you?'

It was Seymour's attempt at a joke.

Cobb didn't laugh. 'No.'

Sarah, on the other hand, found the whole exchange incredibly

374

entertaining. Still, she knew better than to let the awkwardness linger for too long. 'Seymour started in the New Zealand Intelligence Corps. Based on his record, MI6 requested that he be loaned out to help with their caseload. That's how he came to our attention. A few years later he was retired from duty in England and given an official cover in Helsinki through a joint effort with the CIA.'

'Doing what?' Cobb wondered.

Seymour smiled. 'Believe it or not, they had me posing as an auditor for the Internal Revenue Service. I was supposedly there to ensure that those with dual citizenship had filed their tax returns correctly.'

'Hard to imagine,' Cobb joked. If he had all night, he couldn't have thought of a more perfect cover. 'What brought you to Egypt?'

'The climate – I find the cold intolerable.' Seymour smiled as he looked around the pyramid complex. Despite his claims, he continued to mop the sweat from his face. 'What a lovely day. Getting out of the apartment is such a nice change of pace. Pity I don't do it more often. Excursions like this are a welcomed treat.'

'Well, I'm glad you're enjoying yourself. But I have to ask: if your apartment is in Cairo, why meet all the way out here?'

Seymour had anticipated the question. 'First, you can't walk across the street in Cairo right now without someone wondering what you're up to. The bombing in Alexandria saw to that. Everyone's on high alert – the authorities and the general public. Coming out here was the best way to stay off the radar. Here, none of us stands out.'

Cobb was tempted to make a crack about Seymour's choice

of attire, because it *definitely* stood out, but he ultimately decided to keep the comment to himself.

'More importantly,' he continued, 'I asked to meet you here because Giza was one of the last places in Egypt where your target, Cyril Manjani, was seen alive.'

56

The first thing that Jasmine noticed was the ringing in her head. The unavoidable tone enveloped her, drowning out not only sounds but her senses as well.

She instinctively brought her hands to her ears, hoping to block out the incessant noise. When her fingers touched the bandage that covered her temple, a creeping sensation of pain began to take hold. It was a deep, steady throbbing that blended perfectly with the cacophony inside her skull. She knew they were one and the same.

Lying in the dark, she moved her hands around her head, searching for the source of her suffering. The cloth dressing was dry so at least she wasn't bleeding. She strained to open her eyes, but her eyelids felt heavy. The simple act of blinking required tremendous effort, and even then her dimly lit surroundings were little more than a blur.

The thick cobwebs in her mind made it tough to focus.

Just breathe, she thought.

The air was warm and dry. Every breath felt gritty against the parched lining of her throat. She could smell the faintest wisp of smoke, and she knew that flame, not electricity, was lighting the room.

She licked her cracked lips and forced herself to swallow.

Her stomach rolled unnaturally. It wasn't hunger; more like her body's desperate attempt to fend off a foreign toxin. She fought hard against the nausea, hoping it would pass as she continued to gather her wits.

It took some time before she could open her eyes, and once she did, she confirmed her suspicions about the smoke. High above the room, a heavy clay pot of burning oil dangled from a rope of braided reeds. The flickering light was faint and could barely reach the nearest wall. The rest of the space was shrouded in darkness.

Jasmine's mind raced as she tried to recall the last thing she could remember.

A solitary hut in the desert.

Walking desperately through the sand.

The nomads that came to her aid.

And the monsters that killed them.

The muscles in her arms and shoulders ached and her joints were stiff, as if they hadn't been used for days. A dull burning spread throughout her body as she drew her blistered feet toward her chest. The sound of iron chains being dragged across the stone floor left her troubled and confused. She reached down her legs and felt the cold metal that bound each ankle.

She couldn't imagine why she had been shackled.

Or could she?

Slowly, pieces of her adventure started to reemerge.

She knew she had been searching for something deep under the city of Alexandria. She remembered crawling through an unmarked opening into the hidden space beyond, all the while trespassing into areas that were off-limits to anyone but the Egyptian authorities. She quickly considered the very real possibility that she had been imprisoned for her actions. She dismissed the notion just as quickly, knowing that even the Ministry of

State for Antiquities wouldn't throw an American in a dungeon for a minor offense. And they certainly wouldn't kill a bunch of nomads to recapture her.

No, there had to be another explanation.

As she tried to replay the events in her head, she could hear Garcia's voice in her ear, telling her that they weren't alone in the cisterns. She remembered Cobb and McNutt doubling back to investigate while she and Sarah pressed on. Eventually Sarah left her side and headed further into the darkness while she stayed behind to continue her examination of the wall. Then she saw a shadow on the wall and—

Oh my God. I was attacked in the tunnels.

Memories of the assault came flooding back to her.

There was nothing she could have done to stop it.

The assailant had been big and strong and agile.

She was overwhelmed in a matter of seconds.

Haunted by the feeling of helplessness, she staggered to her feet and studied the wall ahead. It wasn't made of cut stone blocks like the walls of the cisterns. It looked more like poured cement, though the crumbling texture meant that it had aged considerably. She thought back to the support pillars she had found in the tunnel and wondered if this too was Roman concrete.

As she stepped closer, she saw that it wasn't cement or concrete of any kind. Instead, the wall was comprised of tightly packed sun-dried bricks – similar to the construction of the desert hut but more uniform and refined. The mortar between them was nearly invisible, giving the wall a monolithic feel.

From experience, she knew that such materials were common not only in Egypt, but throughout the Middle East as well. The only distinguishing feature of the brick was the acrid scent it left on her fingers.

For some reason, it reminded her of the sea.

Even more confusing was the strange sense that she had been transported back in time. The art of drying clay and mud into rough blocks has been practiced for thousands of years. It went hand in hand with the ancient style of oil lamp she had already noticed. Even the iron fetters fastened around her ankles appeared to be forged by hand, rather than stamped by modern machinery.

This place – whatever it was – hadn't changed in centuries.

Rather than succumb to her fear, she channeled it. The ancient lamp was beyond her reach, but the length of chain at her feet gave her freedom to move about the room. Using what little light she had, she began to systematically probe the boundaries for any chance of escape. She quickly made a startling discovery.

It wasn't a door, a window, or an exit of any kind.

It was the unexpected sight of a man.

In the dark corner on the opposite side of the room, the emaciated figure lay curled on the floor. His clothes were soiled and tattered. His sun-kissed flesh was beaten and bruised. Scruffy, unshaven whiskers covered his face, and dried blood from his nose coated his upper lip.

Jasmine hesitated, unsure of how to proceed. 'Hello?'

It was a word that was almost universally understood in any language. She would worry about translating his response later – *if* there was a response.

But there wasn't.

She tried again, this time slightly louder. 'Hello?'

Not only did the man not answer, he hadn't moved an inch. He was perfectly motionless, lying still on the floor.

Summoning her courage, Jasmine moved closer to check for signs of life, but the limits of her chain stopped her short of her destination. She leaned as close as she could, searching for a muscle twitch or the steady rise and fall of his chest – any sign to indicate that the man was still alive.

But there was none.

The only thing she saw were the shackles around his feet.

They were a perfect match to hers.

57

Cobb glanced around the Giza Plateau. He wondered if the news about Manjani would force them to investigate every nook and cranny of the pyramids. He had to admit that he was looking forward to the day when he could tour an ancient landmark just for kicks, rather than a life-or-death mission.

'Dr Manjani was spotted here? I thought he lost his team in the desert?'

'He did,' Seymour replied as he dabbed his brow with his handkerchief, 'but a few weeks before their disappearance, they assembled here in Giza.'

'Do you know why?'

Seymour nodded as he pulled his phone from his jacket pocket. He tapped the screen several times until he found the file that he was looking for. 'They were meeting with this man – a Dr Shakir Farid, of Al-Azhar University in Cairo.'

Cobb and Sarah studied the image that had been pulled from the school's website. Farid's eyes were bright and his smile looked natural. He seemed more like a grandfather reacting to a school play than a professor sitting for a school photo.

'Why did they meet Farid?' Sarah asked.

'Given the proposed length of their expedition and the foreign backgrounds of the students, they all needed official document-ation. Manjani was granted a work visa because he was heading up the team, but the others needed an Egyptian professor to sponsor their student visas. That's where Farid came in. They all had dinner together in Giza so that he could meet everyone before the dig. He even paid for their meals before they were given a private tour of the pyramids.'

Unfamiliar with Seymour's work, Cobb wasn't willing to take everything at face value, so he decided to test him on his methods. 'I know the names of the students were listed in news reports – which, I'm guessing, is what led you to their visas. But how do you know that Farid paid for dinner?'

Seymour was up to the challenge. 'Five double rooms and one single were reserved at a local hotel in Giza. All of these rooms were charged to Manjani's credit card. However, the cards kept on file for incidentals belonged to the rooms' actual occupants. Four of these cards were used that day within a ten-block radius of the hotel for toiletries, souvenirs, and the like. But no one, including Manjani, had a charge for dinner.'

'And Farid did?' Cobb asked.

Seymour nodded. 'On the night in question, he had a substantial charge at a local Kentucky Fried Chicken; the one right across the street from here. Now, I've been known to eat my fair share of fast food, but even I can't consume three buckets of chicken and a dozen drinks in a single meal. Maybe two buckets, but certainly not three.'

Seymour snorted at his own joke. It was an obnoxious sound like a pig sniffing for truffles, but coming from the bow-tied Seymour, it was actually endearing.

Sarah smiled. It had been a while since she had heard his laugh. 'What about recently? Any activity on the students' cards since their disappearance?'

He shook his head. 'There were no hits on their credit cards, their mobile phones, or their e-mail accounts. They disappeared without a trace. Literally. No footprints at all – either in the sand or digitally.'

'What about Manjani?' Cobb asked. 'I was led to believe that he was spotted after the incident.'

'He was,' Seymour confirmed. 'He spent one night in a seedy hotel in el-Bawiti, a small town in the Western Desert, before he disappeared as well.'

'How do you know?'

'Because I'm good at what I do.'

'Let me guess: he used his credit card.'

Seymour shook his head. 'Actually, Manjani was smarter than most. He didn't use a credit card to pay for the room or his cell phone to make any calls. But he did use a payphone to reach out to someone from his past, and that's where he slipped up. On the night in question, he used a payphone across the street from the hotel to call Dr Farid. Not once, not twice, but five times. My guess was to warn him, or to ask for assistance, or both.'

Sarah nodded in understanding. 'He must have been scared out of his mind. Did he ever get in touch with Farid?'

'He couldn't,' Seymour replied. 'Farid was already dead.'

Her mouth dropped open. 'Someone killed him?'

Seymour quickly realized his mistake. 'No, not at all! The man was seventy-eight years old and in failing health. He passed away shortly after the team had left for the desert, which meant Manjani was unaware of his death.'

'You're sure it wasn't foul play?'

'Foul play, no. *Fowl* play, maybe. Three buckets of extra crispy would stop most people's hearts.' Seymour snorted again, even louder than before. So much so that a group of tourists glanced over to determine the source of the obnoxious sound.

Cobb grabbed Seymour's arm and gently pulled him away. The last thing he wanted was to turn up on anyone's radar. 'Tell me more about Manjani. Was he clean?'

'Squeaky,' Seymour assured them. 'The same with Farid and the rest of the team. I've looked into academic records, work histories, credit reports, and every other digital source you can think of. Manjani and Farid were incredibly respected among their colleagues. Every peer evaluation was filled with glowing remarks and notes of admiration. The students all performed at honors level, and none has any challenges to their integrity in their files. Except for a couple of traffic tickets, they're spotless.'

Cobb nodded in appreciation. After working with Dade, a street hustler who talked in half-truths, Cobb loved the military efficiency of Seymour's reports. Although he could do without the loud snorting, the material itself was first rate.

'And the students?' Cobb asked.

'What would you like to know?'

'What were they studying?'

'Everything,' Seymour claimed. 'Archaeology, Egyptology, Roman literature, pagan theology, Greek antiquities, Mediterranean folklore, archaeoastronomy, and a few others. It was quite the diverse collection. I'm not sure how all of these areas fit together, but I can tell you that their divergent backgrounds are decidedly Manjani-esque.'

Sarah didn't understand the reference. 'How so?'

'Dr Cyril Manjani held – or rather *holds* – doctorates in several of the aforementioned fields and has published articles in many others. Based on all that I have read, I am quite comfortable calling him an über-genius.'

Cobb grimaced. If Manjani was as intelligent as Seymour claimed, then there was a damn good chance that he would never be found. And even if he were, it would probably be far too late to do Jasmine any good. 'So, what do you think?'

'About?' he asked, puzzled.

'Can an über-genius be tracked?'

Seymour grinned. 'He might be book-smart, but that doesn't always translate to the street smart. He's good at covering his tracks, but he's not the best. Let me ask you, what's the first thing you do every morning?'

Cobb stared at him. 'I take a piss.'

Seymour snorted. 'Okay, after that?'

'I eat breakfast and clean my gun – but not necessarily in that order. Seriously, where are you going with this?'

Sarah interrupted him. 'Unlike Rambo over here, I tend to be a little less soldierly. The first thing I do is check my e-mail.'

'Me, too,' Seymour laughed. 'And, thankfully, so does Manjani. He's using a brand-new account that's being routed through a web server in the middle of the Aegean Sea, but I'm sure it's your man.'

'The Aegean?' she blurted. 'There are literally hundreds of islands, not to mention thousands of boats, in the Aegean. Any way you can narrow it down for us?'

'Of course I can,' he said proudly, as he tucked his thumbs underneath his suspenders and snapped them against his chest. 'Dr Manjani is hiding on the island of Amorgos.'

58

Thursday, November 6
Katapola, Amorgos
(140 miles southeast of Athens, Greece)

Surrounded by the turquoise waters of the Aegean Sea, the island of Amorgos is located at the easternmost edge of the Greek Cyclades, one of the island groups that make up the Aegean archipelago.

With no airport on Amorgos, those who wish to visit can do so by private boat or on one of the public ferries that service the island's two ports: Katapola in the south and Aegiali in the north. These shuttles – which include catamarans, jet boats, and traditional cruisers – offer daily routes between Amorgos and the nearby islands.

Unfortunately, it was a long way from Egypt.

The quickest way for Cobb and Sarah to reach the Cyclades would have been to charter a seaplane in Cairo to fly them directly to the island of their choice. But Cobb took that option off the table when he learned that air traffic near Amorgos was sparse at best. Circling the island a couple of times on a sight-seeing tour was one thing, but actually touching down just off shore was bound to attract unwanted attention.

Another possibility was to grab a flight to Athens, then work their way south. It wasn't a difficult trip, but it wasn't fast, either. By the time they made their connecting flight from Athens to Naxos and then caught the ferry from Naxos to Katapola, they would have wasted more than a day. They needed to get there as soon as possible if they hoped to catch Manjani when he checked his e-mail as part of his morning routine.

Their answer came in the form of a regional airline that promised to have them in Santorini shortly after dawn. From there, it would take less than two hours to reach Amorgos by boat as long as the weather stayed clear and the sea remained calm. As fate should have it, their quest was noble and the gods blessed their journey.

And no one released the Kraken.

The high-speed ferry arrived at the port city of Katapola just after nine. Cobb stared out the window at the rocky coast of the small island, searching for hidden beaches among the sheer cliffs. Sarah wasn't interested in the sights. She had spent the entire trip curled up on the seat beside him, getting caught up on her sleep.

He couldn't blame her.

It had been a grueling week.

Initially, they had hoped to blend in with the crowd as it left the ferry, but it turned out they were the only ones departing in Katapola. In fact, they were the only ones in sight, as if the entire island had been deserted for an impending disaster.

And yet that wasn't the strangest thing that he noticed.

Or *didn't* notice.

Cobb had visited many ports in his life, and the one thing that all of them had in common were signs for local destinations. In St Petersburg, imposing steel placards with massive Cyrillic letters announced routes inland. In Montego Bay, there were charming, hand-painted wooden planks that pointed to the nearest bar. The signage was distinct for each country, but the goal was the same: to guide new arrivals.

But in Katapola, there were no signs at all.

Sarah noticed it, too. 'How's your Greek?'

'Slightly worse than yours,' Cobb replied.

'Which means it's non-existent.'

They headed inland, hoping to spot someone who could point them in the right direction. Eventually, Sarah spotted a man sprawled on a wooden bench. At first she thought he might be dead, but as they approached he popped upright as if he had been caught sleeping on the job by his supervisor.

She smiled, and the man smiled back.

He even raised his hand and waved.

'Jack, take a look.'

As Cobb followed her gaze, the man stopped waving and signaled for them to come forward, letting them know that he would welcome a conversation.

'You are lost?' he called out. A Scandinavian accent tinged his words, but it was the alcohol in his system that slurred his speech.

'Just a bit,' Sarah admitted.

'Where you going? Maybe Jarkko can help.'

'Who's Jarkko?' she asked, confused.

'I'm Jarkko!' he announced proudly. 'And Jarkko knows the sea like a butcher knows his meat. Yesterday was Athens. Today is Amorgos. Tomorrow is Malta – *if* Jarkko can find it in the dark. The island is quite small, and Jarkko is quite drunk.'

With no other options, she was willing to humor their new

companion. Walking closer, she saw his callused hands and sunburned face. Together with his three-day beard, Jarkko had the look of a man who had spent his lifetime on the water. She scanned the slips nearby, focusing on a battered wreck of a fishing boat.

'Yours?' she asked.

Jarkko looked at the boat and laughed. Then he turned in the opposite direction and pointed to a magnificent yacht anchored far offshore. It rivaled the size and splendor of that yacht that Papineau had secured for them in Alexandria – which meant it cost a lot more than a drunken fisherman could afford.

'That one,' Jarkko bragged.

Cobb rolled his eyes. 'Great. He's drunk *and* delusional.'

Jarkko laughed at the suggestion as he pulled out a Thermos from under the bench. He then filled the cap with steaming brown liquid and offered it to Cobb. 'Kafka?'

Cobb didn't speak Greek, or Swedish, or whatever language the crusty fisherman had just muttered, but a hot cup of coffee sounded pretty damn good at that moment. Despite his reservations about the man himself, Cobb knew that in some parts of the world declining an offer of food or drink was tantamount to a slap in the face.

'Sure,' he said as he grabbed the cup and lifted it toward his mouth. A split second before he took a sip, he caught a whiff of its aroma and turned his head in disgust. 'Oh my God, what is this shit? You said it was coffee. That's *not* coffee.'

Jarkko started to laugh. And not a normal conversational laugh, but a loud, booming chortle that shook his entire body. 'Not coffee. *Kafka*. Mixture of coffee and vodka. My own creation. Is good, no?'

'No!' Cobb objected as he handed the cup to Sarah so she

could take a whiff. 'It's not good at all! It smells like piss that's been mixed with lighter fluid. Seriously, how can you drink that stuff?'

Jarkko patted his belly. 'I am tough guy. Iron stomach.'

'And a pickled liver,' Cobb added.

Jarkko stared at him and burped his rebuttal.

Sensing an opportunity to belittle Cobb while ingratiating herself with a local, Sarah took a sniff of the liquid, shrugged like it was no big deal, and then drank the kafka in a mighty gulp as if she were at a bachelorette party in Las Vegas. To make the moment complete, she glanced at Cobb and sneered. 'You're such a pussy.'

Cobb started to defend himself, but quickly realized that anything he said would fall short of the mark, so he simply held his tongue in silence.

Meanwhile, Jarkko's reaction was the exact opposite. He looked at Sarah with puppy dog eyes and muttered the first thing that came to mind. 'I think I love you.'

Sarah smiled and handed him his cup. 'In that case, I was hoping you could give me some directions.'

'Yes!' he exclaimed as he rose to his feet. 'Jarkko will give you anything! His Thermos! His yacht! His sexy underwear! Tell me, do you like to fish?'

'I do,' she said as she gently pushed him back down, 'but let's start with directions. Do you know a place called Diosmarini's?'

'Yes! Jarkko knows it very well. It is up steep hill. If you climb on Jarkko's back, Jarkko will carry you there – *and* pay for breakfast.'

'As tempting as that sounds,' she grabbed Cobb's elbow for emphasis, '*we* have a previous engagement.'

Jarkko groaned in heartbreak. 'You are engaged? Why you flirt with Jarkko?'

She smiled at him. 'Because you're too sexy to ignore.'

'Yes – Jarkko sees point. Jarkko has forgiven you!'

'Glad to hear it.'

'So,' Cobb said as he glanced at his watch, 'the café is right up the hill?'

Jarkko nodded. 'Yes, keep walking. You find, right there. Look for white sign, white tables, white chairs. It is so bright even *you* can find it.'

59

Jarkko's directions to the restaurant were spot on, much to the surprise of Cobb, who figured there was a damn good chance that the Finn sat on the bench all day, drinking his kafka, and randomly making up directions for wayward travelers in order to amuse himself. Then again, Jarkko's affection for Sarah seemed so genuine that his moment of accuracy was probably intended to impress her rather than to reward Cobb.

Either way, the café was right where it was supposed to be.

And more importantly, so was Dr Manjani.

According to Seymour, the missing professor checked his e-mail every morning at Diosmarini's café, using a local wireless network. Sometimes he remained online for minutes, and other times hours, but he made an appearance every single day. To find him, all they had to do was show up for breakfast.

The smell of roasted beans flooded their nostrils as Cobb tried to distance himself from the memory of the dreaded kafka. Though he longed for the biggest espresso that they were willing to make, he walked through the restaurant to the courtyard beyond where he spotted the professor at one of the ubiquitous white tables.

Manjani's hair was shaggy and unkempt. Thick, bushy eyebrows pushed the frames of his glasses away from his face as he read from his laptop, forcing him to stare down his nose like Santa Claus checking his naughty list. He had dark circles under his eyes and his clothes hung loosely, as if he wasn't sleeping or eating at all.

Cobb had seen several pictures of Manjani from the weeks and months before his disappearance, and the man he was staring at was a shell of his former self. If Cobb hadn't been aware of the tragedy in the desert, he would have assumed that the professor was dying from cancer or some other horrible disease that ravaged its victims over time. Instead, he sensed the only things eating away at Manjani were his inner demons.

Remorse for the students who had lost their lives.

Shame for running away from his past.

Guilt over his survival.

As a former soldier who had lost men in combat, Cobb could identify with those feelings better than most. So much so that he could spot the suffering from across the room, like a pusher spotting a junkie. And yet, even though he felt empathy for Manjani – because based on everything he had heard, the professor was a good guy in a bad situation – Cobb knew that they were there for information, and he was willing to do just about anything to obtain it.

Cobb headed forward until Sarah grabbed his arm.

'Slow down,' she whispered as she pulled him aside. 'So, what's your plan? Are you going to stroll right up to him, tell him who you are, and lean on him for information?'

'Pretty much. But you know, *subtle.*'

She smiled. 'I've seen your version of subtle, and it's typically anything but. How about you sit this one out and let me handle things?'

'Sarah, we don't have time for games.'

'Jack,' she said, 'when you were in the Army, how often did you go up to the enemy, tap him on the shoulder, and ask him questions about his past?'

'Define "tap".'

'That's what I thought.'

'What's your point?' he asked.

'We did things different in the CIA. Much different. The trick is to get all the information that you need without arousing suspicion of any kind. You don't want anyone to clam up because you asked the wrong questions or gave off the wrong vibe. Trust me, it takes a lot of panache to pull it off.'

Cobb grimaced. 'Are you saying you don't like my style?'

'No,' she assured him, 'I'm not saying that at all. I just think this particular job might need a woman's touch.'

'Fine. Who did you have in mind?'

'Very funny.'

'I thought so,' he said as he took a seat at an empty table on the opposite side of the patio from Manjani. 'He's all yours. Let me know if I can help.'

'Just be sure to smile and wave when he looks your way.' She pulled the tie from her ponytail and ran her fingers through her hair. 'How do I look?'

Cobb shrugged. 'Meh.'

She smiled. 'You're such an ass.'

'Not really. I'm just lacking *panache*.'

'Touché,' she said before heading toward Manjani.

The patio overlooked the striking blue water of the Aegean. Waves crashed gently in the background as Manjani worked at the table he had commandeered near the far wall. The carafe of coffee and the empty plates that had yet to be cleared told Sarah that he was a regular, and that the staff were content to leave him alone.

She had to admit. His office had a hell of a view.

As she approached his table, Manjani caught her from the corner of his eye. He instinctively recoiled as he shielded his laptop from her prying eyes.

She caught it all and realized he was spooked.

She knew better than to ignore the reaction.

'Oh, I'm sorry to interrupt. I was just wondering if you're on the Internet right now?' She pretended to catch herself. 'Oh, umm, can you even understand me? Do you speak English?' She started to pantomime her question, suddenly aware that she had no idea what gesture would convey the concept of the World Wide Web.

The bewilderment wasn't part of her gambit, but it fit in seamlessly.

Her moment of honest confusion had broken the ice.

Manjani smiled. 'Yes, I speak English. And yes, there is access to the Internet.'

'Perfect!' she gushed. 'I hate to bother you, but can you tell me who won the game? We've haven't seen a computer since the weekend, and my boyfriend is simply beside himself. The longer he waits, the grumpier he gets.'

Manjani stared at her. 'Which game?'

'Wow, I honestly don't know. Sports aren't my thing at all.' She turned around and waved at Cobb. 'Honey, which game did you care about again?'

Cobb didn't have to pretend or lie. In the chaos of the past few days, he hadn't found the time to check any weekend scores from the NFL. 'The Steelers.'

'The Steelers,' Sarah repeated.

Manjani, who had much better things to do than to check scores for tourists, begrudgingly typed in the data and quickly found the result. 'Pittsburgh won, 31-3.'

'Yes!' Cobb replied with a fist pump. 'Thanks.'

Sarah lowered her voice to a whisper. 'Thank you so much. You just made his day – *and* mine. Maybe he'll shut up now and enjoy himself.'

Manjani reluctantly cracked a smile.

'I hate to push my luck,' she said when she spotted an opening, 'but do you know if there's anything good to see around here? Besides the water, of course. We're going to see enough of that while we're sailing around the islands.'

Manjani stared at her quizzically.

His body was rigid and defensive, but his expression was soft.

Sarah wondered if he was actually thankful for the company.

'Yes,' he eventually said. 'There's a monastery on the eastern side of the island, not far. Near Chora. It's built into the cliffs. Simply beautiful.' He looked at her jeans. 'You will need a long skirt. Women are not permitted to be dressed like this.'

She smiled. 'Lucky for me, I brought one. My friends told me that it wouldn't be tropical this time of year, so I brought plenty of long sleeves for the cool nights.'

Manjani nodded his approval. In the summer months, the temperature in the Greek Islands was typically in the low-to-mid-eighties. But in November, the temperature regularly dropped below sixty degrees.

'Does this monastery have a name?' she asked.

'It is known as the Monastery of Panagia Hozoviotissa.'

'Wow. Try to say that three times fast.'

He smiled. 'It's a mouthful, I know. It's even worse in Greek.'

'Wait! *That* was in English?'

'Yes,' he said with a laugh. This time, it wasn't forced or stilted. After a rocky start, he seemed to be loosening up. 'So, what brings you to Amorgos?'

Sarah stepped closer, placing her hand on an empty chair at Manjani's table. 'We've been meaning to do something like this for a while. We talked about Paris, or maybe Hong Kong, but then I saw the Greek Islands on a travel site. Beautiful scenery, friendly people, and really affordable in the off season. The plan is to bop around the Aegean for a couple of weeks, take in the sights, and eat as much baklava as I can.'

'Sounds like a tasty plan to me.'

She laughed and pointed at the empty chair, asking for permission to join him. He considered the request for an unnaturally long time before he smiled warmly and closed his laptop, as if to say his computer could wait until later. It was obvious that he trusted her enough to chat for a bit but not enough to see what he was working on.

Still, his frosty demeanor was melting.

She eased into the seat. 'Do you have any suggestions on what to see? We checked out the Acropolis in Athens before we caught our boat. That place was amazing. It's, like, there's American history – and then there's Greek history. They're, like, two completely different things. One's modern and the other one's ancient.'

'I'm afraid I'm not much for history. At least not anymore.'

'Really? I find that surprising.'

'You do? Why's that?' he laughed.

She calmly placed her hand on his. 'I was told differently.'

His smile withered. 'By whom?'

'Your old friend, Petr Ulster.'

She saw a flash of fear in his eyes and a lump catch in his throat. Then she noticed his muscles tense as he tried to pull away. With a few simple words, she had triggered his most primal instincts: fight or flight?

Manjani, who was unarmed, was too old for fisticuffs.

But he was very tempted to run.

She subtly shook her head. 'You have nothing to fear. Not from us.'

He stared at her. 'Then why have you come?'

Instead of answering, she leaned forward in her chair. She had only known Manjani for a few minutes, but it was long enough to get a feel for him. Her years of experience had revealed a lot about the man, and she needed to trust her skills.

She could see the guilt in his eyes.

He felt responsible for his team's slaughter.

'Dr Manjani,' she whispered, 'if you want to walk away, we're not going to chase you. Honestly, we won't. We'll leave the island and disappear forever. But just so you know: you are the *only* person on the planet who can save our friend.'

'Your friend? What do you mean?'

She pulled a folded copy of his map from her pocket and showed it to him. 'Your map told us where to start, but we need to know more if we're going to find her.'

'Who?' he demanded. 'Who are you talking about?'

'While we were exploring the tunnels underneath the city, our friend – our *historian* – was abducted by the men who attacked your team. To have any chance of finding her, we need to know what happened in the desert and how you got away.'

It was obvious that Manjani didn't want to talk, much less think, about the details of the slaughter, and yet the guilt he felt was so pronounced it kept him glued to his chair, as if the bodies of the victims weighed him down. 'And if I help you, what are you going to do about it?'

'We're going to save her and kill them.'

Her answer caught him off guard.

So much so, he needed a moment to think.

Manjani stared at his map as a wave of emotions crashed into him like the water against the rocks below. Somehow, someway, he knew that he would eventually be found on the tiny island of Amorgos, but he had always assumed it would be by the shadow priests of Amun, not a couple of Americans who were searching for *them*.

If not for the danger, the irony would be delicious.

'Not here,' Manjani said as he threw money on the table to pay his tab. Then he tucked his computer under his arm. 'Come with me.'

60

Jasmine sat in the center of the dungeon floor staring at the ancient door. The mere sight of it had once lifted her spirits, but now it taunted her. For all she knew, it was the only thing standing between her and freedom.

After spotting the body in the corner of her cell, she had gone back to her exploration of the room. The heavy chain attached to the shackles around her ankles had kept her from investigating the entire space, but she was determined to scour every inch that she could reach. Hindered by the lack of light, she had felt her way around the edges of the chamber until she found the door. The smooth texture of the wooden slab had been easy to distinguish from the rough masonry of the wall.

Finally, she had found the handle.

For a moment, it had given her hope.

Though the keyhole presented a much different challenge than the barrel locks of the handcuffs in the desert hut, Sarah had explained the function of tumblers in great detail during Jasmine's training. By no means was she ready to take on Fort Knox, but she understood the basics of what she needed to do. With enough time and a healthy dose of luck, Jasmine was sure she could unlock the door.

If, and only if, she found something that resembled a lock pick.

So far, that had proven to be a difficult task.

Comically, it wasn't until sometime later that she had faced the larger issue at hand. Even if she had been able to open the door, she was still chained to the wall. And the shackles around her ankles had no locks to pick – they were solid rings of iron that had been hammered into place.

Jasmine winced at the memory of her oversight.

It sounded like something McNutt would do.

She lay back on the floor and shifted her focus to the oil lamp that dangled above, strangely wishing that it had been a candelabrum. At least the melting wax of a burning candle would have offered her a sense of time. She knew it was an arbitrary sense since she had no way of knowing how fast a random candle burned, but at least it was a measurable unit. She would have been much more at ease knowing she had been trapped for three candles . . . or twelve . . . or two hundred.

Instead, all she had was the continuous flame of the lamp.

With nothing else to entertain her, she began to reflect on her predicament. She knew that her exposure to the events of the last couple of months had changed her outlook considerably. She also knew that much of that change was brought about by her growing relationships with the team, particularly Sarah. Before their adventure, she would have resigned herself to the inevitable, patiently waiting to be rescued. But the confidence she had recently gained meant she now understood the need to make her own fate.

Accepting her imprisonment wasn't an option.

Jasmine closed her eyes and thought back to the events in the tunnel when the silence was shattered by a sharp grating noise that echoed through the cell. She couldn't place the direction of the sound because of the acoustics in the room, but she wanted to be ready if she was about to have visitors. She tensed, focusing on the self-defense techniques that Cobb had insisted she learn before their last adventure. All of the repetition, all of the muscle memory – it had led to this moment. Or had it?

She heard the sound again.

This time, she was able to locate the source.

It wasn't coming from the door.

It was coming from the grave.

Amazingly, the man in the corner of the room – the one she had assumed was dead – had suddenly come to life. As he emerged from his drug-induced sleep, he struggled to sit up on his own. Every time he tried, his chain rattled against the stone floor and he flopped over like a toddler learning to walk.

A moment passed before he spotted Jasmine in the center of the room, watching him from afar with a mixture of empathy and fear. His sunken eyes locked on hers as if pleading for his life. Eventually, he mustered the strength to ask a single question, one bathed in desperation and doubt.

'Where . . . are . . . we?'

61

After leaving the café, Manjani led Sarah and Cobb to a barren stretch of coastline near the harbor, where they could talk in private. Sensing anger and distrust from Manjani, Sarah knew she had to repair some of the damage she had caused by her deceit in the restaurant. She wasn't planning to reveal classified details regarding her past, but she felt that she needed to be truthful about some basics in order to gain his trust.

'Dr Manjani, my name is Sarah.' She motioned toward Cobb, who was lagging behind while searching for any signs of trouble. 'And that's Jack.'

'Let me guess: he's not your boyfriend.'

Sarah shook her head. 'No, he's not my boyfriend.'

'Bodyguard?' Manjani asked.

'I'm her colleague,' Cobb answered. They didn't have time to explain the nuances of their relationship; and even if they did, he didn't see a reason to tell Manjani any more details than were absolutely necessary. 'Sorry about dropping in unannounced, but we're in a bit of a hurry.'

'Are you working for the Archives?' Manjani asked.

'No,' Cobb replied, 'Petr Ulster is merely a friend. He offered to help us out when the shit hit the fan. I guess we have that in common.'

Manjani nodded but said nothing.

Sarah took it from there. 'Considering what you went through,

I can understand your reluctance to talk about the incident in the desert. Still, anything that you can tell us about your expedition will be helpful to our cause.'

Manjani remained quiet as they walked along the edge of the water. They could tell from his sluggish pace that events from the past weighed heavily on his mind. The only question was whether or not he'd be willing to share the details.

Eventually, they came across a decrepit wooden bench that looked older than the ground itself, as if the bench was the seed from which the island had grown. Despite its sagging boards and weathered exterior, Manjani looked at it like it was an old friend. When he sat, the bench groaned and creaked but its form held true.

'Sometimes I come here to think,' he said to himself as much as the others. 'And when I do my mind invariably drifts back to that day.'

Sarah was tempted to sit next to him for support but ultimately decided against it – not only to give him some room to breathe, but also for the short-term health of the bench. She honestly didn't know if it could handle additional weight.

Manjani stared at the ripples on the water as he slowly opened up about the past. 'It was our third week in the field when we made an important discovery: a small settlement that had been completely buried in the sand. At first, we assumed the village had been abandoned and that the Sahara had gradually reclaimed the terrain, as the desert was apt to do. And yet, as we dug deeper, we soon realized the village was completely intact, including several male skeletons huddled in the corners of the rooms.'

'A sandstorm?' she asked gently.

'Undoubtedly,' he answered while keeping his gaze frozen ahead. 'Although it was a horrible tragedy for those we found – and I can think of few worse fates than being swallowed by sand – it was a remarkable discovery for me and my team because it gave us an ancient snapshot of a forgotten culture, right down to their archaic swords.'

Cobb winced when he heard mention of the blades.

From that alone, he could guess the rest.

Still, he allowed Manjani to fill in the details.

'Two nights later, I needed some time alone to ponder the significance of our discovery. So I grabbed my GPS and a backpack full of supplies and headed to the top of a nearby dune. I know it's foolish to head off into the desert on one's own – trust me, I would *never* let my students be so careless – but I have spent the past twenty years in the Sahara looking for tombs and pharaohs, so I know a thing or two about navigation.'

'How long were you gone?' Sarah asked.

'Ninety minutes. I even timed it to be sure. Fifteen minutes out, an hour to eat and think about the discovery, and fifteen minutes back. As long as I kept my pace and my direction was true, I would end up in the same place that I started.'

'Did it work?'

'Of course it worked,' he replied. 'As I mentioned, I'm a seasoned veteran when it comes to the desert, and it's a good thing, too, because the wind really started to pick up on my way back to the campsite. So much so, my tracks were completely erased.'

He paused, recalling the horror that followed. 'When I crested the last dune, I could see my team being slaughtered in the valley below. The shadows simply cut them down where they stood

'. . . I couldn't hear their screams over the gusting of the wind, but I could see them . . . They were reaching out to me, begging for help.'

He swallowed hard, fighting back his tears. 'There was one student in particular, a brilliant scholar by the name of Marissa. She was the youngest one in the group. She had this *smile* that could light up a room . . . Everyone adored her, even me. I could see her there in the campsite . . . She was right *there* . . . For a minute, I thought maybe, just *maybe*, I could run down the dune and save her, but before I could . . .'

His voice faded into sobs of grief.

And Cobb felt his pain.

He knew from experience that the worst thing that could happen on a battlefield wasn't death; it was watching someone you cared about suffer. That feeling of hopelessness never went away. In fact, sometimes it worsened. Over the years, Cobb had awoken to his own screams in a tangle of damp sheets more times than he could count, and the lingering nightmare in his head always focused on the soldiers under his command that he wasn't able to save and the family members they left behind.

Those were the images that haunted him.

Not his own death, but the agony of others.

'Trust me, there's nothing you could have done to save her. Absolutely nothing. If you had charged in, you would be dead, too.'

Manjani nodded as he wiped away his tears. In his heart he had known the truth for months, but it was nice to have someone agree with him.

'What happened next?' Cobb asked.

'When it was over, I watched the shadows drag the bodies

into the swirling haze of the approaching storm, knowing that I would never see my team again, knowing that the desert would be their grave. So I wrapped a towel around my face, lowered my head into the wind, and tried to escape.'

'How did you make it out?' she asked.

'Fortunately for me, the sandstorm erased my trail as I made my way toward el-Bawiti. My wallet, my phone, and most of my equipment were still at the camp. I hoped that no one would look for me if they thought I was dead. Eventually, I met a Bedouin caravan kind enough to help me to the coast. From there, I traded my watch to a fisherman in exchange for passage to Crete. Once you've made it that far, you have the whole Aegean to get lost in. I ultimately ended up here.'

Cobb knew that a man of Manjani's intellect would have no trouble finding well-paying work, especially in his native Greece. 'Why did you send the map to the Archives?'

Manjani forced a smile. 'I knew I wasn't going to use it, but a small part of me felt that finding Alexander's tomb would mean my students hadn't died in vain. I guess I was hoping that someone might pick up the trail where I jumped off.'

'Which is where we come in,' said Cobb, who hoped to tie Manjani's efforts directly to Jasmine's disappearance. Not to be cruel, but to guarantee his full participation. 'We followed your map into the tunnels beneath the city. That's when we were attacked. There was something under Alexandria that the bombers were trying to protect – something so valuable that they blew up a city block in order to hide it.'

Manjani nodded knowingly. 'When I saw the reports, I somehow knew it was them. I didn't believe the claims that it was an accident. That didn't make sense to me. The men used swords in the desert, but I could tell they were willing to do anything to accomplish their goals. Tell me, how many people did you lose?'

'Just our historian. They grabbed her before the blast.'

'But why?' Manjani asked. 'I don't mean to sound indelicate, but why would they take her when they were so intent on killing my team? Why would they save her and then kill hundreds on the streets above?'

Cobb shrugged. He had asked himself the same questions over and over again and had yet to think of a reasonable answer. 'I don't know why she was taken. Even worse, I don't know where to find her. All I know for sure is that we came a long way to find you. With your knowledge of the map, we were hoping you could help us.'

Manjani glanced at him. 'With what?'

'The map made note of "the gift of Neptune". Our historian believed this referred to a well that Caesar had dug to ensure that his drinking water couldn't be poisoned.'

Manjani nodded approvingly. 'Ptolemy Theos Philopator and the Battle of the Nile. I'm familiar with the tale. Please, continue.'

'She believed the fortress that was built to protect the well eventually became a Roman temple. She also believed that the priests used the temple to hide evidence of Alexander's tomb when the emperor demanded that the records be destroyed.'

Manjani smiled. 'That's actually quite brilliant.'

Sarah took the compliment on Jasmine's behalf. 'We'd like to think so. That's why we thoroughly explored the cisterns and the temple. Unfortunately, we didn't find any evidence of the tomb's location. All we found were the symbols on the wall and the secret grotto. We were hoping you could shed some light on their significance.'

'I'd love to,' he admitted, 'but I honestly don't know what you're talking about. What symbols? And what grotto?'

Until that moment, Sarah had been confident that Manjani was a guilt-ridden victim who would do whatever he could to help save Jasmine. But now, she wasn't so sure.

'You know,' she said angrily, 'there are few things in life that I hate more than a liar. So we'll give you one more chance to change your story before we start to get mean. What can you tell us about the grotto?'

'Nothing!' he assured her. 'I have no idea what you're talking about! I swear to God, I'm telling you the truth! I haven't lied about anything!'

'Bullshit!' she growled. 'We *know* you were there. I found a glow stick in the grotto, and we traced it back to you. You bought it in Piraeus before your expedition!'

'A glow stick?' he stuttered, completely confused. 'Yes, I bought a case of them in Piraeus, but we only used a few in the desert. I left the rest of them with my equipment at the campsite. For all I know, the whole box is still there!'

Sarah stared at him, searching for any glance or twitch that might indicate deceit on his part, but she saw nothing of the sort. That meant the men who slaughtered Manjani's team most likely raided the equipment before they disposed of the bodies and used the glow sticks in the cisterns. 'You're telling me that you know nothing about a grotto?'

'No!' Manjani shouted.

'Or a pictograph?'

'A pictograph? You found a pictograph? Where?'

'Inside the temple. It was written in ancient symbols.'

'Wait,' blurted Manjani, who was trying to make sense of things. 'You found an ancient pictograph inside of a Roman temple next to a hidden grotto?'

Cobb nodded. 'Yeah. That about sums it up.'

Manjani suddenly smiled. 'Please show me everything!'

62

After discussing it with Sarah, Cobb decided to show Manjani the images of their underground adventure. The viewing wasn't only meant for his benefit, it was also for theirs. Despite his glowing reputation, Manjani still needed to prove his worth. The more insight he could provide, the more they would show him. And if at any point he appeared to be deceitful, they would shut down his access completely.

But first, they needed to go somewhere private.

Since his arrival in Amorgos, Manjani had been living in a small cottage near the harbor. Aside from Internet access, the location gave him everything he needed. The neighborhood was clean and safe, and it was within walking distance to the café, the marketplace, and the port. In less than fifteen minutes, he could be surfing the web, buying groceries, or making a quick getaway to a neighboring island.

And the view was simply breathtaking.

As much as they envied the panorama from Manjani's porch, Cobb and Sarah were taken aback by the lack of décor inside the bungalow. Thanks to their former careers, both of them were familiar with the never-in-one-place-for-long lifestyle, but Manjani's place took that notion to the extreme. His only furniture was a battered table, some mismatched chairs, and a threadbare mattress.

One end of the table served as his office with a mouse,

keyboard, and external monitor for his laptop, while the nearer end was reserved for meals. There was a lone cast-iron skillet on the stove in the kitchen and a single set of tableware in the drying rack next to the sink. It was clear that he had no intention of entertaining guests.

Cobb noted the lack of creature comforts in Manjani's cottage and wondered if it was done out of guilt, as if any enjoyment would somehow disrespect the memory of the students who had died under his command.

As if he viewed *their* deaths as the end of *his* life.

As an ex-soldier, Cobb was quite familiar with the syndrome. Sympathy wouldn't help. Neither would pity.

The best remedy was to give him a reason to live.

At that moment, the merits of interior design were the furthest thing from Manjani's mind. The only things he cared about were the pictograph and the grotto that they had discovered under Alexandria. He walked to the far end of the table and connected his laptop to the peripheral devices. Once he was done, he powered up the system.

'All yours,' Manjani said.

Cobb had rightly assumed that Manjani wouldn't have access to the Internet at his place – he checked his e-mail at the café, after all – which meant they wouldn't have access to the images and footage on Garcia's website. Not wanting to drag an iPad with him to Greece, Cobb made do with what they had. He connected his smartphone to the computer via a small adapter and then, using software that Garcia had stored on the device, accessed the files that had been uploaded to his phone's hard drive.

It wasn't perfect, but it was better than nothing.

Cobb had his choice of dozens of files but started with a video clip of Sarah and Jasmine entering the hole in the wall of the far side of the chasm. Instead of watching the screen, Sarah watched Manjani as he viewed the footage for the first time. She noticed a familiar gleam in his eyes, one that she had seen before. It was the same reaction as Jasmine's when they had reached the concrete pillars.

Manjani practically glowed. 'There's your Roman temple.'

The news wasn't unexpected. Cobb had always been confident with Jasmine's assessment of the underground architecture. Still, it was nice to hear a prominent expert like Manjani support her theory without being prompted.

'Tell me,' Manjani said, 'are you familiar with *assimilation*?'

'The word, yes. How it applies to the video, no.'

'The Romans,' he said as he studied the video, 'were masters of assimilation. So much so that the concept is often referred to as *Romanization*.'

'Sorry. Still drawing a blank.'

'What about *Latinization*?'

Cobb held up his hands. 'Speak to me like I've never read the dictionary cover to cover – because I haven't.'

'Me, neither,' Sarah admitted.

Manjani smiled apologetically. 'It means that the Romans adopted the best things from the cultures before them and passed them off as their own. For instance, the Romans took the Grecian tale of Zeus and created the Roman god Jove. It's basically the same story – they just changed the name of the main character to suit their needs.'

'I did that once in high school: they called it *plagiarism*.'

'Touché,' Manjani said with a laugh.

Cobb pointed at the screen. 'How does that apply to the temple?'

'To understand the temple, you have to understand the historical climate of Alexandria. Although the city is located in Egypt, it was founded by a Macedonian king who encouraged assimilation long before the Romans. In fact, many believe they took the concept from him. I know that America is often called the "world's melting pot", but Alexandria earned that title long before – particularly when it came to religion.'

'How so?'

Manjani glanced at Cobb. 'Long before the arrival of the Romans, the high priests of Amun-Ra, the almighty sun god in the Egyptian pantheon, wielded great influence in Egypt. Not surprisingly, they used their connection to the god for much more than spiritual growth. The priesthood controlled vast tracts of land, as well as nearly all of the country's ships. For a time, they were as powerful as the pharaohs, if not more so.'

'And yet they adopted the Roman way of life?'

'They did,' Manjani replied, 'but only as a means to an end. Their "conversion" was a ruse that allowed them to continue their worship of Amun-Ra in a Roman city despite the wishes of the emperor and the growing popularity of Christianity. They believed the only way to survive was to conform to the Roman standards of priesthood. And yet they never lost their true identity. When Severus ordered the tomb to be hidden from public view, they took it as a personal affront. To the emperor, Alexander was nothing more than a conqueror. To the high priests of Amun, he was the *actual* son of god.'

'Jesus,' Sarah murmured. She caught herself before the others could mistake her words for blasphemy. 'I mean literally. The high priests thought of Alexander in the same way that Christians think of Jesus Christ.'

'That might be oversimplifying it a bit,' Manjani said, 'but the parallels are there. Unfortunately, the emperor's decision to hide Alexander's tomb meant that followers of their faith could no longer worship him properly. This, of course, put the priests in a very difficult position. For decades, they had been hiding in plain sight, dressed in the priestly robes of the Empire while worshipping Amun behind closed doors. But now they were forced to take a stand for the preservation of their religion. They were forced to do something desperate.'

'Like what?' Cobb wondered.

'They decided to steal his body.'

63

Based on the revelation about Alexander's body, Cobb decided to play additional footage for Manjani, starting with the video of the pictograph.

Needless to say, it left him speechless. He simply stared at the screen as the camera moved down the length of wall. An occasional gasp escaped his lips as he studied the symbols. This continued until they reached the end of the clip.

Manjani glanced at Cobb. 'Please show me again.'

'Only if you speak this time.'

'Yes, of course.'

The second time through, Manjani couldn't contain his glee – or his words – as he watched the footage. 'Do you know what this is?'

Sarah nodded. 'It's a timeline of the city, from its creation until Alexander's body was smuggled out to sea. Our historian told me that before she was taken.'

Manjani shook his head. 'Close, but not quite right. I understand her interpretation, I really do, but I'm sorry to say that she was mistaken.'

'Mistaken how?' Cobb demanded.

'The symbols were meant to resemble the traditional markings of the era, but there were subtle alterations that changed the translation. It's like an embedded code – a form of communication meant only for those who were familiar with it. The high priests did this frequently, just in case an outsider stumbled across one of their messages. The outsider would interpret it one way, and the priests would view it another.'

'But you can read it?'

'Yes,' he assured them, 'I am quite familiar with the basics. I studied the language for many months in preparation for my last expedition. Ultimately, it was a message like this that led us to the discovery of the settlement.'

'Really?' Cobb grunted, somewhat surprised. 'I guess we got that wrong. We were under the impression that you were looking for Alexander's tomb.'

'That's correct. We were searching for his tomb.'

'Hold on just a second.' Cobb was starting to get confused. He hit the PAUSE button so Manjani would concentrate on his questions instead of the footage. 'Let's back up and start over. When you assembled your team, what were you looking for?'

'We were looking for Alexander's tomb.'

'But you found the settlement instead.'

'Exactly!' Manjani said. 'On its own, the settlement was a very nice discovery. Not nearly as glamorous as Alexander's tomb, but still a solid find. My students, most of whom were light in fieldwork, were absolutely elated.'

'But not you.'

He shook his head. 'When you're hunting for Moby Dick, a shark won't suffice.'

Cobb smiled. 'Good point.'

Sarah used the moment to reenter the conversation. 'Out of curiosity, what led you to believe that the tomb was where you were digging?'

Manjani glanced at her. 'Are you familiar with the Bahariya

Oasis in the Western Desert? It is home to a modern archaeological site known as the Valley of the Golden Mummies. Since its discovery in 1996, hundreds of bodies have been uncovered there, and I believe thousands more will be discovered – all followers of Alexander.'

Cobb connected the dots. 'You thought the body was moved to Bahariya?'

'It was a working theory,' Manjani said with a shrug. 'You see, the Temple of Alexander is located in Bahariya. It is the only such temple in all of Egypt to honor him. Although there is no tomb inside, we found several records of travelers who asked to be buried near the temple in the belief that it would bring them closer to Alexander. That might not seem like much, but these messages weren't the scribbled notes of commoners. They were written by the personal scribes of noblemen from Egypt, Greece, Rome, and beyond. These people left their homelands to be buried in the middle of the desert, and we thought the reason was Alexander.'

'What about now?' Sarah wondered.

'Now?' he asked, confused.

'You said the tomb's presence in Bahariya *was* a working theory. I noticed that you used the past tense, *was*. Does that mean you've changed your mind?'

He shrugged. 'I suppose I have.'

'Why?' she asked.

'Pardon the pun, but I saw the writing on the wall.'

The look on her face said that she wasn't amused.

'Just hear me out,' Manjani said as he pointed at the image frozen on the screen. 'These three symbols of the spindle, the scroll, and the shears represent the Fates. It means that a prophecy was foretold by the oracle. This square, here, is Pandora's box. Whatever the prophecy was, it wasn't good news. And look here – the horned man inside the block that these people are carrying? That's Alexander. They're moving his tomb.'

Sarah had heard all of this before from Jasmine. 'Right. They evacuated Alexander to a waiting ship. Isn't that what the ram's head on the boat means?'

Manjani shook his head. 'In the language of the priests, the ram's head on a man refers to Alexander. The ram's head by itself refers to his father, Amun. The boat with the symbol of Amun simply tells us that he was directing their attention to the water. You have to understand the context to appreciate what he was trying to convey.'

She was getting impatient. 'What did he say?'

'It's a warning, telling the priests to fear the water. It implores them to remove Alexander's body from the city, because something terrible was coming from the sea. If I had to guess, I'd say it refers to the tsunami in 365 that nearly wiped out the city. Unfortunately for me, the accounts that led us to Bahariya were all written at least a hundred and fifty years *before* the tsunami. That means we were wrong about the Valley of the Golden Mummies because Alexander's tomb was still in Alexandria for more than a century after the noblemen asked to be buried near the oasis.'

'Good,' Cobb said. 'I don't mean to sound insensitive, but that's one less place that we have to check. What else does the wall say? Does it give us a location?'

'None that I saw, but let me check again.'

Manjani fast-forwarded the video and studied the final frame of the pictograph, searching for the smallest of clues. In his excitement, he realized it would have been easy to neglect a crucial detail in the coded message about the tomb. He scanned the image slowly and methodically, looking for a symbol that would point them in the right direction, but he found nothing.

'You're *sure* this is everything? There were no other carvings on the wall?'

'I'm positive,' she answered. 'I looked over every inch of the wall. And Jasmine examined it, too. That's everything we found.'

Manjani cursed in Greek, obviously frustrated.

'What's missing?' Cobb asked.

'I don't know – I really don't – but *something*. There has to be more. There just has to be. Because this doesn't make any sense!'

64

Manjani leaped to his feet and began to pace around the room. 'If the priests were abandoning the city, they wouldn't have left their message so open-ended. They would have been explicit about where they were headed next.'

'Why?' Sarah asked.

'Because they didn't have cell phones and they didn't have e-mail, and they were expecting the city to be swallowed by the sea. This was their one and only chance to get a coded message to their followers, whether it was a priest who was stationed in Thebes or a pilgrim from a faraway land who would read the message ten years later. Keep in mind only those fluent in the priestly language would know how to read the *actual* message. Everyone else would look at the symbols and think that Amun had spared the priests by warning them about the flood. That alone would have kept the priests safe from harm. No one – not even the Romans – would have risked the wrath of their god by chasing after the priests. This wall bought their freedom.'

Cobb smiled. 'Two birds, one stone. It kept the guards away, and it told the followers of Alexander where the priests were relocating to.'

'Exactly!' Manjani said. 'Now all we have to do is figure out the location.'

Sarah, who had more than a little experience when it came to classified information and the acquisition of valuables, viewed things from a different perspective. 'I concede I know next to nothing about history, but I disagree with your assessment. There's no way in hell that I would put all of the pieces to the puzzle in one place. I mean, why put your jewels in a safe if you're going to leave the key in the lock?'

Manjani considered her statement. 'You raise an interesting point. Perhaps they hid the key to the safe but kept it nearby. Do you have any film of the other walls?'

Cobb shook his head. 'Not on my phone.'

'What kind of key are you looking for?' she asked.

Manjani answered. 'It could be directions, a reference to a landmark, or even the actual name of the place involved. I'm not sure exactly, but I know there's something missing from the coded message.'

Sarah shook her head. 'There was nothing like that further down the tunnel. The only thing I found was a series of steps that led back up toward the surface. That's where I found the glow stick.'

'On the steps?'

'No, after the steps. It was in the grotto by the water.'

He nodded excitedly. 'That's right! You mentioned that before but we haven't discussed it. Please tell me everything.'

Sarah glanced at Cobb, wondering how much she should reveal. A subtle nod gave her permission to continue. 'At the end of the steps was a grotto with a number of columns that held up the ceiling. The room was connected to the sea by an underwater channel. That's how I made it out when the bombs went off. I swam to safety.'

Manjani closed his eyes, as if he were praying while he spoke. 'Please tell me you have video from the cave. *Please.*'

Sarah honestly didn't know the answer. Her flashlight camera had been working when she looked around the cave, but she was sure that the footage was a low priority for Garcia. Their focus was the wall, not the tunnel beyond.

Fortunately, Cobb knew that he had the video on his phone. He had seen a clip earlier when he and Garcia had scanned through everything that had been recorded. 'We have some footage of the grotto, but it's not that great. Why are you so anxious to see it?'

'Why?' Manjani asked as he stopped his pacing and sat beside Cobb to plead his case. 'Because of the image of Amun in the pictograph! Remember, he's the god of all gods, and the priests are his disciples. They will do whatever he asks them to do.'

'Which is what?' Sarah asked.

'Think, you two, think! What's he asking them to do in the message?'

Cobb thought back to the image of Amun on the pictograph. A few seconds later, the answer popped into his head. 'I'll be damned. He's telling them to look at the water.'

'Exactly!' Manjani blurted. 'On one level, he's warning them about the approaching tsunami. On another, he's literally telling them to look at the water. And where in the temple would they look at the water?'

'In the grotto!' Sarah answered.

Manjani smiled. After all this time, he finally remembered how much he had missed the thrill of the hunt. Still beaming, he turned toward Cobb and laughed. 'So, does this mean I've earned the right to see the footage?'

'Sure. What the hell.'

Cobb glanced through the files until he found the one that

he was looking for. 'This is everything we have from the steps and grotto.'

As the footage began to play, Manjani stared at the screen. His eyes were glued to the monitor as he watched Sarah make her way up the steps toward the surface. He slid to the edge of his seat as he watched her movement through the darkness, the beam of her flashlight reflecting in the pool just ahead. As she reached the water's edge, she shined her light upward, illuminating the domed ceiling of the dark cavern.

'There it is,' Manjani announced.

Cobb paused the video and stared at the screen. He saw the natural grotto that had been reinforced by elaborate pillars. The ceiling had been chiseled smooth, rounded into the shape of a dome. Though he had seen the image before, he hadn't given it much thought. And, admittedly, he still didn't see anything noteworthy. 'There what is?'

Manjani sat back in his chair. 'The second half of the message.'

'You'll have to do better than that. All I see is a domed cavern.'

'Look closer. You see the markings across the dome?'

Sarah moved in for a better look. 'Yeah, what about them?'

Manjani reached for the mouse. 'May I?'

'Be my guest,' Cobb said.

Manjani clicked through the options of the computer program, searching for the right adjustment. With the click of a button, the picture reverted to a negative image. Suddenly, the once black specks now glowed white against a dark background.

He looked at Cobb. 'Does that help?'

'Are those supposed to be stars?'

'Better than that. You're looking at a star *map*.'

'Great,' Sarah joked, 'the tomb's in space.'

'No,' Manjani assured her, 'the tomb is on Earth. The map above will give us a location below. All we need is an archaeo-astronomer to read it for us.'

'An archaeo-what?'

'An archaeoastronomer is an expert in archaeological astronomy.'

'You're making that up.'

'I swear, it's a legitimate field! For instance, they would be able to tell you how the position of the sun influenced the place-ment of the megaliths at Stonehenge, or why the plumed serpent magically appears in Chichen Itza during the equinox.'

Cobb groaned at the thought of an *additional* expert on his team, particularly one in such a limited field. 'Let me see if I got this straight: based on the position of the stars in the sky, an archaeoastronomer will be able to use advanced math to give us a specific location on the ground. Is that what you're saying?'

Manjani nodded. 'That's correct.'

'Couldn't a regular astronomer do that, or even a computer whiz?'

'Theoretically, yes, if they had the right software to chart the sky.'

Sarah laughed. 'In that case, we're good to go. We have a nerd on staff.'

65

Jasmine should have been frightened by the question.

After all, she had assumed that the person lying in the corner was a corpse. Not only did he smell like a corpse, but he looked like one, too, in the gloom of the dungeon.

Presented with evidence to the contrary, she didn't know whether to appreciate the company or to fear his presence. Ultimately, her instincts took over and she decided to run to his aid. Or at least she tried to. When the slack pulled taut on her chain, the shackle grabbed her ankle and she crashed clumsily to the floor.

'Shit!' she said under her breath.

Despite his condition, the withered old man crawled toward the middle of the room to see if she had hurt herself during her fall. 'Are you . . . okay?'

Jasmine sat up and smiled. 'I'm fine. Are *you* okay?'

'I don't know,' he said between labored breaths. 'I feel . . . strange.'

She knew the sensation. She had felt the same way when she had awoken from her drug-induced slumber. She knew that he was probably suffering from blurred vision, muscle aches, and severe confusion.

'It will go away,' she assured him. She grabbed his wrist to check his pulse; it was slow, but strong. His breathing was similarly steady and deep. 'You're going to be fine. Just give it time.'

He stared at her with confusion in his eyes. 'Who are you?'

'My name is Jasmine.'

'Kaleem,' he said as he closed his eyes and lay on the stone floor. His head was still spinning from the drugs. 'Jasmine, what day is it?'

'Good question,' she said with a laugh. Despite their situation, she was trying to stay positive for his sake. 'If I had to guess, I'd say it's the fourth of the month. Or maybe the fifth. I'm not sure how long I was unconscious.'

He shook his head in dismay. 'May fifth? Has it really been twenty-some days?'

His comment roared through her mind like a freight train. The unavoidable truth forced a lump into her throat: it was November, not May. She stared down at him, temporarily unable to speak out of both concern and pity.

To him, he had survived twenty-some days.

In reality, it had been twenty-some *weeks*.

As hard as it was, he needed to hear the truth.

She grabbed his hand tightly. It was a desperate act of comfort that wouldn't offset the news she was about to deliver. But at that moment it was the only thing she could offer. 'I need to tell you something, and it's going to hurt.'

Kaleem grimaced in anticipation.

'Spring has passed. We're well into fall.'

It was the gentlest way she could think of to convey the news.

Tears flooded his eyes as he groaned in pain. Then his body went limp, as if all hope had been sucked out of him. 'God, just let me die.'

She squeezed his hand. 'Don't say that. You've survived this long. You're not going to die in here. My friends are coming to get me. I promise.'

He did not reply. He merely lay there and cried.

Jasmine knew that she needed to do something to bring his mood back around – a distraction of some kind. She decided to engage him in conversation.

'Tell me about yourself. How did you get here?'

Several seconds passed before the question sank in. When it did, he wiped the tears from his face and began to speak. 'I was . . . I *am* an expert in Egyptian history. I traveled here from Greece as part of an expedition.' He stared blankly at the light above, as if the memories were not readily available. 'We were investigating rumors about Alexander's tomb. We set up a camp-site in the valley and started to dig.'

'Did you find anything?'

He glanced at her. 'An entire village buried beneath the sand. It was remarkable. But before we had a chance to excavate the site, they came in the night.'

'They? Who are they?'

'Hooded men in black tunics. They stormed our camp after sunset, wielding ancient swords. We tried to fight back, but they were too strong. The bodies of the others were dragged into the desert . . . For some reason, I was kept alive.'

Jasmine was familiar with the incident. As a fellow historian, she kept her ears tuned to reports of any developments in her field – good or bad. 'Your expedition made the news. When your team failed to return, the authorities were sent to find you. They spent days searching the desert.'

'Did they find anyone?'

She shook her head. 'All they found was your camp. Everyone was presumed dead. And as far as I remember, there was no mention of an archaeological find.'

He sighed. 'The desert hides its secrets quickly.'

Jasmine knew her next question would sound indelicate, but she also knew it had to be asked. After all, her life was at stake too. 'I hate to ask you this – I really do – but do you have any idea why they spared your life?'

He shrugged. 'I honestly don't know. Sometimes I wish they hadn't.'

'Have they questioned you?'

'Repeatedly,' he answered. 'And I have told them everything that I know. I was merely there to interpret our discoveries. I was not the team leader.'

Jasmine nodded. 'I know the feeling.'

He looked at her. 'What do you mean?'

'My story is similar,' she explained. 'Just like you, the whole reason I was in Egypt was to put my team's discoveries into the proper historical context. And just like you, we were also looking for Alexander.'

'In which part of the desert?'

'We weren't in the desert. We were in Alexandria.'

Kaleem grimaced. 'My dear, Alexandria has been picked clean. They even have a name for those that search there. They are known as the Fools of Alexander.'

She nodded. 'Trust me, I know. I'm very well aware of the reputation. But what if I told you that the fools weren't so foolish after all?'

'Are you saying that you found Alexander?'

Jasmine smiled. 'Not Alexander, no. But we may have found a clue that no one else has seen. We were exploring the tunnels under the city when we came across a wall covered in ancient carvings. It implied that Alexander's body had been moved long ago.'

'Are you surprised by this message? Because I, for one, am not. Alexander's whereabouts have been unknown for centuries. It only stands to reason that his body has been transported elsewhere. The question is not *if* he was moved. It is when? And where? And how?'

'That's three questions.'

Kaleem smiled. 'Yes, I guess it is.'

Jasmine realized that saying anything more would come dangerously close to revealing the secrets that her team had worked hard to uncover, but she thought it was worth the risk. If their captors had interrogated Kaleem, he would know what type of information they were seeking.

She lowered her voice to a whisper. 'What if I told you that I could answer two of those questions?'

A look of hope spread across his face.

66

In case of emergencies, Manjani had memorized a wide variety of escape routes from Amorgos. He knew the schedule of every ferry with service from Katapola and the northern port of Aegiali. He also had the names of a few local fishermen who would be more than willing to take him from the island for the proper compensation.

And yet none of those was good enough for Cobb.

Not with so much at stake.

With a single call to Papineau, he arranged for a seaplane to pick them up near the harbor and whisk them back toward Alexandria. Five hours later, they were touching down in the blue water several miles from the Egyptian coast, where McNutt and the speedboat greeted them. Tired from their journey, few words were spoken until they reached the yacht.

Manjani stared at the vessel in total disbelief. He was used to canvas tents and broken cots, not multimillion-dollar boats. 'This is your base of operations?'

Cobb nodded. 'Make yourself at home.'

As they crossed the aft deck Papineau stepped out from the lower lounge to greet them. He was anxious to hear Manjani's take on things, but he didn't want to pepper him with questions just yet. 'I trust the arrangements were satisfactory?'

Sarah nodded. 'I have to give you credit: you're one hell of a travel agent.'

'Thank you, my dear. I'm glad you approved.'

Cobb patted him on the shoulder. 'She's right. Nice work.'

Papineau smiled. 'For once, it seems I have done something right. Perhaps the tide is turning, and there are clearer seas ahead.'

'Let's hope,' Cobb said with a shrug. 'In the meantime, I need to hit the head. How does the command center in ten minutes sound?'

'Ten minutes is fine, but let's meet in the lounge instead. I think that would be better for Hector.'

Cobb grimaced. He sensed something was wrong.

Before Cobb had a chance to find out, Papineau extended his hand toward their guest. 'Dr Manjani, I presume? I am your host, Jean-Marc Papineau. It's good to have you aboard. Please let me know if I can do anything to make your stay more comfortable.'

Manjani noticed Papineau's designer suit and guessed that it cost more than the cottage on Amorgos. 'Thank you. I appreciate the hospitality.'

Papineau smiled warmly. 'Josh, would you please show Dr Manjani to the lounge? I need to have a quick word with Jack before we start our briefing.'

'No problem,' said McNutt as he took Manjani's elbow and led him inside. 'Hey, are you really a doctor? Because I have this rash on my thigh that won't go away. I can take off my pants, if you'd like.'

Cobb rolled his eyes but let it pass. For the time being, he was more interested in what Papineau had to say about Garcia than Manjani's response to McNutt. 'So, what's going on with Hector?'

'I'm afraid he's rather agitated,' Papineau answered.

'That time of the month?' Sarah asked.

Papineau ignored the wisecrack. 'He's having a few issues with the star map that you asked him to analyze. He can't come up with a solution, and he feels like he's letting us down – particularly Jasmine. Right now, he's a bit of an emotional wreck.'

Cobb appreciated the insight. 'Is it really that bad?'

'I'm afraid it is. I fear he's close to his breaking point.'

Sarah patted Papineau on the back and reassured him. 'Don't worry, Papi. It will be all right. We'll take it easy on him. I promise.'

*   *   *

Ten minutes later, Sarah wanted to scratch Garcia's eyes out. 'We did the hard part! We found the goddamn map! All you have to do is math!'

Garcia yelled back. 'For the last time: I can't figure out the equation if I don't have all the variables! It's impossible! It can't be done!'

'Then tell me what you're missing so we can figure this out!'

'It's not just one thing, Sarah! There are just too many factors involved!'

Cobb heard the commotion and hustled into the lounge. He found McNutt, Manjani, and Papineau standing in the back, watching the fight from afar. None of them was tempted to intervene. In fact, McNutt was eating a sandwich.

Cobb knew they didn't have time for arguments, not at this stage of the game. So he ordered the two combatants to shut the hell up and sit the fuck down at the center table. Then he sat on the chair between them to put a stop to their squabbling.

'Hector,' Cobb said, 'Dr Manjani is here to help you solve the problem. Ask him whatever you need to ask. Hopefully he can fill in some of the gaps.'

Manjani tentatively approached the table.

Garcia took a deep breath, trying to calm his nerves. 'Doctor, I'm not challenging your assertion of a star map. I'm really not. Based on my comparisons with current charts, I agree that the markings on the dome correspond to visible stars in the night-time sky. But my question is this: are you sure that the map is meant to point to some specific location? Is there a chance we're reading too much into it?'

'I believe the map will tell us where to go,' Manjani answered as he settled into a chair. 'The ancient priests spent their lives studying the sky above them, and their understanding of celestial bodies was truly remarkable. Not only were they able to use the stars to navigate through the barren desert, but they actually constructed many of their temples in accordance with astronomic phenomena.'

Papineau was familiar with the concept. 'For instance, the pyramids in Giza correlate to the stars in Orion's belt. Their size, their spacing, their alignment, all mimic what was seen in the heavens.'

Manjani nodded. 'That's nothing compared to the Temple of Amun in Karnak. It was built along the precise rise of the midwinter sun. It is only during that period that the structure is fully illuminated. At all other times, the angles of the inner walls prevent the light from penetrating deep into the temple.'

'What's your point?' Garcia demanded.

Manjani smiled in return. As a college professor, he was used to highly intelligent students with anxiety issues. He knew the best way to calm them down was to relate to them in simple terms. 'Tell me, are you familiar with Indiana Jones?'

Garcia grinned at the mention of one of his favorite fictional characters. 'Of course I am. He's the whole reason I learned how to use a bullwhip.'

'Kinky,' Sarah muttered under her breath.

Manjani ignored her comment and continued. 'Remember the scene in *Raiders of the Lost Ark* where Indy used a wooden staff and a special jewel to create a shaft of light that showed him where to dig?'

'Great scene. One of my favorites.'

'Mine, too,' said McNutt as he rushed forward. 'Please tell me that we're looking for the Well of Souls. If so, I know how to deal with the snakes. *Napalm.*'

Manjani laughed. 'Sorry to disappoint you, but the Well of Souls was discovered a long time ago. Furthermore, it's located in the depths of Jerusalem, *not* Tanis, Egypt, but that's beside the point. The main thing to remember is that the scene with the beam of light was based on real archaeological evidence.'

'Really?' Garcia asked.

Manjani nodded. 'For instance, the Serapeum in Alexandria, which is quite near the grotto, was constructed so precisely that it did not even require a jewel. The temple was designed in such a way that the structure itself would focus a beam of sunlight into an inner chamber and onto the statue of the god Serapis as a way to honor him.'

He glanced around the lounge, making eye contact with everyone on the team. 'As improbable as it may seem, I assure you that Egyptian priests had a masterful knowledge of the stars above and how they related to the earth below. Now all we have to do is crack their map and figure out where it's pointing.'

67

Despite Manjani's impassioned speech about the star map, Garcia was forced to point out the obvious. 'I hate to be the bearer of bad news, but like I told Sarah, I don't believe we have enough information to crack their code. In fact, I'm sure of it.'

'Why not?' Cobb asked.

'Determining latitude by looking at the stars is relatively easy. Once you find the North Star, you can measure its angle from the horizon to figure out your latitude.'

'So what's the problem?'

'There's no horizon on the map. It's just not there. And even if it were, we would run into the much larger problem of longitude. To calculate it accurately, you need to know the time difference between an event that occurs at the prime meridian and when that same event occurs where you are.'

'Wait,' McNutt said, obviously confused. 'How can the same event take place twice in different parts of the world? Are you talking about time travel, or clones? Or time-traveling clones? Oh my God, I'd *definitely* watch that movie.'

'Actually,' Garcia said, 'I'm talking about celestial events that are perceived differently all over the world.'

McNutt grimaced. 'Somehow your explanation made it worse.'

Garcia changed his approach. 'Think about high noon. Not noon on your clock, but *solar* noon – the moment at which the sun reaches the highest point in the sky. That moment happens at some point everywhere on earth, but it doesn't happen at the same time in every location. If solar noon is at 11:56 at the prime meridian, but it occurs at 12:04 where you're standing, then you can calculate your longitude as long as you know the difference in time. At one degree for every four minutes, you'd be two degrees west of the prime meridian.'

Cobb stroked his chin in thought. 'Not to complicate the issue even further, but was there even a prime meridian back then?'

'Surprisingly, there was,' Manjani replied. 'The astronomer Ptolemy defined the first set meridian sometime during the second century. And guess where he was from? *Alexandria*. It's not the same standard used today – his line ran through the Canary Islands – but it was known throughout the educated world and it was definitely known by the priests of Amun. They would know the concept better than most.'

Garcia groaned in frustration. 'Once again, I'm not challenging their expertise. All I'm saying is that this particular star map can't be used to plot longitude and latitude to the level of precision that we'd require. It simply doesn't have enough information.'

Manjani was disappointed, but not defeated. He knew that the map would lead them to Alexander's tomb, he just didn't know how.

McNutt cleared his throat. 'I know this might be a little late – I kind of drifted there when you mentioned time-traveling clones – but I think you're giving these priests way too much credit. I mean, how can they be experts if they can't even draw the sky right?'

Cobb glanced at him. 'What do you mean?'

McNutt pointed at the star map on the screen. 'There are stars on here that don't exist. You know that, right?'

'How could *you* possibly know that?' Sarah demanded.

'This isn't my first trip to the Middle East. I've spent hundreds of nights looking up at this sky, with nothing to keep me company but my spotter and my M40. We used to make a game of it – naming stars after all the things that we missed back home.'

'You memorized the constellations?' Papineau asked.

McNutt nodded. 'And all the other stars, too. We didn't know their real names, so we improvised. The Arabian Goggles. The Rusty Trombone. The Angry Dragon.'

Sarah rolled her eyes, knowing damn well that he probably learned those terms while on leave in Tijuana or Bangkok. 'So what are you saying?'

'A dozen of these stars weren't on my list.'

'You're sure?'

'I'm positive! I never had a chance to use the Arctic Helicopter.'

Cobb glanced at Garcia. 'What do you think?'

Garcia shrugged as he considered the possibilities. 'If we're talking about a couple of stars, then there's always a chance that they burned out during the last two thousand years or so, but if we're talking about a dozen, there has to be another explanation.'

'Such as?'

'Specks of dirt on the lens. Particles of dust in the air. Imperfections in the rock. And, of course, the most obvious choice: McNutt is bat-shit crazy.'

McNutt laughed. 'Maybe so, but I'm not wrong.'

'Then prove it,' Cobb said as he tossed a magic marker to McNutt. 'Show us which stars don't belong.'

McNutt was up to the challenge. So much so, he rushed to the oversized screen and started to circle stars before Garcia or

439

Papineau had a chance to stop him. 'This one. And this one. And this one, too. And both of those . . .'

From his seat at the table, Manjani used a notebook to keep track of the celestial anomalies by charting the dots that didn't belong. Once McNutt was finished, Manjani stared at his drawing in disbelief. 'I'll be damned.'

'What is it?' Garcia demanded.

'Your friend is right. They aren't stars. They're ancient Egyptian cities.'

Manjani drew a frame in the shape of Egypt's border around the points he had plotted, then turned the paper around for everyone to see. 'They follow the path of the Nile, from Abu to Alexandria.'

Papineau was skeptical. 'You're sure?'

'Not *positive*, at least not yet – but it certainly makes sense. To avoid detection in Alexandria, the high priests of Amun hid in plain sight. They blended in with the culture around them. Why should their secrets be any different? This is a map within a map. The star map protects the map of the land, just as they protected the tomb. In their world, it fits perfectly. Even if the grotto was found by those who didn't belong, this was an added level of security that would ensure the tomb's safekeeping. In ancient Egypt, few people studied astronomy on this level. Only the priests would have known how to distinguish the cities from the stars.'

'He's right,' Garcia said as he superimposed a map of ancient Egypt over the collection of rogue dots on the screen. The two layers lined up perfectly.

Papineau was pleased but not overjoyed. 'That narrows our search to about fifty cities, most of which don't exist anymore.

Regrettably, we don't have the resources or personnel for that type of investigation, not with our timetable.'

'What if I can narrow it down for you?' Manjani asked.

'That would be great.'

'How?' Cobb demanded.

Manjani pointed at the screen, drawing their attention to a pair of dots far to the left of the others. Given the location of most of the cities along the Nile, these dots would be found somewhere in the middle of the Sahara. 'One of these isn't a city.'

68

The team stared at the diagram of ancient Egypt that had been superimposed over the image of the dome. It was simply uncanny how perfectly the markings matched the cities. The precision of the priests who had carved the dome was staggering, and all of it had been done without the sophisticated equipment available to modern cartographers.

'Can you center the map on western Egypt?' Manjani asked.

As the image shifted, the group could see that only one of the two dots in the desert aligned with a known city. It was nestled among a cluster of small lakes near the Libyan border. The other dot stood by itself, only a few miles away.

Manjani pointed at the city between the lakes. 'This is Siwa. To the east and west, it is bordered by saltwater lakes. To the north and south, it is surrounded by desert. It is an isolated city hemmed in on all sides by hostile environments nearly incapable of supporting life. And yet Siwa thrives because the land is riddled with more than one thousand freshwater springs.'

Sarah chimed in. 'Are we talking about a few hundred nomads who have settled near a water source, or something more substantial?'

'Considerably more substantial,' he replied. 'Siwa is home to roughly twenty-five thousand people, and most of them are farmers. Despite the salinity of the nearby lakes, the soil in Siwa is perfect for growing olives and dates. And not just a few trees here and there, but thousands of trees, covering considerable acreage.'

Garcia typed furiously on his keyboard. A moment later, a colorful photo of an olive plantation in the Siwa Oasis appeared on the screen, showcasing hundreds of squat, bushy trees, each with dangling green fruit. 'There are approximately seventy thousand olive trees in the region, and more than three hundred thousand date palms.'

McNutt whistled in amazement. 'Wow. That's a lot of martinis and . . .' He turned toward Sarah. 'What do I do with dates?'

'Disappoint them?' she joked.

Cobb smiled. 'Let's move past their agriculture and focus on what's important. What's the connection to Alexander?'

'Plenty,' Manjani answered. 'After establishing his plan for what would become Alexandria, he then set out westward across the coastal road toward Libya. This was not a march to battle – he had left his army behind and was accompanied by little more than his close friends and local guides. This was a quest to better understand his destiny. He traveled along the coast until he reached Amunia, then he turned south, toward Siwa.'

Garcia grimaced in confusion as he entered the locations into his computer. 'Hold up a second. This guy is the greatest conqueror the world has ever known, and yet he travels the long way to reach Siwa? Why would he do that?'

To illustrate his point, he put the map of Egypt back on the screen. First he drew a western line from Alexandria to Amunia – modern-day Mersa Matruh – then continued with a southern line to Siwa. 'I mean, the shortest distance between two points is a straight line, right? So why travel two sides of the triangle when he could just cut diagonally across the desert?'

McNutt rolled his eyes. 'Let me ask you a question. Have you ever schlepped across a desert? And before you answer, sneaking across the US border *doesn't* count.'

Garcia shook his head. 'No, but—'

'Well I have. More than I care to remember. And if you're walking the wrong way in the Sahara, it's brutal. Traveling north and south is fine, but trying to go east or west is a royal pain in the ass. It's just an endless cycle of climbing up the face of a dune, then tumbling down the other side. Up. Then down. It's a fucking grind.'

Manjani agreed with McNutt's assessment. 'Imagine nearly three hundred miles of that same routine. I grant you that Alexander was already well traveled and understood the rigors of such a lengthy journey, but this would have amounted to a seemingly insurmountable challenge – even for him. The alternative, while longer, allowed the group to travel a level path between the dunes.'

'Oh,' Garcia replied sheepishly. 'Well, then I guess that does make sense.'

Manjani started again. 'He went south toward Siwa, seeking an audience with the renowned Oracle of Amun. The oracle was revered in Greece, where its edicts were widely known, and it is presumed that this reputation is what drove Alexander to visit the temple. It's unclear as to what he was hoping to hear, only that he was determined to hear it. Many believe it wasn't so much Alexander's determination that brought him to the oasis, but that he was guided there by divine intervention.'

Papineau spoke up. 'Dr Manjani is referring to a number of events that hindered Alexander's trip to Siwa, and the miraculous ways in which he overcame these obstacles. First, the king ran

444

out of water in the middle of the desert but was saved by a sudden, torrential downpour. It was followed by a sandstorm that disoriented his guides. Amazingly his life was spared when a pair of ravens descended from the sky to lead him in the right direction. Although some historians argue that it was snakes, not birds, that led him through the desert, the point of the fable remains the same: Alexander was meant to reach Siwa, even if it took a little help from the gods.'

Manjani nodded in agreement. 'When he finally reached the oasis, Alexander was immediately taken to the Temple of the Oracle – a magnificent edifice built atop a natural acropolis that rose above the surrounding ground.'

Garcia flashed a picture of a crumbling ruin on the video screen. 'We'll have to take your word on it because the years haven't exactly been kind to the temple.'

Manjani smiled. 'Trust me, in the time of Alexander, the Temple of the Oracle would have been the focal point of the area. If there was one thing that drew people to Siwa, this was it. It would have been cared for above all other buildings, immaculately prepared for those who had traveled great distances to commune with the spirits.'

Cobb was familiar with the influence that these spirits could wield. Whether it was Joan of Arc leading the French army into battle or Kevin Costner building a baseball field in Iowa, there were plenty of people willing to do irrational things when asked by a higher power. Given what Alexander had already accomplished, Cobb wondered what message was possibly worth the journey for the Macedonian king.

'What did the oracle tell him that was so important?'

Manjani smiled. 'Alexander learned that he was a god.'

Sarah rolled her eyes. 'How can you just become a god? I mean, not to sound metaphysical, but isn't that something you're born into? As in, you need to have a deity somewhere in your family tree.'

Manjani nodded. 'You do, and he did – if his mother is to be believed. From the time of his birth, Alexander's mother, Olympias, maintained that he was not the son of King Philip the Second. She claimed that he had been sired by a god in the form of a serpent. Alexander took her word on it and began living his life in accordance with his divine lineage, even though he harbored many doubts. But those doubts were erased on his trip to Siwa.'

'Erased how?' she asked.

'Before Alexander was admitted to the temple to talk to the oracle – which was actually a large statue of Amun – he first met with the High Priests of Amun, who welcomed him in his familiar Greek. As non-native speakers of the language, they blessed him not as their son – "*paidion*" – but rather as the son of god: "*pai dios*".'

Sarah scoffed at the notion. 'One slip of the tongue and Alexander became a god? Is that all it took?'

Manjani shook his head. 'The linguistic confusion was only the beginning. After consulting with the oracle, Alexander emerged from the temple alone and immediately renounced his mortal father. He also proclaimed that he wasn't a son of *a* god, but rather a son of *the* god, Amun. The high priests supported his declaration and heralded his divine provenance, forever linking him to the king of kings.'

69

Sarah was still struggling with Alexander's ascension to the Egyptian pantheon. 'Hold on. Alexander visited the temple alone. Afterward, he claimed he was the son of a god and the priests just took his word for it? How do they know what the oracle said?'

'Because the priests were there,' Manjani explained.

'They were where? Inside the temple?'

'Yes, *inside* the temple.'

'But you said he went in alone!'

'Technically he did, but when the ruins were investigated centuries later, it was discovered that the entire structure was essentially one big performance stage. There was a hidden second floor that could only be accessed through a secret entrance. It allowed the priests to remain concealed while they, not the statue, spoke to those inside.'

McNutt laughed. 'Sounds like the Wizard of Oz.'

'Similar,' he conceded. 'There were also double walls surrounding the statue. The gaps between could only be reached via an underground tunnel that originated behind the temple. From within these walls, additional priests could add special effects to enhance the booming voice from above. Pounding, musical instruments, and hushed echoes were all used in concert with the message being delivered. Anything to convince the visitors that they had, in fact, communed with a higher power.'

Garcia was dumbstruck. 'Why would they trick Alexander?'

'They didn't,' Manjani assured him. 'Considering all of their efforts to protect Alexander even after his death, it would be foolish to assume this was some sort of elaborate ruse. What you have to understand is that the priests truly believed they were the conduits through which the gods would make their desires known. They considered themselves to be mystics, the earthly reflections of the divine rulers. As such, they were the chosen voice of the pantheon, and it was their responsibility to ensure that its will be conveyed to the people. If they told Alexander that he was the son of Amun, it was only because they believed it to be true.'

Papineau agreed. 'That makes sense. From the priests' perspective, only the son of a god could have accomplished his feats.'

Manjani nodded. 'They saw him as the most powerful man on earth. So powerful, in fact, that he could not possibly have been of mortal blood. When Amun sent them word that Alexander was his son, they did not question it. When Alexander accepted his fate, their duty had been fulfilled . . . Or had it?'

'What's that supposed to mean?' Sarah asked.

Manjani pondered the dot near Siwa. 'The priests were the source of his power, and he was the source of theirs. For the remaining years of his life, Alexander showered the priests with tributes, and they, in turn, offered their guidance and wisdom. In the eyes of the priests, the glories of Alexander were hopelessly intertwined with those of Amun. It only makes sense that they would want to bring his body back to Siwa after his death. By placing Alexander's tomb near their holy temple, they would create an eternal bond. They would be linked in death, as they had been in life – just as he had hoped.'

'Alexander wanted to be buried in Siwa?'

Manjani nodded. 'On his deathbed, it is said that Alexander spoke of his desire to be laid to rest next to Amun. It stands to reason that he would want his body returned to the place where he first learned of his divinity, to be forever interred in Siwa.'

Although many historians have suggested that Alexander's body was secretly taken back to the oasis at some point in time, little has ever been discovered to support such a claim. In fact, the ruins in Siwa give the impression of abandonment, not adoration, leading some to speculate that even *if* the body had been taken there, it had been moved away some time later.

He continued. 'In the time of Alexander, the high priests controlled the land. They were the authority, and they determined who was allowed to enter the oasis. Their absolute power made Siwa a logical spot to hide Alexander's tomb.'

Sarah furrowed her brow. 'But the second dot wasn't in Siwa – it was miles away. Why put the tomb all the way out there if you're trying to keep an eye on it?'

Manjani was ready with an answer. 'Having the tomb concealed within the city would have made it easier to guard, but it also would have limited their options. They couldn't build a shrine in the middle of Siwa and still expect to keep their secret. Someone would have questioned their efforts. But constructing a temple in the outlying desert would not only safeguard its exposure, it would protect it from uninvited guests. Remember, this is the terrain that once swallowed an entire Persian army overnight. It has taken millions of lives over the centuries. Two thousand years ago, it was even worse than it is today. It was known to bring nothing but death.'

Cobb stood and walked closer to the screen. 'Hector, can you show me a satellite flyover of Siwa?'

'Sure. Just give me a second.' A moment later, a high-definition reconnaissance photo replaced the image of the ruins. 'What are we looking for?'

Cobb traced his finger to the southeast, circling the approximate location of the mysterious second marking that they had found on the dome. 'Zoom in on this section.'

Garcia zoomed in on a stretch of desert.

Cobb eyed the image carefully. 'What kind of coverage do we have?'

'There are thousands of satellites circling the globe. At any given moment, hundreds of those are focused on Egypt, probably more, considering the civil unrest. Together, they offer a nearly constant stream of information if you know where to look.'

Cobb nodded his understanding. With any luck, he would be able to detect the telltale signs of a compound. 'How close is this to the Libyan border?'

'About thirty miles. Why?'

McNutt leaped to his feet. 'Holy shit – the Semtex.'

'Exactly,' Cobb said.

'What about it?' Papineau asked.

McNutt walked toward the screen. 'Remember what I said before? In all likelihood, the Semtex came from Libya.' He placed his hand to the left of the map. 'That's right about *here*. They're close enough that you could stand in Siwa and piss into Libya. It would only take a quick field trip to secure what they needed.'

Having missed their previous discussion about the explosives, Manjani was trying to piece everything together on the fly. 'Are you saying that the second location is the tomb, and that the priests are the warriors who are trying to protect it?'

Cobb nodded. 'That's exactly what I'm saying. The murders weren't acts of aggression; they were acts of devotion.'

Even Papineau was convinced. 'I must admit, it seems to fit.'

McNutt laughed. 'Papi's so excited, he's rhyming!'

Cobb urged everyone to calm down. 'Right now, it's just a theory. Before we start dancing the jig, let's get some evidence to back it up.'

Garcia looked at him. 'Tell me what you need.'

'I need a much better photo than this. Something focused on this stretch of desert. Preferably one of our birds. We have the best optics from space.'

Garcia typed away, searching for a different satellite.

'I also need a second set of eyes. Josh, are you up to the task?'

McNutt nodded. 'You know I am, chief. What are we looking for?'

'Anything that doesn't belong in the desert.'

'Like polar bears?'

Cobb took a deep breath. 'I might need a third set of eyes.'

McNutt laughed loudly. 'Just messing with you, chief. I know what we're looking for. This isn't my first desert assault.'

'Glad to hear it.'

A few seconds later, a new picture appeared on the screen. The detail of the image was remarkable, as if it had been taken from a helicopter instead of a satellite.

'Much better,' Cobb said. 'Good job, Hector.'

Garcia smiled at the compliment.

Meanwhile, Cobb and McNutt went to work.

Cobb knew there were a handful of ways to spot a subterranean bunker – exhaust vents, power cables, and other topside connections – but if they were there, he needed McNutt to see them without being prompted. It was the only way to ensure that he wasn't simply seeing what he had been told to see.

To the untrained eye, the scene was little more than a vista of endless sand. Fortunately, this wasn't the first satellite reconnaissance that Cobb and McNutt had studied. Slowly but surely, they began to spot the telltale indicators.

'Camouflage netting,' McNutt said as he pointed toward the screen.

Cobb nodded as he pointed out something else. 'Mesh.'

McNutt drew an X over a ripple in the sand.

Then Cobb circled a suspicious shadow.

Eventually, McNutt traced an imaginary border.

Each time, they exchanged knowing nods without speaking.

From where Sarah was sitting, it looked like they were just making things up as they went along. Either that, or they were playing a foreign version of tic-tac-toe, one that she couldn't comprehend. 'Enough already! What the hell did you find?'

McNutt glanced at Cobb. 'May I?'

Cobb nodded yet again. 'Be my guest.'

McNutt grinned and turned to face the others. 'Good news, everybody. Either Jack and I just located the Egyptian equivalent of Area 51, or we just found our target. As far as I'm concerned, we're winners either way.'

70

Jasmine had hinted to Kaleem that there was more to tell about her expedition, but she needed one last moment to consider what she was allowed to reveal. Even in her time of crisis, with her life on the line, she was worried what the others might think.

Eventually, she decided that they would understand.

'What do you know about the tsunami in 365 AD?' she whispered.

'Are you referring to the earthquake in Crete?'

She nodded. 'I have reason to believe that the body was moved at the time.'

Kaleem didn't understand. 'Are you saying that Alexander was washed out to sea? Because I don't believe that for a second. The harbor has been exhaustively searched. And even though they have found ruins, nothing would lead me to believe that his tomb is sitting at the bottom of the water.'

She smiled. For the time being, she thought it best to leave out any mention of the Fates or Pandora's box. Their role in the decision was far less important than the decision itself. 'Alexander wasn't lost in the flood; his body was moved because of it.'

'This is what you learned from the wall?'

She nodded. 'The implication was clear: Alexander's body was relocated so that he would not fall victim to the disaster.'

'Relocated to *where*?'

'I don't know,' she answered. 'The wall only told us when and how it was moved, not where. According to the message, Alexander was smuggled from beneath the city and carried to a waiting boat.'

Until that moment, she had been thrilled by her discovery that Alexander had left the city by way of the coast – if only because it had given them a concrete lead to follow. But hearing it aloud in the stranglehold of the prison, she was struck by how insignificant it seemed. In fact, the more she thought about it, Alexander's departure seemed to raise more questions than it answered. The Sahara was vast, but it was nothing compared to the sea. Suddenly, her optimism waned as she considered the seemingly endless destinations that her story allowed.

She stared at Kaleem, fearful that her tale would not be important enough to trade for their freedom. 'Do you think that will be enough?'

'Maybe,' he said, unsure. 'Is there anything else?'

She shook her head. 'That's everything I know.'

Kaleem forced a smile. 'Then they will have to accept it. The mystery of Alexander has remained for thousands of years. And it will remain for thousands of years to come.' He gently took her hand in his. 'His fate is not yours to determine.'

Jasmine appreciated his attempt to console her. She understood that she could only give them what she knew. The rest was beyond her control.

She reached out and pulled him in for a long hug.

For her, the physical contact was remarkably soothing.

Her worries seemed to melt away in his grasp.

Sadly, her solace was short-lived.

Without warning, the heavy door was flung open and

smashed into the wall as three robed men stormed into the cell. No words were spoken as they charged forward to separate the inmates, but none were needed. Their intention was quite clear.

Jasmine clung to Kaleem, fearing for his life. Having made a connection to the old man, she desperately hoped that they would be permitted to stay together.

But it was not to be.

The sentries made that known as they pried the duo apart.

Jasmine raised her head and pleaded for forgiveness for whatever they had done wrong, but all that did was piss them off. In response, the nearest guard delivered a backhand to the side of her face. The vicious blow sent her reeling across the floor. He charged forward and screamed at her in no uncertain terms that interference of any kind would be punished with violence.

Chained to the wall, she knew it didn't make sense to fight back.

Now wasn't the time to escape.

Meanwhile, Kaleem was pinned to the ground as they removed his leg irons. A minute later, they dragged his frail body toward the exit.

In the last fleeting moment, she caught a glimpse of Kaleem's face as he was hauled from the chamber. He wasn't flushed with panic. His eyes were steely and calm. It was as if he knew his time had come. There were no tears. There were no pleas. He did not beg for his life. He had accepted the inevitable with dignity and grace.

In her heart, she knew that she would never see him again.

* * *

The instant the door slammed behind him, Kaleem rose to his full height. He nodded to his left, then to his right, assuring the guards that he could stand on his own. They instantly released their grasp and backed away.

The charade was finally over.

Waiting in the hallway outside the cell was a fourth man, his robe much more ornate than those of the others. He smiled warmly at Kaleem and offered him a glass of water as reward for a job well done. 'Are you okay, my son?'

Kaleem looked at the high priest with reverence. Even though they were roughly the same age, Kaleem even went so far as to bow his head as he accepted the drink. 'Thank you, elder. I am fine.'

The priest placed his hand on Kaleem's shoulder. 'Perhaps it is time to choose a younger man for your role. The constant sedation cannot be good for you.'

'Amun will keep me safe. Of this, I am sure.'

'Indeed he shall,' the elder said.

For centuries, the shadow priests had always followed the same routine. Whenever their secrets or landmarks were threatened, they responded decisively by killing all but one of the interlopers who dared to stray too close. The only soul that they spared was the most knowledgeable of the group, the one who seemed to know their history, for this was the best way to learn how the infidels had picked up their scent.

Jasmine was simply the latest in a long line of scholars, tourists, and travelers who had fallen victim to Kaleem's ruse. Manjani would have fallen for it, too, if he had not managed to escape in the desert before they had a chance to grab him. The only thing that had stopped them was a freak sandstorm that had erased his trail.

The elder continued. 'What of the girl? Has she told us all she knows?'

Kaleem knew there were cameras and microphones in the ancient cell, but he also knew of Jasmine's tendency to whisper. 'I believe she speaks the truth. She knows nothing about the star map or the location of the tomb. We are safe.'

The elder rejoiced when he heard the news.

Amun had protected them once again.

Now only one step remained.

The historian must be killed.

71

Friday, November 7
Siwa Oasis, Egypt

Establishing a base of operation near enemy terrain takes time – even when someone's life is on the line. In the case of Cobb's team, it had taken an entire day to establish a camp near Siwa. Papineau had docked the boat several miles from Alexandria during the early morning, but it was nearly noon before they had secured transportation and had off-loaded everything that they needed for the adventure ahead.

A journey into protected land.

Protected by the priests *and* the government.

At the turn of this century, Egypt declared most of the territory surrounding Siwa, some 7,800 square miles in all, to be a protected area. The distinction limited the amount of development that could be undertaken and at the same time boosted the number of tourists wishing to experience the area's pristine beauty. Under normal circumstances, Papineau would have gladly greased local palms to ensure that they had the finest accommodations, but such behavior was entirely out of the question on this trip. They wanted to blend in, not stand out, and big-spending foreigners would be noticed.

With that in mind, they avoided the city altogether and set up camp on the outskirts of Siwa. They were not alone. There were hundreds of natives in cloth tents who preferred the old ways of desert caravans to the modern conveniences of hotels. And the government allowed it. As long as campers adhered to the conservative cultural restraints of the area, no one would give them a second look.

Just to be safe, Cobb and McNutt waited until sunset to begin their rekky.

*   *   *

Cobb dug his foot into the soft, loose sand, watching as the chilly nighttime breeze swept it away. He breathed deep, noticing the faintest tinge of salt that drifted with the wind. Though they were hours from the sea, the vast salt lakes a few miles to the north produced the same scent. Cobb ignored the smell and concentrated on the ground beneath him. He instinctively gauged its texture, calculating what type of footing it offered.

The knowledge that came from an on-site investigation – things like the direction of the wind and the traction of the soil – was why rekkys were so important to him. Any piece of information gained might be the one that saved his ass in an emergency.

Cobb and McNutt scanned the area through their night-vision goggles. They had already sidestepped dozens of guards on roving patrols during their steady approach through miles of surrounding desert, but they knew there were plenty more out there. So far, the men they had encountered had disguised themselves as groups of nomadic traders and Bedouins, but there was no reason to believe that there weren't lone assassins waiting to ambush them in the night. Fortunately, even the shadow men's finely honed ability to see in the dark was no match for next-generation military optics.

When Cobb and McNutt arrived at their destination, they could finally see what all of those men were protecting. Everywhere they looked, there were telltale signs of a structure buried beneath their feet. Ductwork popped up from the ground in an irregular pattern, allowing fresh oxygen to be pulled in while poisonous carbon monoxide was vented out into the atmosphere. There was even a trio of massive condensers capable of pulling moisture from the air. With the addition of a microbial filter, these giant dehumidifiers could be used to produce drinking water from the arid winds of the Sahara.

And above it all hung the canopies of camouflage tarps and netting.

To the average observer, the efforts for concealment looked unfinished and haphazard. But Cobb and McNutt knew that the disguises only needed to fool people at a distance. Whoever had taken these measures was only concerned with protecting the site from an aerial view. The guards took care of the rest. No one foolish enough to actually visit the site had ever made it back to describe what had been found.

Cobb and McNutt had every intention of becoming the first.

Cobb broke radio silence to verify that everyone was ready. 'One minute to target,' he whispered. 'Status?'

Sarah answered from the makeshift command center that Garcia had assembled in their tent. 'Bored beyond belief.'

Cobb knew her crankiness was because of him: he had refused her request to join their rekky. It wasn't because he didn't trust her skills – she had more than proven her worth over the last few months – he simply didn't think there was a need for her on this operation. This wasn't an infiltration. This was reconnaissance. Despite her incessant lobbying to get in the game, Cobb had sat her on the bench.

'Hector, you with me?' Cobb asked.

'Ready when you are,' Garcia replied.

'Okay. We're moving in.'

While the others listened in, Cobb and McNutt made their way toward their target, a low, flat shed where Garcia believed they would find the communications system that serviced the underground bunker. If they could hack into the network, they would have access to the entire facility.

They scurried across the sand while keeping a watchful eye for tripwires and IEDs, but neither expected to encounter any. Between the harsh climate and the terrain, few people ventured this far from the safety of Siwa. The brutality of the desert coupled with rumors of deadly boogeymen meant that uninvited guests were seldom, if ever, an issue.

When they reached the shed, they ducked low and glanced in all directions, searching for any sign that their movement had drawn attention. Eventually, McNutt looked at Cobb and shook his head. There were no signs of life or detection.

They had made it inside the guarded perimeter.

They were standing in the eye of the storm.

McNutt let the others know. 'At primary.'

Cobb lifted a hatch on the side of the enclosure, giving him access to the circuitry inside. He crawled into the shed and slithered through the tangled web of cables, searching for the clues that Garcia had explained to him earlier. Once he found them, he was sure that Garcia was right: this was the nerve center of the compound.

'Target confirmed,' Cobb whispered. 'Please advise.'

Garcia walked Cobb through the process of linking his equipment to the system that they had found. And even though Cobb was a layman compared to Garcia, it took him less than five minutes to install the hardware.

Back at the tent, Garcia smiled when his monitors came to life. By physically hacking the signal, he now had access to everything on the network. 'Nicely done, sir.'

'We're good?' Cobb asked.

'GoldenEye is live. I repeat: GoldenEye is live.'

Cobb ignored the movie reference and focused on what really mattered. He wanted a preliminary report on the facility. 'Anything we need to know?'

Garcia grimaced. 'It will take me a while to sort through all of the data feeds, but I can tell you one thing for sure: the bunker is a hell of a lot bigger than we thought.'

72

It was well after midnight by the time Cobb and McNutt reached their camp on the outskirts of Siwa, but they knew no one would be sleeping. It wasn't caffeine that would be keeping them awake, it was the surge of adrenalin that all of them felt now they were back in the field. It was a good thing, too, for each of them had duties to tend to in their effort to rescue Jasmine.

Having already survived one massacre, Manjani had no intention of pressing his luck a second time. He opted to stay on the yacht with Papineau, who would be piloting the boat across the Mediterranean toward Siwa. If Cobb, McNutt, and Sarah failed to accomplish their goals – if they were captured, killed, or otherwise defeated by the shadow warriors – it would be up to Papineau to send in reinforcements.

Unless, of course, he decided to cut bait and run.

He had put one team together. He could always do it again.

In his mobile command center, Garcia pored over the streams of information that he was receiving from the hacked communication lines, while Sarah kept a watchful eye through a narrow slit in the tent for any unexpected visitors.

She glanced away to check on Garcia. 'How's it going?'

Garcia shook his head in agitation. 'It's fine! But this isn't exactly ideal, you know. I've got exabytes of data to comb through, and just two computers. That's like telling a chef to cook a fifty-course meal with only a pot and a pan.'

'First, settle down. I wasn't criticizing; I just asked how things were going. And second, don't mention food. I'm freakin' starving.'

'I'm just saying that I'm working as fast as I can.'

Garcia wasn't exaggerating. If he'd had access to the array of technology at his home, the expensive gear back in Fort Lauderdale, or even the full complement of devices on the yacht, he could have made short work of the information he was pulling from the enemy's network. But with limited equipment in a tent in the desert, the process would take considerably longer. Even with his backup laptop pressed into service, it would still take hours to sort through all of the raw feeds streaming through the system.

'And I'm sorry if—'

'Shhhh,' she demanded. 'Someone's coming.'

She wrapped her fingers around the grip of her pistol as she glanced at her phone. The program she was running was linked to several motion-detectors that McNutt had buried in the sand around the tent before he had left. The tiny capsules, filled with drops of mercury, were known as *rattlers* because they would rattle under the pressure of a foot hitting the ground. According to the sensors, someone was approaching.

Sarah was a split second from ordering Garcia to turn off his computers and to grab a rifle when they heard a familiar voice in their ears.

'Stand down. It's just us,' Cobb said.

'Copy that,' she said, relieved.

A minute later McNutt emerged from the blackness of the open desert and stepped into the tent. 'Honey, I'm home. What's for dinner?'

Cobb entered a moment later. He skipped the pleasantries and cut right to the chase. 'Have you found anything useful?'

'Sure,' Garcia answered. 'At least I think so.'

'Show me,' Cobb ordered as he took off his gear.

Garcia tapped his keyboard, and the single image on the screen instantly split into a grid. Each of the eight squares offered a different feed from one of the cameras inside the bunker. He waited for Cobb to gulp down some water before he started his briefing.

'There are hundreds of camera angles being routed through the system. It looks like every inch of the place is accounted for. Not the best news if you're trying sneak in without being seen, but pretty damn useful if you're trying to map the structure.'

He punched in a different command, and the screen switched from video feeds to an unfinished architectural rendering.

'What am I looking at?' Cobb asked.

'By analyzing all the footage and matching where the angle of one shot intersects with the next, I was able to piece together a rough schematic of the bunker's layout.'

Cobb was impressed. 'Is that everything?'

Garcia shook his head. 'Like I said, there are hundreds of angles to look through. I still haven't seen them all.' He pointed to the map. 'That was drawn by the computer. I just had to choose the right parameters to tell it what to look for as it scanned through the feeds. As you can see, it's still compiling. That's why the map's unfinished. It will keep adding details as it continuously analyzes the incoming feeds.'

Cobb stared at the map, appreciating the advantage it gave them. If they could get inside, they would know their way around. 'Nice job, Hector. Really nice.'

'Don't get too excited,' he replied as he selected a particular camera feed. 'Take a look at this.' He spun on his makeshift seat to face the others. 'You too, Josh.'

Sarah wasn't about to be left out. The three of them crowded around Garcia to see what had caught his attention. Once he enlarged the footage to fill the whole screen, they could see that he had located a depository of some kind. Inside row upon row of wide wooden crates were stacked from the floor to the ceiling. It appeared that each box was marked with a serial number spelled out in a different language.

Sarah squinted at the image. 'What am I looking at?'

McNutt's eyes bulged from his head. 'Holy. Fucking. Hell.'

'My thoughts exactly,' Garcia replied.

'I still don't get it,' Sarah admitted.

'Weapons,' Cobb told them. 'Lots and lots of weapons.'

McNutt pointed at the description emblazoned on one of the crates. 'Those are Ribeyrolle 1918s – French rifles used to lay down suppressive fire.' He tapped a different label. 'STENs, a nine-millimeter sub-machine gun.' He pointed yet again. 'These are—'

Sarah chuckled. 'You can barely speak English, yet you can read all these foreign labels?'

'STENs *are* English. It's an abbreviation honoring the guys who designed them: Shepherd, Turpin, and Enfield.' Despite Sarah's comment, McNutt's tone was playful, not cocky or defensive. There was nothing he liked more than talking about weapons – except using them, of course. 'It's an impressive collection.'

'That much I understood,' Sarah replied.

McNutt shook his head. 'It's not just impressive because of its size, it's impressive because these are *antiques*. Most of these guns date back to World War Two.' He pointed to a final crate. 'Like the Maschinengewehr 30s. MG 30s haven't been used since the 1940s . . . by the Nazis.'

Though most of the battles in Egypt during World War II were fought along the Nile, the Western Desert saw its share of action as well. At one time or another, British, Italian, French, Greek, South African and German soldiers all took up arms in an attempt to capture Siwa and/or control the area extending north to the Mediterranean. Unfamiliar with the challenges of the Sahara, hundreds of these men were never heard from again.

Few were prepared for the heat of the desert.

And none were ready for the shadow warriors.

'It gets worse,' Garcia said as he changed the feed.

This time, there weren't any crates. Instead, they saw an entire wall whose shelves were stocked with large packages of what appeared to be reddish clay.

'Look familiar?' Garcia asked.

Unfortunately, they all recognized the compound.

It was Semtex.

McNutt whistled in amazement. 'Forget about a single block. That's enough to take out the whole damn city.'

'They're stockpiling supplies like an army,' Sarah said. 'But why?'

Garcia tapped a few keys. 'I can't tell you what the guns are for, but let's be clear: they're not *like* an army – they *are* an army.'

As he scrolled through the feeds, they got a much better sense of the underground structure. There were barracks filled with beds, dining halls crowded with tables, even a library lined with books. Though there was certainly a generator powering the bunker – they were staring at a computer feed, after all – such luxury did not extend to every aspect of the facility. Simple oil lamps lit the majority of the space, giving the footage an ominous hue, as if they were staring at an ancient castle.

Despite the dim lighting, each room was buzzing with activity.

Throughout the facility, robed men tended to their duties of preparing food, sweeping floors, and refilling the lamps that lined the walls. Regardless of the task, they went about their business with humble efficiency. Every act seemed to have a purpose. And every disciple seemed to know his place.

It had the look and feel of a monastery.

Only these monks would kill for their cause.

Cobb stepped away from the computer and pondered their situation while McNutt and Sarah grabbed something to eat. Cobb had seen enough to know that they needed a plan – one that didn't involve them charging into certain death while Garcia watched on his laptop. Even with tricks and surprises, he knew it would be impossible to take on the vast number of soldiers below without an army of his own.

There had to be a way to get inside.

All Cobb had to do was figure it out.

Before he had the chance, Garcia leaped from his chair and pointed at the video as if he had seen a ghost. 'Jack! Look at this! Now!'

Unsettled by his urgency, everyone huddled around the screen.

There, chained to the wall, was Jasmine.

73

The arrangement between Cobb and Hassan was simple: Cobb wanted to rescue Jasmine without being chased by goons, and Hassan wanted to kill the men who blew up Alexandria. Though they weren't exactly working together to accomplish their goals, they had agreed to assist each other for the time being.

Or, at the very least, stay out of each other's way.

Cobb still had plenty of reservations about Hassan, but he knew the gangster had one thing at his disposal that he didn't have: a legion of gun-toting thugs who would happily charge into battle if it meant winning favor with their boss.

With this in mind, Cobb had placed a call to Simon Dade, who was running down leads of his own in Alexandria while being shadowed by the giant Kamal, and told him to get word to the crime lord about the compound in the Western Desert.

As for details, Cobb would only provide the GPS coordinates of where to meet, rather than directions to the bunker itself. Cobb knew it would take several hours for Hassan to rally his troops and drive across Egypt. This had given Cobb and McNutt plenty of time to do a rekky, tap into the surveillance system, and formulate a plan of attack.

By 4 a.m. the caravan from Alexandria had made it to the staging ground a few miles east of the bunker. Cobb had chosen this particular patch of desert for its proximity to the thoroughfare that ran between el-Bawiti and Siwa. The spot was accessible, yet secluded. It was far enough away from the bunker to avoid the enemy's patrol, but it was close enough to mount an attack. And their arrival in the dead of night would give them at least a few hours before anyone questioned their presence.

Hassan's men were ready for battle.

All they needed was a target.

When Cobb arrived at the rendezvous point, he expected to see an assortment of beat-up trucks and a ragtag group of criminals. Instead, he saw a fleet of Humvees lined up across the sand and scores of men in desert camouflage. For a moment, Cobb wondered if the Egyptian military had somehow gotten wind of Hassan's activity and had moved in to intercede. But then he saw Kamal, whose unmistakable size stood head and shoulders above the others, and instantly understood who these men were.

Hassan hadn't rounded up a bunch of street thugs.

This was his personal battalion.

Cobb approached the lead car – an opulent Mercedes-Benz G-Class fit for a prince – and sensed that all guns were trained on him. Kamal quickly stepped forward to cut him off before Cobb could knock on the tinted window. From that action alone, he knew that Hassan was sitting inside the luxury SUV.

'Where's Simon?' Cobb asked as the two men came face to chest.

'Safe,' Kamal replied. 'In car.'

Cobb shook his head. 'Tell your boss that Simon comes with me. You don't need him anymore. Tell him that once Dade is free, I'll lead you and the others to the Muharib stronghold. You can kill them all as far as I'm concerned. I just want the girl.'

Kamal retreated to the Mercedes and spoke through a crack

in the lowered window. A moment later, the rear door opened and Dade exited. As he walked toward Cobb, it was clear that he had expected his host to kill him and bury him in the desert.

'Well, I guess I owe you again,' Dade said.

'Nope, just Sarah,' Cobb replied. 'She was worried about you, by the way.'

'Good to know. Where is she?'

Cobb smiled as he extended his hand. 'She's sitting this one out.'

Dade thought the greeting was odd until he felt the small earpiece in Cobb's palm. He fought the urge to smile as he took the device and slipped it into his ear while he pretended to adjust the stocking cap on his head. 'Sorry I missed her.'

Sarah laughed in his ear. 'Don't worry. We'll meet up soon enough.'

Kamal, oblivious to the deception, was growing restless. He hadn't driven all this way to stand around while Dade chatted with Cobb.

'No more talk. Time to fight.'

Cobb nodded in agreement. 'Have your men grab whatever they need. We go the rest of the way on foot.'

Kamal shouted instructions in Arabic, causing five trucks' worth of men to assemble beside him. They were heavily armed and bouncing with anticipation.

Cobb pointed toward the Mercedes. 'What about your boss?'

Kamal shook his massive head. 'He stay here.'

Cobb shrugged. 'Okay then. Follow me.'

* * *

Ten minutes later, Cobb ordered the men to hold their position at the edge of the patrolled territory. It was as far as they could go without risking an ambush. He knew the shadow warriors were out there in the night, ready to defend their land at all cost.

Cobb stared into the darkness. 'Okay, Josh. Help me out.'

McNutt stared through his scope from a half a mile away. From his vantage point atop a small dune, his night optics gave him a clear view of the scene. 'On it, chief. You've got men approaching. Directly at your twelve.'

Cobb looked straight ahead, trying to see the men that McNutt had spotted. But he saw nothing but sand. 'I can't—'

His voice cut off as the shadows seemingly materialized in front of him. One moment they weren't there; the next a half-dozen were heading his way.

Then six became twelve.

And twelve became twenty.

And suddenly, they were everywhere.

A sound like thunder rolled across the desert as Kamal opened fire. A single shot was all it took for the others to know that the battle was on. A second later, Hassan's men fired multiple rounds into the night. Bullets sprayed in every direction as the enemy swarmed, forcing the men to defend themselves from all sides. They tried to fend off the shadow warriors as best they could, but their efforts seemed to be in vain.

No matter how many times they shot, the ghosts just kept coming.

Armed with nothing but ancient blades.

*   *   *

McNutt watched as the shadow warriors rose from the sand, as if they had emerged from the Underworld itself. It was a pretty neat trick, one that kept him on his toes as he carried out his one and only responsibility: protecting Cobb from harm.

As wave after wave of swordsmen charged toward Cobb, McNutt zeroed in on those who posed the biggest threat. With each squeeze of the trigger, another enemy fell – most with a gaping hole in his head or chest.

'Chief,' he said, 'permission to shoot both sides?'

'Not yet. Let the gunmen help us for now, but if they turn on me at any time, you do what you do best.'

McNutt grinned. 'Sweet.'

*   *   *

From their base camp near Siwa, Garcia ignored the firefight that raged in the desert and focused on the activity below. His map of the stronghold wasn't entirely complete, but it was getting close. By cross-referencing the video feeds that he was watching with the blueprint of the compound, he could determine where the troops were headed.

Earlier, while combing through the footage, Garcia had noticed a series of narrow cylinders that rose from the bunker up through the sand. At first he thought they were ventilation shafts, but when he saw someone climbing toward the surface, he understood their true purpose. They were access tubes. Like the tunnels of the Viet Cong that stretched across Vietnam, these access tubes provided the Muharib with multiple entry and exit points all across the desert landscape.

'Jack, you've got twenty more climbing to the north.'

*   *   *

Right on cue, nearly two-dozen warriors appeared. Cobb watched as they stormed in from the hidden shafts just beyond his view.

Despite their cache of artillery, the Muharib carried only swords. The weapons had served them well for centuries, and there was no reason to believe their tradition would fail them now. In their time of need, they relied upon what they knew best.

They preferred ancient blades to antique guns.

Garcia continued his analysis. 'The numbers are looking pretty good. This might be the best chance we get. Most of the men have gone topside.'

'Copy that,' Cobb said with his hand to his ear. 'We're a go for phase two. Repeat. Go for phase two.'

* * *

Dade had arrived unarmed, but that quickly changed during the course of the battle. He borrowed a rifle from one of the dead goons and fired it at anyone with a sword.

Though he was grateful that Cobb had rescued him, he wondered if he wasn't better off back in the Mercedes with Hassan. He was tempted to head back to the car when he heard Cobb's command to commence with phase two.

'What the hell is phase two?' he asked.

It was Sarah who answered. 'Simon, listen closely. Turn west, and sprint like your life depends on it . . . because it does!'

Dade looked to his right and hesitated, seeing nothing but desert. He assumed it was filled with assassins, just waiting to cut him down. 'To where?'

'To me!' Sarah shouted. 'I need your help. Now!'

He took a deep breath. 'On my way.'

* * *

As Dade sprinted forward, Cobb began his retreat.

It wasn't an act of cowardice; it was part of the plan.

Even though the shadow warriors had taken Jasmine and blown up the city, Hassan's men weren't exactly saints. He had heard the stories of how they ruled their territory. He also knew that they hadn't followed him into the cistern to help him out. He was sure that they had been sent to kill him and his team, and he sensed that they still might try once the battle was over.

If that was the case, why help them win?

It didn't make any sense.

So Cobb pulled back to the relative safety of a nearby boulder and took a knee. With McNutt watching over him, all he had to do was separate himself from the chaos and keep his distance while the two sides slugged it out in the desert sand. As far as he was concerned, he hoped that the battle dragged on all night because the war was thinning the ranks of both sides and distracting the Muharib from his team's ultimate goal: sneaking inside and rescuing Jasmine.

74

Dade barreled through the blackness, convinced that he would be killed by the shadow warriors, cut into pieces by their blades.

The fear didn't stop until he spotted Sarah ahead.

She rose from her crouch and signaled for him to duck behind a cluster of shrubs. Then she pointed at a raised, round lip in the sand on the other side of the bushes. It looked like a manhole in the middle of the desert.

'Watch,' she whispered as she crawled toward him.

A moment later, the lid popped open and five cloaked men emerged from the hole. Dade braced himself for a slaughter, but the lump in his throat disappeared as the warriors ran off toward the battle in the distance.

Once they were gone, he turned to Sarah. 'What are—'

'Shhhh,' she said as she cut him off. 'Hector?'

'Hang tight,' Garcia replied.

* * *

He kept a watchful eye on the surveillance feed from his command center and waited for the perfect moment for Sarah to spring into action.

She was positioned near the closest entry tube to Jasmine's cell but had been unable to enter because of the steady stream of guards. Though impatient, she knew if she bided her time that an opportunity would present itself.

At least, she hoped so.

They had yet to discover another way into the lair.

Eventually, Garcia saw their chance.

'Sarah,' he blurted. 'Two guards are headed your way!'

* * *

As the guards emerged from the hatch, Sarah shoved Dade from behind the shrub and out into the open. He instinctively cried out in protest, momentarily forgetting the assassins standing no more than fifty feet away.

Responding to his girlish shriek, the guards spun toward the sound and spotted Dade. They instantly raised their swords and rushed in for the kill.

But Sarah struck first.

Using Dade as a diversion, Sarah had circled the bushes in the opposite direction. In their haste to slaughter Dade, they never saw her coming. She moved behind them and dropped them with silenced double-taps to the backs of their heads.

They were dead before they hit the ground.

She turned toward Dade. 'Sorry about that.'

'No, you aren't! Not at all!'

'Maybe a little,' she said with a smile.

Dade nodded. 'Next time you need a diversion, just leave me out of it, okay?'

Sarah shrugged. 'No promises.'

She hurried over to the fallen warriors and pulled off their tunics. She knew they couldn't roam through the bunker dressed as they were. They would need to disguise their appearance. 'Put this on.'

He didn't argue as he took the tunic, but he still didn't understand her intentions. 'Fine, but at least tell me why. What's the plan?'

Sarah nodded toward the hatch as she got dressed. 'We're going in.'

Dade looked at her in confused horror.

He could tell from her face that she was serious.

*   *   *

Cobb knew what the shadow warriors were capable of. He had seen the shredded remains of their victims in the cisterns, and Manjani had described their handiwork in great detail. A reputation such as theirs did not come easily. It was established over centuries of action and continually reinforced throughout the ages.

Cobb knew their skills were impressive, but not *how* impressive until he saw them in action.

He watched in amazement as the shadow warriors and their ancient weapons bested the horde with machine guns. Though the warriors took casualties – try as they might, they could not deflect automatic fire with narrow, steel blades – it seemed like most of their deaths were selfless acts to protect their brethren by taking out gunmen.

Like kamikazes with swords instead of planes.

Once they had infiltrated a crowd, their every movement was not only graceful, it was calculated. Their angles of attack used friendly fire to aid their cause. By always positioning themselves between their enemies, they ensured that any bullets that missed or passed through their bodies would end up lodged in their opponents.

Combined with their nimble swordplay, it was like watching a ballet of death.

*   *   *

Kamal had seen Dade run away.

At first he had assumed that the coward was simply running

from the fight, too scared to face things like a man, but he quickly convinced himself otherwise. Dade ran with purpose, not fear, accelerating in a straight line. All things considered, Kamal could think of only one justification for his behavior.

Dade wasn't running *from* someone.

He was running *to* someone.

But who?

Kamal was determined to find out.

* * *

Sarah descended first, leaving Dade to slide the heavy steel covering back into place. The chute was much narrower than it had looked outside. It reminded Sarah of the time she had toured a World War II submarine. The tunnel had that same dimly lit, claustrophobic feel.

She looked up at Dade, and noticed that he had to scrunch his shoulders to keep from banging them off the sides of the tube.

The tunnel was that tight.

When she reached the bottom of the ladder, she had to fight every instinct to go charging through the hallways in search of Jasmine. They needed to move quickly, but they needed to blend in as well. She knew the only reason that Garcia had eyes inside the bunker was because it had been wired for surveillance.

That meant someone else was watching.

* * *

Despite their advanced weaponry, Hassan's men were losing the battle. Although the goons were seriously outmanned, it was the Muharib's willingness to sacrifice themselves for the greater good that was the real problem.

The warriors were relentless.

As the cloud cover grew and the moonlight waned, the Muharib were driven by a sense of destiny. They believed that Amun had blessed them with additional darkness – a sign that their actions had pleased their god.

In response, they attacked with renewed vigor, overwhelming their opponents with their superior numbers. Though many on the frontline were gunned down, the surge of humanity quickly enveloped the trespassers. At such close range, the bulky firearms were no match for the agile swordsmen. Skulls were split and organs were spilled as the Muharib sliced their way through the crowd.

The goons continued to fight, but it was only a matter of time.

It was a slaughter in every sense of the word.

Sensing that his window was closing, Kamal slipped off into the darkness, leaving the others to fend for themselves. Despite Hassan's order that Dade was not to be harmed, Kamal intended to make the American pay for his betrayal.

Dade was out there, somewhere in the night.

Kamal would not stop until he had been punished.

* * *

Hassan stood beside his car and watched the massacre through night-vision binoculars. Though it wasn't the same as being there, he could see well enough to know how the fight would end. He cursed his men for not rising to the challenge, then cursed himself for not bringing more men.

People were expendable.

Opportunities were not.

Hassan lowered the device. 'They have failed me.'

Realizing his defeat, Hassan smashed the expensive lenses

against the nearest Humvee in frustrated disappointment. 'A hundred rounds of ammo each, and still they are beaten by men with swords . . . Swords! They insult me with their incompetence.'

He folded his hands behind his head and looked skyward, sucking in the cool night air in an attempt to calm down. 'Come, Awad. It's time to go home.'

In response, the bodyguard drew the long, curved blade he had hidden under his jacket. He had been embedded as a spy in Hassan's camp for years. His job was to keep an eye on the tunnels that ran under the gangster's territory and to notify his brethren in the Muharib if anyone breached the wall of the underground temple.

Ultimately, he was the one who had sounded the alarm in Alexandria.

He had given the order to attack Hassan's men.

He had given the order to abduct Jasmine.

And he had given the order to blow up the temple.

Now he had one more loose end to deal with.

If Hassan had seen it coming, he would have recognized the blade immediately. It was the same weapon that he had just belittled. The same weapon that had just cut through his squad of goons. Now he was about to understand its power.

In a flash, Awad's blade swept across Hassan's throat.

Blood gushed from the wound as he slumped to the ground.

Awad stood over his boss and sneered: 'I *am* home.'

75

Jasmine didn't know how long it had been since Kaleem had been dragged from their cell. Her face no longer ached, so she guessed it had been at least a few hours since she had been struck by the guard. She wasn't sure what would happen next, but she was sure of one thing: the waiting was intolerable.

So much so, she actually felt relief when the door swung open.

Unfortunately, the feeling wouldn't last.

It would quickly turn to fear.

The guard who had slapped her came in first. As he moved toward her, she instinctively retreated to the rear corner of the cell, the farthest point that her chain would allow. Rather than give chase, the guard simply stared at her – as if his only purpose was to ensure that she did not intervene in what was about to happen next.

Jasmine watched in confusion as five more guards entered the room. Each carried a long, slender rod that bowed across his shoulders. The rods were weighted down on both ends by heavy oil lamps that dangled from metal hooks. The additional flames filled the room with an abundance of light and scented smoke.

Not ready for the glare, she shielded her eyes with her hands.

Behind the torchbearers came two more men whose sturdy physiques stretched the fabric of their tunics. Their muscles bulged as they strained to carry a cylindrical stone slab into the ancient cell. They carefully set the ancient relic in the center of the floor before they took their place among the others.

Together, the group formed a ring around the stone.

Finally, the high priest entered the room. Dressed in an ornate cloak, he had a regal air about him that was oddly comforting, as if he knew the secrets of the universe and would be willing to share them for the betterment of mankind.

Jasmine breathed in the smoke and irrationally filled with hope.

Perhaps he was there to explain it all.

Her imprisonment. Their history.

Maybe even the tomb itself.

* * *

Despite his size, or perhaps because of it, Kamal found himself alone in the dark. As he lumbered through the desert, he searched the ground for Dade's trail and eventually found something much more interesting than footprints.

Kamal literally stumbled across two dead shadow warriors, their blades still clutched in their hands. He initially thought that they had been casualties of the firefight – wounded men who had tried to seek refuge – but he knew that didn't make sense.

Injured Muharib would not retreat.

They would fearlessly fight to the death.

Leaning close, Kamal could see that they had been killed efficiently. He also knew that no one who had made the trip from Alexandria – including Dade – would have been able to shoot four rounds so accurately. When it came to shooting, his colleagues relied on the quantity of their ammunition over the quality of their aim.

The marksmanship meant that Dade was not alone.

Kamal crouched low, at least for him, and scanned the darkness for signs of trouble. The shrubbery to his left hid no threats, but he wasn't as sure about the odd ring of cement that he suddenly noticed. He approached it cautiously, his finger on the trigger, ready to fire at whoever or whatever emerged from the hole.

Instead, he found it sealed by a heavy metal plate.

Sliding back the cover, Kamal reached two important conclusions.

This underground compound was the home of the warriors.

And he was way too big to fit down the chute.

*　　*　　*

Sarah had always been a tomboy. Even as a child she had been tall and lanky, with an athletic frame built more for basketball than beauty pageants. Not that she ever minded. She was perfectly happy with a physique that matched her psyche. While most of her female classmates were doing their nails, she just wanted to be one of the guys.

Many years later, she finally had her chance.

With the loose-fitting tunic draped over her body and a hood draped over her head, Sarah looked the part of a Muharib warrior. As long as she kept her face hidden from view, she and Dade could move through the underground hallways without drawing attention. Once they had reached Jasmine's cell, the plan was to put her in a tunic and carry her, as if she had been injured in the battle above.

In truth, the only reason Dade was there was to help carry Jasmine to the surface.

Prior to the mission, Sarah had memorized the map of the complex. She knew exactly which turns to make to ensure the shortest path to Jasmine's cell. If all went according to plan, Garcia would only inform her of the Muharib's movements; the rest would be up to her. Unfortunately, things went to hell almost immediately.

'Sarah,' Garcia said, 'something's happening. A bunch of guards just went into her cell. I think they're going to interrogate her.'

* * *

The priest gazed upon the stone slab in the center of the room. Reverence filled his eyes as he basked in its glory. 'Do you know what this is?'

Jasmine shook her head, surprised by his query.

He had posed it in English, not Arabic.

'This is from the original temple of Amun. It was broken from a pillar two millennia ago, but we have found a home for it here – safely protected within our walls. It is a sacred relic, having borne witness to great acts of honor and adoration.'

Turning his attention to Jasmine, the priest sat on the flat piece of rock. He ran his hands along its smooth sides, as if touching it could summon unearthly power.

'Tell me, what does Alexander mean to you?'

She swallowed hard. 'He was the greatest conqueror the world has ever known.'

The priest shook his head, disappointed with her response. 'You know him only by his mortal acts. But he is so much more. You see him as flesh and bone. But his spirit is everlasting. He is heralded as the vanquisher of all who opposed him, yet you deny the very reason for his success.' He leaned closer. 'You cannot defeat a god.'

He closed his eyes, taking a moment to acknowledge the

importance of the man he and his followers had deified over two thousand years ago. When he opened them again, his tone was that of a lecturer, not a preacher.

'The Vatican. Mecca. The Western Wall. What do these sites have in common? To invade these places is to encroach upon holy ground. Doing so would draw the wrath of millions of followers – each of them eager to see justice done to those who dared to desecrate their faith. Do these numbers alone give credence to their outrage?'

'I . . . I don't understand.'

'Why are the large fellowships of Catholicism, Islam, and Judaism able to profess their concept of god without ridicule, yet you insult our beliefs? Why should we be disrespected in such ways?'

Jasmine pleaded. 'Whatever I've done, I meant you no harm.'

'Harm?' the elder mocked. 'You seek the tomb of our righteous son, the progeny of Amun himself, yet you claim to be without blame? It is that ignorance that threatens our way of life. You yearn for riches and glory in your attempt to find his body. You call yourselves "scholars", "explorers", and "historians", but you are really just thieves in the night. You and your ilk think nothing of disturbing our sacred grounds – all in the name of what? Science? History? Treasure? Tell me, how do you justify your disrespect of our master and your obvious contempt for his followers?'

He waited for an answer, but none was forthcoming.

* * *

The more Garcia listened, the more confused he became.

The interrogator appeared to be more intent on delivering information than extracting it. Not only that, but he seemed to pay no heed to the battle happening above. His voice and demeanor were calm and collected, his actions not rushed in any way. Even with the enemy at his doorstep, he did not exhibit one degree of panic.

His lack of fear was disturbing.

The entire scene was unsettling.

Garcia knew that something was wrong.

76

Garcia had been so caught up in the events in Jasmine's cell that he had almost forgotten about Sarah and Dade. By the time he noticed the four shadow warriors moving toward their location, it was almost too late.

He kept his tone relaxed, knowing that a sudden reaction from Sarah would alert anyone watching the camera feeds from inside the bunker.

'Sarah,' he said, 'you've got four men headed your way, just around the farthest corner. I need you to move into the armory coming up on your left. Keep your pace and you'll make it. You've still got ten seconds to get there . . . nine . . . eight . . .'

In his own head, Garcia was screaming for them to hurry.

* * *

Sarah and Dade moved steadily toward the room in front of them. There was no hitch in their stride or any noticeable change in their movements – nothing that would give them away. As Garcia reached the count of 'two', they pushed through the unlocked door and gently closed it behind them.

Garcia breathed a sigh of relief as the guards walked past. 'See, no problem. A whole second to spare.'

'Thanks,' she whispered. 'Let me know when it's clear. In the meantime, I'm going to check out their supplies.'

'Don't stray too far,' Garcia warned as he searched for her on his computer screen. 'There's a camera mounted above the door. Right now I can't see you. I'd advise you to keep it that way.'

'Will do,' she said as she grabbed Dade's sleeve.

He nodded in understanding. He would stay by the door.

In person, the armory was even more impressive than it had been on screen. The cache that they had accumulated would rival those of the world's most formidable warlords. The guns alone were enough to stage an invasion – if that invasion had taken place fifty years ago, because many of the weapons were antiques.

The real prize, however, was the explosives.

Each pound of Semtex could do the work of a thousand guns.

And that was just the beginning of their arsenal.

* * *

A curious grin spread across the elder's face.

'Tell me,' he said, 'do you understand the concept of faith?'

Before Jasmine could speak, he answered his own question.

'Of course you don't. Your version of faith allows you to pick and choose your level of devotion, paying tribute when it suits you. Meanwhile, our faith is all-consuming. Our devotion is absolute. It has not faltered in more than two thousand years. Even when our city was overrun by Romans, we triumphed because of our faith.'

'You did what was needed,' she said.

She hoped to make a connection.

Instead, it fueled his indignation.

'Do you think you know us? Do you think you understand sacrifice?' He shook his head. 'You know nothing! We planned in advance for the oracle's prophecy to come true – never questioning, never doubting that the flood would eventually come.

Every action in Alexandria was a calculated endeavor, from the feigned acceptance of the Roman doctrine to our adoption of their culture. The clothes we wore, the words we spoke – all maneuvers that allowed us to keep an eye on Alexander. Our forces were always outnumbered, but we were never outsmarted. First we took their temple. Then we took the tomb. For centuries no one suspected our actions, and no one discovered our hidden message. But the moment it was found, we took care of that as well!'

As much as it pained him to destroy a sacred piece of their history – a temple in the bowels of the city that they had maintained over the centuries – the elder had done so without remorse. The preservation of their religion far outweighed the protection of a landmark.

*   *   *

Garcia didn't like what he was hearing. The speech in Jasmine's cell had suddenly gone from educational to heated. The once calm façade of the priest had started to crumble, revealing the furious disposition below.

Garcia worried that the shouting hinted at what was to come.

He feared it was a prelude to violence.

He checked his screen and saw that the hallway was finally clear. 'Sarah, it's time to go! Things are getting loud in there, and I don't like it. I'm starting to get a bad feeling about this – like he's about to erupt.'

*   *   *

Sarah stepped into the hallway, with Dade following close behind. She knew they were close, but she couldn't afford to be careless. Not with so much at stake.

Stay calm. Don't run.

Find Jasmine. Get the hell out.

If their path stayed clear, the only thing that stood between them and Jasmine's cell was a long corridor that ended with two quick turns before it continued on. Sarah knew there were no cameras covering the zigzag section of the hallway. They couldn't linger long, but it offered them one last chance to gather themselves.

One quick moment before they made their final push.

* * *

The elder rose from the block to deliver his final words. 'We have no quarrel with those who mean us no harm. But those who seek to desecrate our lands in search of our relics will be met with the full force of our power. Amun will reward us for our faith. He and his son protect us. They guide us. They are the source of our strength. And our strength is unsurpassed because we are fueled by god.'

As if on cue, the muscular guards charged toward Jasmine and grabbed her. Despite her flailing arms and cries of anguish, they easily dragged her across the floor, delivering her to the sacred stone. The guard who had slapped her earlier grabbed a fistful of hair and yanked her head back as she was pulled roughly to her knees.

* * *

When Sarah reached the twist in the hallway, she paused briefly. She needed to know what Garcia was keeping from her. Firelight danced across the wall in front of her, as if making that final turn would lead her into a raging inferno.

'Hector,' she whispered, 'what's going on? I see flickering flames and a bunch of shadows on the wall. What am I facing?'

'Sarah!' he shouted. 'Go now! Go right now!'

She reached under her tunic and pulled out her gun, waiting for more intel on the situation. 'Tell me what I'm facing!'

*　　*　　*

For the first time, Jasmine could see finer details of the stone.

From a distance, she had believed that the earthy tone was a natural feature of the rock. Her eyes grew wide when she realized the discoloration in each cut was man-made. The crimson stains were dried blood left by centuries of executions.

She stared up at the elder, nearly paralyzed by fear. She watched as a guard removed the elder's cloak and handed him a curved sword. She tried to scream at the sight of the blade, but she could barely muster a sound.

The elder looked down at her. 'You must pay for your indignities.'

'Wait, wait, please wait,' she muttered, summoning the last bit of courage she could muster. 'The tomb! I need to know: where is the tomb?'

The elder smiled, leaned in close, and whispered in her ear. 'That is not for me to say. Amun will tell you himself when you meet him.'

With a subtle nod, the brutal guard slammed her face against the stone. The other two held her arms far to the sides so she couldn't squirm away.

*　　*　　*

Garcia leaped to his feet, knocking over his chair. 'Oh God. Someone—'

He started to hyperventilate. 'They're going to—'

His knees wobbled as he gasped for breath. 'Sarah . . . now!'

*　　*　　*

The elder raised the sword above his head, said a few words in his native tongue, then brought the blade down with all of his might.

The last sound that Jasmine ever heard was the snap of her neck.

A moment later, her head rolled across the floor.

Just as Sarah reached the cell.

One second too late.

77

Sarah stared in horror as Jasmine's head tumbled across the stone. Time seemed to stand still as the gathered priests in the chamber all turned to face the interloper. She could see the confusion on their faces – their utter shock that someone had infiltrated their sacred dwelling and dared to intervene.

In the middle stood the elder, his blade wet with blood.

Once glance was all it took.

Sarah simply snapped.

Their numbers should have given them an advantage, but her Glock more than evened the odds. Before the men could react, she raised her pistol and fired at the elder. In her rage, the shot missed its mark, yet it still accomplished her goal. Rather than striking his body, the bullet shattered the clay lamp that dangled at the elder's side, spraying his tunic with oil. In a flash, the burning wick ignited the fuel, engulfing the elder in a wave of fire.

As the others lunged forward to extinguish the flames, Sarah unleashed hell. Bones broke and lamps exploded as she emptied her clip in a vengeful fury. When Dade reached her side, she tore her backup pistol from his grasp and emptied that as well.

The onslaught crippled the men and set the entire room ablaze. Pools of burning oil crept across the floor, hungrily consuming the fallen priests. They writhed in agony as their bodies were roasted like meat on a spit. Without guns to fire back or the ability to stand, all they could do was burn as Sarah tried to make sense of the scene.

She stood there, dazed, unable to look away.

How could this happen?

Why did you kill her?

What did she do to you?

Sarah had been taught to never leave a colleague behind – even those who had been killed in action – but she had to face facts: there was nothing she could do with a burning body. Her stomach churned in revulsion as she realized that she couldn't take Jasmine with her. As much as it pained her, she had to worry about the living.

At least those who fought on her side.

Just then, one of the guards tried to crawl toward the safety of the hallway, but she slammed the door in his face, sealing him and the others inside. There were no screams of pain, no cries for help inside the chamber. The priests endured in silence. The only sounds were the crackling of the flames and the sizzling of their flesh.

In the corridor, Sarah fell back against the opposite wall, nearly overcome with grief. Reeling from the tragedy, it took a moment to find her voice. 'Jasmine . . .'

'I know . . .' Garcia sobbed. 'She's dead.'

* * *

Cobb's stomach rolled as the news sank in. Despite all that they had done and learned, their efforts had come up short. Regardless of their initial mission in Florida, this had been a rescue operation since the moment they had lost Jasmine in the tunnel beneath Alexandria. She had become the focus, not the tomb.

And now, she was gone.

His years of service had made him resistant to pain, but not immune. Losing a fellow soldier was bad enough, but Jasmine was a civilian, the lone member of their team without government training. Hell, even Garcia had worked for the FBI.

But not Jasmine.

In his heart, Cobb knew that he should have persuaded her to walk away after their first adventure. He should have forced her to take the money and run, but somehow he had convinced himself that he could protect her from danger.

Obviously, he had failed.

'Chief,' McNutt said somberly, 'did I hear Hector right?'

The voice in Cobb's ear snapped him out of his daze. He swallowed hard, forcing the anguish from his mind. He could grieve later. For now, he needed to quell his emotions and rescue the people who could still be saved.

Though their mission had failed, it was far from over.

They still needed to make it out alive.

'Sarah, get out of there. There's nothing else you can do.'

*   *   *

Despite her respect for Cobb, she completely disagreed with his order.

There *was* something else she could do.

She could kill everyone in the compound.

Without saying a word, she turned and sprinted back toward the armory. Dade could barely keep pace as she charged down the long corridor. Fueled by rage, she burst through the door and scanned the room for something to help her cause.

She had plenty of options.

Though she lacked McNutt's expertise, she had received extensive weapons training in the CIA. After grabbing a crowbar from a rack of tools, she pried open the nearest crate. Hoping that the relics had been well maintained, she instead found a collection of corroded firepower that hadn't been touched in more than fifty years.

She cursed her luck as she reached for another lid. She knew they were wasting time. She needed to find something useful, and she needed to find it fast. Unfortunately, the second crate was no better than the first.

'This is junk!' Sarah shouted as she continued to search.

'What do you mean?' Dade replied. 'A gun is a gun is a gun. This isn't the time to be picky!'

Sarah glared at him. 'This stuff hasn't been fired since World War Two. That means more than five decades of neglect. You pull the trigger on one of those, and it's liable to blow up in your face.'

Dade grimaced. 'No wonder they're fighting with swords.'

'Still,' she said with determination, 'there has to be something here that we can use. I don't care if it's old, as long as it isn't rusted.'

Sarah tore open a third crate and nodded. 'Jackpot.'

She tossed the lid aside, revealing a dozen Benelli M4 shotguns. The modern, Italian-made weapon was sturdy and reliable, with a shot pattern that didn't require pinpoint accuracy. The M4 could hold seven shells in its magazine and one in the chamber, and its twelve-gauge rounds could blow a hole clean through someone's chest.

It was more than ideal for what Sarah had in mind.

It was perfect.

'Take this,' she demanded as she handed one of the guns to Dade. She dug deeper into the crate, reaching for the ammunition that had been stored with the guns. She tossed a box of shells to Dade. 'Fill the gun, then fill your pockets.'

He had never seen Sarah like this.

The person he knew tried to save lives, not take them.

Still, he wasn't about to interfere.

Sarah watched as Dade fumbled his way through loading the weapon. 'Do you know what you're doing?'

Dade stared at her, not knowing if she was referring to his clumsy attempt to load the shotgun or to his role in her plan – assuming she had a plan.

He simply shrugged in confusion.

Sarah ripped the Benelli from his hands and quickly filled the magazine, holding it out so that he could understand the process. When she was done, she pulled the shotgun to her shoulder and took aim at the video equipment mounted above the door. She pulled the trigger, and the camera disintegrated, along with a large chunk of the wall.

She tossed the gun back to Dade. 'Got it?'

He nodded slowly. 'Yes.'

'Good,' she growled as she motioned toward the door. 'Shoot anything that tries to come through. If it keeps moving, shoot it again.'

Garcia chimed in. 'Sarah, where are you? I don't have eyes on you anymore.'

'And neither do they,' she snapped at him. 'Don't worry about what's going on in here. Just let me know if someone's headed our way. Got it?'

'Yeah, sure,' Garcia said. 'Whatever you need.'

She glanced at Dade. 'Does your comm still work?'

'My what?'

'Your comm. Can you hear Hector?'

'Yeah,' he mumbled, worried about his friend. He anxiously watched as she turned away from him and searched through the chemical compounds that lined the wall. 'What are you doing?'

'I'm thinning the herd.'

As she inspected the shelves, cartons, and bins that lined the wall, she was shocked and amazed at the variety of explosives that they had hoarded. She knew that compounds like Semtex and C-4 were great for jobs like the one in Alexandria – the explosives were stable enough that they wouldn't explode en route, and they could be molded into a variety of shapes and sizes for maximum effect – but they also had their drawbacks. Namely, each package of explosive required its own blasting cap.

On the other hand, dynamite and other nitroglyccrin-based compounds didn't require a primary blast as a simple electrical charge or standard fuse would trigger their explosion, but their destructive force was relatively weak when compared to plastic explosives. And for a job like this, weak simply wouldn't cut it.

No, Sarah was looking for something between the two products. Something that would fully incinerate the bunker yet could be ignited without the hassle of hundreds of detonators. Something simple yet devastating. A chemical with some serious kick.

Something like ammonium nitrate.

The white powder looked more like laundry detergent than a lethal explosive, but Sarah knew the damage it could inflict. In 1947, a shipload of ammonium nitrate detonated in Texas's Galveston Bay. The resulting blast shattered windows forty miles away in Houston. The shockwave tore the wings off planes flying overhead, and the ship's anchor was eventually found on the other side of the city. The explosion started a chain of destruction that has been compared to that of an atomic bomb.

All because the shipment overheated.

Sarah popped the lid from the plastic drum and stared down at the substance. The ammonium nitrate in this one container would easily take out the armory, the hallways, and the cell where she hoped the priests were still dying a slow, excruciating death. But that wasn't enough. She wanted the entire compound to burn.

Fortunately, there were three more barrels of the deadly mix.

Enough to incinerate the compound several times over.

Sarah smiled at the thought.

To ensure that the chemicals ignited, Sarah pulled a brick of Semtex from the shelf. She rigged the package with an electronic detonator that would allow them to flee before the fireworks started, then she dropped the bomb into the barrel of ammonium nitrate and reaffixed the lid. She could now ravage the bunker with a push of a button, eradicating the minions that called it home.

They had ended her friend's life.

Now she would end theirs.

Sarah secured the detonator in her tunic and grabbed a shotgun of her own. It was time to leave. 'Hector, how's it looking?'

'The hallway is clear. They've all rallied at the holding cell.'

She stuffed a handful of shells into her pockets. 'Simon, we're leaving.'

'It's about time,' Dade mumbled.

He exited first, with Sarah directly behind him. But instead of running, she paused for a moment to sabotage the lock on the armory door. It wasn't a permanent solution, but it would prevent the Muharib from accessing their weapons anytime soon. Once she was done, they hurriedly retraced their steps back toward the exit shaft.

Garcia warned them of potential obstacles. 'There are four guards waiting for you in the room near the hatch. I think they're there to block your escape.'

'Are they armed?' she demanded.

'Only with swords,' Garcia informed her.

'Big mistake,' she muttered. 'Simon—'

He cut her off. 'I know, I know. I'm the distraction.'

Simon took a deep breath then ran toward the exit at full speed. When he approached the room where the guards were waiting, he unleashed a primal scream and ran past their door. The four guards immediately gave chase, none of them bothering to check for intruders that might be approaching from behind. This, of course, was a fatal mistake because Sarah mowed them down like targets in a shooting gallery.

Blood and brains sprayed the walls of the hallway as she opened fire. Round after round tore through them, eviscerating bodies and spilling guts onto the floor.

The guards never stood a chance.

When it was over, Sarah just stood there in the midst of the carnage. Overwhelmed by rage, she could barely remember what she had done. All she knew was that she had wanted them to die, over and over and over again.

Eventually, she looked down at the weapon in her hands.

She was still pulling the trigger on the empty gun.

Dade hurdled the corpses and returned to her side. 'Are you okay?'

'Yeah,' she lied as she tossed her shotgun to the floor.

He followed her lead and did the same. 'Are you sure?'

'Yes. I'm fine. Let's get out of here.'

Due to the weight of the hatch above, Dade opted to go first. Sarah might have been tougher, but he was stronger. There was no doubt about that.

They climbed the ladder as quickly as they could, one after the other, clearing two rungs at a time as they hoisted themselves toward the surface where the battle continued to rage in the nearby desert.

With the detonator in her pocket, Sarah knew it would be over soon.

She had lost a friend, but she would have her revenge.

She would make them pay for her loss.

Unfortunately, Kamal was thinking the same thing.

78

Dade slid the heavy plate from the top of the chute, giving them access to the desert above. He peeked out of the concrete cylinder like a meerkat looking for a predator and quickly learned that they weren't alone.

Unable to use the tunnel himself, Kamal had waited patiently near the hatch, playing a hunch that Dade would exit in the same place that he had gone in. His restraint was rewarded when his former colleague emerged from below. Wasting no time, Kamal grabbed Dade by the neck, lifted him from the hole, then tossed him through the air like a bag of trash before he turned back to deal with his accomplice.

*   *   *

A moment earlier, Dade had been blocking her path on the ladder. Now he was nowhere in sight, as if he had been grabbed by Amun and pulled to the heavens above.

Sarah glanced up to figure out how that was possible.

She had her answer a second later.

Kamal's face filled the space above, soon followed by a glimpse of his gun. In the cramped space of the tunnel, she knew she was an easy target. With those odds hanging over her head – not to mention the ugly brute – she did the one and only thing she could think of to avoid near-certain death.

She released her grip and plummeted to the floor below.

*   *   *

Kamal didn't care how she died, only that she did. With that in mind, he simply stepped to the edge of the opening and fired a single shot at the woman on the ladder. He watched her fall before he slammed the lid shut and refocused his attention on Dade.

His death would not be quick.

Dade, still reeling from the shock of his unexpected flight, rose to all fours while trying to catch his breath. Unfortunately, this made him an attractive target to Kamal, who charged toward him and kicked him as hard as he could in the midsection. The giant smiled when Dade started to cough up blood, knowing that he had broken some ribs.

'Get up, you deceitful slug!' Kamal shouted in his native Arabic. He didn't care if Dade understood him. He was merely venting his anger. 'Stand up and face the consequences of your actions!'

But Dade didn't stand.

He merely groaned in pain.

So Kamal kicked him again, toppling him onto his back.

Kamal glanced down at him without pity and raised his boot above Dade's face. Then, with as much force as he could muster, he tried to stomp his head into the ground, but somehow Dade found the strength to roll out of the way.

The giant smiled at the effort.

He was having fun.

*   *   *

Sarah opened her eyes at the base of the ladder. Her ears were ringing and her head throbbed from her crash landing on the floor, but she was okay.

At least she thought she was.

She patted herself just to make sure.

No blood, as far as she could tell.

Just a bump on her head.

Still gathering her senses, she glanced at the ladder above and tried to remember everything that she had seen before her fall.

The hatch. The giant. His gun.

Then it hit her. 'Simon!'

*   *   *

Dade clambered to his feet. His neck ached and his ribs were broken, but he had to fight through the pain. His quickness was the only advantage that he had over his bigger, stronger opponent, and he couldn't use it lying on the ground.

Kamal raised his fists like a boxer. 'Come. Fight like a man.'

In response, Dade flung a fistful of sand in the giant's face, momentarily blinding him. Then he charged forward, hoping to use the moment of weakness to incapacitate his opponent with a swift kick to the groin. The plan probably would have worked on a shorter man, but due to a combination of things – Kamal's height, poor traction in the desert sand, plus Dade's inability to swing his foot high enough to even reach Kamal's crotch – Dade barely grazed his target. Instead of inflicting excruciating pain, his foot got stuck between the giant's thighs like a car getting wedged between two walls.

'Son of a bitch!' Dade said, embarrassed by his failure.

Soon his shame would turn to pain.

Still blinded from the sand, Kamal couldn't fully see his challenger, but he could feel his foot in a place it shouldn't be. He responded by grabbing Dade's leg and twisting it with so much force that the ligaments ripped in his knee and ankle.

Dade screamed in agony and tried to pull away but was unable to break the giant's grip. He frantically clawed at his tormentor, hoping to break the vise-like lock as the shooting pain in his leg took hold of him. He was on the verge of passing out when Kamal finally released his grasp.

Not out of sympathy.

But to end Dade's life.

* * *

The thought of Dade had driven Sarah to her feet. She knew he was defenseless, having dropped his shotgun before ascending the ladder. She scrambled to find the weapon, knowing that it was still fully loaded.

Dade hadn't fired a shot.

She had seven chances to settle things.

She grabbed the gun in one hand and climbed the ladder with the other. Her progress was slow and lurching as she struggled with the awkward, single-handed climb.

Still, she couldn't give up on him.

Not in his time of need.

* * *

Kamal's anvil-like fists rained down on Dade, unleashing a torrent of pent-up rage: for the indignity that he had suffered at Hassan's house, the humiliation of tracking the Americans through the sewers, the devastating loss of his entire crew, and his displeasure at accompanying Dade in the city and during the long ride through the desert.

It was simply too much to handle.

Enjoying every single moment, Kamal had started low and had methodically worked his way up. Now that he had reached Dade's face, he stared down at him with a crazed look in his eyes. He grabbed Dade's jaw and smiled, making his next target clear.

'For Tarek,' he growled in English.

Dade defiantly spat blood in the thug's face. 'Fuck Tarek.'

Infuriated by the insult to his dead best friend, Kamal grabbed a softball-sized rock from the sand and swung it at Dade's head. The bones of his face collapsed under the pressure, killing him instantly. But Kamal continued to pound away, releasing his hatred with blow after angry blow. The giant never let up, not even as Dade's skull was reduced to nothing but a sopping stew of bones and brains and hair in the arid desert sand.

79

Sarah reached the top of the ladder and crawled into the moon-light. No more than twenty feet away, she could see Kamal hunched over Dade's lifeless body.

The fight was already over.

She was too late to save *another* friend.

The grief was nearly too much to bear – even for someone like Sarah.

If she had wanted to, she could have run to safety. Kamal was clearly lost in his rage, and he assumed that she was dead. It was likely that he never would have noticed her. She could have easily slipped past him and returned to base camp.

But the thought never crossed her mind.

Without saying a word, Sarah lifted the shotgun to her shoulder, trained it on the unsuspecting thug, and opened fire. The shot tore through Kamal's arm, spinning him to the ground. The second shot splintered his leg. He cried out in agony, but she was all out of sympathy and would be for a very long time.

Clinging to life, Kamal did the only thing he could.

He reached for his pistol, determined to go out fighting.

Sarah granted his wish, unloading the remaining rounds into his chest before he could brandish a weapon. With every shot she moved closer, growing more and more satisfied with every pull of the trigger. By the time she reached him, it was very clear that he was dead, but she kicked him a few times just to be sure.

*   *   *

Garcia had watched her carry the shotgun up the ladder, and he had heard the shots shortly thereafter, but he had no idea what had happened. Once she had left the bunker, he could no longer track her movement with the network of cameras.

'Sarah,' he said, 'can you hear me? What's your status?'

Cobb waited several seconds for a response. He wasn't the type to panic, but considering what had happened moments earlier, the prolonged silence was deafening. 'Hector, give me an update. Where's Sarah?'

'I have no idea,' Garcia said. 'I watched her and Simon crawl up the wormhole, but I think they were attacked outside the bunker because I watched her drop back down the chute, pick up a shotgun off the floor, and head back to the surface. Next thing you know I'm hearing multiple shots. And not from a wimpy Glock; something a lot more powerful.'

Cobb had heard the shots as well. Not only in his earpiece, but in the distant desert. Now that he knew they were from Sarah's gun, he needed her to check in. If she didn't, he would have no choice but to track her down.

'Sarah, it's Jack. Are you out there?' He waited a few seconds before he continued. 'If you can hear my voice but can't talk, just tap on your comm and give us a signal. Josh and I will come to you.'

'Don't,' she ordered.

Cobb, Garcia, and McNutt breathed a sigh of relief.

'You had us worried,' Garcia said.

'Don't be worried about me. Be worried about yourselves.'

Cobb didn't like the ominous tone of her voice. He knew that she was hurting from the loss of Jasmine, but now wasn't the time to lose one's cool — not with danger lurking in the desert. 'Sarah, where are you? Are you with Simon?'

'Simon's dead,' she announced as she continued to run from the compound. 'Kamal killed him, so I killed Kamal.'

Cobb groaned. Losing one friend was hard enough, but losing two back to back had to be devastating. 'Sarah, I'm sorry about Simon. I really am. Where are you?'

'Don't worry about me. Worry about yourself.'

'What does that mean?' he said, confused.

'Are you clear of the compound?'

'Yes,' he said, struggling to comprehend.

'What about Josh?'

'What about me?' McNutt asked from his sniper post.

'Are you clear of the compound?'

'Yes, I'm clear of the goddamned co—'

'Wait,' Cobb shouted as a feeling of dread washed over him. From the tone of her voice and her line of questioning, he sensed what was about to happen. 'I know you're hurting, but think things through. Don't do something you're going to regret.'

'I won't regret it.'

'Jack,' Garcia demanded, 'what are you talking about?'

* * *

Sensing trouble, McNutt used his scope to search for Sarah in the darkness. He was shocked to see her sprinting across the desert.

Through the optics of his rifle, she seemed to be completely out of control, as if she no longer gave a damn about herself.

Regrettably, he had seen this type of behavior on the battlefield before, and it never ended well. He prayed a kill shot wouldn't be necessary, but he wanted to be ready just in case she threatened anyone on his team.

'Chief, I've got eyes on Sarah. She's sprinting toward base camp like her pants are on fire. What the fuck is going on?'

'She's running toward me?' Garcia blurted.

'Relax,' Cobb said to them.

McNutt continued to watch. 'Chief, she's got something in her hand. I can't tell what it is. I don't think it's a gun, but I can't tell from here. Just say the word.'

'Sarah,' Cobb said, 'don't do it unless you're sure.'

'Do what?' Garcia demanded. 'Am I in danger?'

'Just say the word, chief,' McNutt repeated.

Now that she was far enough from the compound, she slowed to a halt then turned back to watch the desert. 'Jack, I'm sure about this. This needs to be done.'

* * *

Cobb took a deep breath and nodded in understanding.

He had been there many times before.

He felt her agony. And anger.

Contrary to McNutt's concerns, Cobb knew this wasn't about Sarah losing control. This was about reclaiming it. Two of her friends had died a few minutes apart, and she had been unable to save either. Although she couldn't bring them back to life, she could even the score by killing the people that she held responsible for their deaths. She had already killed Kamal, and now she wanted to kill the rest.

And he wasn't going to stop her.

'Josh, stand down. Repeat. Stand down.'

McNutt did as he was told. 'Standing down. Repeat. Standing down.'

'Josh,' Cobb said.

'Yeah, chief.'

'You might want to watch this.'

'Watch what, chief?'

'The fireworks.'

*   *   *

Sarah started the show with the touch of a button.

A moment later, the Semtex that she had rigged in the armory erupted. The explosion devastated the weapons depot and rocked the foundation of the bunker, but that was just the beginning. As the heat of the blast ignited the barrels of ammonium nitrate, a wall of flame roared through every room and corridor in the complex. And just as she had escaped through the hatch, so did the raging inferno.

Only it used every tunnel, all at once.

Pillars of flame rose high into the air, lighting the sky and turning night into day. For those unfortunate souls in the tunnels themselves, they were set on fire and launched into the heavens like meteorites that had changed their minds. Bodies were silhouetted against the flames as those who remained in battle spun frantically in confusion, searching for an escape from near-certain death. But before they could move, the trembling sands beneath their feet pulled them down into the depths of the earth.

As the fire consumed them, everyone on the battlefield was buried, crushed, swallowed, and scorched by the collapsing terrain. Like a biblical horror, their bodies melted as the heat consumed them. To the Muharib among them, it was as if Amun had brought forth his inescapable wrath to punish them for their sins. They accepted their fate without question.

For Hassan's soldiers, it was much, much worse.

For them, there was no salvation.

There was only death.

＊　＊　＊

By the time McNutt and Cobb found each other in the darkness, the desert was eerily quiet. Despite the glowing purr of the sinkhole and the occasional pop of munitions, there were no more signs of life. The grunts and groans of war had given way to the shrieks and cries of death, but now even those had ceased.

The land had been swarming with activity.

Hundreds of souls, committed to their cause.

Now only they remained.

Cobb looked him over. 'You okay?'

McNutt nodded. 'Yeah, chief. I'm good.'

His usual jovial demeanor had been replaced by a melancholy sadness. While his humor often hid it, he had come to think of the team as family – something he'd never had as a child. Having known Jasmine for less than six months only added to his misery. In his mind, they were just getting started.

They walked toward the road in silence, each contemplating what the future had in store. They knew they still had five million dollars coming to them for their original mission, but the money seemed meaningless. They would have gladly traded it to have Jasmine back. One thing was certain: Papineau would keep all of his promises to her, or they would spend the rest of their lives destroying his.

It was nearly dawn as they reached the makeshift parking lot just off the desert road. As they approached the Mercedes SUV, it was clear that something wasn't right. Though they were nearly a mile from the battlefield, there was blood splattered everywhere. The entire front half of the vehicle was doused in sticky crimson.

They spread out, converging on the scene from both sides.

'What happened here?' McNutt whispered.

Cobb shook his head. 'It wasn't like this before.'

A few seconds passed before they spoke again.

'You need to see this, chief.'

Cobb hustled over, following the trail of blood on the ground until he spotted a body slumped against the door. Stepping closer, he saw Hassan's cold, lifeless face staring up at them. His throat had been cut from ear to ear.

The wound told them everything they needed to know.

There was at least one Muharib unaccounted for.

Maybe more.

80

Sunday, November 9
Mediterranean Sea
(10 miles north of Mersa Matruh, Egypt)

Cobb stood at the helm alone, silently staring at the whitecaps that surrounded them. Though the sky was clear and bright, the winds stirred a heavy chop in the water. The yacht pitched and rolled in the waves, breaking the normal serenity of the sea.

He thought it was a fitting touch.

It had been a bumpy ride.

After picking up Sarah in the desert, Cobb had driven to their base camp where Garcia was anxiously awaiting their return. He had packed and stacked their gear in advance of their arrival and only needed to load it into the Humvee before they could leave. They had worked quickly and quietly, all of them hoping to put the oasis behind them, as if that would be enough to make them forget the tragedy.

Obviously, it did no such thing.

They eventually made their way north to the Egyptian coast where they transferred everything to the yacht before heading out to sea. The plan was to lie low in international waters for a few days before they figured out their next move – *if* there was a next move. The truth was that they were keeping to themselves. Not because they were angry at one another; they simply needed some time alone.

A chance to think. A chance to grieve.

That ended shortly after noon when Papineau joined Cobb on the bridge.

Cobb turned to greet him. 'Did Cyril make it to Athens safely?'

Papineau nodded. 'He arrived about an hour ago.'

With the Muharib stronghold in ruins, Manjani no longer felt the need to hide. If the last few months had taught him anything, it was to make use of whatever days he had left. Between the massacre of his students, the disaster in Alexandria, and Jasmine's execution, he learned how fleeting time could be. With that in mind, he decided to reestablish contact with his relatives, all of who had presumed him dead.

Cobb could only imagine how happy his family would be.

'While you're here,' Cobb said, 'I'd like to talk to you about Jasmine. I need to know that her money will make it into her parents' hands. And not just the payment for our first mission, but all of it: two full shares, tax-free.'

'Yes, of course. The entire amount will be transferred to her family.'

'And they'll still be brought to America?'

Papineau nodded. 'The arrangements have already been made. First class. All expenses paid. The money will be waiting for them when they arrive.'

Cobb could feel the tension in his shoulders start to ease. Jasmine and her family had been weighing heavily on his mind since the desert. He knew that money wouldn't make up for the loss of a child, but he was glad to hear that Jasmine's efforts would not be in vain. Her family would have the life that she wanted them to have.

'Did you tell them what happened?'

Papineau shook his head. 'They know nothing, except that she will not be meeting them at the airport. I assumed that you . . .'

Cobb nodded. 'I'll take care of it. Thanks.'

Per their original agreement, Papineau didn't actually owe anyone a full share for a failed mission, but in his heart he knew it was the right thing to do, particularly with the guilt that lingered in the back of his mind about Jasmine. He knew that he had failed her and the others by not detailing the violent outcome of Manjani's expedition when he had briefed them in Florida. If they had been warned about the attack on Egyptian soil, Cobb would have handled things differently in Alexandria.

His omission had put the team at risk.

As Papineau stared at the sea in silence, Garcia poked his head through the door and cleared his throat to get their attention.

'Jack,' he said tentatively, 'do you have a minute?'

Cobb nodded. He welcomed a distraction. Anything to take his mind off Jasmine. 'Of course. What do you need?'

Garcia lowered his eyes in shame. 'I know I shouldn't be working at a time like this. But, you know, it's who I am, and I needed something to do.'

Cobb stepped forward and put his hand on Garcia's shoulder. Unlike Sarah and McNutt, the computer whiz had never encountered death in the field. 'Are you okay?'

'Yeah,' he assured them, 'I'm fine. It's just, well, I was going through some things on my system, and I noticed something that I can't explain.'

'What kind of something?' Cobb asked.

Garcia looked at him. 'Can I show you?'

'Of course. Lead the way.'

* * *

Cobb and Papineau followed Garcia into his command center and stood in front of the bank of monitors. Each screen was filled with streaming lines of codes, oscillating signal meters, and other images that were beyond their grasp. To Cobb and Papineau, it was hi-tech gibberish – a secret language that only hackers could decipher.

Garcia explained what he had been doing. 'When we first tapped into the security at the bunker, the goal was to pull all the video feeds from their network, so we could see what they saw. To do that, I used a program that selected only what we needed. The criterion was simple: video signals originating from inside the compound. Everything else was filtered out into a digital scrap bin. With only two computers at the camp, I didn't have the resources to sort and scan all the data, but I do now. Over the last few hours, I've been making my way through the trash. Most of it was digital garbage – just like I figured it would be – but then I came across this.'

Garcia tapped his keyboard, and the monitors switched from unintelligible streams of data to a webcam video of a panoramic desert scene.

It was so picturesque it looked like a screensaver.

'Pretty scenic, eh?'

'Very,' Papineau answered. 'When was this recorded?'

'It wasn't,' Cobb said as he studied the image. He knew it had been dark when he had first tapped into the communications shed and the sun hadn't risen until *after* the compound was destroyed. 'This is a live feed.'

Garcia nodded, glad that Cobb had figured it out on his own. 'You're right. It's a batch signal from an outside source.'

'Define *batch*,' Papineau said.

'Eight in total,' Garcia explained. 'They cover a complete panorama.'

With the tap of a button, the main screen was split into a grid of nine boxes. The center block was empty, but the eight perimeter squares combined to offer a three-hundred-and-sixty-degree view of the desert.

The fact that the ground wasn't smoldering and the air wasn't gray with toxic smoke told Cobb that this was not being sent from the bunker site. 'Where is this?'

Garcia clicked his mouse, and a map of the Western Desert appeared on one of his screens. A pulsating red dot drew their attention to a spot a few miles from the carnage. 'It's coming from right there.'

Papineau leaned closer, hoping to see something important.

But all he saw was desert.

He turned toward Garcia. 'What are we looking at?'

'Beats me,' he said. He had stared at the images for several fruitless minutes before he had found the courage to bother Cobb and Papineau. 'I can enlarge the frame a thousand percent, and it's still the same damn thing. It's just sand blowing in the wind. Why the hell would anyone take the time to monitor the barren desert?'

'Bird watching,' McNutt suggested from the doorway.

Cobb turned and smiled, appreciative of the levity.

McNutt made it clear that he wasn't joking.

'Seriously, chief, I've seen this type of setup before.'

'Bird watching?' Papineau muttered.

'Not just birds,' McNutt explained. 'Alligators, elephants, unicorns — you name it. They put cameras like this in the jungle, so why not the desert? Anywhere there are animals humping, there's a pervert who wants to watch. Trust me, I'm one of 'em.'

'A pervert or a humping animal?' Sarah asked as she entered the room.

Her presence was so surprising that it caught everybody off guard. She had been keeping to herself since their return to the boat, only emerging to use the bathroom in the middle of the night. Other than that, she had stayed in her berth.

'Well?' she demanded.

'Both,' McNutt said with a laugh.

From across the room, Cobb made eye contact with Sarah. No words were said, but a lot was expressed with a simple glance. He knew that she was still devastated over the death of her friends and understood that her humor was nothing more than a brave front for the sake of the team. He also sensed that she was looking for a distraction of any kind, even if that meant making fun of McNutt for an hour or two.

Meanwhile, Garcia focused on the problem at hand. He pounded furiously on his keyboard until he came across a secured website that seemed to address their needs. Though he couldn't access the feed itself — the entire site was password-protected, and he didn't have time to break the encryption with everyone waiting — he was able to read the message on the welcome screen.

'You're not going to believe this, but it looks like Josh is right.'

'Bird watching?' Papineau repeated.

Garcia nodded as he read aloud. 'The Western Desert Observation Initiative is an ongoing effort to study the unique wildlife of the region . . . yadda yadda yadda . . . in cooperation with the Egyptian Ministry of State for Environmental Affairs ... blah blah blah ... rodents, snakes, and birds ... and so forth.'

'Told ya!' McNutt bragged. 'Granola-eating tree huggers are everywhere – even in places *without* trees. Tell me how that makes sense.'

Sarah shook her head. 'It doesn't. Wildlife studies concentrate on specific areas of interest like a nest, a watering hole, maybe a food source. That's the exact opposite of this. You don't put cameras in the middle of a giant void unless there's a reason.'

Garcia didn't understand. 'What kind of reason?'

'This isn't research. This is security.'

'Security?' McNutt said with a laugh. 'I realize you're a thief and all – oops, sorry, I mean a "retrieval specialist" – but in every heist movie that I've ever seen, the security cameras are pointing *at* something. You know, something *valuable*.'

'True,' she said, 'but you know what else those movies have in common? The valuables are always stolen because the cameras are in the wrong place.'

'How so?' Cobb asked.

'Think about it,' she explained. 'Cameras are usually placed on the outer walls and are pointed inward at something of value. For some reason, people feel safer when guards are able to keep an eye on things from a distance. However, a system like that has a major flaw. The cameras are located on the periphery of the room. That allows someone like me to sneak in and access the camera feeds before I even set foot inside.'

'And here?'

She studied the video feeds on the screen. 'These guys did it right. Look at that coverage. If you want to make sure something is safe, you set up multiple cameras in the middle of a zone and point the lenses *away* from the thing that you're trying to protect. That way you know what's coming to steal it at all times.'

'*It?* What's *it?*' Garcia demanded, still not connecting the dots in his mind. 'What in the world would someone want to steal in the middle of the desert?'

She tapped on the blank center square. 'The tomb.'

81

The decision to forge ahead was an easy one. The team was still reeling from the loss of Jasmine, and Cobb sensed this was a golden opportunity to work through their grief together. He knew that Jasmine's last thoughts were of Alexander, and while they couldn't bring her back, they could do something that would honor her sacrifice.

Plus, the evidence was too damn compelling to ignore.

As was his way, Cobb insisted on advanced reconnaissance before allowing his team to return to the Western Desert, but unlike previous rekkys that required boots on the ground, he conducted this one without leaving the boat. With assistance from Garcia, he used images from the spy satellites circling overhead and the live video feed from the surveillance cameras at the site to work out the details of their mission.

On the surface, Cobb's plan seemed part-suicidal and part-inspired, but he assured the team that it would work if, and only if, they trusted McNutt with their lives. Not surprisingly, the vote was quick and unanimous: all in favor of the scheme. Despite his wacky ways, they knew McNutt was a first-rate soldier who wouldn't let them down. If he promised that he could protect the team, then they damn well believed it.

After the vote, they spent the next several hours gathering supplies, a process that went smoothly thanks to Papineau's money and connections.

By dawn, the team was packing their cargo into the back of a desert-modified Land Cruiser. When the storage space proved to be insufficient, they loaded the rest of their gear onto the roof of the 4x4 off-road vehicle while saying their goodbyes to Papineau, who would stay behind on the yacht.

Dressed in desert clothes and local headwear to blend in, they reached the periphery of the site a few hours later and were taken aback by the stark terrain. Though they had studied the video feeds in advance and already knew there were no lakes, rock formations, or geographic features to mark the tomb in this flat stretch of desert, the location was more desolate than they had imagined. There was nothing but sand in all directions.

'This place sucks,' Garcia muttered.

'You say that like *sucking* is a bad thing,' McNutt joked.

Sarah rolled her eyes. 'Is it too late to change my vote?'

Cobb nodded. 'That's affirmative.'

'In that case, I'm going to walk the site to get a feel of things.'

'Before you do,' he said while handing her a wire cutter, 'take out the cameras.'

She covered her face and opened her door. 'With pleasure.'

Once the cameras were offline and the gear was unloaded, McNutt established a defensive perimeter by lining the terrain with rattlers – the same devices that had protected their camp near Siwa. If they worked as intended, the tiny motion detectors would alert him to the presence of the Muharib the moment they approached.

That is, *if* they approached.

After planting the devices, McNutt climbed to the roof of the SUV and erected a small Mylar canopy that offered a few square feet of shade. Though the fabric kept him relatively cool, he was far more concerned about the glare. He knew that the high-powered spotting scope he had placed on the small tripod next to his rifle would work best in the absence of direct sunlight.

As an added benefit, the others were jealous of his setup.

While they slaved away in the desert sun, he sat on the roof in a folding chair and peered out over the landscape. From his elevated position, he could see for miles in every direction, prepared to eliminate any threat. His lone job was to keep them safe while they searched for the tomb using ground-penetrating radar (GPR).

Gone are the days when most archaeological discoveries were made through trial and error. Instead, modern explorers commonly use GPR to locate ruins and artifacts before the topsoil is even breached. The low-frequency radio waves are transmitted into the ground by a lawn-mower-shaped device, which is pushed back and forth in a grid pattern. Once the radio waves bounce back to the surface, the onboard computer provides data on the depth of the object and the consistency of the soil, as well as an image of the item itself.

Needless to say, it eliminates a lot of the guesswork.

And saves a tremendous amount of time.

The heat and wind of the Sahara certainly presented their challenges, but the dry, sandy soil was almost perfect for this type of radar imaging. In fact, there were few geological materials that could offer a better picture than sand.

Less than thirty minutes into the process, Garcia was still getting a feel for the device when it started to beep like crazy. He assumed he had done something wrong until he looked at the screen and noticed a large object, roughly seven feet underneath the surface. Having little practice with GPR other than a few test runs in Fort Lauderdale, he decided to keep the information to himself until he was certain of his discovery.

Meanwhile, Cobb and Sarah were busy setting up a search grid with laser pointers, stakes, and string. This would allow Garcia to walk back and forth in straight rows while they marked potential discoveries with tiny flags.

A few minutes later, it seemed entirely unnecessary.

Garcia had seen enough. 'Um, Sarah, I think you can stop.'

'Why?' she asked as she hurried to his side. 'What's wrong?'

'Nothing's wrong,' he assured her. 'I think we found it.'

Sarah looked at the display and could clearly see the flat, wide stonework that he had noticed. It looked like a cobblestone patio; only each stone was roughly three feet across. The clean, straight layout of the pattern was undeniably man-made.

'Find out where it ends,' she said, trying to keep her emotion in check. 'Maybe it's just a walkway.'

Garcia glanced around. 'A walkway to where?'

'Don't argue. Just do it.'

After all that had happened, she couldn't allow herself to get too excited. So far, she hadn't seen enough to start jumping with joy. The stone certainly wasn't a natural feature of the desert, but that didn't mean it was the tomb.

She could hear Jasmine's voice in her head.

Be thorough.

Don't jump to conclusions.

Garcia did as he was told, walking in a straight line while intently watching the display. After ten paces, the image hadn't changed. When he saw the same pattern after twenty-five steps, he wondered if it was the machine, not him, that was making a mistake. He couldn't imagine something that large being buried beneath him. But still he kept on. Finally, after more than fifty strides, the image disappeared. Backing up slowly, he saw the pattern return to view.

He had found the outer edge.

He shouted back toward the truck. 'Jack, grab a marker.'

A few moments later, Cobb drove a thin plastic flag into the ground to identify the boundary. 'What are you guys thinking?'

Neither Garcia nor Sarah was willing to venture a guess.

This was just one wall.

They needed time to map the entire structure.

* * *

While Egyptian pyramids were marvels of engineering that rose triumphantly above the ground, Macedonian tombs were decidedly less grandiose. Instead of elaborate complexes like those found in Giza, Alexander's ancestors were placed below ground in simple stone vaults; their only embellishments were the temple-like pillars that marked their entrance. Despite their differences, each structure had its advantages, the virtues of which could be debated by architectural historians until the end of time.

Not surprisingly – given the way in which the Muharib melded foreign cultures with their own ideals – this structure appeared to exhibit a combination of characteristics. It was buried and flat like Macedonian tombs, with two distinct columns at one end. Yet its considerable size suggested the multi-chambered approach found in Egyptian pyramids.

The only way they would know for sure was to dig.

Garcia studied the layout, then drew an X in the sand. 'You asked for my best guess, so here it is: we aim directly between the pillars. Even if this isn't a Macedonian tomb, that has to be our way in. Why else would it be marked like that?'

Cobb looked at Sarah. 'What do you think?'

She grabbed a shovel and drove it into the sand. 'I think we'd better keep moving.'

Cobb nodded. 'I think you're right.'

At the moment, Cobb had more on his mind than finding an entrance. He stared to the west as the final, lingering streaks of daylight began to vanish, leaving only the darkness behind. He wondered if the Muharib were out there, watching his every move.

Waiting like vampires in the night.

Driven by their thirst for blood.

82

Awad stared at the infidels as they plundered his holy ground.

Disgust filled his face, and anger fueled his rage.

He had known he would see them again.

After killing Hassan, he had escaped to the desert to find his brethren. Though most had perished at the bunker disaster, there were still pockets of disciples spread throughout the barren terrain. He called upon them in his time of need.

He had underestimated the trespassers twice before.

It would not happen again.

For more than a decade, Awad had guarded the ancient wall beneath the streets of Alexandria. His was a life of sacrifice – both literally and figuratively. Not only was he responsible for killing those who ventured too close to the temple, but he had also been forced to protect Hassan. Awad loathed the man and had considered slaughtering him many times before finally getting his chance. Unfortunately, keeping Hassan in power for all those years had been in the Muharib's best interest. As long as Hassan controlled the territory above the ground, Awad could control the tunnel below.

His service to Hassan was just a means to an end.

And it ended with a slice of his blade.

Though he didn't quite know how the infidels had made it this far, it honestly didn't matter. Whether it was Dade's involvement or simply dumb luck, these foreigners had not only escaped the cisterns unscathed, but they had managed to locate the Muharib stronghold. Had he known the level of their resilience in advance, Awad would have personally taken charge of their massacre in Alexandria.

Now, he was the only thing that stood between them and their prize.

For hours he had watched as they desecrated his shrine, biding his time as the sun and the digging exhausted the intruders. The harder they worked, the easier they would be to kill, once the sun disappeared and the darkness arrived.

Theirs was a quest for riches.

His was a chance at redemption.

Only one side would win the war.

* * *

Earlier in the day, McNutt had relished his seat in the shade, but all that changed when the sun slipped below the horizon. The balmy breezes of the afternoon had given way to brisk winds, and the temperature had plummeted into the forties.

Suddenly, he envied the others as they dug.

At least they were staying warm.

Though the process was grueling, Cobb, Garcia, and Sarah pressed on through the night. At first, finding the entrance had seemed like an impossible task as sand kept filling their hole, but now they could plainly see the progress they had made.

They were more than halfway there.

They would reach the doorway by dawn.

* * *

Awad studied the scene from afar. Though the efforts of the intruders were impressive, he knew it wouldn't matter in the end. They might as well have been digging their graves. Blinded by greed, they had forgotten about the threats that lurked in the darkness.

He smiled, knowing that they would soon be defenseless. Even their lookout – once attentive and vigilant – had grown weary of his post. Instead of focusing on the surrounding terrain, he shivered as he glanced aimlessly at his phone.

It was only a matter of time.

Awad knew that the longer he waited, the more convinced they would become that they were alone in the desert. He had seen it dozens of times before. Despite the centuries of rumors that evil forces protected the desert, the lust for treasure always displaced common sense. The anticipation elevated their pulse, but it also lowered their guard.

They were already weak.

Now they were vulnerable.

Soon, it would be time to strike.

* * *

Having finally found their rhythm, the team burrowed deeper by the minute. Their muscles ached, but they fought through the pain, anxious to reach the structure below. As the walls of the pit grew higher, so did their spirits.

Nothing could stop them now.

* * *

Awad watched as the lone guard left his post and strolled toward the crater that the others had created. The moment of truth was finally here.

It was time to launch their attack.

Regardless of their superior numbers, their strategy remained the same. They would use the cover of darkness to approach the site with stealth. Once they were gathered near the edge of camp, Awad would raise his blade and lead the slaughter.

This would be his finest moment.

The son would be protected.

Amun would be pleased.

And order would be restored.

*   *   *

Sometimes plans just come together, and this was one of those times.

Despite the temperature and his apparent boredom, McNutt was highly aware of his surroundings. Thanks to the rattlers in the ground and the comm in his ear, he knew exactly where the Muharib were and when they would attack.

After that, it was all about patience.

He waited for the last possible moment to leave the roof of the SUV to make his way toward the giant hole that his teammates had dug in the sand.

Eventually, the hole would give them access to the tomb.

For now, it would save their lives.

'Get down,' McNutt called out to his friends. 'It's time.'

Sarah and Garcia dropped their shovels and hustled to the bottom of the slanted pit where they would be safe from the attack. Cobb joined them a moment later, after turning off the lantern that had lit their surroundings. For the next thirty seconds, the hole would be the safest place in the desert, guarded by an unseen force.

All that was left was the signal.

Sarah had suggested it, and the others had agreed.

Somehow it seemed appropriate.

McNutt smiled as he pulled the glow stick from his pocket.

He activated the tube with a crack and a shake, and then held it above his head.

To the Muharib, light represented everlasting life.

To the Marines, it represented death.

* * *

Staff Sergeant James Tyson grinned when he saw the signal.

It was about goddamned time.

He and the rest of his Force Recon unit had been waiting patiently from their position just beyond the dunes. For hours they had tracked the shadows in the darkness. Despite their legend, the Muharib were not ghosts. They couldn't escape the infrared and thermal vision employed by the Marines – especially since they knew where to look.

They had McNutt to thank for that.

Ever since their meeting at Biketoberfest, Tyson hadn't been able to shake the feeling that he would be seeing his buddy again real soon. The Middle East was a vast and varied place, but Marines had a way of finding each other when it mattered most. Combine that with their personal penchant for mischief, and it was only a matter of time before someone's phone started to ring. This time, it had been his.

Hell, he had even told McNutt that he would be in the region.

That was an open invitation for trouble.

McNutt had called to offer what he knew about the Alexandria bombing – which was more than the Pentagon. He had explained to Tyson that the men responsible for the tragedy belonged to the same group that had been involved in the Siwa explosion. Their conversation had been short, but McNutt had known all the right things to say:

Unchecked threat.

Regional terror.

Target of opportunity.

By the end, Tyson had been ready to lend his services, and McNutt had been more than eager to accept.

All they needed was a place and time.

Those were here and now.

'Green light,' Tyson exclaimed as he stared through his scope. 'We're a go. Repeat. We're a go. Fire. Fire. Fire.'

* * *

Considering the pain and suffering the Muharib had caused, McNutt wanted to participate in their demise. He wanted to stare them in the eye and pull his trigger. He wanted to watch them die as they gurgled blood at his feet.

Instead, he followed through on his promise.

He signaled the Marines, and then joined his friends in the pit.

A moment later, the horizon exploded with silent bursts of muzzle flare. Pink mist filled the air as the Muharib were cut down where they stood. Skulls were shattered, and brains erupted. Blood showered the sand like crimson rain.

McNutt knew that the desert warriors were known for their ability to strike without warning, but they had nothing on the US Marine Corps. His fellow soldiers had perfected the art, and they relished the chance to show off their talents.

Shadow after shadow fell to the ground.

Until only one remained.

* * *

Moments earlier, Awad had been leading his men into battle.

Now, he was all that remained of their faith.

An invisible force had wiped out his legion in the night.

It was a scene dripping with irony.

And blood.

With nowhere to run or hide, Awad knew he had been defeated. In what should have been his time of triumph, he had failed himself, his brethren, and his god. He only hoped that Amun's punishment would be swift.

A second later, a bullet answered his prayers.

Awad fell dead in the sand.

Despite their defeat, their deaths seemed a fitting tribute to their cause. The Muharib had defended the tomb to the bitter end, dying for what they believed.

In the end, their blood was spilled on holy ground.

And they died next to their god.

83

When the ambush was over, the Marines swooped in to cover their tracks. Since their actions weren't exactly sanctioned, they needed to erase any evidence of their involvement, and that included the bodies of the men they had just killed. When they were finished with their cleanup, all that remained was blood-soaked sand.

The Saharan winds would take care of that.

As his men loaded the last of the corpses into the cargo transport they had secured for the mission, Tyson walked over to the others. Despite his relationship with McNutt, he kept his headcloth drawn tight and his goggles on to conceal his features. Officially, he and his unit were never there. As such, he couldn't risk exposing his face.

McNutt nodded toward the large truck. 'That's not exactly subtle. Are you sure you can stay under the radar in that thing?'

'I got here just fine, didn't I?' Tyson scoffed. He quickly scanned the group for any signs of injury. 'Anyone hurt?'

Cobb shook his head. 'Just fine, thanks to you.'

He saluted out of respect. 'No worries, Major. Happy to help.'

As the son of a Marine Corps brigadier general – and a deco-rated soldier in his own right – Cobb was well known in certain circles. Normally, he hated the recognition, but at that moment he was willing to make an exception. 'If you or your men ever need anything, just let me know. I'll put in a good word wherever I can.'

'I appreciate that,' Tyson said. He turned to McNutt and held out his arms. 'And you – you're buying at Bike Week.'

'See you there,' McNutt answered in the midst of a brotherly hug.

As Tyson backpedalled toward his men, he had one final observation. 'So the giant hole in the ground is for . . .?'

'Giant flowers,' Sarah joked. 'We want to see if they'll grow out here.'

'Bullshit,' Tyson growled.

The entire group tensed, including McNutt.

Tyson stared at them for an uncomfortable length of time before he started to laugh. 'For the flowers, I mean. I hear manure makes all the difference in the world in a climate like this. That and water. Lots of water.'

Sarah smiled. 'Good to know.'

Just like that, their arrangement was clear. McNutt and the others would never mention the Marines, and in return Tyson and his men would keep quiet about the excavation. It was an agreement that worked for all involved.

*   *   *

Cobb waited for the Marines to clear out before his team went back to work on the entryway. With their focus no longer split between the dig and their safety, they made short work of the remaining few feet of sand. As the sun's first rays began to light the eastern sky, their shovels hit something solid.

Even though they had been expecting it, the clang of metal against stone still gave them a moment of pause. In some odd way, it struck them as proof that all of this was real. Only then did they fully comprehend the magnitude of what had happened. They would never see Jasmine again. Their friend was dead, as were those responsible for her death. All to protect whatever was hidden beyond this wall.

A few quick blasts from McNutt's sonic pulse baton were enough to loosen the mortar around the stones. After opening a large enough gap to fit through, they lowered themselves into the chamber beyond. Given all that they had been through, they would face this final leg of their journey together.

Buried beneath the sand, the chamber was as dark as it was silent. They had the sense that no living soul had seen these walls in more than fifteen hundred years, and yet the air inside was remarkably sweet.

McNutt breathed deeply. 'Why do I know that smell?'

'It's honey,' Sarah explained. 'It was a common tribute left for the pharaohs.'

'How do you—' Garcia caught himself. He already had the answer. She knew about the honey because Jasmine had told her. He tried to change the subject. 'That's a good sign, right?'

Sarah shrugged. 'Let's find out.'

One by one, they turned on their video flashlights.

Despite the massive width of the structure that the GPR had detected, they found themselves in a narrow corridor. It was flanked on each side by archway after archway after archway, each leading to a different room. Curious, McNutt ran ahead and peeked inside the nearest cavity. He was shocked by what he saw.

Honey wasn't the only tribute left behind.

'Holy shit!' Before the others could reply, McNutt disappeared into the room. His voice echoed from beyond the wall. 'You guys need to see this!'

A moment later, they found McNutt sprawled on the floor of the large enclosure. He flapped his arms and legs excitedly, as if making snow angels. Only instead of fresh powder, he was frolicking on a massive pile of ancient coins.

'I feel like Scrooge McDuck,' he said gleefully.

Garcia laughed at the scene and decided to celebrate with McNutt. Without thinking things through, he ran a few steps and then dove face-first into the pile.

Instead of a splash, there was an awful *clank*.

Followed by a loud howl of pain.

'Ouch,' Garcia mumbled, face down in the pile of coins.

McNutt scrambled over to him. 'Maria, are you okay?'

Garcia laughed and groaned at the same time. When he flipped over, several coins were stuck to his face. 'That *never* happens in cartoons.'

McNutt flicked a coin off Garcia's forehead. 'That's because cartoons aren't real.'

'Good to know.'

Smiling at the scene, Cobb and Sarah reached down and grabbed a handful of gold and silver coins from the floor. They represented a wide mixture of countries and cultures that had paid homage to Alexander; so many, in fact, Cobb imagined that the priests had shoveled the donations into wheelbarrows instead of bagging them for transport. Tens of thousands of them covered the floor like wall-to-wall carpeting.

Sarah glanced around the room. Everywhere she looked, piles of money glinted in the beam of her flashlight. 'Do you think all the rooms are like this?'

'Beats me,' Cobb admitted.

McNutt sat upright like an obedient dog that had just been asked to fetch the newspaper. 'Not if I *beats* you first!'

The pun had barely left his lips before he sprang to his feet and sprinted through the opening back into the hallway. Garcia followed hot on his heels. As he ran, the remaining coins fell off his face.

Sarah crossed her fingers. 'Please let the other rooms be booby-trapped.'

Cobb smiled and motioned toward the exit. 'Come on, let's make sure they don't do anything too stupid.'

Back in the corridor, they watched as McNutt and Garcia darted in and out of the rooms, breathlessly describing the contents of each space. Looking closer, Cobb noticed inscriptions above each archway and presumed they were a record of those who had left these offerings. He couldn't read any of the names – they had been chiseled in an ancient language that he couldn't decipher – but the gifts they had left were universally recognizable. There were tributes from nations far and wide and the spoils of war from every conquered land, all of it stored for safekeeping.

All of it kept to honor the king.

Meanwhile, Sarah walked further down the main corridor, searching for the priests' most treasured possession. Eventually, her light revealed a gleaming archway that differed from the other walls. As she drew closer, the polished alabaster – the sacred stone of Amun – almost appeared to glow in the darkness.

'Guys, over here!'

Sweeping her light across the length of the wall, Sarah stared in wonder as the others gathered around her. Chiseled in the white surface were symbols that resembled those left behind in the cisterns. From what she could tell, the images picked up where the message in Alexandria had ended. Together, they combined to tell a magnificent story of honor, devotion, and sacrifice.

A tale that few had ever known.

Just like the pictograph had suggested, the tributes left for Alexander over the centuries had been smuggled from the city right before the flood in 365 AD. Removed through the tunnel and taken away by boat, the riches had made their way along the coast before being offloaded in Amunia. From there, a caravan had transported them to Siwa, following the same route that Alexander had taken centuries before.

While the citizens of Alexandria recovered from the devastation of the tsunami, the high priests were busy sealing their treasures inside the tomb that they had constructed in the desert. Though a pyramid had been considered, the largest the world had ever seen, they decided a Macedonian tomb would attract far less attention.

Having claimed their most valued asset from the Roman Empire, the disciples of Amun meant to hide their bounty for all of eternity. Once the tomb was sealed, no one would be granted access – not even the priests – for the risk was far too great.

But today, the seal was finally breached.

Together, the four of them stepped into the final chamber. They stood in awe as the glow of their lights illuminated a towering statue of Amun in the back of the room. As they moved further into the space, they could see that he was not alone.

There, under his watchful eye, was the glass sarcophagus of legend.

Inside lay the body of a king.

The mortal son of Amun.

Alexander the Great.

Epilogue

Two days after the team's discovery, Maurice Copeland had yet to celebrate. As he walked the halls of the tomb for the first time, the treasure that surrounded him barely excited him. To most people, this magnificent fortune would have been a life changer, but it meant little to a billionaire like Copeland, who already had more money than he could spend in ten lifetimes.

To him, the tomb was simply a means to an end.

A way to get the item that he actually desired.

Few historians had ever heard of the Pieces of Eight – a collection of relics that led to a bounty of immeasurable value and incalculable worth – and most who were familiar with the legend viewed it as a myth, like the golden city of El Dorado. But Copeland wasn't like most people. Assured by experts that the Pieces of Eight did not exist, he risked his fortune and his reputation to prove them wrong.

Through bribes and good fortune, Copeland had obtained the first piece at the conclusion of his team's previous mission in Romania. Countless lives had been lost and several million dollars had been spent, but in his eyes it had all been worth it.

The existence of a single piece gave credence to the legend.

The Pieces of Eight were real.

Copeland had immediately turned his attention to the second piece, which was rumored to be buried in Alexander's tomb. Finding the tomb had been Papineau's responsibility, but that's where his duties ended. He knew nothing about the Pieces of Eight and neither did his team. To keep them in the dark, Copeland thanked Papineau for his discovery, then told him to evacuate his team before they were linked to the violence in Siwa. Anxious to leave the desert and to put the bad memories behind them, the team didn't argue. They concealed the entrance and left immediately.

Their mission was over, and they were headed home.

Meanwhile, Copeland's crew moved into position.

Just as he had done in Romania, Copeland had arranged for a separate team to remove the treasure after it had been found. There was no need for multi-lingual historians, computer geniuses, or stealthy thieves. Instead, Copeland had hired a private security force that would follow his every command and keep their mouths shut. These men couldn't care less about the historical significance or cultural value of the items inside the tomb. All they cared about was Copeland and his bank account.

He paid handsomely to protect his life and his secrets.

In exchange, his men would do anything that was asked of them.

After locating the entrance and establishing a perimeter, the recovery team locked down the burial site without even going inside. That would happen later. For now, they had more important things to worry about than the treasure.

Copeland's men had no way of knowing if the entire Muharib force had been eliminated, and they wanted to be ready if more swordsmen arrived to defend their legacy. In addition, the destruction of the compound near Siwa had drawn the attention of a dozen governmental entities, everything from the Egyptian Army to the Environmental Affairs Agency. Because of their investigations, not to mention the hordes of satellites that were focused on Egypt because of the tragedy in Alexandria, the scene was still too 'hot' to risk the removal of the treasure.

It would be another week before they could act.

But Copeland couldn't wait that long.

He needed to know if the second piece was inside.

And he needed to know *now*.

As he stared at the glass sarcophagus, Copeland wondered how many great men had come before him. He knew that kings and conquerors throughout the ages had made the pilgrimage to Egypt to pay homage to Alexander. He also knew that many of them believed that Alexander's body somehow made its owner invincible.

Copeland chuckled at the concept.

Those are the true Fools of Alexander.

The hope of divine intervention had no place in Copeland's philosophy. He too had fought battles and shed blood in the pursuit of his goals, and his experiences had taught him the only way to accomplish greatness was to be smarter, faster, bolder, and more committed than his opponents. Those were the qualities that separated leaders from followers; it had nothing to do with blessings from the great beyond.

It was a tenet that had served him well.

Copeland took one last look at the casket then casually turned and walked away. He realized that the body would be heralded as the crowning jewel of the discovery, but that didn't mean it was the most valuable. For those in the know, there was a greater prize hidden in this vault.

Fortunately, he knew exactly where to look.

As he strode confidently through the tomb, Copeland studied the names engraved above each archway. He was quite sure that each chamber contained riches far beyond the comprehension of normal men, but he was uninterested in these baubles. There was only one name he was searching for, and the object he sought would put the rest of the collection to shame.

And then he saw it. A single name in an ancient language emblazoned across the stone. A sign – a literal sign – guiding him toward what he had come to find.

TIBERIUS CAESAR AUGUSTUS

Copeland grinned at the sight. Despite the name on the wall, he knew that the second emperor of the Roman Empire had never visited the tomb. Instead, his tributes had been delivered by a legendary general in the Roman army – a man named Paccius.

As one of Tiberius's most trusted confidants, Paccius played a major role in the expansion of the Empire before he mysteriously vanished on a trip to the British Isles. Some believed he had been killed on the battlefield; others suspected he had faked his death in order to carry out secret missions for the emperor. Whatever the case, it had happened long after Paccius's trip to Alexandria.

His heart pounding in anticipation, Copeland stepped inside the alcove. He didn't have to wait long to find the item that he sought. Sitting there in the far corner of the room was a large pedestal meticulously carved from a single block of marble. The sturdy construction of the platform was needed to support the weight of the offering that it cradled: a golden sphere encrusted with sparkling gems.

The precious stones caught the beam of Copeland's light and bounced it throughout the room like a multi-colored disco ball. Ruby red and sapphire blue reflected from the surface, painting the floor. Deep purple hues of amethyst and striking green shades of emeralds danced across the walls. And beneath all the gems, the fiery glow of the polished gold seemed to illuminate even the darkest corners of the space.

Though he was struck by the beauty of the shimmering tribute, Copeland concentrated on the task at hand. He set his flashlight on the marble base and attempted to lift the basketball-sized artifact from its platform. Just as he suspected, the sphere was heavy but not unmanageable.

Rolling it in his hands, he was stunned by the details. Despite being constructed more than two thousand years ago, the globe displayed a likeness of the modern world. North and South America were clearly defined, their basic shapes outlined in gleaming opal and aquamarine. The inclusion of these continents struck him as odd, given that Roman cartographers in the time of Christ had no knowledge of their existence. These lands wouldn't be discovered for another fifteen centuries.

Besides, the map shouldn't be round at all.

It was built at a time when everyone thought the world was flat!

In an instant, he understood the importance of his discovery.

The object in his hands was the oldest known globe in the world.

One that predated all others by more than a thousand years.

And yet it was merely a vessel for the prize inside.

His research had told him that the sphere was hollow, formed by two halves connected along a hidden seam so well designed it would take an X-ray to spot it.

Like a child examining a plastic egg on Easter, he gently spun the globe in his hands as he poked and prodded, twisting it in every direction, searching for some clue as to how it opened. Yet the gems didn't budge, and the halves showed no signs of separating.

Desperate to breach the shell, Copeland considered prying loose the magnificent diamond that represented the South Pole, hoping that its removal would allow him to reach inside. But he fought his urge to pull the gem free and pushed it inward instead.

The act was counterintuitive, but it worked.

The stone sank beneath the golden casing.

Righting the orb, Copeland watched as fine, white sand poured from the gap he had created. His eyes flashed with excitement. He somehow knew that each flowing grain brought him closer to his goal, like an hourglass counting down to destiny.

Once the sphere had emptied, Copeland twisted the hemispheres again.

This time, the globe separated at the equator.

As he raised the upper half, Copeland uncovered the core of the device – a secret compartment created to protect the very thing that he had longed to possess.

A smile spread across his face as he lifted the object from the hidden cavity.

His faith and his risks had been rewarded.

He had found the second piece of the puzzle.

IF YOU LOVED READING ABOUT
THE HUNTERS

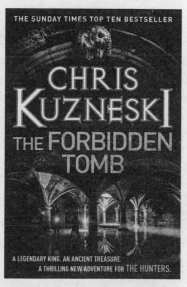

LOOK OUT FOR THE THIRD NOVEL IN THE SERIES

OUT AUTUMN 2015

The Hunters

Chris Kuzneski

THE HUNTERS:

A billionaire philanthropist hires an elite team – an ex-soldier, an historian, a computer whiz, a weapons expert, and a thief – to find the world's most legendary treasures.

THE MISSION:

Fearing a German victory in WWI, the Romanian government signed a deal with Russia to safeguard the country's treasures. In 1916, two trains full of gold and ancient artefacts were sent to the Kremlin's underground vaults. But in the turmoil of war, the treasure was scattered – and lost. Almost a century later, the haul is valued at over 3.5 billion dollars. Despite hundreds of attempts to find it, its location has remained a mystery. Until now . . .

Can the Hunters find the treasure and succeed where all others have failed?

From the international bestseller comes the first in an exhilarating new series.

High-octane action. Brilliant characters. Classic Kuzneski.

Praise for Chris Kuzneski:

'Kuzneski's writing has raw power' James Patterson

'Excellent! High stakes, fast action, vibrant characters . . . Not to be missed!' Lee Child

978 0 7553 8649 9

headline

The Einstein Pursuit

Chris Kuzneski

A lab destroyed.

An explosion in Stockholm claims the lives of an elite group of scientists. Evidence suggests the blast was designed to eliminate their research. It's up to Interpol director Nick Dial to uncover the truth.

A scientist on the run.

When Dr Mattias Sahlberg learns of the incident, he knows he is in danger. Turning to ex-Special Forces operatives Jonathon Payne and David Jones, he seeks protection from the forces that want him dead.

A miraculous discovery.

As Dial's case intertwines with Sahlberg's past, Payne and Jones uncover hidden truths involving the world's greatest minds. But some will do anything to keep such radical advances firmly in the dark. Can Payne and Jones stop them before it's too late?

High-octane action. Brilliant characters. Classic Kuzneski.

Praise for Chris Kuzneski:

'Kuzneski's writing has raw power' James Patterson

'Excellent! High stakes, fast action, vibrant characters . . . Not to be missed!' Lee Child

978 0 7553 8653 6

headline

THRILLINGLY GOOD BOOKS FROM CRIMINALLY GOOD WRITERS

CRIMEFILES

CRIME FILES BRINGS YOU THE LATEST RELEASES FROM HEADLINE'S TOP CRIME AND THRILLER AUTHORS.

SIGN UP ONLINE FOR OUR MONTHLY NEWSLETTER AND BE THE FIRST TO KNOW ABOUT OUR COMPETITIONS, NEW BOOKS AND MORE.